PRAISE FOR JOSEPH FINDER AND HIS NOVELS

Guilty Minds

"Nick Heller is a breath of fresh air in the world of private investigators as he will go to any lengths to succeed for his clients. His background and skills are an asset, making him almost a superhero. . . . *Guilty Minds* is a compelling thriller."
—Associated Press

"Smooth and polished—and classy enough for troubled characters to pause and make a big deal about the relative merits of rye whiskeys like Old Overholt and WhistlePig."
—*The New York Times*

"Finder shows off his top-notch storytelling skills, moving with ease from high places to low in the nation's capital."
—*Kirkus Reviews*

"Finder really knows his way around a thriller, and his sensibilities about Washington, scandal, and the immediacy—and threat—of digital publishing and electronic surveillance seem chillingly plausible. This is an exciting, insightful thriller with finely sketched characters."
—*Booklist* (starred review)

"[A] tight plot, sharp dialogue, and a cast of intriguing characters keep the story a cut above the genre pack."
—*Publishers Weekly*

"Finder shows off his clever storytelling skills by packing action, politics, and modern detective techniques into a complicated plotline that leads to murder."
—*Library Journal*

"This is a dark tale of intrigue and underhanded politics. . . . If you're a Finder fan, this book will not disappoint you. If you're not, you might become one after this read." —*Suspense*

"The plot of *Guilty Minds* . . . is taut, rapid, and tensely recurring." —*Harvard Magazine*

"Finder is one of the best contemporary thriller writers." —*Connecticut Post*

"*Guilty Minds* crosses the finish line a winner—suspenseful, swift, surefooted, and entertaining to the end." —*New York Journal of Books*

"*Guilty Minds* balances its thriller tenets with solid characters . . . razor-sharp dialogue, and a breathless plot that careens from one realistic twist to another." —*Mystery Scene*

The Fixer

"A master of the modern thriller." —*The Boston Globe*

"If you're in the mood for tense, witty angst about closed-down career opportunities and dirty money cleansed by family redemption, *The Fixer* is the way to go." —*The New York Times Book Review*

"Joe Finder moves from action to psychological thriller in his scintillating, Boston-based new novel. . . . There's a wondrous noir aspect to *The Fixer* that also recalls Dennis Lehane at his best. But Finder, thankfully, isn't nearly as dark or bleak and remains a storytelling maestro whose latest hits all the right notes." —*Providence Journal*

"*The Fixer* is [Finder's] most personal book. . . . A lively page-turner with smart, tight dialogue."
—*Houston Chronicle*

"Joseph Finder takes a familiar story and gives it a unique spin in his latest page-turner." —Associated Press

"Finder returns with another thriller that will have you . . . turning the pages to find out what happens next."
—*Kirkus Reviews*

"Finder can make reading about someone walking across a room excruciatingly suspenseful. . . . This is a thriller that is as much about redemption as it is about escape. A remarkable exciting read." —*Booklist* (starred review)

"Joseph Finder has written a tense, fast-moving thriller bearing the warning that there may be things you don't know and should know about your family."
—*The Washington Times*

"Adroitly told with a riveting cast of three-dimensional characters and enlightening reveals aplenty, Finder's latest standalone should be on everyone's summer reading list."
—*The Strand Magazine*

"So many surprises, this book is a definite page-turner and a whole lot of fun to read. A thriller that will keep you up late to find out what will happen next. Five stars for this one!" —*Suspense*

"*The Fixer* is a page-turner with deep emotional resonance as it explores the mysteries between all fathers and sons."
—*CT News*

ALSO BY JOSEPH FINDER

GUILTY MINDS

JOSEPH FINDER

A NOVEL

DUTTON

DUTTON

An imprint of Penguin Random House LLC
375 Hudson Street
New York, New York 10014

Previously published as a Dutton hardcover.

First Dutton premium mass market printing, 2017

Copyright © 2016 by Joseph Finder
Excerpt from *The Switch* copyright © 2017 by Joseph Finder

ISBN 9780451472588

Printed in the United States of America
10 9 8 7 6 5 4 3 2 1

In memory of my dad, Morris Finder
1917–2013

GUILTY MINDS

1

Lies are my business. They keep me employed.

If you believe scientific studies, we all lie, several times a day. Can't help ourselves. Sure, white lies are the grease that keeps the social engines running. But lies—real lies—are the source of all trouble. My job is really nothing more than figuring out who's lying and why, and catching them at it. That's all there is to it.

Fortunately, I have a knack for detecting lies. At least on my good days.

I was sitting in the reception area of the Boston office of the international law firm Shays Abbott Burnham, which was as sleek and polished as a missile silo and just as lethal. Every surface was hard and glassy—the white stone floors polished like glass, the glazed white partitions, the glass-topped coffee tables, the frosted glass walls, the sharp-edged white leather sofa. Even the receptionist, with her brassy blond hair and poreless skin and gleaming carmine lips, perched like a Gorgon behind a curved rampart of gleaming steel you might find in a Swiss bank vault.

The décor wasn't meant to put potential clients at ease. You want soft and fluffy, it said, go to a spa. This place had the machine-tooled precision, the gun-oil gleam, of a well-made semiautomatic. It reassured like a Glock under your pillow.

Which was exactly the point. Shays Abbott Burnham was one of the biggest law firms in the world. It had more than three thousand lawyers in its offices, in twenty-six countries around the world. It was a one-stop shop. They did white-collar crime and corporate litigation. They defended giant oil companies and Big Pharma and Big Tobacco. They launched hostile takeovers and defended against them.

They didn't mess around. Their clients came there with serious battles to fight. They came seeking blood.

But not me. I was there to hear about a lie.

I'd received an urgent call the afternoon before from a Shays partner named John Malkin. He'd been given my name by another lawyer who'd hired me a few months earlier for a discreet job. John Malkin had a client who needed my help immediately—wouldn't say who or why, and couldn't discuss it over the phone. We had to meet in person, and as soon as possible. In advance he e-mailed me a nondisclosure agreement and agreed to pay my consultation fee.

Whatever he wanted to discuss, it was obviously something serious.

I never meet with potential clients without doing at least a backgrounder, to make sure I'm not stepping into trouble. So I'd read a complete dossier on the man. John Epsworth Malkin: Dartmouth, Duke Law summa cum laude, member of the Order of the Coif, which sounds like something you might find framed on the wall of a barbershop. His area of practice was regulatory compliance. If I had to do that all day I'd probably scratch my eyes out.

Malkin greeted me in the reception area with a damp handshake and an undertaker's solemnity. He had round horn-rimmed glasses and silver hair brushed straight back. He dressed with the raffish eccentricity that only a senior partner could get away with: pink broadcloth button-down shirt with a threadbare collar, missing one collar button; a gray pinstriped suit whose wide lapels might have been stylish in the 1970s.

In one glance I understood him in a way no dossier could ever convey. He hated his job and probably never enjoyed practicing law. He was tired of pumping up his billables and writing memos that no one ever looked at. He was an academic wannabe. He fantasized about retiring early to teach law at a small New England school with smart students and intellectually engaging and genial colleagues. He read every Churchill biography ever published. He cared about his shoes. (His were bespoke, probably from John Lobb, in London.) He collected first editions and maybe fountain pens—the ink blotches on his fingers told me that he wrote with a fountain pen. And (one sniff confirmed it) he was a pipe-smoker but only at home. Maybe he even collected South African cabernets and was inordinately proud of his EuroCave wine cellar.

Also, he wasn't the guy who was really hiring me.

He was the beard. I was sure of this. They didn't want to give me advance notice of who my client really was.

Malkin thanked me for coming. "Does anyone know why you're here?"

"*I* don't know why I'm here."

"Good point," he said. He led me down a corridor. We probably weren't going to his office.

"And, er, who knows you're meeting with me, or even with Shays Abbott?"

"Just my office."

"Your office . . . ?"

"My office manager and my forensic tech. But they don't get out much."

"That's your whole office? Two employees?"

"It's how we maintain our low, low prices."

He didn't smile. He probably had no idea what my rates were and wouldn't care if he did.

"Mr. Malkin," I said. "I'm on the clock. You're assured absolute confidentiality. Why don't you take me to your leader."

He ducked his head and motioned for me to follow him around a corner and down another hall. When we reached a long conference room, I was astonished to see through the glass walls, sitting alone at the head of a long black table, the man I was really there to meet.

2

His name was Gideon Parnell, and he was a Washington legend.

A national legend, actually, the subject of countless profiles in the *Times* and the *Post*. I think *60 Minutes* had twice done stories on him. He'd been on the cover of *Time* magazine.

He was a tall, handsome, regal black man of around seventy-five whose close-cropped hair had gone white. His life story was the stuff that newspaper feature writers fantasize about. Raised in poverty on the southeast side of Washington, he'd marched with Martin Luther King, Jr., in Selma. He'd become one of the great civil rights heroes and had golfed with every president who golfed since Lyndon Johnson. Every president, Republican and Democrat, had considered him a friend (to the extent a president really has friends in Washington). He was the ultimate Washington insider, a power broker with extensive connections and friends everywhere. Now he was "senior counsel" at Shays Abbott, though I doubt he actually practiced much law. The more powerful lawyers become, the less they seem to practice.

Given the circles he moved in, his being here meant that this had to be serious. Likely he'd flown in from DC to meet me. My curiosity was piqued.

He rose, all six feet seven inches of him, and crossed the room in three strides. He enfolded my hand, which isn't small, in what felt like a weathered old catcher's mitt. His other hand grasped my forearm. A classic politician's handshake, but somehow, with him, it felt sincere.

I'm pretty big myself—six four and broad-shouldered—but Parnell had more than size going for him; he had *presence,* and no point pretending that it didn't make a hell of an impression. His charcoal pinstripe suit looked hand-tailored. He wore a silvery tie and a crisp white shirt.

There are very few people I genuinely admire, but Gideon Parnell was one of them. The man was a giant, and not just in size.

"Mr. Heller," he said, "thank you so much for meeting with us." His voice rumbled like the lowest *C* in the organ at Washington National Cathedral. He waved a hand around at the conference room, at his colleague lingering in the doorway like a family retainer awaiting further orders.

A few people passed by and looked curiously through the glass wall. "John, it looks like the morning rush has begun, so could you . . . ?"

John Malkin nodded and touched a button on a

switch plate just inside the doorframe. The glass wall immediately turned opaque, like a glass of milk.

"Thank you, John," Parnell said preemptively. Malkin flinched and then nodded. "Mr. Heller," he said, tipping his head in my direction. He eased out, closing the door behind him.

Parnell poured coffee from a thermal carafe into a couple of white stoneware mugs. "You like coffee, and you like it black, I'm told," he said without looking up.

I smiled to myself.

He handed me a mug and gestured toward the chair next to his at one end of the long black table.

"So let me ask you something," I said as I settled into an expensive-looking leather chair. "What was the point of making me sign an NDA? You obviously checked me out. You did your due diligence. You even know how I drink my coffee. So if you'd really done your homework, you know about my reputation for discretion."

"Please don't take this the wrong way, Nick—may I call you Nick?"

I nodded.

"It's not you I'm concerned about."

"Then what are you concerned about?"

"Others who may be watching this office and me in particular. I have to be extraordinarily careful."

"Well, even paranoids have enemies," I said.

After a long pause, he said, "A dear friend of mine—I won't say *client*, because he's not and *can't* be a client, for reasons you'll soon understand—is about to be viciously defamed by a scurrilous gossip website."

"Okay."

"This is a gentleman I have known for decades. A man of impeccable moral character. An eminent, I would say *great*, man. If these outrageous charges are allowed to be published, his entire career will be destroyed."

"Is the story true?"

"Absolutely not."

"Then what's he worried about? Truth is the absolute defense."

"Not anymore. Not in the Internet era. I'm not sure you appreciate the gravity of the situation."

"Well, you wouldn't have asked to meet with me if it weren't serious. Tell me, Mr. Parnell. How bad is this story?"

"It alleges that my friend had a regular relationship with an escort. A call girl. A prostitute."

"Is your friend the pope? I could see that being a career ender for His Eminence, maybe."

Parnell wasn't amused. "In his position, my friend can't afford the slightest hint of impropriety. His entire career rests on his moral authority."

I held his gaze a moment. "And you're not going to tell me who it is."

He lowered his head, clenched his jaw muscles, shook his head. "Not until you agree to take the job."

"The job is—what? To discredit this story?"

He nodded, took a sip of his coffee. Checked his watch. Finally I spoke.

"Mr. Parnell—"

"I can't tell you," he said.

"And I won't take the job until I know who it is." I started to rise. "So I'd say we've reached an impasse."

I realized then the secret to Gideon Parnell's success. It wasn't his dignity or his gravitas or his integrity. Not even his storied career. It was his face. The large liquid eyes, the disarming smile: They made him look vulnerable, eager, defenseless. Like a puppy. You wanted to protect him, take care of him. It was disconcerting. But his expression could toggle to stern in an instant.

"I want to make sure we're both on the same page before I tell you any more."

"Everything you say to me is covered by the NDA I signed."

Parnell compressed his lips like a petulant child.

"All right," I said. "You want me to discredit a false story. What am I missing here? Why give it any attention?"

"Because the story has been meticulously prepared. On the surface, it looks plausible. The website claims to have copies of e-mails, even a video interview with the escort in question. Once this story gets out there, unwinding it will take some time and the damage will be done."

"If the story's so solid, why haven't they run it already?"

"Because I've made a deal with them. They're giving us forty-eight hours before the piece goes live."

"What's the website?"

"Slander Sheet."

"Hoo boy." Slander Sheet made even the edgier gossip websites like Gawker and TMZ look like *The Econo-*

mist. It was one of those trashy, sensationalist websites that no one admitted looking at but everyone did. Or knew someone who did. Unlike old-fashioned newspaper gossip columns, which might run a cutesy blind item about, say, "a certain sixtyish real estate magnate with a much younger trophy wife," Slander Sheet came right out and named names. It was fearless and vicious and just about everybody in the public eye was scared of it.

"Well, that sucks," I said.

"Indeed. That's why ignoring it won't work. The story will have legs, as they say. It's going to be picked up, and it's going to get a lot of attention. Like the old saying goes, a lie gets halfway around the world before truth has the chance to put its pants on."

Maybe not the best expression to use in this situation. I tried not to smile. "Here we are, sitting in the offices of Shays Abbott, the biggest, scariest law firm in the country. Can't you guys just shut this thing down? Threaten an injunction or whatever? Isn't that normally how it plays?"

He shook his head slowly. "There's not a damned thing we can do to stop them."

"If the piece is false and libelous, can't you get a judge to order them not to publish?"

"That's called 'prior restraint,' and it's unconstitutional in this country. Violates freedom of speech."

"That doesn't stop you from threatening to file a massive libel suit against this lousy little website. Scare the crap out of them. Kill the snake. Everyone from the White House on down would cheer you on."

"And that would just feed the flames. Give the story oxygen, which is exactly what they want."

He had a point. "So how do you know what's in the story?"

"The reporter e-mailed a list of questions."

"To you? Or to this unnamed friend of yours?"

"To him."

"Did he answer them?"

"He ignored them."

"And they're running the story anyway?"

He nodded.

"I don't like this."

"Neither do I."

"No, that's not what I mean. Something doesn't smell right about this. Like maybe there's more to the story than you're letting on. I'd put this in the 'where there's smoke, there's fire' category. Meaning that there's at least some truth here. So I'm thinking the real reason I'm here is that you want me to do a scrub."

Parnell fixed me with a steely stare. No more frightened puppy dog. "If you mean, do I want you to conceal evidence and make witnesses disappear or what have you, you don't know me. As I told you, this entire story is false."

"Mr. Parnell, I can't take this on until I talk to your friend."

"I'm sorry. That's just not possible. And I'm Gideon."

"I understand." I rose and extended my hand, but Parnell didn't take it. "I'm sorry we wasted each other's time."

"Sit down, Mr. Heller. Please understand, this is not someone you can just go in and interview."

"Well, until I've talked to the guy, I won't do it." I remained standing. "You know damned well you can easily find someone else. There's no shortage of investigators who'd jump at the chance to work for Shays Abbott. I'm in the fortunate position of being able to pick and choose."

This was an out-and-out lie. In the past few months I had taken work I once swore I'd never do. Times were hard for everyone.

"Perhaps I can arrange for you two to talk over the phone."

"I need to look him in the eye, Gideon. Either I talk to him face-to-face or I'm just not interested."

"As I say, that's not possible."

"Why not?"

"Because he's a Supreme Court justice."

I slowly sat back down. "Now I'm interested," I said.

3

"Which one?"

Parnell took a sip of coffee, put it down, and drew a breath. "Jeremiah Claflin."

He wasn't just a Supreme Court justice, he was the chief justice. I didn't show any reaction.

"Now you understand the sensitivity."

I nodded.

My mental image of Claflin was of a man in his midfifties, one of the younger justices on the court. Pleasant-looking in a square-jawed way. He was fit. The first thing he did upon being named chief justice was order a renovation of the court's run-down gym.

So unlike some of his more geriatric colleagues on the high court, you could actually imagine him having a sex life. But would anyone believe he'd hired a prostitute?

Yeah, probably.

He was a regular churchgoer. The news media would salivate over a story like this. We all love seeing the mighty topple, but a lot of people find it particularly gratifying to have someone famous and morally upstanding exposed as a hypocrite and brought low.

"How long have you known Slander Sheet was investigating the chief justice?"

"Only since yesterday. The reporter had been calling his office for a week or two. Eventually they bounced her over to the court's public affairs office, which did what it usually does."

"Stonewalled."

He nodded, took another sip of coffee. He leaned back in his chair. "Yesterday she e-mailed this long list of very specific questions and said the story was going up whether he returned her calls or not. The chief justice called me in a panic."

"What kind of questions?"

Parnell pulled a couple of pages from a brown file folder and handed them to me. "This is a copy they Fed-Exed me yesterday."

The first page was headed HUNSECKER MEDIA in an elegant font like it was *Vogue*. It was a letter to Chief Justice Claflin, cc'ing Gideon Parnell.

"Hunsecker Media?"

"Publishers of Slander Sheet."

I quickly skimmed the questions.

"The reporter's name is Mandy Seeger," I said. "Why is that name familiar?"

"She used to be at *The Washington Post*."

"That's right." Seeger was a hotshot investigative reporter who'd won a Pulitzer Prize for some big series of

GUILTY MINDS   15

articles about . . . something, I didn't remember, some
government scandal. What the hell was she doing working at Slander Sheet? "Her byline on the piece is going
to give it instant credibility."

"One of the reasons I'm taking this seriously."

I continued scanning the letter and the attached list of
questions. "This looks pretty damning."

"It's an elaborate setup."

"Hold on. It says the justice's . . . meetings with the
escort were paid for by Tom Wyden." I knew the name.
Wyden was a well-known casino magnate, the CEO of
Wyden Desert Resorts in Las Vegas.

Parnell shook his head in apparent disgust. "Wyden
recently had a big case decided in his favor by the Supreme Court. If this story were true, it would be an im-
peachable offense. But it's completely bogus."

"Do they even know each other, Claflin and Wyden?"

Parnell nodded. "Yes. Not well, but they know each
other."

"This is looking worse and worse. You say you made a
deal with Slander Sheet. What kind of deal?"

"I told them I'd give her an interview if she gave me
forty-eight hours."

I groaned. "A mistake. You just effectively confirmed
the story."

"Not at all."

"Why else would one of the most powerful attorneys
in Washington bother to call some low-rent gossip website, if he wasn't worried they were onto something?"

Parnell looked at me for a few seconds, a glint of

amusement in his eyes. "I'm not known for leaving fingerprints. I told her I would be happy to speak with her,
but the justice would not."

"So now she can report that the chief justice's attorney, Washington insider Gideon Parnell, denied the account. Which is another way of saying 'the allegations
are obviously true or else one of the heaviest hitters in
Washington wouldn't have taken time out of his busy
schedule to try to make it go away.' You just gave the
story the street cred Slander Sheet wanted."

"Wrong," he said patiently. "First of all, as I told you
and as I told her, I am not the justice's attorney. I'm just
a friend. Second, I made it clear that my condition for
speaking with her was that our talk be off the record, including the fact of any conversation. They agreed not to
run the story until the reporter had spoken with me."

I nodded. "So basically you bought yourself some
time."

"Until she meets with me, they're not going to run
the story."

"And when's this meeting?"

He looked at his watch, a gold bezel with a big white
face on a brown crocodile strap. It looked expensive.
"Tomorrow at five P.M."

"Nowhere near enough time. I'd need a minimum of
two weeks, and that's if we get lucky."

"Get lucky faster."

"Sure. No problem."

"That's all the time we have, Nick. I was surprised
they agreed to hold off as long as they did."

"I'm going to need to talk to the chief justice. In person."

"I doubt he'll agree to it, but let me ask him."

"One more question."

He inclined his head.

"How many other firms turned you down before you had Malkin call me?"

"No one turned me down."

"I was your first choice? Somehow I don't believe that."

"Of course not. I don't know you. I had to make some inquiries about you first."

"That's not what I mean. I'm in Boston, and this is a DC case. You could get anyone you want in DC, without having to pay travel. Including the obvious choice."

He knew I meant Jay Stoddard, my former boss, whose firm was the best known in the private intelligence business, a man who'd got his start working for Richard Nixon. Stoddard had recruited me from Defense intelligence and taught me the tricks of the trade. I learned a lot from him—a bleak education—until we had a falling out and I quit to start my own firm.

He heaved a sigh. "Jay has too many close ties to powerful interests in Washington. Whereas you're an outsider."

"Is that a polite way of saying I've made some enemies?"

He shrugged. "It is what it is." One of those annoying catch phrases that seem to have caught on like herpes. "Everyone in DC is in bed with someone. And this feels like some kind of inside job. An attack like this doesn't come out of nowhere. Someone went to a lot of trouble to put this thing together, and I can't take a chance with the local talent."

"Let's be clear about something. You want more than information. You want me to do certain things in ways you can't be associated with. Correct?"

"I want you to do whatever it takes to kill this story. I want you to strangle the baby in its cradle. And yes, you're absolutely right, no one must ever know that you're working for me."

"And why is that so important?"

A long, long pause. "Candidly, the senior partners in this law firm are deathly afraid of Slander Sheet. No one wants to be fed into that wood chipper."

"I appreciate the honesty. The chief justice is going to have to be just as open with me."

"I'll see if he agrees to meet. He can be prickly. He's very private."

"One more thing. If I find out the story's true, I'm off the job. I'm not interested in helping cover something up. If that's what you want, I'm not the right guy for this."

He smiled. "Oh, I know that well. I believe the phrase Jay Stoddard used to describe you was 'loose cannon.' He made it eminently clear that you're not controllable."

"I have a feeling he put it more colorfully than that."

He gave a low, rumbling chuckle, glancing at his watch. "I have a meeting with the Boston partners, and I want to reach the chief justice before that. I'll let you know what he says. Let me have your cell phone number."

I gave it to him. "The sooner the better," I said.

4

In the cab on the way back to my office, I read over my copy of the letter Slander Sheet had sent to the Supreme Court's public affairs office. I started to formulate a plan, in case I did take the case.

It looked really bad for the chief justice. They were highly specific questions and implied a pretty solid article. The questions weren't part of a fishing expedition. *If* Gideon Parnell was right that the story about the chief justice and a hooker was a total lie, then it was a fiendishly clever hoax. And not the work of amateurs. From what I could put together from the list of questions, the chief justice had—*allegedly* had, to be fair—three trysts with an escort hired from a website called LilySchuyler.com, "the world's leading online service for discreet encounters."

I thought about Gideon Parnell. The fact that he was inserting himself in the middle of this battle was significant. His reputation was towering. He had much to lose, being associated with something as tawdry as this, true or not. He must have been a good friend of Justice Claflin's.

And I mulled over the question of why they'd contacted me. Was Parnell on the level when he said he wanted someone outside DC? In a situation like this, in which speed and discretion are of paramount importance, it would make a lot more sense for him to hire someone in town he knew. The question kept coming back: *Why me?*

If the chief justice did agree to meet with me, I'd have to fly to DC immediately, which would mean rescheduling a few meetings and appointments I'd lined up for tomorrow and possibly the day after.

I had the taxi drop me off on High Street, at the old brick, converted lead-pipe factory in Boston's Financial District where I have an office. It was still early, but by then my office manager/receptionist, Jillian Alperin, was in. She stood, back to me, struggling with a printer, trying to feed it paper.

Jillian was in her early twenties and had all sorts of piercings and tattoos. If I saw a lot of clients at the office, she wouldn't have been a good hire. She was a little young, a little rough around the edges, not exactly business-appropriate. But she was competent and tried hard and I'd grown to like her.

"Nick," she said, "Dorothy was looking for you. Also a couple of queries came in—I forwarded them to your e-mail." Dorothy Duval was my forensic tech and researcher.

She sounded uncomfortable saying my first name. It had taken her a long time to stop calling me "Mr. Heller."

"Thanks."

She turned around. "Also, a client called—Shearing?—and wanted to talk to you right away."

Her face was red, and she looked like she'd been crying.

"Hey," I said gently. "Everything okay?"

I didn't know her very well and tried to stay out of my employees' personal affairs. But not to ask seemed cold-hearted.

She sniffled. "Yeah, I guess."

"Okay."

"It's just . . . that guy, Shearing, you know?"

"What about him?" Shearing was a lawyer at a midsize firm in New York who'd hired me to do due diligence on a German businessman. The German was the CEO of a company in Düsseldorf and was being considered for a US company's board of directors. I'd asked a colleague in Munich to work the case. Most of my clients come to me through lawyers, which has its plusses and its minuses. Dealing with a lawyer was often easier than dealing directly with clients, who could be emotional. Lawyers tended to be more professional. But some lawyers were just plain assholes, and Bob Shearing was exhibit A.

"He just called up looking for you, and I told him you were tied up with a client. And he demanded your cell number." She sniffed a couple of times. "And when

I told him I couldn't give that out he got . . . really abusive. He said, 'Goddamn it, I'm a client and I want his cell phone number now!' And 'Listen to me, bitch, you better give me that number now, or I'll have your job.' " She looked miserable, her eyes and nostrils red.

"He said that?"

She nodded, reached for a tissue on her desk, and blew her nose. Then she said, "I don't know if I made a mistake. If I was, like, angering a client. But you told me you're the only one who can give out your cell number. And now I don't know if I lost you a client!"

"He called you a bitch?"

She nodded. "I'm sorry, Nick, if I screwed up."

"Can you put me through to Shearing in two minutes?"

She nodded again.

I went to the coffee station. Dorothy was already at the Keurig, filling a mug that said JESUS SAVES, I SPEND. She was wearing a turquoise raw-silk blouse and black pants and very high heels. She always dressed well, though she didn't have to—as my tech, she rarely met with clients. She could wear jeans if she wanted to. But she usually didn't want to.

She gave me a questioning look. She knew I'd just come from a supersecret meeting with a potential client and wanted to know what happened. The answer wasn't as simple as thumbs up or thumbs down. I wasn't sure I was going to take this new client on. "Meet me in my office in five, okay?"

She nodded. "Uh-oh."

In my office—I have the corner office with a view of the street and a glimpse of the waterfront—the phone was buzzing. Jillian's voice came over the intercom: "I have Mr. Shearing on hold on line one."

I picked up the phone. "Bob, it's Nick Heller."

"There you are, Heller. Your damned secretary wouldn't give me your goddamned mobile phone number."

"She told me."

"I need the word on Kleinschmidt today," he said.

"Did you call my receptionist a 'bitch'?"

"I told her it was urgent but she kept saying she wasn't allowed to give out your number. I said, 'Hey, I'm the client here.' You gotta train your girls better."

"Well, Bob, I'm afraid I can't help you either."

"What are you talking—?"

"With Herr Kleinschmidt, I mean. I'm too busy to take on your case."

"Too busy? You already took the goddamned case."

"My schedule has gotten crowded all of a sudden. I don't really have time to work for assholes." And I hung up.

I noticed Dorothy lingering at the threshold of my office. She entered, eyes wide. "Am I hearing correctly? Did you just fire a client?"

I nodded. "I never liked the guy anyway," I said.

"Nick, our clients are a little thin on the ground. Can we really afford to lose one?"

"Dorothy," I began, but then my mobile phone rang.

It was Gideon Parnell. "The chief justice has agreed to meet," he said. "Can you be in DC this afternoon?"

"Absolutely," I said.

"He'll see you at four o'clock. Your name will be on a visitor's list at the court."

I ended the call and looked at Dorothy. "Looks like we just may have a new client," I said.

5

The Supreme Court is, I think, the most beautiful building in Washington. It's a gleaming Greek temple, its exterior bright white Vermont marble, chosen because it was so much whiter than the marble of the buildings that surround it, including the US Capitol. It was modeled after the Temple of Artemis, one of the Seven Wonders of the Ancient World, with its frieze and the Corinthian columns and such.

But mostly I've always thought of the Supreme Court building as a triumph of branding.

It was built fairly recently, in 1935. Prior to that, the justices were jammed into close quarters in the basement of the Capitol building. They got no respect. But once they got their own temple of justice, they had a clubhouse, a headquarters, a logo, and a mystique. And along with that mystique came power.

A big chunk of that power and legitimacy, after all, is based on perception and persuasion. So you had a glistening marble landmark, quite prominent, in which nine invisible judges deliberated in absolute secrecy. Like the great and powerful Oz, with the smoke and green fire, and a small man behind the curtain working the props.

When I first moved to Washington, working covert intel for the Defense Department, you could walk right up the grand front steps of the Supreme Court and enter through the heavy bronze doors. But ever since 9/11, the front entrance has been closed off. You have to enter through a basement door on the southwest side.

I'd caught a late morning flight to DC. After I'd landed, I had three hours before I had to be at the court building. That was just enough time to do some quick research.

Later, standing on the plaza in front of the court, I made some phone calls. When I'd gotten what I needed, I called Dorothy.

"Any progress?" I asked

"So far it's a dead end." I'd asked her to dig up whatever she could on an escort named Heidi L'Amour, who was employed by LilySchuyler.com, which marketed itself as a high-end escort service in DC.

"According to the Lily Schuyler website it says she's on vacation. So there's no way to set up a date with her. That leaves us with just a name, and, you know, there's a teensy-weensy chance that this name might be fake."

"You think?" I smiled. "What about trying a Google image search for her picture, see if it comes up on any other adult websites?"

"Already tried it. Nothing."

"Means she probably doesn't work for other escort services. The odds are she'd use the same photos if she did."

"You could call the phone number and offer a bonus if she'll come back from vacation. You know, you like her look and she's the only one you'll settle for."

"Maybe. But I'm guessing she's gone into hiding. She knows all hell's about to break loose, as soon as that article's published."

"I'll keep at it," Dorothy said. "Maybe I'll have a brainstorm."

Then I joined a long line of tourists and passed through a metal detector, up a short flight of stairs to a large open hallway where clots of tourists were milling around. A few others strode by with a sense of purpose. Lawyers, I assumed. They were too well dressed to be reporters.

I took the elevator up one flight, as Gideon had instructed me, and when I got out I looked around for the marshal's office, where I was supposed to check in. A large, beefy uniformed cop with a blond crewcut and ruddy cheeks approached, a metal clipboard in hand.

"Help you, sir?"

"The marshal's office?"

"Do you have a visitor's pass?"

"I have an appointment."

"With?"

"Justice Claflin."

He nodded, looked at his clipboard. "Name?"

"Nicholas Heller."

"May I see some form of government-issued ID?"

I showed him my driver's license.

"Right this way, sir."

I followed him to a bank of coin-operated lockers outside a cloakroom. "You need to check any laptop computer, cell phone, PDA, iPad, or any other electronic device. If you prefer, you can use one of these lockers."

I nodded, fished around in my pockets for a quarter, but I didn't have any. He slid one into the slot, pulled out the key, and handed it to me. I thanked him.

"Good idea to check your stuff in a locker," the cop said. "Can't trust anyone around here."

6

Jeremiah Claflin, the chief justice of the Supreme Court of the United States, had a bland, almost generic look about him: short graying brown hair, small nose, fine features. You'd call him nice-looking but not handsome. There was nothing interesting about his face. As soon as he was out of your sight, you'd forget what he looked like. He had deep lines on his forehead and crow's feet around his eyes. He looked like he spent a lot of time in the sun, probably sailing.

He greeted me politely but gave off a vibe that he had a lot more important things to do. "Jerry Claflin," he murmured as we shook hands in his paneled waiting area. He was in shirtsleeves and a tie, no jacket.

He gestured me to a couple of wingback chairs on either side of a large fireplace. His office was lined with old law books and had oriental rugs on the floor and a killer view of the Capitol dome.

"So, Mr. Heller," he said, "you're—what, a private

eye?" He said the words with a moue of disgust, the way you might say "carbuncle" or "abscess."

"If you want."

"Then what do you call yourself?"

"A private intelligence operative."

"Is that like being a 'mortician' rather than an 'undertaker'?"

I smiled. He was known for his acid sense of humor. I decided to give some back. "Maybe more like being 'justice' instead of 'judge.' There's a difference."

He laughed, pleasantly. Touché. I wasn't particularly bothered by his contempt for me. He needed me a lot more than I needed him.

Then he blinked a few times and smiled thinly. "I have to tell you, it's not at all clear to me why you're here."

"I'm beginning to wonder the same thing. You're a busy man, so let's get right down to it. Apparently Slander Sheet is about to publish an exposé about your relationship with a call girl. Which I assume is entirely false, right?"

He pursed his lips, scowled. "I'm not even going to dignify that."

"I'm afraid you're going to have to dignify it. Did you have a relationship with a call girl from the escort service Lily Schuyler?"

"That's preposterous on the face of it."

"Which means—what? True or false?"

Claflin peered at me askance, as if wondering whether I was a moron.

I said, "You're going to have to put it in plain English for me. Sometimes I miss the subtleties."

"You're asking me if I had sex with a hooker? The answer is absolutely not. No, I did not. Is that unsubtle enough for you?"

"And you've never met a woman named Heidi L'Amour, is that right?"

"That's right. I'd never heard the name before this e-mail came in." He gestured vaguely at the printout of questions I was holding.

"Now, one of the reporter's questions asks—the most serious charge—whether it's true that this escort you claim you never met was a gift of sorts to you. Whether her fee was paid by Tom Wyden, the gambling mogul. You're a friend of Mr. Wyden's, is that correct?"

"No, that's not correct."

I arched a brow.

"I once attended a function at his home in Las Vegas. Before I was appointed to the court."

"Have you been in touch with him since being named to the court?"

"He's invited me to various functions, and each time I've declined."

"So you haven't seen him since coming to work in this building?"

"That's right. Do those questions allege otherwise?"

I shook my head. "Is he a friend?"

"No. We've shaken hands once or twice."

"Does he have a reason to want to bring you down?"

"Quite the opposite. A few months ago we handed down a decision on *Wyden Desert Resorts v. PokerLeader*. A decision that came down in his favor."

"All right. Now, this reporter alleges that on three nights this past month, you had, uh, sessions with this Heidi L'Amour."

"Which I've already told you is false."

"Right, but can you account for your whereabouts on those three nights?"

He hesitated for an instant, but long enough to put me on alert. "I was at home," he said.

"Actually, on one of those nights, weren't you at the annual Mock Trial and Dinner of the Shakespeare Theatre Company at Sidney Harman Hall on F Street?" That was in the quickie background file Dorothy had prepared for me by the time I landed at Reagan National Airport. It was a star-studded event the Supreme Court justices seemed to do every year.

"No. I had to cancel my appearance at the Mock Trial. I was feeling a little under the weather."

Dorothy had missed that. He must have been scheduled to appear, but the website hadn't been updated. "So you were at home all three of those nights?"

He nodded pensively.

"Excellent. So your wife can establish your alibi."

He paused. "My wife and I are separated. This is not generally known. It's also nobody's business."

But I already knew this, of course. I'd wondered whether he would try to gloss that over with me. "This is Washington," I said. "Everything is everybody's business. So do you live in the Chevy Chase house or does she?"

"She does. I live at the Watergate."

"I see."

"I live alone. So that, uh, won't work as an alibi."

I could have tormented the chief justice further, asking whether the doormen or the lobby attendants would back him up, but I'd done enough. "You actually weren't at the Watergate on those nights, were you?"

He gave me a look that I couldn't quite read. Was he surprised or offended or just taken aback? He didn't reply right away, so I went on, watching him intently. "For that entire week, you were somewhere else." Just before our meeting, I'd gone to the Watergate and asked a few questions, dispensed a little cash. I'd done my due diligence.

Now he looked away. I noticed a reddening in his cheeks, but I wasn't sure whether I was seeing a flush of anger or the sting of embarrassment. I remained silent. I'm a big believer in the power of silence.

"It's irrelevant where I was," Claflin said.

"If we want to blow this story out of the water, I'm afraid it's entirely relevant. The simplest refutation is to establish an ironclad alibi."

"Then I think we're going to have a problem."

I waited, said nothing.

"Your challenge is to prove I never met with this prostitute. I'm afraid I can't help you beyond what I've already said."

But I persisted. "The court was in recess that week.

You had no public appearances, gave no speeches. There's nothing on the public record for that entire week. The Watergate's security cameras, the parking lot cameras, they're all going to reveal you weren't home at the time of the alleged incidents. Did you travel somewhere?" I was bluffing, of course. I didn't have time to check out security cameras.

He continued looking away. Finally he turned toward me and spoke. "Can I trust your confidence?"

"Of course."

"If this gets out I'm going to have real problems."

"I understand."

"The reason I wasn't home that week is that I was at Sibley Hospital, in the inpatient mental health clinic. I was having electroconvulsive therapy."

I tried to hide my astonishment. "Electroshock therapy?"

He nodded. "For depression. You can understand why it's important to me that this be kept private."

"So you have an alibi we can't use," I finally said, because it was all I could think to say.

7

Who else knows?"

Claflin shrugged. "No one except you and my wife and Gideon, as far as I know. My wife and I may have our differences, but she'd never betray my confidence. I'm certain of that."

"Are you still being treated?"

"No. I had twelve sessions at Sibley."

"Did they work?"

He smiled, unexpectedly. "They did, thank you."

"Maybe it's not a coincidence."

"What's not?"

"That each of the occasions you allegedly saw a call girl occurred at the same time as you were being treated at Sibley. Whoever is setting you up must know about the treatments."

"I don't see how it's possible. Unless someone at the hospital . . ."

"Anything is possible." I thought for a moment. "You

allegedly met with this girl in a room at the Monroe."
The Monroe was one of the finest hotels in DC, a few
blocks from the White House. "Have you ever stayed
there?"

"Why would I stay in a hotel? I live here."

"When you moved out of your house, for example."

He shook his head.

"I've never stayed in a hotel in town."

"The questions refer to hotel records at the Monroe,
claiming you reserved a room for each of those nights."

"How would anyone know that?"

"Obviously they had a source at the hotel who
checked the guest registry database."

"But it's not true. How long do we have before they
decide whether to run the piece?"

I looked at my watch. "As of five P.M. yesterday it was
forty-eight hours. By my count, there's twenty-seven
hours left."

"That's impossible. What can you possibly hope to ac-
complish in twenty-seven hours?"

"I guess we'll find out." I stood up. "Now I'd better
get to it."

The white marble corridors downstairs were mostly
empty now. The floors gleamed. My footsteps echoed
distantly. I found the bank of gray metal lockers, located
mine, and opened it.

And stared at the empty compartment.

Nothing was there. My laptop, my iPhone: gone.

I double-checked the number on the key. It matched the number on the locker. I had the right locker, and my belongings had vanished.

At the end of the rows of lockers was a cloakroom where you could check your coat or umbrella or whatever else you couldn't stuff into a locker. The attendant on duty was a matronly black woman with large sleepy eyes behind elaborate eyeglass frames that swooped down from the temple to the earpiece. Her black hair glistened with pomade. She spoke in a gruff, gravelly contralto.

"Honey, you know what kind of rush we get before court starts? I got a line halfway out to the street. Even if I could see the lockers from here, which I can't, I sure don't have time to look. I'm sorry, dear. I wish I could help you."

"You keep the spare keys here, right? I'm sure people lose locker keys all the time."

She blinked a few times, looking like she was on the verge of drifting off to sleep. "Less than you might think. I'm sorry, I don't understand. You're telling me you think someone took stuff out of your locker, right? So why're you needing a spare key?"

I tried not to show my impatience. "Maybe someone took one of your spares and opened my locker. Would you mind checking to see if one's missing?"

She shrugged and reached down to get something from under the counter. Then, key in hand, she unlocked a gray steel box mounted to the wall. I saw the row of green plastic key fobs, and even though I was too far away to read the numbers, I didn't have to. There was no gap in the row of keys. None was missing.

She turned back, shook her head. "Nope."

"The policeman who brought me over here," I began.

"What policeman would that be, sir?"

"He met me when I came in, an hour or so ago, and brought me over here. Big tall blond guy, brush cut? Did you see him come back here at any point?"

She shook her head slowly with an exaggerated swing from side to side. "Doesn't sound familiar. One of our Supreme Court police?"

I thought for a moment, remembering his uniform. "He was Washington Metro Police."

"I doubt that. We have our own Supreme Court police. You see the tan patch on his left shoulder?"

He had no tan patch on his shoulder. "Thanks," I said, spun around, and began striding down the hall.

8

Whether he was a real cop or not, the guy with the blond brush cut who'd so politely guided me to my locker—even providing the quarter—was obviously the one who'd emptied it. He'd picked out my locker in advance, which meant he had a copy of the key. He didn't need to take one of the spares. He'd just waited for me to leave and then removed my laptop and iPhone. Had I been on alert, and had I known what to look for, I'd have noticed that he was wearing the uniform of a DC city cop. It had been a simple if brazen move, and the only reason it worked was that I hadn't been operating with my usual wariness.

The question was, who was he and how did he know I'd be here?

This I couldn't yet figure out.

I stopped mid-stride. I had a strong feeling that I was being watched. That the guy was somewhere nearby, within eyesight.

It was more than a feeling, of course. It was the result of "situational awareness," which is the military's fancy term for knowing what's going on around you. In combat, your life can depend on whether you notice anomalies: the scuff of a boot, the glint of a weapon. I sensed a stillness at my eleven o'clock and turned. There, at the head of the staircase at the other end of the great hall, was a familiar blond crewcut. A man in a policeman's uniform.

I walked casually in that direction, as if I hadn't seen anything, but the man began going down the stairs, so I accelerated my pace until I was almost running. He must have realized he'd been spotted. By the time I reached the steep marble stairs, he was nowhere in sight. These were stairs meant for dignified procession, not hot pursuit. They were also not stairs you'd want to take a header down.

The problem was that I didn't know the building's layout at all. I'd had no reason to acquaint myself with the exits, not when I was just having a discreet private meeting with a Supreme Court justice. I hadn't expected trouble because I figured no one knew I'd be here.

But obviously someone knew.

At the ground floor, I stopped, oriented myself. To my left was the visitors' entrance. It wasn't an exit, just an entrance. Maybe someone in a policeman's uniform could slip out that way. The long, broad corridor was sparsely decorated with display cases. Down at the other end I saw a cafeteria and a gift shop. There seemed to be only two exits for the general public. One was upstairs, outside the courtroom, through the huge bronze doors. You couldn't enter that way, but you could leave. The other exit was on this level, straight ahead of me. It appeared to lead to the plaza behind the court building, on Second Street. There was no security here. People were strolling out casually.

I had to make a decision. Try to force my way out the entrance, race for the exit onto Second Street, or stay inside the building and look for him here. It was possible he hadn't left.

I went out the Second Street exit, looking in all directions, but it was no use. He wasn't there.

That was all right. I didn't have time to look anymore. I had far more urgent business to get to.

9

I'd forgotten what life was like without a cell phone. I had phone calls to make but no way to make them. I had to walk two blocks to find a pay phone that worked. It was covered with an ad for Red Bull. The holes in the mouthpiece were clogged with some mysterious brown substance that probably wasn't Red Bull. When I remembered I had no quarters, I got change at a deli on East Capitol Street. I returned to my Red Bull pay phone, fished out Gideon Parnell's business card from the breast pocket of my suit jacket, and called his mobile number.

He answered right away. "This is Gideon Parnell," he said in his basso profundo.

"It's Nick Heller."

"You've spoken to my friend."

"I'll take the case."

"Excellent. You have everything you need?"

I told him I thought I did and that I'd call back immediately if I didn't. I understood that we were on a tight deadline—we had barely twenty-six hours before Slander Sheet's deadline.

Next I wanted to call Dorothy, but her cell number was programmed into my iPhone, and I couldn't remember it. Not so long ago I took pride in my ability to memorize numbers, but that seemed to be decaying, an evolutionary casualty of technology. Instead, I called my office and asked to be transferred.

"I called you a couple of times," Dorothy said when she answered. "You must have been in your meeting with the justice."

"What's up?"

"I had that brainstorm I was talking about. How to hack into LilySchuyler.com."

"Tell me."

"I used an old tried-and-true hacker trick—SQL injection. I found the customer log-in area on the website and started running script against the username and password fields. Trying to cause a buffer overflow."

"Right," I said, though I had no idea what she was saying.

"So I created a query in code, thirty characters long, and put that query into the username field. It dumped me into the back end of the website—the index."

"I thought you were uncomfortable doing hacker stuff like that."

"I am. But time is really short, and I was desperate. Also, it's Gideon Parnell. I'd do anything for that guy. You know he marched with Martin Luther King?"

"Yep. I appreciate it."

"I'll e-mail you when I have something useful."

"Oh, that reminds me. I don't have a phone or a lap-top anymore."

"Anymore?"

"I'm temporarily back in the Dark Ages, and I don't like it as much as I thought I would."

I explained.

"Well, they're both password-protected, the phone and the MacBook Air," she said, "so you're not at risk of losing information. More interesting . . ." I heard her tapping away at her keyboard. She seemed to be talking to herself.

Dorothy had set up both my phone and my laptop and given them to me plug-and-play. I'm no computer savant, but in my business you can no longer be ignorant about technology, unfortunately. At the very least you need to hire people who are good at it and let them do their thing. She insisted that Macs are extremely secure devices, and that the iPhone is the most secure phone you can get. I do what she recommends.

"Hold on one second," she said. There we are. You have Find My iPhone turned on, very nice, and . . . oh, crap."

"Now what?"

"They just turned it off."

"How do you know this?"

"I see you had it at the Supreme Court building, but then it goes dark. That tells me they turned the phone off as soon as they stole it, and probably the laptop, too, to defeat the tracker. Someone knows what they're do-ing. That's too bad."

"I'm going to need my phone and computer replaced."

"Stop in at an Apple Store. There's a couple in the district. Or else I can bring them to you."

"How's that?"

"You're going to be in DC for at least a couple of days. My brother's in the hospital in Prince George's and I want to pay him a visit."

"I'm sorry to hear about your brother." I wasn't aware that she had a brother. She was extremely private when it came to her personal business. "Ask Jillian to book us a couple of hotel rooms in DC," I said. "It's being billed to Shays Abbott, so make it a high-end place, something nice. Would you mind taking a piece of luggage for me?"

"Your go-bag?"

"Right." In my office I always keep a packed carry-on case with a few days' clothing and a shaving kit and miscellaneous necessities. Just in case I have to go somewhere out of town at the last minute.

"Sure. Nick, how did they know it was you?"

"The guy who stole my laptop, you mean?"

"Right."

"I haven't figured that out yet, but I will." I told her I'd check back in with the office a little later on, since I was no longer reachable anywhere, and I hung up.

I summoned a mental image of the fake cop who'd guided me to my locker at the Supreme Court. I concentrated, did a mental inventory and download. I remembered him being about my height but broader and heavier. He had a blond buzz cut and his face looked flushed. Eye color? Gray, maybe, or light blue, but light in any case. Age? Somewhere in his thirties. I was putting together what birdwatchers and military types call the GISS, which stands for "general impression of size and shape." For birders, it's a way to make a field identification when you don't know a bird's species.

I turned away just when the pay phone rang. I picked it up.

"Nick Heller's line."

"Nick?" It was Dorothy.

"Yup."

"Oh, good. As long as you stay by that pay phone all day, we should be fine. I've found our girl."

10

Her real name is Kayla Pitts. Kayla spelled with a *K*. She's twenty-two, and she comes from Tupelo, Mississippi."

"How do you know all this?"

"Employee records on their server."

"You find a phone number?"

She read it to me. It had a 571 area code, for Virginia. I wrote it down in my little black notebook.

"Address?"

She read that aloud, too, and I wrote it down.

"Now what?"

"Now I go to see her."

"How?"

"I'll think of something."

Three hours later I was sitting in a rented black Chevy Suburban parked outside Kayla Pitts's apartment building on Glebe Road in Arlington. It was a huge crablike complex built of white brick that belonged on the outskirts of Moscow: like late Soviet-era public housing built on the cheap, almost defiantly so.

I had with me my new phone and MacBook Air—I didn't want to wait for Dorothy, so I made a stop at the Apple Store—and I was browsing LilySchuyler.com's website, piggybacking on someone's Wi-Fi signal, probably one of Kayla's neighbors'.

So my computer screen was filled with color photos of women in various states of undress, four across. Some of them were nude, with the pertinent areas blurred out. Some wore elaborate black lace bustiers with fishnet stockings and spike heels. Or caged corset teddies with sheer side panels and lace fronts. Or tiny bikini bottoms, or thongs. It was like an L.L. Bean catalog of women for almost every taste. At the top of the page, LILY SCHUYLER appeared in gold script letters that were probably meant to look high-end. I clicked on "About Us" and learned that it was an "exclusive and discreet social introduction service that provides upscale companionship to sophisticated and discerning gentlemen." They offered "the most beautiful, exquisite, and sensual young ladies ever to work in the escort industry." All the girls were "ladies," and all potential clients were "gentlemen."

A few of the exquisite ladies had what's called the "girl-next-door look," though no girl like these ever lived next door to me. They appeared to be pure, innocent, "collegiate." Almost demure, if you could call a woman who posed in a lacy pink bra on a call girl website "demure."

All of the pictures looked Photoshopped, some more than others. Some had their faces blurred out entirely, some didn't. They had names like Savannah and Sabrina, Bethany and Kendra, April and Sydney and Sierra and Giselle.

Heidi L'Amour—Kayla Pitts—was one of the demure collegiate ones. Also one of the prettiest, so far as I could tell. At least you could see her face clearly. Her photo showed a young woman in her early twenties with lustrous blond hair down to her collarbone. She wore a simple black top with cap sleeves, cut low enough to reveal the cleft of her bosom but not so low it looked trashy. God forbid the photos on a call girl website should look trashy. Her chin rested on her left hand.

Photoshop can disguise blemishes and flaws and even give a chunky girl a slender waist, but it couldn't simulate this kind of natural beauty. She had delicately arched brows, a pert nose, a sweet smile. She had an open face and a kind, vulnerable expression.

HEIDI VACATION, the caption said, as if *Vacation* were her last name. When I clicked on her picture, her profile page came up. More photos, including one in a lacy bralette and matching G-string, side-tie. Her arms raised, hands behind head, a dreamy look in her eyes. Here it said Heidi L'Amour was on vacation and gave no end date:

22 years old, 5'5", 125 lbs, 36D natural. Very Open-Minded GFE.

Heidi is a stunning young blonde beauty with a face and accent as sweet as a Georgia peach. She's new to the DC area and is a brilliant and accomplished college student with a girl-next-door look. She loves fine dining and is as comfortable at a five-star restaurant or a cocktail party as she is sitting in front of the fire drinking red wine. She has insatiable desires, longing for fulfillment, and can always be relied upon to give you the ultimate GFE.

I knew that GFE meant "girlfriend experience," which basically meant she kissed, along with everything else. Men paid extra for a prostitute who could pretend to be in love with them, which I find a little sad.

No prices listed. Just a row of five diamonds. Maybe if you had to ask you couldn't afford it. I clicked around the website some more and saw that some of the girls had as few as three diamonds. No one had more than five.

The answer to the price mystery turned up on the "Services & Rates" page. Five diamonds represented "our most highly rated tier of model." In other words, the most expensive girl. They even offered five-diamond packages. One hour with a five-diamond girl cost $4,000. A package of "three unrushed decadent hours over drinks and dessert" was $10,000. Another package, for "gentlemen with savoir faire," offered a full night of "ultimate pampering." That would set the discerning gentleman back $22,000.

Heidi L'Amour did not come cheap.

So this was the girl Justice Claflin had allegedly hired. I didn't believe it.

*   *   *

Now I knew approximately what she looked like. Her
GISS, at least. For half an hour I had been watching people come and go from the apartment building. If I saw
anyone who vaguely resembled Kayla, I was ready to
jump out of the car and approach her. But no one looked
remotely like her. I was looking for a small, blond young
woman of slight build. I saw a few guys in their early
twenties, an elderly woman with a walker, a middle-aged
woman with a few kids. But not her. If she were at home,
she'd have to emerge eventually. But I could be sitting
here in a rented car waiting for twenty-four hours, and I
didn't have the time.

Besides, it wasn't even a sure thing that she was at home.

I decided to try the direct approach. I got out of the
car and entered the lobby, which was large and garishly
lit. It was lined with mailboxes on either side. Oversized
envelopes, which didn't fit in a mailbox, were lined up on
a shelf.

At the front was an intercom system where you
searched for the resident's name and it pulled up a number to punch in. I grabbed an envelope and searched the
building directory until I found PITTS, K.

I entered her number in the intercom and waited for
it to ring. I could hear the ringing through a tinny
speaker, but nothing more happened.

After a minute, I rang again, and I waited some more.

My plan, if she answered her door, was to tell her I
was a courier with a package that required her signature.

An old trick that usually worked. That would likely bring her downstairs, out of her apartment.

But after five minutes of waiting, I began to believe that she wasn't at home, and I started mulling over my options.

Since I had her mobile phone number, there was an array of trickery at my disposal. More if I wanted to bring in Dorothy, but she was probably on a plane by now.

There was an app on my iPhone—the kid at the Apple Store had "restored" to my new phone everything that had been on the stolen one, which I'd deactivated—that would enable me to "spoof" a number. That meant that when I called someone who had caller ID—and on cell phones, everyone does—they'd see that the call was coming from whichever number I chose.

I could call or text her from the phone number belonging to Mandy Seeger, the Slander Sheet reporter. That number was on the note she'd sent to the Supreme Court's public affairs office. It was a fair assumption that the reporter had been in close touch with Kayla over the past few weeks or so. They might have texted each other. A text from Mandy Seeger asking her to meet somewhere might bring her in from wherever she was.

But that trick would only work so far. The moment she texted the reporter back and reached the real person, the ruse would be over. *What are you talking about? I didn't ask you to meet!* Mandy would reply.

So . . . there was a variation on that trick that might work a little better.

Another app on my iPhone called Burner would give

me a temporary phone number in almost any area code I chose (except, for some reason, New York's 212 area code) that I could use to call or text her. She could call or text me back on the same number and reach me without ever seeing my real phone number, which had a 617 area code, for Boston. I needed a number with a Washington area code.

I still liked the idea of pretending to be the journalist. Kayla probably had a relationship of trust with her, reporter and source. If Mandy asked to meet, she was likely to agree to it. If that didn't work, I'd try something else.

I left the lobby and returned to the car. Then I took out my phone and fired up Burner. I chose the area code for Washington, 202, and texted Kayla's phone:

Kayla, it's Mandy on a new phone. We have to meet.

Then I waited.
More than a minute.
Then a text came back:

When?

Relieved—it had worked—I texted back:

Now. 30 min.

A pause, shorter this time, then:

OK, where?

I thought a moment. As soon as she saw me, she'd figure out that I had impersonated the reporter from Slander Sheet. I'd have to talk fast or do something to convince her I wasn't a danger. That was best attempted in some public space.

I texted her the name and address of a Starbucks I'd passed not too far from her apartment building.

OK, she replied. 30.

Meaning she'd be there in half an hour.

I got to the Starbucks ten minutes later and found a table with sightlines to both entrances. I sipped a black coffee. The table wobbled. I looked around to see if she'd arrived early, but I didn't see anyone who resembled her. Just the usual assortment of Starbucks customers. A young intern in a rumpled white button-down shirt placing an order for eleven beverages including a banana chocolate Vivanno, whatever that was. A couple of hipsters. A businessman in a suit and tie looking at an iPad, probably between appointments. A guy and a girl, college-student age, chatting awkwardly, maybe on a date.

After I'd been sitting for fifteen minutes, a petite blond woman entered. She was wearing heavy black-framed glasses, an oversized sweatshirt, and flip-flops. The sweatshirt said CORNELIUS COLLEGE in red block letters. She was small, vulnerable-looking. Her hair was pulled back in a ponytail. She scanned the interior, back and forth.

She looked frightened. That's what grabbed my attention most of all. What was she afraid of?

Finally she sat down at a table and took out her phone. She glanced at it, looked around some more. I got up and approached her table. It was crowded enough in the coffeehouse that it didn't necessarily seem creepy when I said, "Can I join you?"

She looked up at me, scrunched her eyes. "Sorry, I'm meeting a friend."

I nodded. "Mandy asked me here."

"Who are you?" she said with suspicion.

I stuck out my hand. "Kayla," I said, "I'm Nick Heller."

11

What happened to Mandy?" she said. She was wearing no makeup and was young enough that she looked beautiful without it. Her skin was nearly translucent. I noticed purplish circles, like bruises, under her gray-blue eyes. Her eyes were pretty, but they were red-rimmed.

"It's just me," I said.

"I don't get it. Who are you? Besides Nick whoever? I mean, a lawyer, a reporter, what?" She had a fairly thick southern accent.

"I'm a private investigator. I've been hired by Slander Sheet to verify your story."

She kept her handbag on her lap. It was a Chanel. I wasn't sure, but I had a feeling by the way she clutched it that it might not be counterfeit. "An investigator?" She narrowed her eyes in suspicion.

"They're really going out on a limb on this story, so they want to make sure it's solid." I was lying, sure, but I justified it to myself on the grounds that she was, too. "They want to make sure they don't get stuck with a bad story the way *Rolling Stone* magazine did, with that UVA story."

"I don't know what you're talking about."

"It's not important."

She looked around the coffee shop. "So Mandy's not coming?"

"Right." She seemed anxious.

I'd known a few call girls, and I recognized the basic profile. They tend to be materialistic. They like their Chanel bags and their Jimmy Choos. They like to dress well because they know they look good. Call girls and escorts, unlike ordinary prostitutes, have a certain self-regard. Men pay good money to be with them, and not just for sex. It's like having a mistress without the inevitable obligations. From the girls' standpoint, they go to nice restaurants and black tie events and get to see a life they'd otherwise never see. In some ways it's not a bad gig.

"And how do I know you're for real?" she demanded.

"Here's my business card." That didn't answer her question, but she took the card and glanced at it quickly. I'd written my cell number on it.

"Are you even licensed? I want to see your license."

I was impressed. You'd be surprised at how few people ask to see my license. I took out my wallet and removed my Commonwealth of Massachusetts private investigator license. She glanced at it.

"That doesn't do you any good. That's a Massachusetts license. You have to be licensed in every state you work in, and we're not in Massachusetts."

I couldn't help smiling. Smart girl. She was right. I fished around in my wallet and found my DC license, which I'd kept up to date since my days of working in the district. The picture showed a younger Nick Heller. Also a less jaded one. Back when I started, I didn't know much about how the world worked. I'd learned a lot since then.

I handed it to her. She looked at it, shook her head. "We're in Virginia. Not DC."

I didn't have that one with me, though I had a Virginia license, and a Maryland one, somewhere back in Boston.

"Kayla, I need to ask you a few questions about the chief justice."

"I already told Mandy everything."

"I know. I just need to go over your answers. Sort of kick the tires. Make sure everything's rock solid."

She shrugged. Warily, she said: "What do you want to know?"

"How'd you first meet him?"

"How? I mean, they told me to go to the Monroe, room such-and-such, and all that. I thought, fancy hotel, that's a relief, that means the client's probably not some sleazeball."

" 'They' is . . . ?"

"My boss. My manager."

The hooker booker, I thought. The person who handles incoming calls and assigns girls to clients.

"And . . . you knew right away he was the chief justice of the Supreme Court?"

She shrugged.

"You watch a lot of news, Kayla? You a big C-SPAN junkie? Not a lot of people would recognize the chief justice. You went to his hotel room and you went, 'Hot damn, the chief justice of the Supreme Court'?"

"Of course not. He was just some guy." Her eyes kept roaming the coffee shop, looking for something, for someone. She turned around and looked some more.

"Yet you somehow figured out who he was."

She took a breath. "After my second date with him I was watching TV and I saw something about the Supreme Court and they showed video of him and I knew that was the guy from the Monroe. I thought, huh, that's cool."

"So you saw his picture on TV."

"Once, when he was in the bathroom, I looked in his wallet."

I nodded. A good answer. If she'd claimed she recognized a Supreme Court justice at first sight, I'd know she was lying. So either she was telling the truth—a remote possibility—or she'd rehearsed her answer. The breath, the pause, the way she replied all told me she was probably recalling something she'd been coached to say.

"Did he request you?"

"It . . . it wasn't like that, far as I know. I see this guy Tom Wyden sometimes when he's in Washington. He always asks for me."

"Wyden, the casino guy?"

She nodded. "I guess he wanted to gift me to the guy."

"*Gift* you?"

"He paid my fee in advance. As, like, a present to his friend."

"And you know this how?"

"Cindy, my manager, told me. She said we got a special request. Why do I have to go over all this again?"

"Slander Sheet is insisting on it. I'm just doing my job. So tell me, what's your usual fee?"

She shifted in her chair, clutched her Chanel bag. "Four to six thousand, depending."

"On what?"

"On how much time, and is it travel or not, and what they expect."

"That's a lot of money."

She shrugged, looked uncomfortable. Under her breath she said, "So maybe I'm worth it."

"How much of that do you keep?"

"Why do you want to know?"

"It's all part of the fact-checking. To make sure there's no problems later on. You're going to be asked questions like this. Probably a lot more intrusive ones."

"Usually I get fifteen hundred out of every four thousand."

"And how do you normally get paid?"

"Cash, most of the time. I give them the take, and they give me my cut. But the judge was prepaid. I got my cut later."

"Fifteen hundred each time?"

"Right."

"Now, I'm going to ask you some fairly explicit questions."

She shrugged. Like, *I don't care, I'm unshockable.* "Go for it."

"Claflin a kinky guy?"

She hesitated, just a beat. Looked around again.

"Plain vanilla. Mostly mish."

She meant the missionary position.

"Bareback?"

"Covered full service."

Coitus with a condom. She was either a pro, or a well-trained actress. Both, I decided. She was comfortable with the language of the professional escort, but she was at the same time highly anxious. I could read it in her facial expressions, in her vocal instrument. She was being pressured into telling this story, I was increasingly certain.

"So is he cut or uncut?" It wasn't a comfortable subject, but it had to be asked.

She shook her head, rolled her eyes, sighed exasperatedly.

"Fifty percent chance of guessing right," I said.

She wasn't going to answer. She didn't know whether Claflin was circumcised or not.

Then she snapped, "Screw you, Uncle Pervy. I know I'm one to talk, but how about we leave the guy his last shred of dignity?"

I liked that. "You don't have to do this, you know," I told her.

She blinked a few times. "Do what?"

"You're in trouble, aren't you?"

She smiled uncomfortably. One of her front teeth was snaggled, cutely.

"Maybe I can help."

Her smile faded. "I have no idea what you're talking about." It was a halfhearted protest.

"Someone's putting the squeeze on you, and they've got you scared. I want you to know that I can help."

"Screw you."

"You know, sometimes you've got to trust someone in life. You think you're being clever by being mistrustful, but that's not the answer. You probably think you're alone in this. But you don't have to be."

For a moment she looked as if she was affected, as if maybe I'd gotten through to her.

I probed a little deeper. "Someone's paying you to lie, that's pretty clear. But you're not just doing it for the money. They've also got you scared, right?"

Her red-rimmed eyes glistened with tears.

"Whoever they are, I can protect you," I said. "You don't have to be alone in this."

A look of anxiety suddenly came over her face. Her eyes swept the room once again. "You're not with Slander Sheet! You're a goddamned *liar*!"

"Kayla, hold on, listen to me."

She leaped up from the table. "Get the hell *away* from me!" She grabbed her handbag and threaded her way between the tables.

I got up and went after her. She was racing through

the Starbucks. People were looking up from their con-
versations, craning their heads, staring back at me. It
looked like a quarrel, or just a bad date.

Then I noticed someone loping out after her: a large
man of about thirty, entirely bald, dressed in a navy suit
and tie. I did a mental rewind, recalled him entering the
Starbucks half a minute or so after Kayla. He hadn't
drawn my attention, because he looked like any other
businessman, though maybe bulkier than average.

By the time I got to the door of the coffee shop, Kayla
was most of the way down the block. The bulky bald man
was now bounding in her direction. I considered chasing
after her but decided it wasn't worth it. I'd gotten from
her what I needed. And besides, the guy was clearly her
guard, a watcher, a minder. At the end of the block she
scrambled into a car, a VW, and it pulled away from the
curb before the bald guy could catch up with her.

She was fast.

The bald guy pulled out a phone.

I decided to introduce myself.

12

The bald man was punching digits into his phone. As I approached, I sized him up. He was a few years younger than me, and taller and bigger. He had a low, sloping forehead and deep-set eyes. As I came closer, I saw that his head was shaven to cover up the fact that he'd gone bald on top, typical male-pattern baldness. He looked like someone who worked out a lot in a gym. He also looked uncomfortable in his navy suit, like he didn't wear suits very often.

He looked up and saw me and stopped dialing. His ears, I noticed, were cauliflowered. He was a boxer. It took a beat or two for him to recognize me as the guy who'd been sitting with Kayla. I could see his face go through a whole series of reactions, as gradual as a cartoon: suspicion, slow-dawning recognition, hostility, aggression. He was not a quick thinker.

"You screwed up, man," I said.

"The hell you talking about?" His voice was high and choked.

"The way she gave you the slip. The boss isn't going to like that."

He squinted, and his face went through another series of reactions: bafflement, more suspicion, anger. Like: Who the hell are you?

I said, "Yeah, you're shadowing her, I'm shadowing you. Operations assessment, call it."

"That's bullshit."

"Call the boss and see. Go ahead. Call him right now, come on."

The bald guy hesitated, frowned, then held up his cell phone. He looked at it and punched a couple of keys.

I shot my right arm out and grabbed at his phone, but his reflexes were quicker than his cognition, and he closed his left fist over the phone so I wasn't able to wrench it out of his hand. In the next instant, he jabbed his right fist toward my abdomen, at center mass, aiming for my solar plexus. A boxer for sure. Good technique. I torqued my body to one side so that his fist missed, just grazing my midriff. He was clutching his phone in his left hand, which handicapped him, limiting him to his right hand.

Boxers are trained to punch as hard and fast as possible, and they follow gym rules. One of the rules is that you don't kick your opponent in the balls. Which is exactly what I did, slamming the stiff leather toe of my brogue hard into his crotch, sinking in, connecting with a sickening crunch.

There are no rules in street fights.

For a moment he looked stunned. He made a low *oof* sound. His right fist loosened, then the phone dropped from his left fist, and he crabbed forward and collapsed into a heap. I could hear the breath expelled from his lungs. He was all folded into himself, and he clutched his sides, letting out a high-pitched, almost feminine squeal, as the freight train of agony came at him a hundred miles an hour and he was vaulted into a realm of unworldly pain, like nothing else a man will ever experience, a pain that would crescendo and then explode, reducing him to a pile of limp rags.

I snatched up his phone from the sidewalk where it had clattered a few seconds before, and I jammed a hand into his hip pocket and extracted his wallet. Then I raced away for a block or two before I slowed down to a walk and disappeared into the crowds.

13

Still a little light-headed from the surge of adrenaline that was only slowly dissipating, I ducked into a Panera and sat at a table and examined the phone, a cheap no-brand throwaway. It looked okay, a bit scuffed up but not damaged by dropping to the sidewalk. An iPhone may be more secure, but it also would have had a shattered screen. Not this thing. The advantages of a cheap phone.

The bald guy had punched in a speed-dial sequence of digits but hadn't had a chance to hit SEND. The saved number he was about to call was identified as Home Base. As in "base of operations." He was checking in with his boss, his controller.

Which meant that I now had his boss's phone number. Which was a potentially significant piece of intelligence. Whoever was watching her—either to check up on where she went, because she was unreliable, or to protect her—was a phone call away.

Now at least I understood why Kayla had seemed so scared: She was being followed, openly and obviously. In a way meant to menace.

I pocketed the phone to use later and examined the guy's wallet. His name was Curtis Schmidt, and he was a Maryland resident with about a hundred dollars in twenties, a small sheaf of credit cards, a health-plan card, and a state of Maryland license to carry Class 3 large capacity firearms.

Then I found something extremely interesting.

It was an ID card issued by the District of Columbia Metropolitan Police with a red stripe on it. It said that Curtis Schmidt was a police sergeant, retired.

Kayla was being followed by an ex-cop.

I thought about Kayla some more. I've learned to trust my instincts at reading people. She was lying, that seemed a certainty. But what was especially intriguing was how smoothly she was lying. Her lies were plausible, well thought out and well studied and expertly memorized. Her lies were built to withstand media scrutiny. She had been well prepared.

Figuring that the bald guy was out of commission for a while, I stayed in Panera and made a few calls on my new iPhone.

I glanced at my watch. Twenty-two hours remained. Time was slipping away.

Unfortunately, I had a lot of questions and not much time to answer them.

Who was behind Slander Sheet? Who owned it? If I could find out who owned Slander Sheet, I'd be closer to finding out who was spearheading the effort to destroy Claflin.

I still had sources in Washington, including a senator I'd done work for previously, and confidentially, when I lived here. Senator James Patrick Brennan had become a friend. He was precisely the kind of guy who knew where the bodies were buried. He knew a lot about the internal workings of Washington. He was savvy and connected and he'd been around the Capitol for several decades. He might know about Slander Sheet. If he'd see me. He was a busy man.

I called Pat Brennan's chief of staff, Kelly Packowski. Kelly had been new in Pat Brennan's office when I lived in DC. Lovely and elegant and ferociously smart. She was still there, fortunately, and she picked right up. "Nick Heller!" she said. "How the hell are you?"

We chatted for a few seconds—she disliked small talk as much as I did, so it was pretty much pro forma—and then she said, "I have a feeling you're calling for the senator."

"I need to talk to him. In person would be best." I thought, but didn't say, that earlier in the day would be a lot better than later. Pat Brennan was a drinker—that was an open secret in Washington—and late in the day, after many bourbons, he became less than coherent. But it was already late afternoon. I'd see him when he could see me. If he could see me.

"It's a tough day, Nick."

"Isn't it always?"

She sighed. "Today's even worse than usual. Right

now he's in a meeting, but let me check in with him when he's out and see what I can do."

I gave her my cell phone number and hung up. Then I called Dorothy.

She answered without preface: "I think I got something on the call girl."

"Yeah?"

"Right. Her sister's had three meth arrests. One more time and she's facing life without parole."

"But does Kayla have a criminal record herself?"

"Not that I can find. Her father's dead and her mother's in a nursing home. She did two years at Cornelius College, which is a women's college in Virginia, but it looks like she dropped out. How was she in person? Did she clam up?"

"Well, she talked, but it was all memorized. Someone's got her really scared. I feel bad for her. She doesn't know what she's in for."

"The girl's a prostitute, right? She's chosen the life."

"That's kind of harsh, don't you think?"

"I'm just saying."

"Well, there's something about her. I like her spirit. She's tough."

"Mmhmm."

"Listen, I need you to run a phone number. And do some background on an ex-DC cop named Curtis Schmidt."

"Who's that?"

"That's the guy who was following Kayla just now."

"How'd you get his name?"

"I borrowed his wallet."

"I won't even ask."

"Also, I need you to see what you can find about who owns Slander Sheet. I'm sure it'll be some media corporation owned by a shell company or whatever, but see what you can pull up. How close you can get to who really owns it."

"What about the hotel? Claflin allegedly stayed at the Monroe three times to meet with this call girl. The hotel must have a record of that—or not. My money's on not."

"That's where I'm headed right now."

"If Claflin never stayed there, that cuts the legs out from under this bogus story."

"It should," I said. "This shouldn't be too complicated."

For some reason, though, I wasn't feeling particularly optimistic.

I had no idea what was coming.

14

The security director of the Hotel Monroe was a fussy little man named Kevin Chung. He wore a slim gray suit and a white shirt with short little collar points and a skinny black tie. The sides of his head were shaven so close you could see the white of his scalp, and on top of his head the black hair stood up in serried ranks of bristles. If the hair on top were longer, it would have been a Mohawk.

The walls of his small windowless office were covered with cheaply framed certificates for various security courses he'd completed and professional security organizations he belonged to. The surface of his desk was uncluttered, though: nothing more than a computer monitor and a desk set and a plaque with his name on it that faced the visitor's chair, just in case you'd forgotten who you were talking to. The plaque was unnecessarily big: He obviously considered himself an important man.

"I wish I could help you, Mr. . . ."

"Heller."

"Mr. Heller. But it's a question of privacy. If I were to confirm whether this person was a guest in our hotel, I would be legally liable. I'm sure you understand. Anything else?"

His response didn't surprise me. Most hotel security directors won't cooperate with private investigators. You have to know the guy, or know somebody who knows the guy, so they'll do it as a favor. But I was here cold. Some security directors you can slip a hundred to and buy cooperation. Sometimes it takes a more sizable bribe.

But Kevin Chung was an officious jerk, and I knew at once that a bribe wasn't likely to work. I needed a different approach.

"That's too bad," I said. "I was hoping we could settle this case quietly, without dragging the hotel's name into it."

I caught a spark of concern in his eyes before he masked it with a studied neutrality. "I don't follow," he said.

"You remember when the Mayflower got caught up in that whole Eliot Spitzer thing. It was ugly."

His cheeks flushed, and he sat up a little straighter in his chair. He knew immediately what I was talking about. Everyone in Washington remembered when the governor of New York had hired a call girl on several occasions. It was a huge scandal. One time he saw the prostitute at his room at the Mayflower Hotel. Room 871 at the Mayflower was briefly famous. As a result, the

Mayflower's reputation was tarnished a bit. Not a lot. But enough. Even today, if you Google "Mayflower Hotel Washington, DC," one of the top auto-suggestions is "scandal."

In reality, of course, call girls frequent the best hotels all the time. They just tend to be discreet about it. The management knows but says nothing. As long as it's not blatant, there's no need to interfere. But fine hotels don't want news stories about call girls on their premises. It looks bad. Tacky, even. It damages the brand.

"What does the Mayflower have to do with us?"

I sighed. "Simple. Slander Sheet is working on a story claiming that Chief Justice Jeremiah Claflin met a prostitute here at the Monroe on three separate occasions."

"Slander Sheet?" He looked appalled.

I nodded.

"Right, and of course it's a hoax. Someone must have gotten hold of one of his credit card numbers and a fake ID and checked into the hotel under his name."

"But . . . why?"

"He's being set up. Extortion, maybe. I don't know. But you can look in your property management system and prove he never stayed here. Which will kill the story. And which will keep the Monroe's name out of Slander Sheet. That's all it takes."

Chung pulled out a keyboard tray and stared fiercely at his monitor. His fingers flew over the keys. "But . . . it does look like Mr. Claflin stayed here, let's see, three different times in the past year."

I nodded again. That didn't surprise me. If I only

wanted to establish whether Claflin had been a guest of the hotel on those dates, I could have slipped a fifty to Barb at the front desk. That was probably all the reporter from Slander Sheet had done.

I'd taken a walk through the hotel before coming to see Kevin Chung. I'd familiarized myself with the property. I'd noticed the security cameras behind the front desk and in the lobby and in the elevators and the hallways.

"Can you pull up video from the front desk camera and get an image of the guy when he checked in?"

He hesitated. "Depends on how long ago that was."

"How long do you keep recorded video?"

"Our policy is seven days."

"But in reality?"

"It varies. They're all on motion sensors. Depends how much activity is recorded."

It took me a moment to understand what he meant. Then I got it. Security cameras now record not on tape but on hard drives. It's all digital, not analog. The more activity a camera senses, the longer it records and the more disk space it takes up. When the hard disk gets full, it starts recording over the old stuff.

"Well, these three dates were, let's see, a lot more than seven days ago," I said. "The most recent was a little over a month."

"We're not going to have video that old."

I nodded. That was a bummer.

Then I remembered something. The hotel, like most hotels these days, used proximity keycards. You held the keycard against an electronic reader mounted on the

room door, and it beeped and flashed green and unlocked the door.

"Can you tell whether room keys were issued?"

Clackety-clack. Then: "Yes. Two keys each time."

If the Monroe was like any other hotel I'd ever stayed
in, it used a piece of software called a property management system, which kept track of every time a guest
room door was opened from the outside using a keycard.
So there was always what's called an audit trail.

"Okay. Now look at the first date. Can you tell whether
anyone used that key to enter the assigned room?"

"Of course," he said, sounding offended. He tapped
and clacked some more. "He—strange . . . That key was
never used."

"Right. Check the next date."

More *clackety-clack*ing. "Wasn't used then either."

"Probably the same for the other date. So someone
came by the hotel on three different days and checked
into the hotel, but never actually went upstairs to the
room." The guy was impersonating a Supreme Court
justice, and the less time he spent in the hotel, the better.
The less chance of his image being captured on video.

Granted, without video of the impostor who was pretending to be Justice Claflin, all I had was a negative: the
fact that no one had checked into his room. But that
wasn't nothing—it proved that Claflin couldn't have seen
a call girl here.

Not in a room he never entered.

Whether this was enough to kill the Slander Sheet
story, I was about to find out.

15

Sitting in a cab that smelled powerfully of curry, I reached Gideon Parnell at dinner. In the background I could hear the clinking of silverware against china, and crowd hubbub, and someone's raucous laugh.

"I talked to the call girl."

"You *what*? How?"

"A little research and a little footwork." The less I told him about what we'd done, the better. We'd broken any number of laws, and he was a lawyer. "The bad news is that she's well prepared and well rehearsed. I couldn't shake her story, and I tried."

"I didn't think you'd be able to get to her. I'm impressed."

I considered telling him about the watcher, the ex-DC cop, but decided to hold that back until I'd figured out whether the guy, Curtis Schmidt, was there to protect her or to monitor her. Also, I had more interesting news to give him.

"Whoever's setting up Claflin is good. They had someone check into the Hotel Monroe under his name with a fake ID and credit card. But we found a hole in the setup. No one actually entered the room. They checked in but never stayed there."

"Really? You can prove this?"

"Yes. That should be enough to jettison their story."

There was a long pause. "I don't think so," Gideon said at last. "It's subtle. Too subtle."

"You think?"

"We need to determine who's behind this. Who's doing it. When we hit back, we need to hit back hard. We need to be as thorough as possible. We need to show those gossip mongers what a giant fraud this whole thing is."

I sighed. Actually, he was right. The fact that no one checked into a room was enough to discredit the story in a court of law, but not in the court of public opinion. In real journalism, but not in gossip. Slander Sheet operated in the world of perception, not the legal system.

"Well, we still have time," I said. "A little over twenty-two hours, by my watch. When's your interview with the reporter?"

"I'm seeing Ms. Seeger tomorrow morning at nine A.M."

"I thought we had until tomorrow at five."

"That's when they press the button and the story goes live. Unless we disprove it before then. My deal with them, the way I bought forty-eight hours, was I'd give them an interview. And by the way, I'll want you present for that."

"Of course. But I want to talk to Seeger before that. Like tonight, if possible."

"I'm not so sure that's a good idea."

"I need to size them up. See what else she's got."

"Then be my guest. But be careful. These Slander Sheet people, they're scorpions."

Another call was coming in. After the 202 area code, the first three digits of the phone number were 224, which told me it was a Senate phone number. I said good-bye to Gideon and took the second call.

"Nick, it's Kelly again."

"Hi, Kelly."

"The senator's had a cancellation in his schedule. If you can get over to his hideaway office in the next fifteen minutes, I can get you in to see him before his dinner with constituents."

I looked at my watch. It was seven o'clock. More like bourbon o'clock, for Senator Brennan. "How's he doing—I mean, you know, this late in the day?"

Her reply sounded a little stiff. She knew what I was asking—how drunk was the guy?—but she was still the protective, and discreet, staff member. "He's had non-stop meetings this afternoon, so he should be okay." Meaning he hadn't had a chance to take a nip, presumably. Though I wondered whether Pat Brennan carried a hip pocket flask around during the day. It wouldn't surprise me. She gave me directions. I thanked her and hung up.

16

Senator Pat Brennan's hideaway office was on the third floor of the Capitol building, behind an unmarked door. I would never have been able to find it if the senator hadn't dispatched an aide, a pretty young redhead, to meet me at security and take me through marble hallways and up winding staircases, through several locked doors.

All senators have hideaway offices in addition to their offices in the Senate office buildings nearby. Some are nicer than others. Some are cramped little closets. They're given out based on seniority. They're generally used for quick meetings, a place to escape the press of business, avoid reporters, take naps. During Prohibition, some senators used them as speakeasies. Lyndon Johnson used to invite young women in to "take dictation," as he called it, in his hideaway. Most senators insist on keeping the location of their hideaways secret from all but their closest aides.

Senator Brennan opened the door himself. He was in

shirtsleeves, his bow tie askew. He was a tall, chubby man with stooped shoulders, a ruddy face with a pixielike expression, a high domed forehead, and a shock of white hair that was usually mussed.

"Nicholas Heller!" he boomed. "Good Lord, how long has it been?"

"A couple of years, Senator."

"In this office, I'm Pat. Please."

I nodded. "Thanks for taking the time, Pat."

"I bagged my evening fund-raising calls, which is an obligation I detest, so I should thank *you*. Come, come."

He put a hand on my shoulder and escorted me in. I could smell the liquor on his breath. Based on the fluidity of his speech, his articulation, I concluded he was still on his first bourbon. Which was good. He was normally coherent through his first two or three drinks.

His hideaway office was one long and narrow room with a high arched ceiling. A marble fireplace, built-in bookcases, a bathroom; and, in one corner, a bar with a mini-fridge, where he led me.

"You, my friend, get the good stuff," he said. "Pappy Van Winkle twenty-year-old Family Reserve."

"I'm honored."

He glugged a couple of fingers of bourbon into two glasses and handed one to me. Then he clinked his glass against mine. "In the words of Horace, *fecundi calices quem non fecere disertum?*" He paused, and then translated. "Whom have flowing cups not made eloquent?"

Brennan was a former professor of government at Harvard who'd served in the White House as adviser to the president and was later elected senator from Massachusetts. He was a classics major at Harvard, was erudite, and was obviously not shy about showing it off. The more he drank, it seemed, the more Latin he spoke.

He was also Jeremiah Claflin's biggest champion. He'd pushed for Claflin's nomination to the US Court of Appeals. Later, he'd lobbied the White House for Claflin's appointment to the Supreme Court. They'd been Harvard colleagues—Claflin at the law school—and friends, and Brennan had quarterbacked his confirmation process in the Senate.

I took a sip. "Excellent," I said. It was bourbon, it tasted fine, and it was no doubt wasted on me.

I'd done a job for Senator Brennan a few years back, when I was with Stoddard Associates in DC. He had a leaker on his staff who was causing him great damage. To make a long and complicated story short and simple, I smoked the traitor out.

He lowered himself heavily onto the corner of a yellow brocade sectional sofa next to a low table, and I sat in a chair facing him. "Let me get right to it," I said. "I know your time is tight. I have to tell you something in absolute secrecy." Though I'd signed an NDA, the urgent circumstances justified telling him, I decided. "Cone of silence, right?"

He put up his palms like a priest conferring a benediction. "*Sigillum confessionis,*" he said. "The seal of the confessional."

Then I told him about the Slander Sheet story on Claflin.

"Oh, dear God," he said when I finished, and he took a swig. He looked out the window. The view of the Washington Monument and the National Mall was post-card-perfect. "Slander Sheet. I detest that website with every fiber of my being."

"Everyone does, but everyone reads it just the same."

"It's funny, Nicholas. Everything old becomes new again. Our republic had slander sheets even before it had newspapers. They were mudslingers, that's all. Every printer belonged to a political faction, and they put out gazettes that endlessly circulated lies about their opponents. Defamation sluiced through those pages like sewage. Adams was declared a bugger, and Madison a spy, and Jefferson—what was it now?—was supposedly keeping a slave mistress!"

"Actually, about that—"

"So I will freely grant: Our newborn electoral government was as shit-stained as any infant's diaper. But something has changed, Nicholas. The Internet has supercharged the gossip pages. Weaponized them. These low-minded rags are like those smallpox-infected blankets we once gave the Indians. The japes and jeers of old now form permanent lesions. And American politics has become gravely disfigured as a result."

I nodded.

"Let me tell you a story. In confidence." He arched his great white brows. "I know I can trust you."

"Of course."

"About a year and a half ago, one evening, I had a few drinks with some Senate colleagues. Right here, in fact.

Maybe I had a few too many. Well, there's no *maybe* about it, I had a few too many. I was driving back to my house on Foxhall Road, and I may have gone through a red light, though I still maintain it was yellow. And I was pulled over by the police, who wanted to know if I'd been drinking."

"Was Congress in session?" I asked.

"Ah, very good. Unfortunately not."

It's a little-known fact that members of Congress cannot be arrested or detained while Congress is in session, except for treason or felony. "I told him who I was, and he said, 'Shit,' and he made a call. And after a long while he got out and told me to get into his cruiser and he took me home. And that was that, except for a nasty hangover. We managed to keep it quiet. Well, a few months after that, my office got a call from a reporter at Slander Sheet. Somehow they'd found out about the incident, and they were threatening to publish a story. You can imagine we went into something of a panic. What do you do? How do you induce them not to publish? Back in the day, if it was *The Washington Post*, I'd call Ben Bradlee, and we'd do some horse trading. I'd offer him an exclusive on something . . . A splash more, Nicholas?" He poured himself another few fingers of bourbon.

I shook my head. "I'm good."

"But Slander Sheet is a new creature entirely. Who owns it? Who calls the shots? The editor in chief is a loathsome little toad named Julian Gunn, but he's not the owner. And he doesn't exactly play ball. My aides tried to negotiate with him, but no dice. So I called this

Julian Gunn myself and said to him, 'Look, what can we do here? Surely your readers don't care about some antiquated senator from Massachusetts and what he does in his off hours!' I promised him an exclusive, I offered him special access, but he wasn't interested in any of that."

"He wanted dirt," I said.

"Exactly. Anything personal on the president, the vice president, the secretary of state, what have you. He wanted dirt, and he wasn't going to settle."

"You gave him something, I assume, because I never saw the drunk-driving story."

Brennan bowed his head. A line of sweat beads had broken out across his forehead. "I did something I regret to this day."

I nodded sympathetically and waited. He looked genuinely agonized.

"I gave them dirt. I gave them Steve Frazier."

"The congressman?"

"Former." He nodded. "And former friend." Representative Steve Frazier was a powerful conservative congressman from upstate New York who'd recently resigned after Slander Sheet had published a story revealing that, in the course of some rocky divorce proceedings, his wife had filed a domestic violence complaint against him, which she later rescinded. "Someone in my office had learned about the allegation from someone in Frazier's office. But I gave it to them. I gave them Steve Frazier's head on a platter. Really, I traded my head for his. So that's why I'm still here and Steve is gone."

"But there's a difference," I said, "between your

drunk-driving incident and the Claflin story. The DUI story was true. Whereas this thing about Justice Claflin is a lie."

He was quiet for a long time. "Let me refresh your drink," he said. I offered him my glass this time, just to be sociable. He poured some more into my glass and then his own.

"Gideon and Claflin—" I began.

"Good men. A real partnership."

"How so?"

"Well, Jerry Claflin is sort of Gideon's protégé."

"I figured."

"I know I get all the credit for pushing his confirmation through the Senate, but the plain truth is, it was Gideon who greased the wheels behind the scenes. Prepared him for the big-time oppo that hits any candidate for the high court." By "oppo," he meant opposition research. "Which was a sort of passing of the baton, you might say, because back in the days when Gideon's name was bounced around for the court—he's too old at this point—Jerry played that role. He was Gideon's cornerman, his defender and confidant. You see, the thing about Gideon and Claflin—their relationship is all about loyalty. In both directions. In a town where loyalty is as scarce as spotted owls."

I nodded slowly, taking it in.

"Jerry Claflin is a deeply honorable man," Brennan went on. "Perhaps a bit of a stickler, to my taste. But a brilliant jurist. You know, I'm sure, about his contribution to *mens rea* law."

"*Mens rea*? I forget . . ."

"Criminal intent. Literally, 'guilty mind.' "

"Right."

"It matters whether the defendant intended to commit the crime. What the defendant meant to do. Anyway, Jerry will always be celebrated for clarifying the vexed 'conditional intent' problem of *mens rea*. Adam Liptak in the *Times* compared his decision in *Hagedorn* to 'a bed with hospital corners and sheets tucked so tight you could bounce a coin off them.' " He chuckled with pleasure.

"I didn't know."

"But this story is just scurrilous, and it will damage him. As Virgil tells us in *The Aeneid, fama, malum qua non aliud velocius ullum*. There is no evil swifter than a rumor."

"So who's trying to destroy him?" I said. "Who has the animus and the resources to do something like this?"

"The proper question is, who's driving the story? Is it a plant by someone angry about one of the court's decisions, and Slander Sheet is innocent? Or did Slander Sheet initiate the attack?"

I nodded again. "If it originated with Slander Sheet, do you think it was political?"

"Here's the thing, Nicholas. Most of the time, owners of magazines and newspapers don't hide their ownership. They *want* to be known as the owners, right? They want to be courted and flattered. The fact that we don't know who really owns Slander Sheet tells me it may *not* be someone with a political agenda. If you look at the pattern of their hit jobs, I'm not sure there's a political slant. They came after me, and I'm a liberal, of course. In my place they took down Steve Frazier, who's as right-wing as they come. Then again, maybe there's a subtle figure in the carpet. Hard to say."

"So who benefits from the destruction of Jeremiah Claflin's career?"

"Ah. That old shopworn phrase *cui bono*—who benefits? And I'll tell you the God's honest truth. I don't have the slightest idea. It's a goddamned mystery."

I got up. I had more work to do that night. "Can I give you a ride home?"

"Don't worry," said the senator. "I have a driver now."

17

Slander Sheet's DC offices were located on the third floor of an old bread factory in Shaw, at Seventh and S, a few blocks from the Shaw metro stop. Until the riots of 1968, Shaw was the center of the black middle class in DC. After the riots, most people who could move out to the suburbs did. Now it was the center of a thriving Ethiopian community as well as home to a lot of recent college graduates, who lived in the once beautiful Victorian row houses. It had also recently become the funky home for small businesses and nonprofits and Internet enterprises like Reddit.

It was early evening, and dusk was beginning to gather, but the lights in the old bread factory were blazing. Including the third floor. The lobby of the building was open and unattended. There was a lot of exposed brick and glass and steel. A depressing old relic of a building had been gussied up into a lively, edgy workspace. People were leaving work for the day, and most of them looked to be in their early to midtwenties. A wall plaque gave Slander Sheet's offices as number 301.

I took the elevator, a big clanking thing that looked like it was once used exclusively for freight, to the third floor. I was the only passenger. Everyone else was going down and out of the building. Fifty feet down a narrow corridor, a glass door was labeled HUNSECKER MEDIA. The name sounded vaguely familiar, and after a few seconds I recalled it as one of the names associated with the Slander Sheet operation.

I pulled open the door, surprised that it wasn't locked, and looked around. It was all one big open space. More exposed brick here, and pipes, and a pressed-tin ceiling. Around a dozen people, all in their early twenties, were seated at several long tables that ran the length of the room, computer stations on either side. There was room at the tables for around fifty. No one seemed to be in charge. Mounted to the ceiling was a huge TV screen displaying article headlines. Next to each one was a number, probably for the number of page views they'd received, and a green up arrow or a red down arrow, probably indicating how each post was trending. The most popular one, the one at the top, was titled CON-GRESSMAN DICK: REP. DICK COMPTON SEXTS HIS MAN PARTS TO A CONGRESSIONAL PAGE.

Just about everyone tapping away at their computers was wearing headphones. They were all quiet except for an occasional laugh. It was a digital sweatshop.

I stopped the first person I came to, a heavyset guy

with pork-chop sideburns. I touched him on his arm. He took off his headphones. "Yeah?"

"I'm looking for Mandy Seeger."

He looked around. "She normally sits on that end." He gestured with his chin. "But I don't see her. I think she's gone for the night."

"You got a way to reach her? It's important."

He glanced at me for a moment, incuriously. He shrugged.

I noticed on his monitor a small box on the side that looked like a chat window. I said, "Could you message her for me, please?"

"Uh, like, who are you?"

"Tell her it's about Gideon Parnell."

"Gideon Parnell?"

I nodded.

"You don't look like Parnell." Even a low-level staffer at Slander Sheet knew who Gideon Parnell was.

"I'm with Gideon. She wants to talk to me."

He typed something into his chat window. A few seconds later came a reply.

"She says she's seeing him tomorrow morning at nine."

"Tell her I know. This is an extra interview, if she's interested. A special offer."

More tapping. "She wants your name."

"Nick Heller."

He typed my name in the chat window. He waited a few seconds. Then the answer came back.

"She says to meet her at Lobby on Capitol Hill in half an hour."

I knew Lobby. It was a dive bar: two-dollar beers, beer-and-shot combos with clever names, and Skee-Ball.

"I'll be there."

18

The bar was just as I remembered it: crowded and low-ceilinged, authentically working class, smelling of beer and french fries. The bar back was still painted red, and the beers were listed on a blackboard in different colored chalks. License plates from all fifty states hung on the wall. All types of people still came here: college students and construction workers, Capitol Hill staff, marines from the barracks at Eighth and I, Capitol Hill police, nurses out of DC General, lobbyists. Lobby opened at eight in the morning and closed at two A.M. when the law said they had to.

I found Mandy Seeger holding down a booth. She was in her midthirties, with pale skin and coppery hair, amused light brown eyes, and a lively intelligence in her face. She was not beautiful, yet definitely attractive, and she wore a floral, hippyish dress and large hoop earrings. She didn't look like a reporter, though I couldn't say what a reporter was supposed to look like. Just not like this. In front of her was a tumbler of cola. Diet, I was guessing.

She waved at me. "You've got to be Nick Heller."

I sat down on the other side of the booth. "How could you tell?"

"You're too old to be a college student, and you're not nerdy enough to work on the Hill. Also, you look like a guy who can kick ass."

"Not at all. I'm a pacifist. I prefer to mediate."

"Well, you look like someone who could have been in the Special Forces. Or some kind of soldier, ten pounds ago."

I had no doubt that Kayla Pitts had already told her about me. But I played along. "You did some Googling."

She laughed. She had a great, throaty laugh. "You barely exist on Google. You don't even have a website."

"I don't need one."

"Well, la-di-dah. I had to do a hell of a lot more than Google."

"And yet you're still willing to meet me."

"Morbid curiosity."

A waitress came by with a pad.

"Another Diet Coke," Mandy said.

The waitress turned to me.

"I'll have a Natty Boh."

When the waitress left, Mandy said, "Natty Boh, huh?"

I shrugged. That was localese for National Bohemian beer, which I knew they served here on tap. "Russian owned, by the way," I said.

"No, actually, it's owned by Pabst."

"Right. And Pabst is owned by a Russian oligarch now."

"Well, who knew?" She shrugged, conceding the point. I had a feeling she didn't like being wrong. "So you're almost a local boy, aren't you?"

"I spent some formative years in DC."

"Working for some supersecret unit of Defense intelligence. I know."

"Everything in the Pentagon is classified. Lunch menus in the cafeteria are classified. You must know that."

" 'Classified' is just a red flag to me." She smiled. "And after the Pentagon you went private, working for Jay Stoddard."

I nodded.

"Working for big companies and politicians and the rich and powerful."

"Largely. But not always."

"Not a lot of people know about you. But the ones who do had mostly good things to say."

"Clearly you didn't talk to everybody."

"So Gideon Parnell hired an investigator. That's the best news I've heard all day."

"Why's that?"

"If my story weren't totally solid, they wouldn't bother to put someone like you on it."

"Not at all. Most people are afraid of Slander Sheet. A lie this outrageous, you take it seriously. You do what you can to make sure it dies a proper death."

"I think Gideon hired you for clean-up duty."

"I don't do that."

"Come on. You're an attack dog for the rich and powerful."

"Not exclusively."

"Only the rich and the powerful can afford you."

I didn't want to tell her that I took this job because I believed the story was a lie, and I could see where this conversation was going, so I took a detour. Decided to try my best to defang her. "You did some great work at the *Post*."

"You have no idea what kind of work I did," she said with a grin.

"Not true. You did that major series on the out-of-control secrecy in the US government a few years back. That was huge. What'd you say, like almost a million people hold top-secret security clearances? More than the entire population of Washington, DC?"

She shrugged. "Right."

"And you were also the first one to write about the CIA's secret prisons overseas—that was a big deal, too, that piece. And the one about the abuses at Walter Reed."

She actually seemed to blush. That I didn't expect. "You did some Googling, too," she said.

"I didn't have to. I remember. You were good."

"Still am. Just get paid better. And you're here to threaten me, I bet. Scare me off the Claflin story. Well, you might as well stop wasting your time."

"I never threaten. I don't need to."

"Not the way you look, you don't. You don't have to. You just glare at people and they fall in line."

I wasn't sure that was a compliment, but I said thanks anyway.

The beer came, in a tall plastic tumbler, along with her Diet Coke. I tipped mine toward hers. "To morbid curiosity."

She smiled and took a sip of her Coke. "You're very charming and very smooth. And nice-looking. In another set of circumstances, I could be swayed."

"So you've moved on from the CIA's secret prisons to pictures of Congressman Compton's dick?"

"Less charming all the time. That's actually not my piece, to be fair."

"It's trending number one, right? Over a million views already."

"Hey, Compton's the one who texted the picture of his dick to a Congressional page. Not us."

"You're just making it available to the masses."

"We blur it out. You have to click through to see the not-safe-for-work version in all its glory. Which is not much glory, by the way."

"What's Hunsecker Media? Who's Hunsecker?"

"Burt Lancaster," she said.

"Huh? I mean the sign on the door of your office. It says 'Hunsecker Media.'"

"Right. Like I said. It's from an old movie called *Sweet Smell of Success*. Burt Lancaster plays a powerful gossip columnist, J. J. Hunsecker."

"Now I get it."

"Hunsecker Media is the parent company for Slander

Sheet New York and Slander Sheet DC and Slander Sheet LA."

"So are you Slander Sheet's J. J. Hunsecker?"

"If I've got a good story and I'm onto the truth, sure."

"See, that's the problem with your Claflin piece. It's not true."

"Says the corporate mouthpiece."

"It's just like my beer and the Russkies. You'll see I'm right."

"Really." She smiled again, but this time it was an unpleasant, sardonic smile. "And what, Heidi L'Amour doesn't exist either?"

"Well, strictly speaking, you're right, Heidi L'Amour doesn't exist. She's Kayla Pitts, from Tupelo, Mississippi."

"You *are* an investigator." She said it archly. "And I suppose you think Kayla is lying."

"Most certainly. Though she's very good at it. She'd probably fool most people. I'm sure she's good on camera. You guys are obviously paying her a lot."

"Nothing illegal about paying a source."

"I'm not talking about illegal. But a big payday is a good incentive to lie."

"And what makes you so sure she's lying?"

"For one thing, I can tell. It's called trusting your gut. I've learned to look for a thousand tiny signals and reflexes. How to read body language. People speak a whole lot when they're silent."

"Oh, is that right?"

"I'm sure you pay close attention to your gut instinct when you're reporting a story."

"I do, and my gut tells me this is for real. So do the facts."

"Then you've got a problem with your gut instinct. Also, with the facts. Like the fact that she's not familiar with certain intimate details about the justice."

"Oh yeah?" She meant to sound sarcastic, but her curiosity was getting in the way. She couldn't help sounding intrigued.

"Yeah."

"And are you going to share these details with me?"

"Sure. She doesn't know whether he's circumcised or not."

That silenced her for a beat. Then she laughed dismissively. "She may not want to tell you. That doesn't mean she doesn't know."

"Yeah, maybe she's just too well bred a girl to discuss such impolite topics. So you're certain about that, huh? Certain enough to stake your entire hard-earned journalistic reputation on it?"

"I've got Kayla on tape, I have hotel records, and I have a horny middle-aged Supreme Court justice, separated from his wife and in need of company. And an escort paid for by Tom Wyden. Who had a case before the court, conveniently decided in his favor." She took another sip of her Diet Coke. "It's a huge story. And it's going to explode. I understand why you'd like to talk me out of it. Or discourage me, or intimidate me. Or whatever. Believe me, I've been threatened with probably forty lawsuits and have never been sued, not once."

"I'm not threatening you with a lawsuit. Let's be clear about that. I'm not a lawyer and never wanted to be one."

"I did, once upon a time."

"I'm here to tell you there are holes in your story. Let's take one little detail. If Kayla really saw Jeremiah Claflin on three occasions, where do you think they met?"

"The Monroe. He stayed there on three different dates."

"Sure, because you have records from the hotel guest registry."

She smiled, nodded.

"Which tells you that someone with a credit card in Jeremiah Claflin's name checked into the hotel."

"And Claflin's driver's license." She took a long swig of her Diet Coke, finished it off.

Something in the back of my mind bothered me, but I couldn't quite grab hold of it. "Sure," I said. "But whoever they were, they never entered the room. Not one time."

"And you know this how?"

I paused. Ordinarily I wouldn't give away operational details like that. But this wasn't an ordinary circumstance. She had to be convinced I was right so she'd back off the story.

"The Monroe uses software that keeps track of room keys electronically. How many keys are issued. When keys are used. Every time a hotel room is opened from the outside, the system records it. So someone posing as Claflin checked into the hotel but never, not once, entered the room."

There was a spark of something in her eyes. "Oh, and of course a hotel's computers can't be tampered with, right? You're going to have to do a lot better than that. Kayla told me about your little ruse. Tricking her into thinking she was meeting me. You people, you'll stop at nothing."

"I've only been at this a couple of hours, and already I've punched a serious hole in your story."

"Look, uh, Nick, I've got a heap of evidence, and the best you can come up with is some easily manipulated piece of computer data? I don't think so. You're going to have to do better than that. This isn't going to move my editor at all."

"Your editor is . . . ?"

"His name is Julian Gunn. And he's as battle-hardened as they come. He'd laugh in my face if I brought this to him."

"You know, I think you're missing the real story. It's right in front of your face."

She was starting to look annoyed now. "And what's that?"

"The fact that someone's setting Jeremiah Claflin up to damage him, to discredit him. Who would do something like that? You see, I think you're being used. The question is, by who?"

"By whom."

"If you prefer." I waited.

"Well, Nick Heller. Nice try. Thanks for playing."

There didn't seem to be much more to say, so I put down some cash and said, "Drinks on me."

"You can expense it," Mandy said.

19

The hotel that Jillian, my office manager, had booked for us was nicer than the hotels I normally stay in. When I'm traveling on my own dime, I'm partial to the kind of budget hotel that has a coffeemaker and refrigerator in the room and a waffle iron in the breakfast area off the lobby. When someone else is paying for it, though, I like to live well. I work hard for my clients; why shouldn't I enjoy the perks? This hotel had sumptuous décor and five-hundred-thread-count bed linens. My suite had a separate living room and an ergonomic desk chair. It was a nice hotel. No in-room coffee machine, though.

I unpacked quickly, changed into sweatpants and a T-shirt, and called Dorothy. Her room was directly across the hall. She said she was in her bedtime attire but would quickly change and knock on my door. I ordered a steak from room service. Dorothy said she'd already had her dinner.

A few years back I'd hired Dorothy away from the private intelligence firm in DC where we both worked, Stoddard Associates. Jay Stoddard had hired her out of the National Security Agency. She was skilled at cyber investigations, and digital forensics, and she was unshakably loyal to me. I was loyal right back—there were certainly better digital forensics people around but no one as persistent and determined as Dorothy. I'd uprooted her from a comfortable life in Washington, and, though she never reminded me, I never forgot it.

She knocked on the door long before room service arrived. She was wearing jeans and a white T-shirt. She always wore her hair short, but recently she'd been wearing it practically buzzed, to go with the complicated arrangement of piercings on the helixes of her ears. (I was the only one in our office whose ears weren't pierced.) She was barefoot. Her toenails were painted the same bright shade of pink as her fingernails.

"How's your brother?"

"Don't ask."

"Too late, I just did."

"It's a long story. I'll tell you some other time."

"Tell me now."

She surveyed the room as she entered. "How come you got the executive suite, with the separate living room and everything? You probably have two bathrooms, too."

"Just one. All I need." I ignored her question. "Are you going to tell me about your brother?"

"Some other time."

"Okay." I usually knew when to stop pushing.

"Internet's blazing fast for a hotel, by the way."

She took a glass from atop the minibar and filled it with water from the bathroom sink. Then she sat down in the big wingback chair in the corner of the living room.

"Did you see Representative Compton's member?"

"I didn't click through. But I saw the piece."

"Why are we worried about a trashy online gossip site that runs pictures of congressmen's dicks? Who's going to pay any attention to what they report?"

I poured myself a Scotch from the minibar. I wanted ice but didn't feel like going out to the ice machine or calling room service again, and neat was fine anyway. "It's all about the life cycle of scandal," I said. "Everyone pays attention to Slander Sheet, whether they admit it or not, but the serious news establishments, like *The New York Times* and *The Wall Street Journal,* aren't going to report any scandal that comes out on Slander Sheet until it becomes just too big to ignore. And when they do, they'll report it at a slant. They'll report on the *existence* of a scandal, a controversy. Holding their noses. Meanwhile, they'll send their own reporters to reweave the case. Pretty soon they've done their own wave of stories. Then come the ancillary stories, the featurettes on the principals. You can just see the piece on Kayla Pitts, can't you? Young college girl from rural Mississippi comes to the nation's capital and gets corrupted. Innocence meets the dubious morality of DC. Very *House of Cards.*"

"You know it."

"By then they own the story. They've got an equity stake in the narrative."

"But if you've got the proof it couldn't have happened . . . ?"

"Remember the Duke University lacrosse case? These three poor college guys, members of the Duke men's lacrosse team, were accused of rape. Their lives were turned inside out. Turns out it was a false accusation. Totally made up, by someone with a history of that kind of thing. Yet it took the mainstream media eight months before they acknowledged the whole story was just a hunk of pulp fiction."

"I know. I remember."

"So a false allegation like Slander Sheet's about to run could do Claflin some serious damage. Once the mainstream media picks it up."

"You think Slander Sheet's really going to run with it?"

"For now, that's what it looks like." I told her about getting a beer with Mandy Seeger and how badly the meeting had ended. "Can you do a little digging into her?" I said.

"What about?"

"Why in the world she left *The Washington Post* for Slander Sheet, of all places. I don't get it."

She nodded. "You told her about the evidence you found, right?"

"She doesn't believe it. But I get a feeling it's not up to her."

"Who's it up to, then?"

"Sounds like her boss is the one who's going to make the decision on whether to run with it or kill it."

"Who's her boss?"

"A bastard named Julian Gunn. He's the editor in chief of Slander Sheet. Supposed to be a real asshole. He'll run whatever makes the page views blow up."

"Even if it discredits his own website?"

"I'm sure he doesn't want to *knowingly* trash his own creation by breaking a 'news' story that's going to turn out to be false."

"Right."

"But he won't have a problem running a sleazy story that can't ever quite be disproven. Like those adhesive stickers that always leave a gummy trace, no matter how hard you scrape."

"So what does Mandy Seeger think, you're flat-out lying to her?"

"She must truly believe I'm trying to sell them a crock. That we've, I don't know, manipulated the hotel's computer system. Deleted the digital records."

She laughed. "*I'd* believe it. I've seen it done. I know how to do it."

I was quiet for a few seconds. Was it possible? "You think someone might have done just that? Hacked into the hotel's property management system to make it look like the justice never stayed there?"

"Someone working for the justice?"

"Right."

She shook her head. "That's nutty. If you're going to mess around with the hotel's property management system, why not delete the whole guest record? So it looks like no one named Jeremiah Claflin ever checked into the hotel?"

"Fair point."

"You don't seriously think that, right?"

"I consider all options. But no, I don't seriously think that."

"Good."

"But the fact remains that somebody made off with my laptop and my iPhone, and I don't think that happens very often inside the Supreme Court building. Someone was very interested in who I am and what I'm up to. Which means that somebody was tailing me."

"That doesn't entirely surprise me. The stakes are huge. We're talking the chief justice of the Supreme Court. Whoever's setting this up wants to make sure no one pulls it down. Who was following Kayla Pitts?"

I took the wallet from my back pocket that I'd grabbed from the guy whose balls I'd kicked. "An ex-DC cop named Curtis Schmidt."

"You got his phone, too, right?"

"Right," I said, and I took that out and handed it to her.

"Cheapo burner piece of crap," she said, turning it over. "Disposable phone you buy at Costco, comes with a prepaid half hour of phone time or whatever. You think this ex-cop is protecting her, or spying on her?"

"My gut says he's protecting her. Making sure nothing happens. They're going to need her."

"You mean, to do interviews and such."

I nodded. "That girl was frightened. Like she's signed on to do something she wishes she never had."

"Whether she serviced Claflin or not, she's about to face an avalanche of publicity, and it will not be fun."

"*Whether* she slept with him or not?" I said. "She didn't. It didn't happen. That I'm sure of."

"If you say so. When it comes to men and their sex drives, as far as I'm concerned all bets are off. Anything's possible. I don't care if you're the president or the pope."

"Fair enough. But it never happened."

"Okay." She held up the flip phone. "The call history on this thing will be very illuminating."

"He only called one number."

"His boss, I'm betting."

"No doubt."

"So what do you want to do with it? Are you going to call it? Call the boss?"

"First I want to find out whose number it is."

"You already tried?"

I nodded. I'd tried the usual databases—Skip Smasher, Tracers Info, TLOxp, IRBsearch—where you can look up mobile phone numbers and find who owns them. All I learned was what I already knew, that it was a prepaid phone. Unregistered. No name associated with it. "It's a drop phone, that's all."

"What about Montello?"

Frank Montello was an "information broker" who lived and worked in suburban Maryland. Not a friend, but a valuable contact. I didn't know exactly how he practiced his dark arts. I just knew that if I needed to find an unlisted phone number or someone's home address, and I'd had no luck with the traditional databases, he was the guy I'd reach out to. He knew how to dig deep. He could find out whether someone had had psychiatric problems or was an alcoholic. He could get anyone's birth certificate or motor vehicle records. I used to find it creepy how much he could find out for me, but I'd gotten jaded. In any case, he was extremely expensive, and sort of unpleasant to deal with. He was usually overworked and slow. I used him selectively and reluctantly.

"He came up empty, but I asked him to keep working on it."

The doorbell rang, and I opened the door for room service. The woman rolled in a warming cart and began to set up my dinner. The porterhouse looked perfectly cooked. I thanked her, tipped her, and she left.

"You realize I scarfed down pizza at the airport," Dorothy said, "while you're dining out on steak."

"Happy to split it with you. I don't need the whole thing."

"I'm not hungry. Just giving you a hard time."

"Whatever makes you feel good." I cut off a forkful and took a bite. It was hot and delicious. A solid hit of umami. Hotel room service rarely does a good job with steak. It's hard to get the timing right. But this one was great.

"What I want to know is who's behind this," I said. "It circles back around to the editor of Slander Sheet, this Julian Gunn guy, and what his motivations are. Gunn is leading this, but I'll bet he's taking orders from whoever really owns that piece of crap website. Once we find out who the money is behind Slander Sheet, who the real power is, and bring that out, everything will fall into place. We'll know why this is happening. And we'll have a way to disprove this thing with some real credibility."

"That's not going to be easy, I can tell you that."

"What have you found?"

"SlanderSheet.com is owned by HunseckerMedia.com. HunseckerMedia.com is owned by some proxy, some limited liability company called, uh, Patroon LLC. Which has to be a shell company. I can't find anything about it. And I don't think I'm going to find anything in the next eighteen hours, or whatever we have left."

"Seventeen."

"Right."

"So maybe cyber isn't the way to find out who owns Slander Sheet. Maybe it's old-fashioned door knocking and shoe leather and phone calls."

"I'll keep trying."

"Wake me if you find anything."

"I will. Seventeen hours left. My batteries are running down, Nick, but I'll do as much as I can."

"You want to order coffee from room service?"

She glanced at her watch. "I don't know if coffee's going to help me at this hour."

"Tomorrow morning Mandy interviews Gideon, off the record, and I want to be there for that."

"She's *Mandy* to you now?"

I shrugged. "She's not the enemy. If my theory is correct, she's being used, too. She thinks she's really onto a huge scoop and she doesn't want to back down. Probably because her boss doesn't want them to back down."

"Then who's the enemy?"

I held up Curtis Schmidt's phone. "Right here."

I had another Scotch while I checked my e-mail and then e-mailed Montello, the data broker, again. I was beat—it had been a long day, but I had a feeling tomorrow would be even worse.

The five-hundred-thread-count sheets were smooth as silk but cool and creamy. The mattress was firm but not hard. The bed was extremely comfortable. I fell asleep fairly quickly.

The phone rang some time later, an unfamiliar purring ringtone, and I jolted awake. "You got something," I said.

"This is Gideon."

"Oh, sorry—Gideon? What's—" I looked at the digital clock. It was 6:05 in the morning. I'd been asleep for five hours or so.

"It's online," Gideon Parnell said.

"What's online?" It took me a moment to realize. "Slander Sheet? I thought they were giving us forty-eight hours."

"They ran it anyway," he said.

20

While I waited for Dorothy to throw on some clothes, I went online to SlanderSheet.com. The piece was the first thing that came up. In huge red type against a stark white background were the words:

SUPREME COURT JUSTICE IN CALL GIRL SCANDAL

Above the headline was an unfortunate headshot of Jeremiah Claflin, in black judicial robe and tie, smiling like a cat in catnip.

I clicked on the headline. A short article came up, Mandy Seeger's byline right at the top. All around it were ads with photos of women in bikinis with huge boobs. Atop the article was another headline:

NATION'S TOP JUDGE IN ROMP WITH WYDEN HOOKER

Here was another picture of Claflin, this one in casual attire, getting out of a car. Next to that was a picture of Heidi taken from the Lily Schuyler website.

The piece began:

Jeremiah Claflin, the chief justice of the Supreme Court of the United States, has had at least three trysts with a high-priced escort in DC, sources tell Slander Sheet in an exclusive. The escort, identified as Heidi L'Amour, 22, works for Lily Schuyler, a pricey call girl service that charges upward of $3,000 an hour.

Reliable sources tell Slander Sheet that the country's top jurist, who is believed to be separated from his wife, did not pay for the prostitute's services himself. Instead, the sordid trysts were funded by casino mogul and Claflin pal Tom Wyden, who benefited from a favorable decision by the Supreme Court just recently.

The assignations took place at Washington's ritzy Hotel Monroe on three separate evenings this spring.

. . .

The office of the chief justice of the Supreme Court of the United States did not respond to requests by Slander Sheet for comment.

Below the article were headlines about one of the Kardashians, and one about Angelina Jolie, and one about Britney Spears, and a report on Beyoncé buying "$312,000 diamond shoes."

Then Dorothy knocked on my door and we were off.

*   *   *

In the cab, Dorothy checked Drudge Report and Gawker and Perez Hilton, TMZ and RadarOnline.com, and Celebitchy. All the gossip websites she could think of. The Claflin story hadn't appeared on any other website yet. But it was early. The piece had just gone up.

"Check this out," she said, handing me her phone. It was the most viewed column on SlanderSheet.com. Number 1 was "SUPREME COURT JUSTICE IN CALL GIRL SCANDAL."

It wasn't even seven in the morning.

"It's only a matter of minutes before Drudge links to this story," she said. "Or Wonkette. Then it's going to blow up big-time."

"Not if I can help it," I said.

Fifteen minutes later we arrived at Shays Abbott Burnham's DC offices, on M Street near where it crossed New Hampshire Avenue. Gideon met us in the law firm's reception area. He was dressed in khakis and a light blue button-down shirt, open at the neck. His shirt looked crisp and unwrinkled, as if he'd just put it on.

But in contrast to his fresh clothes, he looked depleted and exhausted. Although I barely knew him, I could see the strain he was under. It showed in the deep lines creasing his face, the prominent bags under his eyes, the cluster of wrinkles between his brows. His large eyes glistened, seemingly with tears, but probably from exhaustion.

The overhead fluorescents were off, but in the dim light I could see that the DC headquarters of Shays Abbott were decorated in the same hard white glossy surfaces as the Boston offices—the white stone floors polished like glass, the frosted glass walls, the sharp-edged white leather sofas.

Dorothy seemed a little flustered to meet Gideon Parnell. Even at a time of urgency, this was a fan girl moment for her. She tried not to show how thrilled she was to shake his hand, to be in the presence of such a historic figure. But she couldn't hide it from me. I had never seen her smile so much and act so deferential. It was as if Jesus Christ himself had come to visit.

Gideon was gracious but terse, and obviously distracted. He led us through a maze of hallways to his office.

"What happened to the forty-eight hours?" I asked.

"Just minutes before the story was posted," Gideon said, "I received an e-mail from the editor, Julian Gunn, saying that they believed they were in imminent danger of being scooped by a competitor, so they had to run it immediately."

"That's a lie," Dorothy said. "They saw how hard we were pushing back and they wanted to get it out before we disproved it."

"No," I said. "That's not the reason. If they thought we were really going to prove it false, they wouldn't risk running it. Too damaging to their reputation."

"We disagree," Dorothy said to Gideon.

It was out of character for her to contradict me in a meeting with a client. It was a little unprofessional. Not that I cared, particularly. I cut her some slack; she wasn't herself; she was in the presence of greatness.

"What about the interview with Mandy Seeger this morning?" I asked.

"I canceled it. They broke their side of the deal."

"I can't help but wonder whether they ran it earlier because I was rattling the cage," I said, and Gideon said nothing.

His office looked exactly as I'd expected: spacious, classical, fastidiously neat. Decorated to impress, for public display. There was a long mahogany conference table. A bottle of Old Overholt rye on a shelf. Two of the walls were ego walls, walls of fame, crowded with photographs of Gideon with a litany of the great and the powerful and the famous. My eye was caught by a photo of him in a golf cart with Barack Obama and Bill Clinton.

His assistant, a plain middle-aged blond woman named Rose, who must have come into work early, offered us coffee. It was a little weak, but it did the job.

"We need to talk," he said.

21

We gathered around the mahogany table. Gideon sat at the head.

"We are well and truly screwed," he said. "Has it been picked up by any other websites yet?"

I shook my head.

"Give it a couple of minutes," Dorothy said.

"I'm sorry about this," I said. "I really thought we'd have killed this thing by now."

"Don't blame yourself," said Gideon. "This was always a Hail Mary pass."

"We're not done yet," I said.

Gideon looked at me, tilting his head. "What the hell are you talking about? It's out there now, Heller."

"Lots of things are out there on the Internet. Websites about how reptile extraterrestrials are running the US government."

He shook his head, as if in disgust, his eyes closed. "The world has changed since the Kennedy administration. Back then, everybody knew that Jack Kennedy had a parade of women coming through the White House. But not a word of it ever made the papers. Now, anything and everything does. Absolute rubbish gets reported on the basis of nothing more than rumor."

"Not true," I said. "It's just gotten a lot more complicated."

"If someone snapped a picture of the president with a hooker today, it would be online in minutes."

"Sure. There's always some website that'll publish anything. But the Claflin story hasn't been picked up by the mainstream media yet. Meaning it hasn't been validated. That usually takes a while."

Gideon tilted his head like a Jack Russell Terrier listening to his master's voice. "I hope you're right. Go on."

"You see, right now it exists only on the Internet. As long as it stays an Internet-only story—Slander Sheet, Gawker, TMZ, Drudge, Vice, whatever—it's just gossip. It's not news. It doesn't become permanent until it's validated by the old 'legacy' media. The mainstream media. *The Washington Post, The New York Times, The Wall Street Journal.* The NBC evening news, NPR, CNN. At that point it's written in ink. It's permanent."

"And when does that happen?"

"You probably know better than me. I don't know the exact timing. Doesn't the *Times* have a morning news meeting or whatever?"

Gideon looked at his watch. "At ten o'clock this morning, *The New York Times* has their front-page meeting."

"There you go. Someone's going to mention the rumor about Claflin and a call girl. They're not going to ignore it."

"No, probably not."

"Who runs the meeting? There's always one person. It's not a democracy."

"The executive editor. I've met him."

"Okay, so the editor's going to ask, 'Who else is running with it?' What they really want to know is, Is anybody *else* in the mainstream media covering it? Any of the other big dogs? But it's not going to be any of them. Not this fast. Not in two and a half hours."

"But this thing's going to spread like gonorrhea."

"No doubt. It'll be picked up first by BuzzFeed or Drudge or TMZ. But that's not enough to push it over the line into the mainstream. So maybe the *Times* assigns a couple of reporters to poke around the Slander Sheet story, see if there's any solid evidence there."

"But it's also going to be picked up by some of the more respectable websites like Politico and Roll Call."

"Maybe. But not the big dogs. Not yet. Does *The New York Times* have another front-page meeting today?"

"At four-thirty."

"That's the one we have to worry about. Four-thirty. Enough time will have gone by that they can at least do a piece about the reaction to this rumor."

"You're right. Four-thirty."

"That's nine hours from now. Not much time." I got to my feet. "So what are we doing, sitting here, talking? Dorothy, come on. We've got work to do."

22

Gideon gave us a conference room to use.

It was like every other office conference room I'd ever seen, only nicer. There was a long, coffin-shaped table, made of mahogany. Around it were arrayed high-backed chairs that seemed to be upholstered in leather. Starfishlike speakerphones were placed every four seats or so. Down one wall ran a long credenza.

Dorothy pushed a button somewhere, and a panel on the far wall slid away, revealing a large video projection screen. She hooked up her laptop to some port built into the table—she worked without hesitation, seeming to know what she was doing—and the bright red Slander Sheet logo came up on the screen.

SUPREME COURT JUSTICE IN CALL GIRL SCANDAL remained number 1 in the most viewed column. She clicked around to TMZ. The Claflin story had been picked up. The headline read:

UH-OH
DISORDER IN THE COURT
TOP JUDGE SCREWS AROUND

"Shit," I said.

"That took almost an hour," Dorothy said. "Longer than I expected. I have a feeling it's just going to accelerate from here."

She quickly went through a series of websites—OK! Magazine, RadarOnline.com, Star Magazine, National Enquirer, PopSugar, ETonline—and found nothing. She entered "Jeremiah Claflin" into Google and pulled up the British tabloid *The Daily Mail*.

"It's here, too," she said. "Does this count as a news site?"

"Not even close. But it's on the border between gossip and real news. All right, look. We have an ironclad alibi we can't use. So let's focus on Kayla."

"Nick, you've already shown that neither of them could have been at the Hotel Monroe. What more do you think we're going to get?"

"Absence of proof isn't proof of absence. We need to focus on proving a positive, not proving a negative. We already know Kayla wasn't at the Monroe on those three nights. You have a backdoor into the Lily Schuyler website. See if she had any other clients those nights."

"Nothing. I already checked."

"Well, she must have been *somewhere*. What about her Facebook page?"

"That was the first place I looked. Nothing there ei-

ther. I've looked on Tumblr and Pinterest and everywhere I can think of, and nothing. But I have an idea."

I looked at her.

"You know how you can post a picture on Facebook
and it auto-suggests the names of the people in the picture?"

"You know I don't have a Facebook account."

"Right. Well, it freaks me out. Facebook is using facial
recognition software for that, and for most people, those
photos are visible to any of the billion people on Facebook. So I'm thinking there's got to be a way to run a
search of all DC-area Facebook accounts using a picture
of Kayla and facial recognition."

"Huh. Worth a try, I suppose. But you're giving me
another idea. Surveillance cameras."

"Sure."

"Traffic cameras, toll cameras, pharmacies, parking
garages, supermarkets, gas stations, gyms, banks . . .
that's a lot of cameras. All we need is a time-stamped
video of her on one of those nights."

"You're talking about searching all the surveillance
cameras in her neighborhood? That's impossible. In nine
hours? We'd be lucky to get a gas station and a CVS and
a Safeway."

"No, we'd have to focus on places we know she fre-
quents."

"How?"

"Her credit card statements. See if she made any
charges those nights."

"And how do we get her credit card statements?"

There was a knock on the door. Gideon Parnell was now wearing a suit. "I think my e-mail in-box is going to crash our servers," he said. "I'm getting e-mails from colleagues and friends and journalists from around the globe. This thing is really blowing up."

"Hang tough," I said. "This is going to go all over the web before the day is through. But as long as it's slugged to Slander Sheet and doesn't make the legit news websites, we'll be okay."

"I don't understand, what makes you so confident you can still kill this snake?"

"Because the media establishment doesn't yet own the story. Gideon, with all respect, let us do our work without interruption. Really, it'll be better for all of us."

After a beat he nodded at me. "Excuse me," he said, giving me a long steady look. "You're absolutely right." He slipped back out and closed the conference room door behind him.

"Heller," Dorothy said. "You don't talk to Gideon Parnell that way."

"He'll get over it."

"*I* won't."

"I was hoping you'd have a way to get into her credit card statements."

"Well, she's got an American Express card and a Citibank MasterCard, and I've tried to get in the usual ways. I tried guessing her passwords, tried all the obvious ones, but no luck. You think Montello might have a way in?"

I shook my head. My information broker, Frank Montello, had e-mailed me back last night. All he'd come up with on the number programmed into Curtis Schmidt's flip phone was that it was another throwaway phone, a burner. That was no more than what I already knew. "I don't think he can get it to us in time."

"It's worth a try."

I nodded, reluctant.

Montello picked up his phone after six long rings. His voice was faint and muffled, as it always seemed to be, as if you'd just interrupted him doing something far more important than talking to you. He operated in the gray zone between law enforcement and private investigation, a place I tried not to go except *in extremis*. That was the place where money changed hands, where laws were broken: the sort of thing that could lose you your license. You had to be really careful.

Montello knew people at phone companies and credit card companies and banks, people who were willing to sell you inside information. I had no moral objection to paying someone off to get me information I needed. I just preferred to put some distance between the source and me. Montello's neck was on the block, and he knew it, and that was why he charged so much and acted so squirrelly.

I asked him if he had any sources at Citibank's credit card division or at American Express.

"No one I trust," he said, and he disconnected the call without further comment.

I looked at Dorothy and shook my head.

She said, "Then we're out of luck."

"No, we're not," I said, and I explained my plan.

23

There was a uniform shop in Silver Spring I used to frequent when I worked for Stoddard Associates. This place sold everything from chefs' toques to lab coats to security officers' blazers to hospital scrubs. I had a good contact there named Marge something, who used to get me whatever I needed, without asking too many questions. When you're working undercover it helps to have access to a variety of uniforms.

Luckily, they had what I needed, and Marge still worked there.

Forty-five minutes later I rang Kayla Pitts's apartment door buzzer. She didn't answer. But that didn't necessarily mean anything. She could still be at home. It was ten in the morning; she was likely still asleep. Last time I tried her buzzer she didn't answer either, even though she was probably at home.

She was surely frightened. Maybe she was hunkering down in her apartment, bracing for the explosion of attention she knew was coming, if it wasn't already here. Journalists around the world were probably hard at work Googling "Heidi L'Amour" and "Lily Schuyler" and pulling up her page on the escort service's website. It was only a matter of time before some smart and enterprising journalist figured out that Heidi L'Amour was actually a young woman named Kayla Pitts. Maybe a friend of hers would turn up and give away her real name. A classmate from Cornelius College might want to sell an interview to the *National Enquirer*. Or one of her colleagues at Lily Schuyler.

But it hadn't happened yet. No TV vans idled in the parking lot.

If she was at home, I was going to surprise her.

I hoped she wasn't.

I waited a few minutes for someone to emerge and let me into the building. But it was a slow time of day, and no one came. So I did the old courier trick, rang a couple of random units until I found one that answered. I said, "package" and sure enough, a few seconds later the buzzer sounded, unlocking the front door.

Naturally, as soon as I passed through the front door, someone was exiting. It was a middle-aged woman with auburn hair, wearing a green business suit with a skirt. She looked at me, then looked away. Even if I didn't have the uniform on, she'd probably not stop me. The building was too big for anyone to know all the neighbors. But I didn't want to take a chance.

I took the elevator to the seventh floor. The hallway—worn beige wall-to-wall carpeting in an ugly pattern, a long corridor with identical doors, the overhead fluorescent lighting flickering—was empty. Most of the residents who had jobs had probably already left for work. An odor of fried eggs hung in the air.

Apartment 712 was halfway down the corridor on the right.

I rang the bell. It made a pleasant *bing-bong*. I turned to my side so she couldn't see me through the security peephole, if she was at home. She wouldn't forget my face.

I waited. Adrenaline pulsed through my veins. If she was home, and if she opened the door, I had to move quickly. I had to get into her apartment whether she invited me in or not.

No answer. I listened for any movement within but heard nothing. I rang again and listened. After a couple more minutes I was as sure as I could be that she wasn't home.

I knew it was possible that she was sitting there in bed, headphones on, ignoring the outside world. Given what was about to happen to her, I couldn't blame her at all for wanting to escape. Not one bit. That girl's life was about to be pulled inside out. She was lying—of that I had no doubt—and I should have felt contempt, but I still couldn't help feeling bad for her. Who knew what pressure she was under. Who knew what sordid life circumstances compelled her to take part in this scam.

I unzipped the small black nylon briefcase and pulled

out the lock-pick set I'd borrowed from a friend who lived and worked in Old Town Alexandria, doing roughly my kind of work. He didn't have a snap gun, which is my preferred tool for picking locks, but I hadn't forgotten how to use a pick and a tension wrench, the old-fashioned way.

I knelt in front of the door, and in a couple of minutes I realized that I was actually a little rusty. Picking locks is all about the technique, and I found myself fumbling. It was taking me far longer than it should have. I didn't do it all that often.

A door opened across the hall.

An older woman with gray hair cut in bangs and thick-framed black glasses was standing there, wrapped tightly in a cherry blossom kimono. "Hello?"

I turned around.

She saw my uniform. It was an all-purpose repairman's uniform, a navy tunic with snaps over a white T-shirt, pens in a breast pocket protector, matching navy Dickies. Stitched over the left breast was "Allied HVAC." My friend Marge at the uniform outfit had plucked it from another customer's order. They always ordered a few extra. I didn't have much choice—that was all she had at the moment, apart from lab coats and hospital scrubs—but I figured it would work. A uniform from a locksmith's would have been ideal, but she didn't happen to have any in stock.

"How ya doin'?" I said.

"Are you working on her lock?" She had a high, bird-like voice.

"Yep."

"My lock is sticking."

I turned back to Kayla's door. "I'll see what we can do when I'm done repairing hers."

"You're not from DC Locksmiths. I thought we could only call DC Locksmiths."

I didn't turn around. "Yeah, well, I got the call."

"Why are you from Allied HVAC? I thought that was just heating and air conditioning and so on and so forth."

"We have a locksmith division." It was all I could think of to say.

"Allied HVAC?" she said.

Just then the tumblers lined up and the lock turned. I turned the knob and opened Kayla's door.

I turned around and smiled. "I'll see about your lock when I'm done here."

The old lady just looked at me and then closed her door.

I had a bad feeling about this woman. I'd seen mistrust in her face, and a kind of determination. It was the look of someone who intended to call the police. She didn't buy my flimsy cover.

I had to move quickly. If she called the cops—and I had to operate on the assumption that she would—I had no more than ten minutes. If that.

24

Entering Kayla's apartment, I closed the door quietly behind me. The lights were off. I looked around quickly. I was in a living room. Along one wall were sliding glass doors that gave onto a shallow balcony. The curtains were halfway drawn.

Strong morning sun blazed a large oblong across the room, a short sofa, a couple of matching chairs, a glass coffee table. To the right was a kitchenette, partitioned off from the living room by a breakfast bar with three stools. On the other side of the living room was an open door to a bedroom. I crept quietly through the room, just in case she was asleep in bed.

Once I was halfway across the living room I could see straight into her bedroom. The bed was made. She wasn't here.

I detoured to the glass sliders. The balcony looked out over the parking lot in front of the building.

No cops yet, but it was too early. I glanced at my

watch again. In nine minutes it would no longer be safe to be here.

The bedroom smelled faintly of perfume. Near a window was a small wooden desk. On it were only a lamp, a textbook, a legal pad, a silver clock, a yellow highlighter, and a small stuffed giraffe. No laptop. I scanned the legal pad. Nothing of interest. I gave the room another once-over. Looked in the adjoining bathroom. It was heart-breakingly neat. A lineup of lipsticks, a bottle of Scope mouthwash, an electric toothbrush. Nothing there.

I went back out into the living room, glanced outside again and saw no police cars. Not yet. When I turned around, I noticed a laptop on an end table next to the couch, a well-used Lenovo with stickers all over its case.

There it was. What I was hoping to find.

I opened it and attached a small, preconfigured USB drive. When it mounted, I double-clicked on it. This little device was pre-programmed to plant something called a key logger on her laptop. The key logger would secretly record every keystroke Kayla made on that machine and transmit it wirelessly to Dorothy.

I entered the commands she'd given me.

As I finished typing, I heard the siren.

I leaped up and went to the balcony. A police cruiser was pulling into the parking lot and the siren growled to a stop. The neighbor had called 911, just as I expected. But the police had responded more quickly than I would have thought. Three cheers for the Arlington Police Department.

Not good for me.

There was a lot more I needed to do.

I went to the front door and put my ear against it and listened. Nothing yet. Everything now depended on how quickly the police gained entry to the apartment building. Once they were buzzed in, they'd be up here within a minute or two. By the time I heard the elevator arrive on the seventh floor, by the time I heard it *bing*, it would be too late.

Now it was a matter of calculation.

I returned to her laptop and opened her Safari browser. I selected History. And there it was: days, maybe even weeks, of her browsing history. Every website she'd visited. Like most people, she didn't clear her browser's history.

My eye was quickly caught by one entry:

American Express Credit Cards . . . Travel and Business Services

She'd gone online to look at her American Express statement, maybe pay the bill. I found another entry in her history:

American Express Login

So I pulled that one up and clicked on it, and her login page came up. The username field was already filled in: KPitts. And the password field was filled with a series of dots for her password. I clicked "Log In," and her American Express card statement came up.

I found the list of posted transactions. Charges for CVS/PHARMACY. A bunch for GIANT, a supermarket. Charges for AMAZON and "VZWRLSS," which meant Verizon Wireless, her mobile phone company. A lot of taxi and Uber charges. A lot for ITUNES.COM/BILLITUNCU-PERTINO CA, which I assumed were iTunes purchases or rentals. A lot of STARBUCKS charges. GRUBHUB SEAM-LESS, which was probably food delivery.

Then I noticed an entry: US AIRWAYS PHOENIX. I clicked on it, and it expanded into a separate window. FLIGHT DETAILS, it said on the right. Washington, DC, to Jackson, Mississippi. It gave a ticket number, passenger name (Pitts/Kayla), and date of departure. June 6.

The day before the first alleged rendezvous with Justice Claflin, she'd flown to Jackson, Mississippi. The return date was June 8. I jotted down the flight information on the little field notebook I always carry with me.

I had to leave. The longer I spent here, the more likely it was that I'd be caught.

And that couldn't happen.

Theoretically, the police could be waiting in the lobby of the building for ten, fifteen minutes while dispatch tried to reach the building superintendent to let them in.

Or the super could have been waiting for them downstairs.

The elevator could arrive on the seventh floor any second.

It was a game of chance. But I had one more thing to do. Dorothy had brought from Boston a couple of mini real-time GPS trackers. I wanted to plant it somewhere

where we could keep track of her movements, some-where where she wouldn't find it. Her car was the obvi-ous target. Was there something in her apartment that she was likely to take with her? Her Chanel purse wasn't here; she'd probably taken it with her. A coat or jacket? The tracker would likely end up sitting in the closet. The only place that seemed to make any sense was her laptop case, even though she obviously didn't take it with her very often. Maybe she took her laptop out of her apart-ment on certain occasions, for long trips and so on.

I slipped the tracker in one of the many compartments and pressed down on the Velcro closure. Most people don't look through all the compartments in their laptop bags. It wasn't likely to be detected there.

Then I went back to the front door, looked out the peephole, saw nothing in the hall. The neighbor across the hall was probably hiding in her apartment, awaiting the cops. I listened, heard nothing. No elevator chime.

I'd already located the stairwell. It was off to the right of Kayla's apartment, whereas the elevator was on the left. Taking the elevator meant far too great a risk of run-ning right into the cops. They wouldn't climb the stairs to the seventh floor. So the stairwell was the safer exit.

My heart was thudding. Everything had been reduced to one crystal clear choice. Stay here and continue to capture more of her browser history and risk being caught. Or call it enough and leave the apartment before the police arrived.

It was time to go. I ejected the USB drive and pock-eted it, closed the laptop, returned it to the end table.

Glanced around quickly to make sure I hadn't left anything. Went back to the front door, looked out the peephole, listened for a moment.

Heard the elevator chime.

The escape route was simple: a right out of the doorway, down the hall about two hundred feet to the door that led to the stairs.

I heard voices in the hallway coming closer. The police, it had to be. I'd stalled too long.

If I left the apartment now, they'd see me emerge. They'd see me in the hall.

Now it seemed to me there were only two choices. To hide somewhere in the apartment, probably in the bedroom closet, and hope that the police didn't do a very thorough search. Not a risk I wanted to take.

Or . . .

I opened the sliding glass doors and stepped out onto the balcony. I did a quick calculation. Eight-foot ceilings meant approximately ten or eleven feet per story. Seven stories up was about seventy-five feet off the ground. Directly below was a narrow strip of grass and shrubs. Theoretically I could drop from the balcony and survive.

Or not.

Assuming I dropped onto the grass, I could sustain a broken ankle, which would be extremely inconvenient.

The adjacent balcony was twelve or fourteen feet away. Too far to swing and realistically hope to make it.

The balcony railing was about four feet high, a little less. The balcony directly below was a drop of ten or eleven feet. I'm six foot four, and with an arm extended,

I can span around eight feet. That meant a drop of only a couple feet to the balcony below.

As long as no one was watching the front of the building, I could—

And at that moment I heard muffled voices outside the front door.

I couldn't risk any more time thinking; I had to move.

Clutching the top of the railing, I pulled myself up, then lifted first one leg and then, with a quick readjustment of my hands, a second leg, and I was over the side. Hanging by my arms. Doing a pull-up. I felt a cool breeze in my hair. I could smell cut grass and hot asphalt. I lowered myself, my feet dangling in midair, the railing below just out of reach.

From the apartment I could hear the metallic scrape of a key turning in the lock.

I had to *move*.

Drop straight down and hit the dirt, maybe the asphalt. Likely injury, even death.

No, I had to swing my feet inward. Toward the interior of the apartment below. With one big swing I let go of my hands, and I dropped to the floor of the balcony below, relaxing my stance, knees bent, hands protecting my head, the impact hard and shuddering through my knees and thighs, my back thumping hard against the glass of the sliding door.

I craned my head and looked around and saw, through the parted floor-length curtains, the light on in the sixth-floor apartment.

Someone was home.

25

The floor-length curtains were half open. I didn't see anyone, which probably meant that nobody had seen me. But almost certainly someone was there.

I did a quick survey of my limbs. I hadn't broken or sprained anything. My legs were a little wobbly from the fall.

Then I had a disturbing thought: *Is it locked?*

It wasn't out of the question that the sliding doors to this apartment were locked. That would mean I was stuck out here. I'd have to make my way down to the balcony below and try there.

Another thought: *Who'd lock a sliding door to a sixth-floor balcony? Who could possibly come in?*

I tried the door, gripping the recessed handle, pulling with my fingers, and the glass door scraped open a few inches, moaning as it went. It was unlocked, but apparently seldom used.

I stopped pulling it. I didn't want to alert whoever

was there, presumably in the adjoining room. Maybe in bed. Maybe in the bathroom.

I inhaled deeply.

A tendon in my right calf went *twoingg*.

Waiting out here on the balcony for the right moment was a bad idea. What if he or she chose at some point to look out through the glass doors? I'd be spotted immediately. The balcony was shallow and not very big; there was no place on it to hide.

I had to enter while I could and hope I wasn't seen.

So I edged the door along its track slowly and steadily and as quietly as possible until it was open just wide enough for me to slip in. I parted the curtains, slid the door closed behind me, and entered. I was in what looked like a living room.

I heard the loud mumble of a TV in the next room, booming and vibrating in the walls.

This was good.

Whoever lived here was watching TV in the adjoining bedroom.

At first glance, the layout of this apartment appeared identical to Kayla's, one flight up. That meant that, depending on where in the bedroom the bed was positioned, the occupant either did or did not have a sightline into the living room.

I had to proceed on the assumption that he or she did. Even if only peripherally.

Given my height and build, I probably wasn't going to slip by unseen. Neither moving slowly nor sprinting by.

I'd be seen.

Standing there in the living room of a stranger's apartment, hoping the resident didn't see me here, I looked around and noticed a walker and a spare cane. So she was elderly. An old woman or an old man. Maybe both. Only one walker, so probably just one person.

Let's assume it's an old lady. If she saw me in her apartment, she would almost certainly scream and then call the police, and I couldn't have that.

Since the lights in the apartment were on, I also assumed that she'd awakened for the morning, turned on the lights, maybe had a little breakfast, and then got back into bed to watch TV.

Based on the volume of the TV, I assumed also that she was hard of hearing. But not necessarily blind. It was fifteen or twenty feet from where I was standing to the front door, with an open bedroom door in between.

I didn't know what to do.

So I began to game out my options.

One: I brazen it out, just walk boldly to the front door, open it, and leave. She'd probably see me and panic. Scream and call 911. The police dispatcher would immediately notify the police on the scene. I wouldn't have time to run down six flights of stairs, or take the elevators.

This seemed like a bad option.

Two: I glanced at the light, lacy curtains that hung next to the glass sliders. There were six panels of curtains, each curtain about six feet long.

Knotted together, losing about a foot in length for each knot, that was thirty feet.

I could sustain a drop of around thirty feet to the grass or bushes below, if I had to. If I fell right.

Quickly I thought it through. I couldn't do it without making noise. Plus it would take me at least ten minutes to remove the curtains, then remove the hooks from the fabric, and turn the curtains into a long rope and climb down from the balcony. Since this apartment, like Kayla's, faced the front of the building, I'd risk being seen by anyone driving up—and by the police, if they happened to be leaving at the time.

Not a feasible option. I was stuck with the bad option. Brazen it out.

Walk across the living room, as quietly as possible, and just hope that somehow I wasn't spotted.

I took a breath, exhaled, and then began moving slowly, as light on my feet as I could be, toward the front door. One foot in front of the other.

When I took a third step I was able to see into the bedroom. I saw a slice of a bed, a brown bedspread or coverlet. A lump in the bed. Someone's legs, presumably. The pallid blue-gray wash of the TV, just out of sight.

I took another careful step. Now I would see her head and shoulders, and she'd be able to see me. Unless her attention was riveted on the TV. Maybe her head was turned at such an angle that she wouldn't see me in her peripheral vision. The door was about ten feet away from me. The TV chattered and blared and barked and reverberated.

The floor creaked audibly underfoot.

My insides clenched.

Would she hear the squeak over the clamor of the TV? Maybe. Maybe not.

Then I saw that the bed was empty.

What had, a moment ago, looked like someone's torso or legs under the coverlet was in fact just a heap of bedding.

So if she wasn't in the bed, and the TV was on, where—?

A toilet flushed.

I thought quickly. He? She? Was in the bathroom, off the bedroom, and she was probably about to emerge.

For a split-second I froze.

Stop or advance? When she came out of the bathroom, the odds would greatly increase of her spotting me in her peripheral vision.

Decided, then.

I took three quick steps and reached the front door.

The door locks here were identical to Kayla's, upstairs. Two thumb latches that turned counterclockwise to unlock the dead bolt.

I turned the top one, and it made a loud clunking sound, audible everywhere in the apartment, no question about it.

I turned the second thumb latch and yanked the door open.

Without waiting another second, I vaulted through the door, and leaving it open behind me, ran down the corridor toward the stairwell.

26

You can't count on always being lucky, even if you consider yourself a lucky guy, as I do. I'd just escaped a jam—a disaster averted—but it had been a close thing. At least I'd gotten something out of it, I told myself, something valuable: proof that Kayla had bought tickets to Mississippi for the day before she'd allegedly serviced a Supreme Court justice.

In retrospect, as I drove the black Suburban back to the Shays Abbott office at M Street and New Hampshire, it had seemed worth the risk. I just had to remind myself that I wouldn't always be this lucky.

I'd broken into her apartment hoping to access her credit card bills so I could identify places she frequented—health clubs, bars, restaurants. Armed with that knowledge, I figured, maybe I'd eventually locate surveillance cameras that had recorded her. A long shot, no question.

But discovering in one of those credit card bills that she'd bought plane tickets: that was far better than scouting around for CCTV cameras in DC.

"You didn't get in to her apartment," Dorothy guessed as I arrived in the conference room. I'd changed out of my HVAC uniform and back into my street clothes. I was limping slightly, apparently having pulled something in my right calf.

"O ye of little faith." I gave her a swift recap of what had happened.

"Heller," she said. "Man." Then she laughed. "At least she wasn't home at the time. You plant the GPS?"

I nodded, told her what I'd found out about the US Airways flight.

"Jackson, Mississippi," she said. "I wonder why."

"Going home, I figure."

"But home is Tupelo, and Jackson is almost two hundred miles away."

"It's probably the closest airport. I doubt there are any direct flights from DC to Tupelo, Mississippi."

She shook her head. "I don't know. Then she flew back two days later. That's a lot of driving for less than two days at home. Why wouldn't she take a connecting flight to Memphis?"

"Good question," I said.

"Well, the important thing is that it proves she couldn't have been with Claflin at the Hotel Monroe on those two nights."

"Almost."

"You don't think that's enough?"

"We have proof she bought airline tickets. That's not proof she flew to Mississippi. Or that she was actually there. What would really nail this thing down would be her CDRs."

She groaned. "I can't, Nick. It's impossible."

CDRs are call detail records generated by cell phones and kept in the mobile phone company's databases. They contain all sorts of data, like phone numbers dialed or received, the start time and length of each call—and then the really useful information: the location where you were when you placed or received a call.

As everyone who watches movies or TV knows, our cell phones are constantly pinging cell towers. Mobile phone companies know where our phones—i.e., we—are at all times. It's undeniably creepy. A CDR documents which cell towers a mobile phone pinged during the course of a call. If you know the location of the nearest cell towers, their longitude and latitude and nearest street address, you know where the caller was.

If we could get the CDRs for Kayla's phone, we could prove she was in Mississippi and not in Washington during two of the nights in question.

The problem was, if you weren't law enforcement, it was next to impossible to get someone's CDRs—even your own, for that matter. Not so long ago, you just had to know someone in the phone company. Money would change hands under the table. But the companies had begun putting in logging systems that keep close track of who accesses call detail records. She was right: She couldn't get Kayla's CDRs.

"I hate to ask Frank Montello," I said, "but I don't think we have a choice."

When I told him what I wanted, he said, "No can do, Heller. Not anymore. Verizon Wireless is really cracking down. All the cell cos are. Everyone's gotten scared."

"Is it a matter of money?"

"It's a matter of no one wants to risk their job anymore."

"My client is willing to pay extremely generously," I said, and I mentioned a range I was willing to pay.

Instead of blowing me off, or hanging up, he suddenly sounded interested. He countered.

Then I countered back, and fairly quickly he admitted he *might* know a software guy who worked for Verizon Wireless who *might* be able to defeat the logging system and get CDRs for me. I suspected that his source at Verizon was someone he didn't like to go to very often, someone easily spooked, but for the right price . . .

There's almost always a right price.

Montello told me he'd get in touch with his source and see what he could do. It might take a while. He wasn't sure. I offered a twenty percent premium on my already generous offer if he could get me something that afternoon.

Even before I'd finished talking to Montello, Dorothy had put a website up on the projection screen. It was the gossip site TMZ. The lead story, in a box with a red border, had a headline in big black type: HIJINKS IN THE HIGH COURT. This was over a big picture of Justice Claflin with a wild, leering look on his face. I recognized the photo. It had been taken at a party for his sixtieth birthday when he was about to blow out the candles.

I put down the phone and groaned.

"The story's starting to spread big-time," she said. She pulled up the Drudge Report. The same picture appeared there under the headline THE LOVE JUDGE.

"Shit." Drudge was a gossip site, but it had first broken the story about Bill Clinton and Monica Lewinsky, so it had a certain residual credibility. "What about the *Times* or the *Post*?" I asked.

"Nothing there. Not yet."

"Good. How about Perez Hilton?"

"Nothing. But check this out." She clicked on Politico. On its front page was a small box with a photo of Claflin, apparently at a State of the Union speech. Over it was the headline CLAFLIN IN POSSIBLE CALL GIRL SCANDAL?

"That's not good," I said. "Politico is mainstream. At least it's a question mark."

Probably the best headline was the one in Vox: JUSTICE SERVED?

BuzzFeed ran a listicle about the top ten DC sex scandals, from Monica Lewinsky in 1998 to Senator Gary Hart and his girlfriend Donna Rice in 1987. A congressman caught sending lewd messages to young male pages in 2006, and a senator arrested in a Minneapolis airport bathroom in 2007 soliciting sex from an undercover police officer.

It must have been hard to narrow the list down to just ten. I could think of quite a few more.

"How much time do we have?" I asked Dorothy.

"Just about six hours."

"Six hours to blow this story up."

"Nick, this story is spreading like wildfire. Way faster than I expected. I think we have enough to go to Slander Sheet and demand a retraction."

I cupped my chin in my hand and thought. True, the Claflin story was going big faster than I'd expected. None of the standard bearers of the old-guard legacy print media had picked up on it yet, but it wouldn't have surprised me if their online versions ran something with a question mark, and soon. It was just too explosive a story to ignore.

"I'm going to talk to Gideon," I said.

27

I wandered through the maze of hallways until I found Gideon Parnell's office. His door was closed. His admin, Rose, sat at a desk right outside. She was on the phone. She nodded, smiled at me, held up an index finger.

When she hung up I said, "Rose, I need five minutes of Gideon's time."

She looked at his closed door, then back at me. "His phone hasn't stopped ringing. Can it wait till things slow down?"

"I don't think they're going to slow down any time soon," I said.

"He's on the phone with the chief justice. I'll let him know you're here."

She tapped at her keyboard. I sat down in one of the visitor chairs lined up outside his office.

After a moment, I remembered about the bald man who'd been following Kayla, Curtis Schmidt. I had a source within the Washington, DC, Metropolitan Police who I'd worked with on a previous case, involving my brother, Roger. The last I knew, Detective-Lieutenant Arthur Garvin was with the Violent Crime branch, on a retirement waiver. When I worked with him, a few years back, he was just past the department's mandatory retirement age of sixty, though they made exceptions in certain cases. But only up to sixty-four. He had to be retired by now.

I called him on his personal cell number. He answered right away, crisp like the cop he was for so long. "Garvin."

"Art, it's Nick Heller," I said.

A pause. "Heller!" he said. "Uh-oh. You in some kind of trouble?"

I laughed and got right to it. "Do you happen to know a retired police sergeant named Curtis Schmidt?"

There was a pause. "Not that I can recall."

"I need to find out what I can about the guy. What he's up to, who he's working for, whatever you can get."

"I can make some calls, maybe dig around. What's this about?"

Gideon's office door opened and he emerged.

"I gotta go, Art. I'll fill you in next time we talk. I owe you." I ended the call and stood up. "You got two minutes?" I asked Gideon.

"Of course. Come on." He led me into his office and closed the door behind him. "You have something?"

I nodded. "How's the chief justice holding up?"

"He's despondent, as you can well imagine. His office is directing people to the court's public affairs office, and they're giving out a statement that I crafted. What do you have?"

"Enough to go to Slander Sheet and demand a retraction," I said. I told him what we had.

"Do we know she actually took those flights?"

I smiled. The same question I'd asked. And I wasn't even a lawyer. "Not without getting the flight manifest from US Airways, and that's something only law enforcement can do."

"That seems like a hole, don't you think? She might have bought tickets and not flown."

"It's a hole, but a minor one. We have less than six hours, and I think the smart play is to go to Slander Sheet with what we have. It's enough."

"Not yet," Gideon said. "We need proof she was in Mississippi and not in DC at the time."

"I think we're in a strong enough position now."

He shook his head. "I want that accusation discredited once and for all, no ambiguity about it, no games, no waffling."

"I understand, but I think we can work with what we have." I found myself in an unusual position. Normally I'm on the other side, pushing for more evidence, a more conclusive case. "They'd be idiots not to issue a retraction."

"I'm the client," Gideon said firmly. "And I'm asking you for more."

"The problem is, for me to get anything more definitive could take a few days, and by then it's too late. We have less than six—"

My phone rang. I glanced at it: Frank Montello. "Excuse me," I said, and I answered the call. "Frank."

"You're not answering your e-mail."

"You have something?"

"Check your in-box," he said. "You owe me a chunk of change."

When I explained to Gideon what call-detail records were, he broke out in a broad grin.

28

Gideon inhaled deeply, then exhaled slowly.

"Thank God. And thank you." His chin tipped up ever so slightly. "It's time we paid Slander Sheet a visit."

"Not you," I said.

"Not me? And why the hell not?"

"It paints a big target on your back. Draws their attention to you. I think you should remain behind the scenes and let me be the up-front guy. The flak catcher. That's what you pay me for."

After a long moment of silence he said, "You're right."

On my phone I forwarded the call records to Dorothy— I was surprised at how big the file was—and then spent ten minutes with Gideon as he suggested to me some legal language to use with Slander Sheet.

When I got back to the conference room, Dorothy got up and threw her arms around me. I couldn't remember the last time she'd done that.

"You did it," she said.

"We can celebrate when Slander Sheet issues a retraction. Why is the file so big?"

"It's a whole lot of data. A lot of the time she was using a navigation app on her phone that kept pinging the cell towers. Communicating, broadcasting nonstop. So the data is almost continuous, back-to-back. We can see where she went for hours at a time. Showing an almost perfect path of travel."

"And where'd she go?"

"When she arrived in Jackson, she traveled from the airport to a Budget Rent a Car agency on the airport grounds. Then she drove about four miles to a town called Pearl, Mississippi, on the outskirts of Jackson. That's where she spent most of her time. In the town of Pearl."

"What's there?"

"The Central Mississippi Correctional Facility."

"Who'd she visit?"

She nodded. "I searched the Vinelink inmate locator under the name of Pitts, and I found a Raelyn Pitts, twenty-seven years old."

"Her big sister."

"Right. She was visiting her sister in prison. She stayed at a Comfort Inn near the prison both nights, June 6 and 7, and went to visit her sister twice."

"You got all this from the latitude and the longitude of the cell towers?"

She shook her head. "They also give you street addresses. So I did some cross-referencing."

"That just leaves one night unaccounted for. June 12."

"Wrong. We got that, too."

"How so?"

"They sent a month's worth of call records, a full billing cycle. On June 12, she spent the evening at a sports bar in Arlington, Virginia, for most of the night. Never left Arlington."

That meant that all three nights were accounted for. All three nights when she was supposedly with the chief justice she was provably somewhere else.

I called Slander Sheet and tried to get an appointment with the founder and editor in chief, Julian Gunn. I was told he was tied up. But once they heard I represented Gideon Parnell, Gunn freed up some time. He probably wanted to dance a victory jig in front of me.

I felt good. We had evidence that was rock solid, even better than I'd expected to come up with.

But there was something about this case that still bothered me, that had begun to nag at me, and I couldn't quite put my finger on it.

29

In the hour before my meeting with Julian Gunn, I got on the phone while Dorothy combed the Internet, and fairly quickly I had a decent working profile of the guy.

He was British, graduated from Cambridge University, in England, and after college worked at *Private Eye* magazine for a few years. Then he moved to New York and started a few Internet ventures that made him reasonably rich. He'd started Slander Sheet in his Tribeca apartment, with a friend of his from Cambridge, but they'd had a falling out.

Slander Sheet gradually caught on, then he spun off Slander Sheet LA, for Hollywood gossip, and then Slander Sheet DC, for political gossip. Pretty soon he had an online gossip network. Slander Sheet seemed to publish items about almost anyone. The only people off limits, as Slander Sheet targets, were his friends (mostly journalists), and his college classmates. Actually, he didn't seem to have many friends. "He's the kind of guy even his friends don't like," someone told me. Two adjectives I heard about him repeatedly were "odious" and "loathsome."

A couple of years ago, he'd sold Slander Sheet, but no one was sure who he sold it to. The sale was handled in great secrecy. Gunn remained editor in chief. He split his time among LA, New York, and Washington.

I showed up at the Slander Sheet offices in the old bread factory right on time, but Gunn kept me waiting. One of his minions, a white guy in his midtwenties with dreadlocks, explained that Julian had been doing interviews all day, with TV and radio and publications all around the world. He'd be with me as soon as he could get off the phone.

Gunn didn't have an office. He worked at one of the long tables just like all his employees. Presumably he wanted to make a point about how democratic Slander Sheet was. So I was shown to a glassed-in conference room and seated at another long table.

After twenty minutes, Julian Gunn showed up, accompanied by an attractive but dour blond woman in a pink suit he introduced as his general counsel. Gunn was a small man with an oversized head, an acne-ravaged face, and receding pale-blond hair. He was wearing dark jeans and a shiny dark blue striped shirt.

"So sorry to keep you waiting," he announced. "It's a crazy day. We've never had such traffic. It's *mad*. We're up to almost ten *million* page views on the Claflin story."

"Wow," I said without enthusiasm.

Turning to his general counsel, he said, "We're approaching the all-time record for page views—those photos of Kim Kardashian's butt, in *Paper* magazine. Those got eleven million."

He sat at the head of the table, his general counsel to his right. I sat on his left.

"So your name is Nicholas Heller, and you're here to talk about our Jeremiah Claflin story, is that right?"

I nodded.

"I take it the great Gideon Parnell is too busy to make it here himself?"

I smiled. "You'll have to settle for me."

"So, Mr. Heller." He opened his hands, palms up. "Have at us."

"Have you set a sale price yet?"

"Excuse me?" He gave me a slow blink. He reminded me of a lizard, or of a frog about to flick out its tongue and catch a fly.

"On your little hacienda in the D.R. See, I figure you can get two point five million for it. You'll need all of that and more."

He looked puzzled, as I expected him to be. He'd recently bought a house on the beach in the Dominican Republic, but not many people knew about it.

"I thought you were here to talk about Jeremiah Claflin."

"Exactly. Because if you don't take down that fraudulent story by four o'clock this afternoon, and issue an abject apology on your home page, you're going to be hit with a massive lawsuit that's going to shut down Slander Sheet and wipe you out personally. You're going to need to sell every asset you can."

"Oh, please. Sue me." He fluttered his fingers in the air. "Get in line. I've lost track of how many lawsuits we've been threatened with." He turned to his general counsel. "We must get ten legal threats a week, right, Emily?"

"At least," she said.

He turned back to me. "I know who you are, Nicholas Heller. Mandy Seeger did some checking. You dropped out of Yale to enlist in the Special Forces, in Iraq and Afghanistan and all those godforsaken places. Who knows what you were up to? I'm sure if we do a little digging, we'll find some My Lai in your past. Some raped Iraqi woman, some bayoneted Afghan boy, maybe. And my goodness, your old man was that scoundrel Victor Heller. Who's currently serving twenty-eight years in prison." He shook his head. "I don't imagine your clients would appreciate the sordid truth about your background coming out. Anyway, if you're here on Gideon Parnell's behalf, I assume you're here to lodge a complaint." He interlaced his fingers and steepled them. "Well, then. Lodge away. You have a problem with Mandy's reporting?"

"Mandy Seeger is a top-notch reporter, but she got taken in by a clever hoax. Jeremiah Claflin never had a relationship with a call girl, period. Full stop."

"Of course not," Gunn said with a smirk.

"You jumped the gun. You ran the story without giving Mandy the chance to meet with Gideon Parnell, who would have set her straight. That's what the lawyers call reckless disregard for the truth."

"We put the story up this morning because our intel told us we were about to be scooped. That's all. It turns out to be the biggest story we've ever run, and it's getting us attention all over the world. That's what I'd call a successful story."

"If you'd waited, as you and Gideon agreed, you'd have learned the truth. You would have learned, for instance, that although rooms in the Hotel Monroe were booked under Claflin's name on three different evenings, at no times were the keys used to enter the room. Claflin never stayed there. Here's a printout of the audit report." I slid a file folder of documents across the table to him.

He shrugged. "That's the best you've got?"

I went on, ignoring his taunts. "You were used by a call girl. Someone paid her to get in touch with Mandy Seeger and you fell for it. As a result, you've done grave damage to the integrity of the chief justice of the Supreme Court."

Gunn blinked again, slowly. One, two, three. "You work for the powers that be, Heller. I work against them. You'll forgive me if I don't immediately credit your claims. And claims are all they are. Are we done here? TMZ TV is waiting to interview me."

I slid a tall stack of paper across the table.

"More printouts from the Hotel Monroe?" he asked.

I shook my head. "These are call-detail records. From Kayla Pitts's cell phone. That's Heidi L'Amour's real name, in case you didn't know. Proving without a doubt that she couldn't have been meeting with Justice Claflin in the Hotel Monroe. She was in Pearl, Mississippi, on two of those nights, visiting her sister in prison. On the third night she was at a sports bar called the End Zone, in Arlington, Virginia."

Gunn blinked again, slowly, twice, and pulled his hands away from the stack of printouts as if they were hot to the touch. He looked at the top page and then looked at his general counsel. He muttered something to her, then took out a cell phone. He pressed one key and put it to his ear. "Eric, I need you to take a look at something. Yes."

He ended the call.

A moment later a scrawny redheaded man wearing a lime-green polo shirt entered the conference room. He went up to Gunn and tapped the stack of documents.

"This?" he said.

Gunn nodded. "This is Eric Ziegler, my chief technology officer," he said.

Eric took the stack of paper with him and left the room.

"Uh, the chief justice is a public figure," Emily said crisply. "It's extremely difficult for a public figure to sue for libel."

"Not at all," I said to her. "As you know, his lawyers simply have to prove 'actual malice.' The malicious and reckless disregard for the facts. Which is going to be nice and easy, since your reporter was given the opportunity to meet with Gideon Parnell and learn the truth. Before you ran the story. A meeting you canceled."

"Is this true?" Emily said to Gunn.

He shrugged dismissively.

"So you didn't do your due diligence," I went on. "The fact that you had the opportunity to correct your fabrications and you didn't take it shows actual malice. I don't know how you put a dollar figure on the reputation of the chief justice of the Supreme Court, but we're going to start at one hundred million dollars and go up from there. Which will put Slander Sheet out of business and you into personal bankruptcy."

"You'd never get that," he said.

I went on, "You see, Julian, juries these days are turning against the power of irresponsible media to destroy the lives of innocent people. Maybe one hundred million dollars in damages is too small. Maybe we go for half a billion."

Gunn's phone rang. He answered it with a smug smile. "Eric?"

He listened for a moment. I watched as his expression molted from arrogant, self-satisfied gloating to what looked a lot like sea sickness. Without another word, he ended the call. He seemed about to throw up. He stood up feebly.

"Emily?" he said, and his general counsel got up as well, and the two of them left the conference room.

While I waited, I checked my e-mail, then my voice mail. I'd gotten a call from my DC cop source, Art Garvin. I recognized his cell number. I was about to call him back when Gunn and his general counsel returned to the room.

"Okay, Heller," Gunn said quietly. "Appears that you've won this battle. But you've just set out on a long road that has no turning."

"What does that even mean?" I said.

"I'm going to loose the investigative hounds on you. You'll be a ruined man. I am not an enemy you want to have, as you'll soon—"

"What do we need to do?" Emily said, cutting him off. And I realized right then that she was calling the shots. Not Julian Gunn. "What do you want, Mr. Heller?"

30

I checked SlanderSheet.com in the Suburban on my way back to the Shays Abbott offices, and sure enough, the Claflin piece was gone, replaced by a notice, bordered in black:

A Note to Our Readers

This morning Slander Sheet posted an item concerning the private life of Supreme Court Chief Justice Jeremiah H. Claflin. We published the article in the firm belief that it was accurate. Given new information received by Slander Sheet, however, we have come to the conclusion that we were mistaken in publishing this item, and we extend our deepest apologies to Chief Justice Claflin and his family.

Ordinarily I should have been feeling some satisfaction, the glow of victory—I'd accomplished what I'd set out to do, what I'd been hired to do—but that wasn't how I felt at all. I felt uneasy. I knew that something was very wrong.

The call girl, Kayla Pitts, had obviously been coerced into making a false accusation. She was scared. She had some ex-cop following her, protecting her or watching her. What was her story? How had she gotten involved in a scam targeting Justice Claflin? Who else had been involved? Who was behind it, and what was the objective?

This case was over, but it didn't feel that way to me.

I called my office in Boston. Jillian answered and filled me in on what was happening there, which wasn't a lot. "I've decided to stay in Washington another day," I told her. "To tie up loose ends. Keep me in the loop by e-mail, and call if there's anything urgent."

I returned to the hotel and told Dorothy the plan. "That's fine with me," she said. "I was planning on staying a few days longer anyway, take some personal time. Also, I think we should have a celebratory dinner somewhere nice."

"Absolutely."

"Restaurant Nora okay with you?"

"If you can get us in, sure."

"Oh, Nick, you asked me to look into why Mandy Seeger left *The Washington Post*?"

"Oh, right." I laughed. "I forgot about that. Why *did* she leave the *Post*, anyway?"

"She got fired."

"Really?"

"Yeah, really. Apparently she violated the *Post*'s policy against lying to sources—she pretended to be a defense contractor or something when she was working on some big story about corruption in the Pentagon. The *Post* doesn't allow its reporters to misrepresent themselves, to lie about who they are to get a story. She went too far."

"Huh."

"Sound familiar?"

I smiled innocently. "How so?"

"You know damned well how so. You'll stop at nothing, too, when you're on a case."

"Yeah, well, no one says I can't lie if and when I have to. I'm not a reporter."

"I'm just saying."

"Interesting," I said. "Thanks." I remembered about the message that my retired police detective friend had left. Without listening to it, I called Detective Garvin back.

"Nick," he said. "That guy you asked me about, Curtis Schmidt?"

"Yeah."

"He's bad news."

"Tell me about it."

I meant it sarcastically, but Garvin answered anyway. "He's a bad apple. He got out when the going was good."

"Why?"

"I had a buddy check the PPMS, the MPD's Personnel Performance Management System. He and some other cops scammed the department out of almost a million bucks in fraudulent overtime pay requests, for court appearances they never made."

"But he has a red-stripe card. He's retired. Not fired."

"The department had to handle this on the DL for fear of jeopardizing any criminal prosecutions these a-holes were involved in. So about four, five years ago, they were all forced to take retirement."

So Curtis Schmidt was a bad cop. That was obvious to me from the moment I found the red-stripe card in his wallet. Obviously he'd found a new source of employment. But was it connected to Slander Sheet? If so, how?

Garvin said, "You want me to dig around some more?"

I thought for a moment. It no longer made a difference, did it?

"That's okay," I said. "I've got what I need. Thanks."

And I ended the call.

31

Slander Sheet had become a laughingstock.

When we returned from dinner, I flipped from channel to channel on the hotel TV while Dorothy checked online. Even though the Claflin story never got any serious traction in the mainstream media, it had been splashed all over. It wasn't just the story that had been discredited, it was the website itself, mocked and derided and lampooned.

On the *Tonight Show* on NBC, Jimmy Fallon opened his monologue with a photo of Vladimir Putin next to him. "Huge news today," he said. "Russia's Vladimir Putin is transitioning into a woman. That's right." Then the photo turned into a Photoshopped picture of Putin as a very butch-looking woman with lipstick and flowing tresses, in a low-cut dress. "It's got to be true," Fallon said with a straight face. "I just read it on Slander Sheet."

On ABC, Jimmy Kimmel announced that his show was now number one in the time slot, and after the applause, added with a blank look, "It was on Slander Sheet, didn't you see it?" Each of the late night hosts did some riff on Slander Sheet. Online, the ridicule was widespread.

Dorothy said, "You have to admit, this feels pretty good."

I nodded. "Yeah," I said tonelessly.

Gideon Parnell called me, profuse with gratitude. I didn't know a man of his gravitas was capable of gushing, but he did. He'd put Claflin on the line, who was more restrained but still heartfelt in his thanks.

I should have been exultant. But something about this victory felt hollow.

Thoughts raced around in my brain that evening. I didn't sleep well at all.

32

The next day passed in a blur of meetings, congratulatory messages, debriefs at Shays Abbott. Dorothy went to visit her brother again. I sent my nephew, Gabe, a text and met him after school for a late lunch at a vegan café he liked, not far from St. Gregory's, the private all-boys school in DC he attended and loathed. The café was a tiny place, mostly for take-out, with a few tables. I knew at a glance that I wouldn't be eating. They featured faux meat sandwiches made out of tempeh, and soups and salads. Gabe had a veggie burger. I had coffee. I took one sip and put it down. It tasted like something brewed by someone who disapproved of coffee.

Gabe was dressed all in black, his usual fashion. He wore skinny black jeans, a studded leather belt, black Chuck Taylors, and a Bullet for My Valentine T-shirt that showed a skull adorned with red roses. The only thing different was his hair. He used to dye it jet black, but he'd let his natural dark-brown hair grow out. I guess you'd call him "emo," though he never did the whole emo thing, the lip rings and the eye makeup and so on. His only piercing was a gold stud earring in his left ear.

He was an interesting kid. He was my brother, Roger's, stepson, but Roger was in prison, and Gabe didn't get along with his mother, Lauren. He was brilliant and insanely talented. He wrote and illustrated graphic novels—not comics; he was always correcting me—that were as good as anything I'd ever seen in a bookstore. He liked me a lot and I liked him. He was the closest I'd probably ever come to having a kid of my own.

He wolfed down two-thirds of his "burger" before stopping to talk. "How long have you been in town?" he asked.

"A couple of days."

"Thanks for the heads-up," he said, heavy on the sarcasm.

"It was a last-minute trip. Plus the case got really busy all of a sudden."

"What's the case?"

"You ever hear of Slander Sheet?"

He smirked. "Yeah. Piece of shit gossip website."

"Pretty much. It was about trying to get them to take down a fraudulent piece about a Supreme Court justice."

"I heard about that. That was you?"

"Yup. Heller Associates."

He took another bite of his veggie burger. "Very cool."

"How's senior year?"

He paused. "What do you think?"

"I imagine you hate it as much as you hated junior year."

He looked away. "More."

"Because of the college application stuff?"

He drew a pattern on his napkin with a fingernail. After a few seconds he said, "College is for losers and suckups. I'm not going to college."

"Did you apply and not get in?"

"Please. I didn't even apply."

"What do you mean?" I hadn't heard anything about this from his mother. She must have been desperate.

"College is bullshit. It's all about the admissions process. The guy who founded PayPal says college is just the final stage of a competitive tournament. The kids who get into the top colleges defeated all their, like, opponents. It's like *The Hunger Games*. That's all it is."

I shrugged.

"It's just a conveyor belt for upward mobility. Mark Zuckerberg dropped out of college, and so did Bill Gates and Steve Jobs. And hey, didn't you drop out of Yale?"

"Don't use me as an example. I dropped out to join the army. Are you planning to enlist?"

"Me? No way!"

"So maybe you're an entrepreneur now, like Steve Jobs or Mark Zuckerberg?"

"What? No. I just refuse to be a drone. I'm not gonna join the herd."

"Because you're special and the rules don't apply to you."

He shrugged.

"There are people in the world who think the rules don't apply to them," I said, "and my job is to take them down." I paused a moment. That sounded like sanctimonious crap. Surprisingly, Gabe didn't call me on it.

Sanctimonious, maybe, but it made me think. *There are people in the world who think the rules don't apply . . .*

Why were we looking for an organization, a group, behind the scam to take down a Supreme Court justice? Couldn't it just as easily have been an individual with an individually tailored agenda, a highly *personal* reason to want to bring Claflin down? If so, that would mean looking for a different pattern of evidence.

I found myself mentally withdrawing from the conversation with Gabe, not being fully present.

An hour later I was back at the hotel making calls.

I was in the shower around six when my cell phone started ringing. I let it ring to voice mail. There was no call I was waiting for, no one I needed to talk to.

It rang again immediately, but I had a headful of shampoo, and I let it go to voice mail again.

When I was drying myself with one of the hotel's big, very thick bath towels, the phone rang a third time.

This time I picked it up.

The caller ID showed a number with a 571 area code. It looked familiar. I decided to answer it.

"Mr. Heller?" a voice whispered.

"Yes?"

"Nicholas Heller?" Still a whisper.

"Yes?" I said again, annoyed. It sounded like a prank call.

"Mr. Heller . . . I'm sorry . . . I need your help. Please."

"Who is this?"

"It's Kayla."

For a moment I wasn't sure I'd heard correctly. "Who?"

"Kayla Pitts."

The call girl whose lies had launched this whole thing. Of all people to hear from. How had she got my cell number? Then I remembered handing her my business card.

Her voice remained a whisper, but it sounded frantic.

"Please, help me. I think they're going to kill me. Please. Oh, God. Please help me. No, I—"

33

The call ended abruptly, then there was a jostling noise, and then silence.

It sounded like the phone had been grabbed out of her hand.

I stood there a moment, dripping water, trying to make some sense of what had just happened. The girl had sounded genuinely in distress, but why would she be calling me? I found the call in my Recents and hit the button to call it back. It rang and rang and then went to voice mail: "Hi, this is Kayla. You know what to do." It was the same number I'd used when I'd spoof-texted her, pretending to be Mandy Seeger.

I dried myself off and dressed quickly, thinking all the while. What was the girl up to? My phone showed two voice mails, both from her. I played them.

The same whispered voice. "Is this . . . Nicholas Heller? It's . . . Kayla . . . Pitts, you know . . . I need your help. I'm . . . I'm in a van, I don't know where they're taking me . . . please help me."

And then the next message: "It's Kayla again. If you get this . . . just, please, you've got to help me. They won't tell me where I'm going and . . . just call me, please, I'm scared."

The two messages were fragmentary and frantic enough to sound genuine. But were they? I picked up the hotel phone and called Dorothy's room.

"It's obviously a setup," Dorothy said, once she'd listened to the messages.

She'd just come out of the shower herself and smelled of shampoo or conditioner. Her close-cropped hair glistened with tiny droplets of water. She wore a white T-shirt and gray sweatpants.

"They hired this girl because she can act, right? She could say she had sex with a Supreme Court justice she never met and be convincing at it. Now they're using her to draw you out somewhere so they can . . ." She fell silent, thinking.

"So they can what?"

"Whoever's trying to set up Claflin is probably royally pissed off that you screwed up their plan. And they . . ." She paused again. "I don't know, Heller, I don't like this. It's a trap of some kind."

"The girl sounds terrified. Like she's been abducted."

"But why would she be calling you? You work for the other side."

"I don't know. It sounds genuine to me."

"So what do you want to do about it?"

"Can you locate her phone?"

She looked at me, eyes wide, shrugged. She did not like to disappoint. "Not without physical access to it."

"How about the Find My iPhone thing you used to locate my stolen phone?"

She shook her head. "I can't think of a way. We don't know her Apple ID. Her—what about the GPS tracker?"

I nodded. "It's in her laptop bag. If she was really abducted, she's not going to have her laptop with her, right?"

"Who knows. Let me get *my* laptop and we'll see."

She went to her room and was back a minute later with her laptop and her iPad. She set them both down on the suite's dining table, which we'd been using for work. Both machines had been preloaded with the GPS program.

"It's still in Arlington," she said. "Hold on. It's moving."

I came over and looked at her laptop screen. A green dot was inching slowly over a map of northern Virginia, along a road identified as Route 66.

"Let's go," I said.

34

I'd parked the Suburban on the street, and not in the hotel garage, exactly for a time like this, when we needed to move fast. While I maneuvered the SUV through the streets of Washington, Dorothy located the moving dot on her iPad. We crossed the Potomac on Memorial Bridge and continued on the interstate, Route 66, heading north and then west.

I was tempted to speed but didn't want to risk getting stopped. The dot, blue on her iPad, was still in Arlington, but considerably west of us. We were heading due north along Custis Memorial Parkway, which was what Route 66 was called in Arlington. It was rush hour, it was getting dark, and the traffic was heavy, a sluggishly flowing metal river of vehicles.

"I still think this is a setup," Dorothy said.

"I hear you. We disagree." I gave her a meaningful look. "Notice I haven't heard back from Kayla since the call was cut off?"

"So?"

"Seems inconsistent with a setup. If they're trying to lure me, they'd have her keep talking to me, keep stringing me along. The way it happened, it's more likely they found her talking on the phone and grabbed it."

"I'm not going to say it again." She looked at me, then back at her iPad. "They're in Falls Church now."

"How often does the tracker update?"

"Every sixty seconds."

"You charged it before you gave it to me, right?"

"Huh. I forgot. Very funny, Heller."

"How long does the battery last?"

"Thirty days at rest. In motion, considerably less, but it should last the rest of the day at least. Probably a couple of days. They're still on the interstate, in Falls Church, heading west/northwest."

"Take my phone," I said, "and try texting her again, just in case." I took my phone from my jacket pocket and handed it to her.

"And say what?"

"Just 'where are you?' "

It had just begun to rain, a few droplets splashing against the windshield. I put on the wipers, which only smeared the glass, so I flicked on the washers, and that cleared it up. But the rain only came faster, thrumming against the SUV's hood.

"No reply?" I asked.

"Nothing." She was silent for a time, and then went on, "Nick, what do you think's going on? What's your theory, why she called you?"

"She knows what I do for a living. She knows I have some idea what she's involved in. I think she called me out of desperation—she doesn't know what else to do or who else to turn to. She's scared. That's what I think."

"So what's happening to her? Hold on—they're at the junction with 267, and they just took the exit onto the Dulles toll road. Where are they headed, do you think?"

"Dulles airport," I said.

"Why?"

"Their whole plan just collapsed and they want to get her out of town before it spins out even further."

"Who's they?"

"That's the question. It's whoever wanted to take Jeremiah Claflin down."

"And getting her out of town means—what?"

"That I don't know either. She was the most important part of this conspiracy, whatever this conspiracy is, but also, I'm guessing, the soft spot—the most vulnerable part. She's a frightened young woman who could easily spill the truth about what's going on. And who put her up to it."

"Nick, they're turning off. They're approaching what looks like an airport."

"It's way too soon to be Dulles."

"It's not Dulles, it's . . . it's a small private airport. The Middleton Regional Airport, it's called. A general aviation airport. They're turning in there."

"Oh, shit."

"What?"

"We've got to move it. General aviation means private

planes, and private planes means no set schedule. They can take off as soon as they get there."

The rain had become torrential, coming down in sheets, splashing up from the road. The visibility was poor. We drove in anxious silence, the windshield wipers beating a quick tempo. I took the turnoff onto Route 267, which would become the Dulles access road.

I passed a few slower-moving vehicles, but I couldn't floor the accelerator. Traffic had slowed to a crawl; I couldn't go faster than the cars ahead of me. The four-lane highway had given way to two lanes, plus there were traffic lights.

"The dot's stopped moving. They've come to a stop."

"The airport's probably ten minutes away. Check the map—is there a faster way?"

"We're on the most direct route. The exit's three point five miles ahead."

But we were moving at no more than twenty miles an hour, so another quarter hour passed before we finally saw a sign that said MIDDLETON REGIONAL AIRPORT NEXT LEFT.

"Is the dot still stationary?"

"Just started moving again."

"Shit."

I signaled left, shifted into the leftmost lane, waited at the red light. I had no choice but to wait; the oncoming traffic was steady. I pounded the steering wheel in frustration. Finally the light turned green.

I gunned it. After about two hundred feet, another sign for the airport loomed into view, and I turned into the airport access road. Very soon I reached a parking lot where no more than five or six vehicles were parked. Next to the lot was a chain-link fence that enclosed the tarmac. There was a small brick terminal building, and there didn't appear to be an airport control tower. A small private airport. I pulled into a space and left the SUV idling.

"What's the plan, Nick?"

"Is it still moving?"

"No."

"How accurate is this thing?"

"Very. Up to a foot."

"So can you figure out where it is?"

She looked at her iPad, swiped at it a few times. "She's on the tarmac."

"Or at least her laptop bag is."

She pointed. "There's a security booth at the entrance to the tarmac."

"Okay. Can you get out the scope?"

"The monocular . . . ?"

"The Canon."

She took out from her bag a pair of 18 x 50 binoculars, and handed them to me. I put them to my eyes, turning them toward the tarmac. Once I got oriented, I located a plane on the airfield and zoomed in on its tail number.

"Could you write this down?" I said. "November one-five-five-X-ray."

"What's that?"

"A tail number."

"Which plane?"

"No idea. Now, how about you go into the terminal building and look for her. See if she's waiting somewhere. It's not a big building—shouldn't take too long."

"What are you going to do?"

"Drive onto the tarmac."

"You can't."

"We'll see."

She got out of the SUV and ducked down in the heavy rain, heading toward the terminal building. I drove over to the perimeter fence gate. There was a booth, but it was dark and empty. The entrance was blocked by a barrier gate arm. I drove up to the booth and found an intercom and a phone handset mounted on its side. A few feet above it was a security camera. I lowered my window, pressed the button, and picked up the phone. Rain doused my shoulder and my sleeve.

After a few seconds, a voice said, "Yeah?"

"I've got a load of luggage for November one-five-five-X-ray."

"One moment . . ." A pause. Then: "November one-five-five-X, go ahead."

I hung up the phone and rolled up my window. The barrier gate lifted and I drove on through.

I wasn't surprised. In most airports, even the big ones, the perimeter security is minimal to nonexistent. For all the ludicrous security measures they put passengers through, the tarmac is the least defended part of an airport. General aviation airports, for private planes, are even more lax. Plus, I was driving a black Suburban, which looked official, like a government vehicle.

Still, I didn't know where I was going.

I passed a refueling truck, an unmarked low brick building, then the one-story brick terminal building. No one was gathered on the pavement in front of it. No passengers preparing to board. But a small plane, a Cessna, was being refueled from a truck on the tarmac about two hundred feet away. That was the plane. I knew it instinctively. This was no setup. Kayla Pitts had been taken to this private airport to fly her somewhere. Some place she didn't want to go.

I drove on another hundred feet until I reached a hangarlike building whose overhead door was rolled all the way up. The bright light spilled out onto the asphalt. I could see vending machines, tables, and desks. A few guys standing around. It looked like it might be a pilots' briefing area. In one glance I saw what I needed.

I parked the Suburban next to the building, alongside a truck. I consulted the iPad once again. The green dot still hadn't moved. It appeared to be about a hundred feet outside the terminal building. That would be exactly where the Cessna was being refueled. I assumed that meant that Kayla's luggage, including her laptop bag, had already been loaded into the plane's cargo hold.

Then I switched off the ignition, got out, and went over to the hangar. On the way, a walk of no more than fifty feet, I got drenched. I entered the hangar looking like a drowned rat. Three guys standing around a coffee-maker, foam cups of coffee in their hands. One of them glanced over at me. I smiled, said, "How's it going?" and kept on moving to the back corner of the hangar, where a row of rain slickers were hanging on a rack along with reflective vests. They were for the airport maintenance and service crew. I grabbed one, as if it had my name on it, and put it on. Over it I put one of the orange-and-yellow reflecting safety vests. I noticed an array of big Maglite flashlights on a narrow table below the safety vests. I took one and put it in the front pocket of the slicker. It was one of the high-intensity, super-bright, tactical Maglites. They got as bright as five hundred lumens, almost.

If you act like you belong somewhere, most people assume you do. For all they knew I was one of the fixed-base operator crew, starting his evening shift, caught in the rain. The three guys were laughing, saying something about the Redskins game last night. No one said anything to me. I belonged.

My phone buzzed, and I took it out of my pants pocket.

"I found them," Dorothy said. "Two guys and a girl who looks like Kayla. They're in the waiting area."

"Does she look like a captive?"

"She does and she doesn't. It's not like she's in handcuffs or anything, but these two guys look awfully intimidating, and she looks scared."

"Can you tell if either of the guys is armed?"

"I don't have the eye for it the way you do, but not from what I can tell."

"Okay."

"But please don't take my word for it, Nick."

I thought a moment. "I think I see their plane refueling. If you can plausibly hang around there without being detected, keep your eyes on them. I want to make sure they're not going anywhere but out on the tarmac. Call me if you see any unusual movements."

I flipped the hood of the slicker up over my head and went back out into the night. The rain was easing a bit by now, less torrential, steadier. The fuel truck was pulling away from the Cessna, having finished the refueling.

I stood in the rain a few hundred feet from the terminal building and watched the glass doors.

I looked at the plane and noticed the tail number and memorized it: N483C.

After about five minutes my phone rang.

"It's them. They're heading out to the tarmac."

"Okay."

I saw three people approach the glass doors from inside and then emerge into the rain. Two large male figures, both in black rain ponchos with hoods up, flanking one smaller figure, a woman. One of the men was holding an umbrella over the woman's head. They were being considerate, which surprised me. Was she their hostage or not? Was she being taken against her will or going voluntarily?

The man who wasn't holding the umbrella was walking in front of the other two, moving more briskly than the others. He half-walked, half-ran. Then he clambered up the short flight of steps and into the plane.

I took out the Maglite, grasped it backhanded, pulsed it with my right thumb a few times to get their attention. Both of them turned to look at me, squinting in the darkness to make out my face.

Then I angled the beam slightly to one side and pulsed it on, then off. Pointing it directly at them would blind them—five hundred lumens would do that; a beam that bright was downright dangerous to the cornea—but I only wanted to see their faces. A cone of brilliant light flashed on for a brief moment and then faded away, but it was enough for me to confirm that the woman was Kayla.

And her escort was the bald man.

Curtis Schmidt.

35

Had he recognized me?

"Excuse me," I said to Schmidt. "We're gonna need a CRM for your flight plan."

Schmidt said, "Huh?"

"Your CRM, sir. We never got the filing."

I was talking officious nonsense.

"You're not cleared for takeoff," I said. "We need you to hold short of Bravo."

With a swift sudden movement, I grabbed Kayla's free hand and yanked her toward me. I was counting on her recognizing me up close—she'd texted me, after all—or at least going along compliantly.

"That way," I said to her, pointing. "Run."

"Heller, you goddamn son of a bitch," Schmidt said in his high choked voice, lunging at me.

I backhanded the flashlight to the right side of Schmidt's head, aiming for the temple and a quick knockout. But he had jerked his head around to his left, and I hit his cheekbone instead. I felt something crunch.

He winced, yelled, but he kept on coming at me, swinging his right fist at my head. Which was stupid: He should have tried to wrest the flashlight out of my hand. I had a weapon, and he didn't, at least so far as I knew. I had the advantage, and he should have removed it from me.

So I pressed the advantage as best I could. He shouted something at me, something obscene, and I swung again, hard, whipping it up from waist level, scything through the air, slamming into his chin from beneath his open mouth, cracking his teeth together hard.

Schmidt shook his head like an enraged bull and took up a boxer's stance. His left fist shot out and clipped me on the chin. My head rocked back. I saw stars.

"Watch out!" But I knew he was readying the right-handed knockout blow. Boxers are dangerous, but they're also predictable, and they rarely think about anything below the belt. So just as he stepped forward to get the range he wanted, I stomp-kicked him in his left knee with my right foot.

It connected. His knee hyperextended, the pain immense, he leaned over at the waist.

A woman's cry: Kayla's.

I glanced up in time to see the second guy charging out of the plane and down the steps. He fumbled under his poncho for something. Not good. It had to be a weapon.

I grabbed Schmidt, who was screaming in agony and staggering around. I got hold of the hood of his poncho and yanked, hard, pulling him in toward me, a human shield.

I could make out the second guy's silhouette in the darkness. I could see a gun in his hand. He was maneuvering to take a shot without hitting Schmidt.

I intended to make it hard for him.

The second guy moved in closer, now ten feet away, his gun extended, angling the weapon around to miss Schmidt.

That was when I hit the Maglite's POWER button with my right thumb, aiming it at his eyes, hitting him in the cornea with five hundred lumens, dazzling him. His hands flew to his eyes and the gun went off, a wild shot, the round pitting the asphalt five or six feet to my left.

Now I shoved Schmidt to the ground and reached out to grab the barrel of the second man's gun. It was blisteringly hot. I yanked and twisted it out of his hand and immediately dropped it, too hot to handle.

I drop-kicked the second man in the groin. It wasn't original, but it worked.

He bellowed in pain and tumbled to the ground near Curtis Schmidt.

I leaned over and scooped up the gun in my burned hand, this time by the grip, and ran toward where Kayla was standing, a few hundred feet away.

She was crying. "Come on," I said, taking her by the

elbow and leading her toward the Suburban. "I need you to run."

But she stood still, weeping. I couldn't make out what she was saying except for "Oh my God."

"Come on," I said, gently this time, taking her hand. "Hurry. You're safe now."

36

By the time we were on the main road outside the airport, Kayla Pitts had stopped crying. She seemed embarrassed about it. She sniffed a few times, said, "Oh, Jesus. Oh, Jesus." Her blond hair hung down in straggly tendrils and dark wet clumps.

Dorothy, sitting in the row behind the front seat, watched her warily. She seemed not to know what to make of our passenger.

"Where are you taking me?" Kayla said in a weak, quavering voice.

"Not back to your apartment," I said.

"Okay." She wiped her eyes with the back of her right hand. "Good. So where?"

"A hotel."

To Dorothy I said, "Do me a favor and call the hotel and reserve another room. See if we can get one of the rooms that adjoin my suite."

"How did you find me?" Kayla asked.

The rain had slowed to a light spattering. I signaled left and merged into traffic, which was considerably lighter now, the worst of rush hour over.

When I didn't reply right away, she asked, "Did you trace my phone or something?"

"Something like that," I said. I didn't want to tell her I'd slipped a GPS tracker into her laptop bag, which would have necessitated telling her I'd broken into her apartment. That would only introduce an element of distrust and paranoia I wanted to avoid. "Tell me what happened."

"These two guys showed up at my apartment and told me to pack my things. They gave me fifteen minutes. They told me they were taking me out of town."

"Did they break in?"

"I let them in."

"Did you know them?"

She shook her head. "I recognized one of them, the big bald guy. He was supposed to keep watch over me."

I had a tremendous number of questions I wanted to ask, but I wanted to keep her on track as much as possible. "They didn't tell you where you were going?"

"Just out of town. They put me in the back of a van."

"What made you think they were going to kill you?"

"I was in the back, but when I put my ear to the front compartment I could hear them talking about me. One of them said something about 'without a trace.' The other guy said something like, 'look like she was running' and something about 'before a body turns up.' And I saw when they were taking me to the van that one of them had a gun. I was scared out of my mind. I didn't know what to do, who to call. I don't trust the cops. So I called that reporter at Slander Sheet, but I got a message saying the phone was disconnected. So . . . I called you."

"Why?"

She was silent for a long time. She shook her head. "When I met you . . . ? I got the feeling, I don't know . . . you were one of the good guys."

"Okay," I said. I'd take that.

"I kept calling, and I kept getting your voice mail. And then when I finally reached you, one of the guys must have heard me talking because he grabbed the phone out of my hand."

"You were brave to do that. And smart."

"Yeah, but now what? Now what happens to me?"

"We're going to keep you with us, keep you safe, and I'm going to need your help in finding the people behind this."

"But I don't know who they are!"

"You know things. Little details that might not mean anything to you. We'll talk, and we'll help each other."

We all fell silent for a moment. I turned off the windshield wipers; the rain had stopped. After a long while, Kayla said, "Tell me something."

"Okay."

"I don't understand. Why did you come for me?"

"Because I think you can answer some questions for me," I said.

"And what if I can't?"

"Doesn't matter," I said. "You're still worth saving."

37

The hotel had an available room adjoining mine. We put Kayla there and opened the connecting doors. I wanted to keep a close watch on her. I assumed that Curtis Schmidt and his comrade would be out of commission for a while, but others might come for her.

She knew that. She was frightened and distraught.

While Dorothy went out to pick up some toiletries for her, Kayla and I talked.

"Keep the security latch on at all times," I said. "Don't open your door for anyone. I don't care if they say it's housekeeping or room service, nobody comes in. Don't call room service. If you need something, just ask one of us. Come get me, or call on the room phone." I fixed her a drink from the minibar, a vodka and tonic, because she needed it. I couldn't find any rocks glasses, so I used a wineglass. In another wineglass I poured myself a Scotch.

"Can I at least use a computer?" she said. "I left my computer on the tarmac and they took my phone, and I want to check in with a couple of my friends. Otherwise they're going to worry about me. I just want to say I'm okay."

I shook my head. "You've got to keep your head down. Don't let anyone know you're in DC."

"So, like, I'm basically a prisoner here."

"For the time being. To keep you safe."

"How long?"

"Until it's safe."

"When's that gonna be?"

I shook my head again, more slowly. "I'll let you know."

She sipped her drink. "Why are you being nice to me?"

"Because I need your help." The simpler answer was usually better.

"Okay."

"Tell me how you got into this."

"What? The life? Or this . . . scam?"

"The scam."

She sat down on the edge of the bed. I sat in the chair next to the desk and drank some Scotch. She had the faint smell of patchouli about her.

She let out a long sigh. "Okay. So, like, three months ago, I had this date, with a client, at the Willard, right? Gary something. When I got to his hotel room, he paid my fee, right up front—that's unusual. Guys always do it after. Nicely dressed, suit and tie and all that. He said he just wanted to talk to me. I thought maybe he wanted something really kinky, but no, he wasn't there for the sex. He told me he worked for an organization of businessmen and they wanted to hire me. They had a . . . a *proposition* for me, he called it."

"Did you get the guy's name?"

"No. Just 'Gary.' He said they wanted me to talk to a reporter at Slander Sheet and tell her that I'd had three dates with this Supreme Court judge named Jeremiah Claflin. They said they'd prepare me to talk to the reporter, they'd take care of everything, and they said they'd pay me a hundred thousand dollars—ten thousand up front, the rest later."

"And you said yes."

"No. Not yet. I was freaked out. I asked why."

"Okay. What'd he say?"

"Just that this Claflin guy had to be taken down, for the good of the country."

"Did he say who this 'organization of businessmen' was?"

She shook her head and gulped her drink like it was lemonade. "I didn't ask. I didn't really care. I was just afraid if I did this, I could go to prison. He said that would never happen. He said I could probably have my own TV reality show."

"Is that what you wanted?"

"Are you kidding?"

"But you said yes to the proposition anyway."

"No, I didn't. Not until they . . . threatened me."

"Threatened you how?"

She finished her drink and put the glass on top of the bed next to her. "So I said no to the guy." She hadn't answered my question, but I waited.

"You said no to a hundred thousand dollars?"

"I don't know, I was scared shitless. Maybe I didn't believe him about the money. I mean, he took out ten thousand dollars in cash and showed it to me and said I could have it right then and there if I agreed. It was all mine. Just do it. But how did I know he'd actually come up with the rest of the money when it was all over?"

"So what did you tell him?"

"I still said no. I mean, a hundred thousand dollars, that's more money than I've ever had, enough to buy me out of the life. But how could I be sure I didn't get exposed as a liar? I told him I had to think about it."

"Sure."

"He said don't take too long. He said they knew about my sister. She's—in prison. In Mississippi. For a drug bust. She was dealing meth."

I knew that but didn't want to let her know. "Okay."

"He said they had ways of getting to her in prison. If I didn't agree to do this thing, or if I told anybody about it, they'd hurt her bad. Or worse. So I flew to Jackson to visit my sister in prison. She'd just come out of the infirmary. But they let me see her. She got stabbed in the thigh. She was hurt bad. She told me she got shanked in the commissary. Some inmate came up to her in line and stuck her and said this is only the beginning, if your sister doesn't cooperate. So when I came back to DC I called this guy Gary and said okay, I'll do it." She looked at me, eyes shining, vulnerable. "I didn't have a choice, you know? It wasn't the money."

"I understand. Do you have Gary's number?"

She shook her head. "It's in my phone. I need another drink."

"You didn't write it down anywhere?" I got up and began fixing her a second vodka and tonic.

"I don't remember. I don't think so. So I met with him and he gave me the ten thousand."

"They prepared you? They told you what to say?"

"That guy Gary did, yeah."

"How many times did you meet with him?"

"Just one more time. To get me ready to talk to the reporter."

"He gave you the name?"

"Mandy Seeger, yeah."

"Just her? No other reporter?"

"Just her."

"Any idea why?"

She shook her head again.

"Did you ever get the rest of the hundred thousand?"

"No. I think they were about to pay me when the story fell apart. They think I leaked to you. I told them that was bullshit, but they said they knew I met with you. Because they had this guy watching me all the time, this big bald guy."

"I saw that. He was the same one who came to take you to the plane."

"Right. Him and this other guy."

"Gary?"

"No. It was someone I never saw before. But Gary called me today and said they were getting me out of town. I—I'm worried about my sister. If they did something to her because they think I—" Her voice broke as a sob welled up. "I'm so . . . I'm scared," she choked out. She slumped forward and spilled some of her drink on the comforter cover. I got up from my chair and took her drink from her and sat down next to her on the bed.

"I want to go to sleep," she said. "I'm so wiped out."

"Do that. We'll talk in the morning."

There was a knock at the door. I went over to the peephole and saw Dorothy. I opened the door. She was carrying a couple of plastic shopping bags, one from CVS and one from Macy's. She looked at Kayla, then at me, wonderingly.

I opened the room door again and hung a DO NOT DISTURB sign on the outside door handle. Then I fastened the security latch. It was too easy to defeat those hotel security latches with a length of stiff wire. I'd done it myself. So I got a towel from the bathroom, rolled it up, and stuck it under the door's lever handle. That would foil any attempts to beat the latch.

I had to move her as soon as possible. Tonight I would make some calls and get her a safe house outside of DC.

"I got you a toothbrush and toothpaste, honey," Dorothy said gently, setting the bags down on the bed next to Kayla. "A nightgown. A pair of pants that might be too big, now that I look at you, and some T-shirts."

"Thank you." Kayla sniffed. "You know, in my line of work there are always these guys who want to *save you*. They're the worst. You want them to just get the hell away, you know? But it's different when you actually need . . ." Her words were once again swallowed up by sobs.

"Come," I said to Dorothy. "Let's let Kayla get some sleep. I have something I need to do."

38

"Nick," Dorothy said quietly, "what are we doing?"

We sat in the living room of my suite, the connecting door to Kayla's room open. I'd set down my wineglass of Scotch and ordered coffee from room service.

"About what?"

"With her? She's a scammer and a grifter, and need I remind you, she also happens to be a prostitute."

"And a victim."

"Of her own making."

"It's complicated."

"Not to me. If it wasn't for her, we wouldn't be here."

"If it wasn't her, it would have been someone else. Anyway, she may prove useful."

"But that's not why you rescued her."

I shrugged. What could I say? She was right; I'd saved the girl because she was being used; she was a pawn in a struggle I didn't yet understand. And because I liked her for some reason. But I didn't want to argue with Dorothy. She had her moral code, a complex one, and I respected it, but she didn't view Kayla as damaged goods, a victim of circumstance, as I did.

A knock at my door. I checked the peephole. I could see a young woman in a hotel uniform with a rolling cart. I opened the door, and she rolled in the cart and set up the coffee.

I offered Dorothy some, and she accepted. She had work to do. She was determined to trace the ownership of Slander Sheet and she had a few online leads. She sat at her laptop at the dining table/work station. Meanwhile, after I'd had a few sips, I called Mandy Seeger's cell phone and got a message—not hers, but a robotic female voice from the phone company saying, "The number you dialed has been changed, disconnected, or is no longer in service."

So I called the main number for the Slander Sheet offices in DC, figuring that there'd probably be staffers working at night.

A young-sounding man answered the line. "Slander Sheet."

"Mandy Seeger, please."

A pause. "Uh, yeah, she doesn't work here anymore. Sorry."

That was fast, I thought.

"Do you have any contact number for her? I'm a friend."

A pause. "Hold on." He sounded reluctant.

He put the phone down. I heard voices in the background. He came back on the line and dictated a phone number. I thanked him and hung up.

I wanted to talk to Mandy Seeger because she was another victim in the Claflin business. She, too, had been used, like Kayla, only in a different way. Now that she'd been fired, I suspected she would be happy to tell me what she knew about who owned Slander Sheet.

Her phone rang and rang and went to a recording of her voice. I left a message.

Then I found Curtis Schmidt's wallet, the one I'd taken off him, and took out his Maryland driver's license. It listed his home address. I looked it up on Google Earth and then switched to Street View.

One of the great advantages of Google Maps and Google Earth is that they enable you to do a kind of close reconnaissance of houses. That's why criminals like Google. Now they can case their targets remotely.

Curtis Schmidt lived in Bethesda, on Moorland Lane. His house was a handsome three-story brick colonial with a detached garage, situated on a small but nicely landscaped plot of land graced with mature trees. The house and the neighborhood were too nice for a cop to afford, and it made me wonder when Schmidt had gone bad. I surveyed the house and the neighbors' houses from every angle I could. The houses were unusually close to one another, I noted.

I checked the address in the usual databases to see whether Schmidt had a wife and family, but from all indications it appeared that he lived alone. Then, using my burner phone, I called Schmidt's home number, which Dorothy had found in one of our databases. It rang eight times and then went to voice mail, a muffled male voice that said only, "Leave your name and phone number at the tone."

I changed into my Allied HVAC uniform, assembled a small bag of tools, and said good-bye to Dorothy and went down to the Suburban.

As I drove up Connecticut Avenue, heading northwest toward Maryland, my iPhone rang.

It was Mandy Seeger.

"Did you call to gloat, is that it?" she said.

"I called because I want your help. It wasn't your fault. Kayla lied to you. She was paid and blackmailed, both."

"How—how do you know?"

"She told me so. She got paid twice. Not just by Slander Sheet. How much did you guys pay her, by the way?"

"Ten thousand bucks. What do you mean, she got paid and blackmailed? By who?"

"That's just it. She doesn't know."

"Where is she? I tried to call her, but no answer. I thought she was screening her calls and didn't want to talk to me."

"She's with me."

"With *you*?"

"We're keeping her safe. The people who paid her tried to grab her and take her out of town, fly her somewhere."

" 'People'? Like who?"

"I'm trying to find out. I thought you might want to help me."

Slander Sheet had just destroyed her credibility as a

journalist and then fired her. She had to be hopping mad.

"Hell yeah, I want to help you. Not tonight, though. I'm wiped out. I can barely talk."

"Tomorrow as soon as you're up, give me a call."

"I will. And—Heller?"

"Yeah?"

"Thanks."

39

I found Schmidt's house easily—I recognized it from Google—and drove past it slowly. The house was dark; the lights were off. I tried his home phone one more time, calling from my burner, and there was no answer.

It was a fair assumption that he wasn't home, but I couldn't be sure. Where was he? Hospital, maybe, getting something done to his hyperextended knee. Though there wasn't much that could be done. Surgery, maybe, if a ligament was torn. A lot of physical therapy. Ice.

Tax and residential records confirmed that he lived alone, without a wife and/or kids. But that didn't mean he might not have a girlfriend visiting, asleep in the house. Or he could be there alone and just not answering.

So I circled around and pulled into his driveway, behind the detached garage, where I parked. That seemed less suspicious than parking a few blocks away and approaching by foot. If neighbors were watching, they'd see a big, official-looking black Suburban in the driveway; nothing furtive about that. Hence the service uniform. The direct approach was often best.

I got out and went right to the front door, the way a legitimate repairperson would, and I rang the doorbell. Was the place alarmed? He was an ex-cop; I had to assume it was. I didn't see any alarm sign on the front lawn or by the door. Which didn't necessarily mean anything.

I rang again. To the left of the door was a window through which I could see into the house, into the foyer. Inside I could see a red LED glowing in the dark. Odds were good it was an alarm panel. Security experts believed you shouldn't have your alarm panel within view of the entrance, because that made it too easy for clever burglars who might have somehow obtained the secret code. But Schmidt, the ex-cop, probably wanted it visible, an overt display, a deterrent.

I noticed a point-of-entry magnetic sensor on the window jamb. That confirmed that he had a classic, old-school security system. Nothing wrong with that. In fact, the old-school systems were just about impossible to beat.

There were often ways around them, though.

I returned to the detached garage. Its overhead door was locked. I pulsed on my small penlight, looked through one of the small windows, and saw what I expected: an automatic garage door opener.

That was good.

One of the tools I'd brought was a coil of steel strapping, the sort of thing that's used to secure pallets of lumber and so on. At one end it was bent into a V. I straightened it and inserted it into the top of the door, between the door and the weather-stripping. Inside, hanging down from the door-opening mechanism, was a manual release, a string with a red handle on it. That was standard on all automatic garage door openers, for use in case of a power failure.

It took about a minute, but eventually my improvised slim-jim hooked onto the handle of the manual release, and I was able to yank it, hard.

Now it was a simple matter to raise the garage door by hand.

The garage smelled of gasoline and motor oil. I found the light switch and flipped it on. No car here. I looked in the obvious places for a key to the house. Nothing.

Then I noticed the eight-foot aluminum ladder mounted on large steel hooks on the wall. I took it down off the hooks, switched off the light, left the garage, and rolled down the overhead door behind me.

I carried the ladder around to the rear of the house and leaned it against the wall, in the shrubbery that ringed the house, just below one of the second-floor windows. It's extremely unusual to find alarm sensors on the upper stories of a residence. It happens, but I've seen it only once.

The window was unlocked. Also not unusual. I edged it open by pressing up against the muntin until the window came open an inch, then I grasped the bottom rail and pulled it up. Feet first, I slid in.

A guest bedroom, by the look of it. A neatly made

bed, an end table, a desk and chair. Not much else. No signs of habitation.

It was dark inside the house and smelled faintly of mildew and cigarette. Wall-to-wall carpeting covered the hall floor. I switched on my penlight and illuminated a path. The next room was a bathroom. Next was another bedroom. This one looked like it was where Schmidt slept. A king-size bed, lamps on end tables on either side. A giant flat-screen TV mounted on the wall. In front of it, an exercise bicycle. A chest of drawers. I pulled open the top drawer and found socks.

I thought of something and checked under the pillow on the bed. On the right side was a weapon, a Glock 26 pistol. I pulled it out and stuck it into my tool bag. I had no weapon with me in DC—they were back home, in Boston—and it occurred to me that I might need one sometime.

I switched off the penlight and descended the carpeted stairs to the first floor.

Here I had to be careful. There might be motion sensors. They were cheap and easy to install and often considered part of the basic security package. I stopped on the third-to-last step and surveyed the darkness.

I saw the glowing red LED dot on the alarm panel in the foyer, but nothing else.

I switched on the penlight, traced it around the crown molding on the ceiling, looking for motion sensors, but found none. So I continued the rest of the way down to the landing. There I stood for a moment. The downstairs was neat and clean and looked almost uninhabited.

Through one open door I saw a roomy kitchen with a dining table covered in Formica. One door was closed. I opened it and found a half-bath. A roll of paper towels in a wall dispenser, one rumpled towel. I opened a second door, pointed my penlight, saw a desk and a file cabinet, another big flat-screen TV, a bookshelf. A safe. This was his study. The safe was probably where he kept his guns, the ones that weren't hidden under his pillow. Maybe other things in there, too. On the desk were an old-looking laptop computer and a couple of framed photos. I glanced at the pictures. They showed Schmidt with his arm around a woman on a beach somewhere, probably Cancún. Another one was of Schmidt and a male friend, with a bristly mustache, who was triumphantly holding up a big bluefish. I tugged at the top file cabinet drawer, but it was locked.

A flash of light caught my eye. I looked up and saw the red light of a motion sensor come on.

My heart began to pound. I'd set it off.

Here was where he placed the motion sensors. Here, where he probably stored his sensitive stuff, the room he was most worried about.

A loud Klaxon blared from speakers throughout the house, a deafening clanging sound, and a tinny pre-recorded voice that proclaimed, "Leave immediately! Leave immediately!"

Then a phone trilled.

That would be the dispatch service, calling to check whether this was a valid alarm, or whether it had been triggered mistakenly by the homeowner.

I grabbed his desk phone.

"Bethesda Alarm Service," a woman's voice said.

"Yeah, that was me," I said. "I screwed up. Can you turn off the damn alarm? I'm going deaf here."

"What is your name, sir?"

"Curtis Schmidt."

"Sir, I'm going to need your code word." She had an Indian accent.

"My code—dammit, I don't remember, my wife chose that." I remembered suddenly that Schmidt wasn't married. But the alarm company wouldn't have a record of that.

"I need to hear the code word, sir, or I'm required to notify the police."

"I don't—look, I'll look around and see if she put it on a sticky note somewhere—can you turn this off in the meantime?"

"No, sir, we're not allowed to do that until we hear the homeowner's code word."

"Will you hang on?"

"Yes, sir, certainly."

I dropped the phone, looked around frantically, realized I had to get out of there at once. The response time for the Bethesda police could be as quick as five minutes and as long as twenty. There was no time to run upstairs and climb down the ladder, and the alarm had been triggered anyway, so I might as well exit through one of the doors on this floor. I took out my phone and snapped a picture of the framed photo of Schmidt and his buddy fishing, and I raced to the kitchen. I unlocked the double locks on the back door and pulled it open.

Outside, the alarm was clanging loudly, piercing the still night, loud enough to alert the neighbors. I went around to the driveway, walking not running, and got into the Suburban.

I backed up the driveway to the street at a deliberate speed and drove off into the darkness.

40

What I'd hoped to find was a file, in a drawer or on a computer, or something else that might clarify who Schmidt was working with or for. All I'd ended up with was a picture of Schmidt and a fishing buddy.

Now he knew someone had broken into his house. He'd know who.

My nerves didn't stop jangling, and my heartbeat didn't return to normal, until I reached Connecticut Avenue.

I parked the Suburban in a space on Sixteenth Street and returned to the hotel. I nodded at the doorman and found the bank of elevators. We were on the third floor. My suite was number 322. Dorothy, across the hall, was 323. I touched the keycard to the sensor above the lever handle and it winked green to let me in.

It was close to ten o'clock in the evening, and it had been a long day. I was exhausted. I checked my e-mail to see if anything had come in, but there was nothing that required my immediate attention. The connecting door to Kayla's room was closed. I had left it open. Maybe she had closed it for privacy. I preferred it left open.

I changed into a T-shirt and a pair of sweats, and then knocked softly on the door, in case she was awake. No answer. I opened the door and peered around. The room was dark but a light in the bathroom was on.

Her bed looked empty. She was probably in the bathroom. I entered her room and knocked on the bathroom door.

The door was slightly ajar, I saw.

"Kayla?" I said.

No answer.

I knocked again, and the door came open an inch or so.

"Kayla?"

Still no answer. Odd. Maybe she wasn't in the bathroom; she'd gone somewhere, left the room. Exactly what I told her not to do.

Tentatively I pushed the door open, and what I saw next at first didn't register.

I smelled blood, dark and sweet and metallic. My stomach flipped and my heart began to clatter. I saw Kayla slumped down in what looked like a bathtub filled with blood. Her eyes were open and staring at nothing. Her face was pale, lifeless. Her lips were bluish. Her breasts and abdomen were covered in blood. I took another step and saw one hand curled against her belly, long parallel gashes cut into her wrists, lengthwise. Another couple of gashes at her neck, one that apparently had severed the carotid artery. My eyes were caught by a glint of light. I turned to see, on the bathroom sink, a broken wineglass, the shards scattered across the vanity. One particularly large shard, smeared with blood, twinkled on the edge of the tub. I put a couple of fingers on her neck, next to her windpipe, and felt no pulse, just cold flesh, and I knew it was too late.

41

The paramedics canceled the ambulance as soon as they arrived. There was no need for it. There was no question whether she was dead. I heard one of the uniformed officers in Kayla's hotel room calling for homicide, which was standard—homicide detectives showed up to investigate any death outside a medical environment—and adding, "but I'm pretty sure it's a suicide."

An investigator and a driver from the medical examiner's office showed up shortly thereafter and began murmuring to each other and taking pictures and measurements. Dorothy and I sat in the suite living room, mostly in stunned silence, in a state of shock. Dorothy cried. I was feeling hollow.

I was surprised at how torn up I was by Kayla's suicide. On some level it felt like my fault. She was on track to make a hundred thousand dollars with a concocted story about Justice Claflin. Until I came along. I'd set off a chain reaction that ended in her feeling alone, desperate, scared, and hopeless. If I hadn't gotten involved, she might still be alive. And what if I hadn't broken into Schmidt's house but stayed here instead? Maybe she'd have had someone to talk to. Maybe she wouldn't have felt so alone.

I barely knew the girl; I should not have felt her death so powerfully.

Around ten minutes later a homicide detective from Washington Metro Police showed up. He introduced himself as Detective Balakian. He was a young guy, couldn't have been much more than thirty, with a gold stud earring in his left ear and a Kurt Cobain goatee with chin strap. He was snappily dressed in a skinny black tie, a white shirt with short collar points, skinny trousers, and a quilted Barbour-looking coat. He wore cool-nerd eyeglasses. On his right inside wrist, I noticed when we shook hands, he had a tattoo of an infinity sign. He was the hipster cop, and I took an immediate dislike to him. Most cops at that hour smell like Burger King; he smelled like *bánh mì*.

While the medical examiner's investigators and the mobile crime unit people were photographing Kayla's body and taking measurements, the groovy cop started asking us questions in a soft-spoken voice. He took down our names and brief descriptions of who we were in a small flip-down notebook.

"What's her name, the deceased?"

I told him.

"What's your relationship with her?"

"None," I said. "She asked me to pick her up at a general aviation airport in Fairfax. She was being taken somewhere against her will."

That naturally piqued his interest, so he asked me to explain, and I did.

"She's 'Heidi'? From—Slander Sheet?"

The hipster detective kept up with the tabloid news. I nodded.

"*I* see. So you're a private investigator?" He smirked. "Like, one of those cruller-munching divorce dicks, that it?"

"Huh," I said. "Is that what you learned from *21 Jump Street*?"

He nodded. Touché. "Does she have a purse or wallet with an ID?"

"No."

"Does she have a phone or a laptop?"

"Not here."

"No phone?"

"It was taken away from her en route to the airport."

"Do you know who her next of kin are?"

"I know she has a sister in prison. Apart from that, I don't."

"Did she have a criminal background, to your knowledge?"

"I don't know." But I knew what he was really asking. If she had a criminal background, if she'd ever been arrested, her fingerprints would be in the system somewhere, and they'd be able to make a positive identification of her body. Without next of kin or any ID, they were going to have problems.

"I didn't find a note," Detective Balakian said. "Did either of you find anything that looked like a note?"

I shook my head, and Dorothy said no.

"How about her mental state earlier tonight? Was there anything about her, thinking back on it now, that may have indicated she was contemplating killing herself?"

"No."

"But you did talk with her?"

"We talked, yes. But nothing indicated she was considering suicide. Absolutely not. Though she didn't like being what she called a 'prisoner' here."

"Was she?"

"Not at all. She could have left at any time. Though I urged her to stay here."

"So why did she call herself a prisoner?"

"Because I told her not to answer the phone or the door. To let no one in."

"How would you describe her mental state?"

"She was frightened of the people blackmailing her; that was pretty evident. She was afraid for her sister in prison, what they might do to her. She was scared."

"All right. I found some little bottles of Scotch and vodka in the trash. Did you witness her drinking?"

"She and I each had a drink or two."

"So that wasn't all her."

"Right."

"She'd just been humiliated publicly," Detective Balakian said. "Did she indicate how that might have affected her?"

"We didn't talk about that."

"When you left her this evening, she seemed fine?"

"That's right. Upset and scared, yes. But not suicidal."

"Where did you go this evening?"

I paused for an instant. *Breaking into an ex-cop's house.* Yeah, *that* would go over well. I couldn't claim I'd met with someone or he'd want to know who. If I said I went out for dinner, where did I eat?

But Dorothy was quick. "He was on a stakeout."

"A stakeout?"

"Yeah," I said. "Couple hours of sitting in a car. I'm sure you've been there."

He looked at me for a beat, as if reassessing. I wasn't so sure he'd ever been on a stakeout, actually. He seemed awfully young to be a homicide detective. "You say she was being taken somewhere against her will, which is why she called you. Where was she being taken?"

"I don't know."

"Why didn't she call the police?"

"I don't know."

"And who were her would-be kidnappers?"

"I don't know that either."

"You say you live in Boston?"

"That's right."

"How long have you been in town?"

"A couple of days." I'd already been over this with him.

"Sounds to me like she'd been under a great deal of emotional stress. Would you say that's accurate?"

"I would."

"Between the attempted kidnapping by an unknown party and the very public nature of her, uh, accusation against a Supreme Court justice."

I nodded.

"She was in a fragile state; is that fair to say?"

I nodded again.

"Yet you left her alone in this hotel room with a mini-bar full of alcohol."

"She was exhausted. She wanted to go to sleep."

He turned to Dorothy. "Did you check on her at any point this evening?"

"I was asleep myself," she said.

He turned back to me. "So she called you to help rescue her, and you brought her to this hotel room and then left her here?"

"I don't think I like what you're implying," I said.

"That you left her here in a vulnerable state? That's not accurate?"

"You're trying to make it sound like it's my fault."

"I didn't say you did it, Mister, uh, Heller. I said you let it happen."

"I told you, we had no idea she was suicidal. And I don't think she was." I heard myself: I sounded more defensive than I wanted to.

"Hey, don't beat yourself up about it."

"Let me ask you something," I said. "How sure are you that this was really a suicide?"

"Do you have any reason to believe it was something else?"

"She was afraid, and she had cause to be afraid."

"Uh-huh."

"She was almost abducted. There were people who didn't want her to talk."

"Well, we'll have to open a separate investigation into that. But there are far easier ways to kill someone than by slitting their wrists and their neck. It takes a while to bleed out, and I didn't see any signs of struggle. There were even hesitation marks, which is textbook—the first couple of times she tried, she was probably surprised at how painful it was and stopped. This is *textbook*, man. We've got a young prostitute, probably mentally unstable, probably with family issues, maybe substance abuse. Who was undergoing a lot of emotional pressure."

"And didn't leave a note."

"Sometimes they leave notes; sometimes they don't. Plenty of times they don't. I know it's hard to accept that someone you care about committed suicide. I understand why you might prefer to think it wasn't a suicide."

"So you've worked a lot of homicides?"

He didn't reply.

I wanted to ask him how long he'd been out of homicide school. I had a feeling it wasn't long at all. He was also here by himself, without a partner. You send an inexperienced homicide detective out solo when you're fairly sure you're not dealing with a homicide. When you're dealing with an apparent natural death or a suicide. That way the newbie investigator develops his chops. It looked like a suicide, so he was investigating it as if it was a suicide.

But what if it wasn't?

42

After Detective Balakian had been there for barely an hour and a half, the people from the medical examiner's office zipped up Kayla's body in a bag and took her away on a stretcher. I watched them do it, feeling numb.

They drained the tub first to make it easier to remove the body, the blood-tinged water leaving a brick-red residue. Spatters of her blood remained on the tub surround, the lip of the tub, the adjoining vanity.

My phone rang. I glanced at my watch: 12:30 A.M.

Then I took out the phone and saw the caller ID and recognized the number. "Yes?" I said.

"Oh my God," Mandy Seeger said in a hushed voice. "Is it true?"

"What are you talking about?"

"Kayla's dead?"

"How—where did you hear this?"

"It's on Slander Sheet."

"*What?*" How was that even possible? But then I realized that Slander Sheet probably had tipsters in the Washington Metro Police Department. Hell, one of the tipsters could have been in this hotel room an hour ago, a mobile crime scene tech or a uniformed officer, texting Slander Sheet on the sly, making a quick buck. I found SlanderSheet.com on my laptop, and there it was.

CALL GIRL WHO CLAIMED AFFAIR WITH HIGH COURT JUDGE TAKES HER OWN LIFE

The headline ran over a photo of Kayla, a.k.a. "Heidi," from the Lily Schuyler website.

"I got a call a couple of minutes ago from Steve, my replacement," she said. "He had some questions."

"When?"

"Like fifteen minutes ago."

"Who tipped him off?"

I was fairly certain that the only one in the room who knew the identity of the deceased besides me and Dorothy was Detective Balakian.

"Julian."

"When?"

"Hold on, he e-mailed me first, before he called. Here it is, he forwarded an e-mail from Julian time-stamped eleven fifteen P.M."

"Julian Gunn knew it was Kayla at eleven fifteen?"

"So?"

"Man, that's barely fifteen minutes after the police got here."

"Slander Sheet has sources everywhere," she said.

43

Mandy Seeger arrived twenty minutes later. I'd asked her to come over. She'd said she couldn't sleep, and I was wide-awake anyway. Dorothy had gone to bed.

She was wearing dark jeans and a black top and looked solemn. Her eyes were red-rimmed.

It was almost one in the morning.

"I don't believe it," she said, entering the suite and looking around curiously.

"You don't believe what?"

"Kayla. I don't believe she—committed suicide. I just don't think she was the kind of person who'd kill herself. She was tough. She was a survivor. Maybe that's why we hit it off."

We sat in the living room of the suite. I'd closed the door to Kayla's room. It didn't seem right to be there anymore. A night manager had come an hour earlier and asked if it was okay if he had housekeeping service the room, or did they need the scene preserved? Detective Balakian said they had what they needed. So housekeeping would come in the morning. Until then, Kayla's blood remained splashed on the walls of the bathroom. And on the floor.

Mandy wanted details, and I gave them. She was silent for a long time after I finished.

I said, "Do you still have friends at Slander Sheet you can get in touch with?"

"I just got fired, Heller."

"What was the reason Julian gave for firing you?"

"He was furious. He said I'd disgraced Slander Sheet. Like that's even possible. I should have investigated the story even more thoroughly than I did, he said."

"Wasn't he the one pressuring you to get it out there?"

"He was. He just told me to pack up my cubicle and go. My e-mail and my cell phone were immediately cut off."

"So who was pressuring *him*?"

"The S.O., I'm sure."

"The . . . 'S.O.'?"

"It's a joke. That's what we lowly employees called Slander Sheet's shadowy owners. S.O. for 'shadowy owners.' Because no one knows who they are. It's kept a deep dark secret."

"Hunsecker Media, right?"

"Right, but they're owned by some holding company, and that's a black box."

"There must have been rumors, at least."

"Plenty of rumors. But nobody knew anything. Can we get some coffee? They must have room service in this joint."

I picked up the phone, called room service, and asked for coffee for two.

When I'd hung up, I said, "How did this story first come to you?"

"Through Julian. He gave me Kayla's phone number."

"And you think he was fed the story by the owners?"

She nodded. "He never said. But it wouldn't surprise me."

"Does he have his own sources? Does he do any reporting?"

She shook her head. "None, and no. He's not a reporter. He's the 'big picture' guy." She waggled two fingers on each hand to make scare quotes.

"I always assumed the whole story was cooked up by someone who wanted Claflin out. For political reasons. An enemy."

"Maybe."

"So maybe the shadowy owners are political opponents of Claflin."

"Maybe."

"You don't seem so sure."

"Maybe politics had nothing to do with it. Maybe it was someone who didn't like him personally."

"Good point."

"This story was a really big deal for Slander Sheet," she said. "If it wasn't for you, this story would have put us on the map."

"And a big deal for you, personally."

"More than you know."

"What does that mean?"

"It's times like these that I really want a drink."

"Happy to make you one."

She shook her head. "I don't drink anymore."

"Okay." I remembered she drank Diet Coke instead of beer at the bar a few days ago.

"It's one in the morning and I'm still in shock, and maybe I should shut my mouth."

"I get it. You're on the wagon. Your drinking days are done. That have anything to do with your departure from the *Post*?"

"You think they canned me because I was a lush?"

"I didn't say that."

"Okay."

"But what's the real story?"

She settled back in her chair and took a deep breath.

And I waited for her to lie to me. People always lie about why they left a job. *A personality conflict with my editor*, I figured she'd say, or *I couldn't do the kind of pieces I wanted to.* Or, *I just like the tempo of the Internet better—it's the future, right?* I wondered how she was going to spin it.

"The thing is," she said, "I actually got fired."

"But you were a star there. I don't understand."

"For a while, yeah. But then I went too far. I crossed the line a couple of times."

"Crossed the line?"

"I got too aggressive on a couple of stories. One time

I was working on a story about defense contractors and bribery and the Pentagon, and I pretended to be working for a defense contractor. And I offered the deputy undersecretary of the Air Force for acquisition a bribe. All a lie, of course. But she agreed to it."

"Uh-oh."

"Yeah, you can't do that at the *Post*. You can't go undercover or pretend to be someone you're not. You're not allowed to lie. It's a legal thing."

I was surprised, pleasantly so. She'd got fired because she lied. And now she was telling me the truth about her having lied. I admired that. I nodded. "It's always the lies that get you."

"Yeah. Well. So they fired me. I guess I can't blame them. But Slander Sheet didn't have a problem with aggressive reporting. They didn't care. They wanted a big name from the mainstream media, and that's what they got."

"You start drinking after you got fired?"

"Exactly. A lot. Starting when I got up in the morning. My mom's an alcoholic, so it runs in the family. And I was afraid . . . I knew where this was going."

There was a knock at the door. I peered through the peephole and opened the door for room service. The guy wheeled in a cart and put the tray on the dining table. I tipped him and poured coffee for both of us: black for me, cream for her.

"But I got help in time," she went on. "I signed up with Slander Sheet, and then I joined AA. I figured a few big stories there would catapult me back into the mainstream. I was working on a couple of pieces, and then this Claflin story came along. And now look where I am. I'm washed up as a journalist. My career's over. And it's a little late to go to law school."

"I'm sorry." I hesitated—I didn't mean to apologize for debunking Kayla's story. "I'm sorry to hear it."

"Need a researcher?"

She laughed, then I laughed. "You don't want to work for me," I said. "The boss is an asshole. But I wouldn't mind taking a look at your Claflin files."

She nodded. "Sure. At least Slander Sheet's reputation has gone to shit. That's some small consolation. So why do you think Kayla lied? Did someone pressure her?"

"Kayla told me she was offered a hundred thousand dollars in cash to lie about Claflin. Also they threatened to harm her sister in prison if she didn't cooperate."

"Christ," she said, glancing at me, looking queasy. "She cooperated all right. She did a great job. She fooled me."

"Is it possible the owners of Slander Sheet were behind this? That they were the ones who pressured Kayla to make this accusation, for whatever reason—and then had to cover it up?"

"It's possible, yes. When you say 'cover it up' . . ."

"Made Kayla's death look like suicide."

"Wow," she said. "You mean, did they have her killed? I guess I wouldn't rule it out. Do the police think it was a suicide?"

"The homicide detective is a novice. This may even be

the first homicide he's investigated, I don't know. And it looks like suicide, so he convinces himself it's suicide. His mind is locked in to the suicide theory. He's got tunnel vision. Confirmation bias. It happens all the time, especially with inexperienced detectives."

"What makes *you* think it wasn't suicide?" she asked.

"Because I talked to her a few hours earlier. And she wasn't suicidal. And if it was murder, that's on me. I'm the one who promised to protect her."

She finished her cup of coffee and avoided my eyes. "That girl was a pawn. It breaks my heart." A pause. "So, a question. What did you want me to come over for?"

"Because I want to find out who murdered Kayla Pitts and flush them out. I need someone who can help with the Slander Sheet end of things. I want to know who the shadowy owners are. And I wondered whether I could count on your help."

She gave a half smile. "I'm here, aren't I?"

44

At a few minutes after seven I sat bolt upright in bed and remembered that Kayla's room was going to be cleaned this morning and I didn't want that to happen yet. No matter what the DC police wanted.

Mandy and I had talked until almost three in the morning, and I wasn't going to last long on four hours of sleep. But I forced myself to get up. I ordered coffee from room service and opened the connecting door to Kayla's room. It was dim: The drapes had been drawn, probably by the mobile crime techs last night, for privacy. I checked the door to the hallway, found that the DO NOT DISTURB sign was still hanging on the handle. Maybe the sign would have kept the housekeepers from entering the room. But maybe not; maybe the night manager's orders would override the sign's authority.

The room still smelled of Kayla. I could detect a very faint waft of patchouli near the rumpled bed. Her clothes were discarded on the floor nearby. I suppose I was looking for signs of struggle, but I am not a homicide detective. Then again, neither was Balakian, really.

I took a deep breath and then went into the bathroom and turned on the light. The blood on the tub and the tile wall had dried. There was blood on the floor as well, next to the tub. It was reddish brown and glossy. It was no easier to see it this morning than it had been last night. I stood and surveyed the scene. I saw the broken wineglass and the shards of glass on the vanity and the floor and decided I'd better get into some shoes or, barefoot, I'd get cut.

When I returned wearing a pair of sneakers, I stood at the verge of the bathroom, looked around again. Slowly. I tried to imagine how Kayla did it, if it was really a suicide. She'd been deeply frightened, no question, but would simply being frightened lead someone to kill herself? No, it didn't make sense. But maybe the feeling of hopelessness caused by the situation she found herself in. That might be enough to do it.

Possibly. I thought it through.

So having decided to end her life, she looks around the hotel room for something to do it with. She's going to slit her wrists, because she's heard you can bleed out that way and die peacefully.

It wasn't true, of course. The vast majority of people who cut their wrists survive. As many as ninety-nine percent. It's most often a form of self-mutilation, a display, a cry for help, not an effective means of suicide. And it's quite painful.

But maybe she doesn't know this. Someone has to be in the one percent.

She doesn't have a knife. She doesn't even have a shaving razor. But she has a wineglass. She smashes it on the bathroom vanity and selects the sharpest shard.

She runs a bath, because that's how she's heard it's usually done, in a bath. She tries; she pokes the shard of glass into the delicate skin on the inside of her wrist and discovers that it's extremely painful. She runs it along a vein and then stops because it hurts so much. Those were the so-called hesitation marks that Detective Balakian had noticed. Homicide detectives look for hesitation marks as evidence of a true suicide. *Textbook*, Balakian had called it. *This is textbook, man.*

I stopped.

Textbook.

Either poor Kayla really did kill herself or someone made it look that way. And if someone killed her and set it up to look like a suicide, whoever did it was no amateur. No, it was someone who knew what a suicide scene should look like. Right down to the hesitation marks.

It was a professional. It had to be. Someone who knew what a homicide detective would look for.

I couldn't help but think of Curtis Schmidt, a former DC cop.

A former cop.

But I realized I was getting ahead of myself. I had no reason other than instinct, gut feeling, to believe it wasn't a suicide.

The doorbell sounded in the next room. It had to be my coffee.

I went back to my room and let in the room service guy with the trolley. I had some coffee, then took a shower and got dressed. I looked respectable even if I felt like a wreck. A caffeinated wreck, at least.

After my third cup of coffee, I called down to the hotel's front desk and was told the security director wouldn't be in until nine. So I returned to Kayla's bathroom. I stood and looked over the blood spatter and tried to find meaning and logic in it, a pattern of some sort. The tub had been emptied, but dried blood remained on the tiled wall behind the tub, on the tub's ledge, and on the floor. Most of the blood, I assumed, would have come when the carotid artery was severed. That would have been a gusher, spewing blood everywhere, as far as the floor beyond the tub.

And that was what I was struggling with. If someone had killed her—slashed at her neck and wrists while she was in the tub—he'd have been hit with blood. He'd have tracked it elsewhere in the bathroom or in the hotel room in general. He couldn't help it. It would have gotten on his clothes, on his hands, and there would be traces of it here and there. Smeared on the door handle or on the toilet's flush lever. In the sink or on the vanity.

But there was nothing. The place was clean. I scanned carefully the bathroom walls and floors and the toilet and the vanity. And didn't see any blood. I turned and faced outward and got down on my hands and knees and crawled around the carpet, searching for a dark fleck, a smear. A trace of blood. I was doing the sort of minute search that Detective Balakian and his crew should have done, and might have, if they weren't so convinced it was a suicide.

Nothing.

I stood and, hunched over, examined the carpet, the path between the bathroom and the door. But nothing. After twenty minutes of this, I stopped. I was starting to lose focus.

Kayla's killer, if there was a killer, had been neat and thorough and extremely careful.

Or maybe there was no killer. Maybe she had really killed herself, a tragedy of another sort.

I went to the bathroom to wash my hands, which were soiled from running them across a carpet that needed to be vacuumed better. The killer, if there was a killer, would have washed his hands right here. He'd have gotten blood on his hands, for sure. He'd have gotten blood on the basin, maybe on the faucet handles. But they were clean. I shut off the hot and cold handles, and then some little tickle in the back of my brain caused me to look at them more closely. I turned the cold lever all the way on, and there, on the back side of the lever, was a dark stain.

At first it looked like rust. But I looked closer and confirmed: It was a splotch of blood.

I shut the water off and then peered again at the back-side of the lever. It was definitely dried blood.

But how did it get there?

It couldn't have been Kayla. Someone in the process of killing herself wouldn't bother to wash her hands. If it was Kayla, there would be blood drips visible elsewhere, between the tub and the sink, on the vanity, on the floor.

Someone had cleaned the bathroom thoroughly but missed one out-of-the-way spot.

To me, it said homicide. But I was no expert.

45

At nine o'clock I tried the hotel security director again. I told him I was a hotel guest and had a few questions for him.

"Oh, you're in the suite, number three twenty-two," he said. "Yes, I just heard, I'm so sorry." He told me to come to his office on the first floor behind reception.

He was an elegantly dressed, dark-skinned man named Wanyama. His accent, his British-inflected diction, sounded African, probably Kenyan. He was soft-spoken and polite in manner. He sat at a small desk, crowded with loose-leaf binders and manuals, that probably was shared with others.

"My condolences," he said. "It's so painful when a loved one takes her own life."

I didn't want to tell him I barely knew her, so I just said, "Thank you."

He nodded.

"I'd like to know whether she used her keycard at all last night."

"Her . . . key?"

"Yes. I know your PMS, your property management system, records all uses of room keys. There's a log. An audit trail. I'd very much appreciate it if you'd check your database."

"I understand. I'm awfully sorry, but we can only give out that sort of information to the police."

"It's my room. I paid for it. I have the right to know if she left the room at some point and then came back in."

He looked at me for a few seconds. Then he nodded and turned to his computer. He entered a few keystrokes. "The key was issued at 7:16 P.M. last night, and according to our system it was used just once."

I thought for a moment. I'd escorted her to her room and used her keycard to open the door to her room. I'd considered withholding the key from her so she didn't get any ideas about leaving the room and going someplace where I couldn't protect her. But in the end I left the card on the desk in the room. I'd asked her to stay in the room, and she did.

"What about the door?" I said.

He nodded again. "It was opened, let me see, five times. Once at 7:16, of course."

"And then around eight or so?" When Dorothy had returned bearing clothes for Kayla. That had been the second time.

"Yes. At 8:07 and then at 8:11."

I closed my eyes, nodded. Dorothy entered at 8:07. A few minutes later, I'd opened the door again and hung the DO NOT DISTURB sign on the outside handle. Then I'd stuffed a towel under the inside handle.

"Then at 9:36, and again at 10:25."

I was gone by nine. I didn't return until after midnight. At nine thirty-six I was probably in Curtis Schmidt's garage.

"But no keycard was used?"

"Correct."

"Which means the door was opened from the inside."

"That's right."

It had to have been Kayla who opened the door. But for whom?

"Can you tell if the room phone was used?"

"Yes, one moment."

He tapped some more and opened a different database. "Yes, just once. An outgoing call was placed at 8:47."

"Can you see the number that was called?"

"No, for that you need to go to the phone company. AT&T. We don't have that capability."

"I'd like to take a look at your surveillance video."

He smiled, a pained smile, and shook his head. "Only for law enforcement. I'm very sorry."

I thanked him, and he expressed his condolences again, and as soon as I left his office I called Detective Balakian.

46

"What can I do for you, Mr. Heller?" Balakian said.

"I have some information for you about Kayla Pitts."

"Information?" Balakian sounded distracted. He was drinking something. Probably kombucha. I could hear the crinkle of paper, a cough in the background.

"A couple of facts that raise some interesting questions."

"Go ahead."

"There's a splotch of blood on the back of the water faucet in the bathroom. Not very big, not easy to see. I'm pretty sure your guys missed it. If it's Kayla's blood, you have an interesting situation."

"How do you figure?"

"You have to wonder how it got there." I didn't want to spell it out for him. That would be insulting. "And there's more."

"Okay." More crinkling of paper. Balakian took another sip.

"According to the hotel's security director, she placed an outgoing phone call at 8:47 P.M. Then at 9:36 P.M. and 10:25 her door was opened. From the inside."

"Uh-huh."

"That may have been when she let someone in. Her killer."

"That's a pretty big leap. She let someone into her room, so it's homicide, not suicide, is that what you're telling me?"

"It's a piece of evidence you need to know."

"There could be a thousand reasons why she opened her room door. She went out to get ice. She went out for a cigarette break. She went down to the lobby."

"If she left the room for some reason, she had to have come back in. Which means the door would have been opened from the outside with the keycard after that. But it wasn't."

"Anything else?"

"Sure. See if there's any security footage. They won't let me view it. And you might want to check for drugs in her system like ketamine. Something that was used to knock her out."

"That'll come from toxicology in a couple weeks. But if they find evidence of drugs in a prostitute's body, well, that's not exactly going to be front-page news."

Balakian was not going to be moved from his theory that Kayla was a suicide. It was infuriating, but I was just wasting my time trying to convince him. I knew the girl had been murdered. I didn't need him to confirm it for me.

There were far more pressing questions to answer.

I said good-bye and hung up, and within seconds my phone rang. It was Mandy Seeger.

"I think I have something," she said.

47

We met for breakfast at a no-frills diner a few blocks from the hotel. She ordered waffles, the house specialty, and I ordered eggs over medium and a half-smoke. They brought coffee without being asked, and I downed half a mug right away, nearly scalding my esophagus.

She looked surprisingly fresh, for someone who'd gotten hardly any sleep. Her skin was dewy and she smelled like soap. For the first time I noticed that she had freckles across her nose. It was cute. Her hair was pulled back. She was wearing an old, faded pair of jeans and a black T-shirt.

She took a few tentative sips of the hot coffee, and I told her what I'd found out from the hotel security guy.

"You think she let her killer into the room?" she asked.

I nodded.

"So it was someone she knew and trusted."

"Seems that way. Unless she thought it was someone from the hotel, room service, or security, or a manager. Even though I told her not to open the door for anyone."

"Oh, man. You know these homicide detectives are supposed to treat every suicide as a homicide until it's proven different."

"That's right."

"But there's always other pressures. Numbers pressures. Stats. Like maybe they don't want to add to the homicide rate."

"Could be that. Or it could be simple incompetence. Balakian's new and doesn't know what he's doing." I took a swig of coffee, then said, "So you said you had something?"

"I think so. All right. As we know, Slander Sheet is owned by Hunsecker Media. Which is in turn owned by a company called Patroon LLC, right?"

"Okay."

"But Patroon LLC is a black box. And for a long time that stumped me. So then I had an idea: pull my payroll tax forms. I looked at my W-2 tax forms from Slander Sheet. And it says that my salary was paid by something called the Slade Group."

"Another black box, I assume."

She nodded. "So I went online and searched the electronic database of the State Corporation Commission in Virginia and found something interesting. The Slade Group was incorporated by a law firm, Norcross and McKenna." She looked at me, expectantly. Her light brown eyes twinkled.

I nodded. "Interesting."

"You know who they are?"

"I'm pretty sure they represented my dad once. I recognize the name."

"You know what they're famous for?"

I shook my head.

"You know what 'dark money' is, right?"

"Sure." Dark money was like the slurry trough of campaign fund-raising in the United States. The superrich, and corporations, could take advantage of a loophole in the law to secretly give unlimited amounts of money to their favorite candidate by passing the contribution through a nonprofit corporation. They could influence elections and do it in secret. It was totally corrupt, but that's our political system. God bless America.

"I did a piece on dark money for the *Post*. And I kept coming across the name of this one particular law firm, Norcross and McKenna. It specializes in forming phony corporations and nonprofits as a way to hide donors' names. The firm is based in Leesburg, Virginia, but that's all I know about it."

"Sketchy-sounding firm. No wonder my father did business with them. So Slander Sheet is owned by the Slade Group, which is one of these phony nonprofit corporations."

"That's right."

"A corporation formed by this law firm."

"Right."

"Do you have any names?"

"For this law firm?"

I nodded.

"They have a website that's pretty bare-bones."

"This is great, Mandy. That's our next move."

"The law firm?"

"Right."

"They're not going to talk to you."

"Maybe. Maybe not."

The waitress appeared with two plates on her arm. She put the eggs in front of me and the waffles in front of Mandy and topped off our coffees. She returned a minute later with syrup for Mandy and sriracha sauce for me. Mandy tucked right into her waffle without waiting. I liked that. I like a woman who likes to eat.

When she finally took a break, she said, "So, your dad was Victor Heller. Wow."

"The dark prince of Wall Street himself, yep." My dad was a prominent Wall Street tycoon who turned out to be a fraud and a liar. A brilliant man, a financial genius, but a twisted soul.

She dribbled syrup on the remains of her waffle. "Is he still in prison?"

"In upstate New York, doing twenty-eight years. He'll probably die there."

"Do you ever see him?"

"I visit him from time to time. As rarely as possible."

"Interesting guy."

"That's one way to describe him."

"So you must have been a smart kid—didn't you go to Yale?"

"I dropped out. And I'm sure I got in only because Yale figured I was a rich kid and they'd snag some big contributions from my dad. That he'd hidden money away somewhere."

"Did he?"

"A damned good question. I think so, but he's not talking."

She nodded. "You're in Boston, right? How come you're not based here?"

"Because I don't enjoy living in Washington, DC. Never did. Boston's my town. Besides, my mother lives there, and she's not going to live forever. So there's that." I gulped some coffee. "Is this a job interview? Want to know my biggest weakness?"

She smiled. "So why are you doing this?"

"Doing what?"

"Aren't you done with this job? For Gideon Parnell?"

"As far as Gideon is concerned, I'm done. But as far as I'm concerned, I'm not finished till I find out who killed Kayla and why."

"And then what?"

"When I find out?"

She nodded.

"I'll see when I get there," I said.

48

Gideon Parnell's admin, Rose, got me in to see him between appointments.

He greeted me with a kind of handshake-hug. He was wearing a dove gray suit, a French blue shirt, and a maroon tie. His cologne was peppery.

"I'm surprised you're still here," he said. "I thought you'd be back in Boston by now."

"I have some unfinished business I need a bit of help on."

He looked a little perplexed. "Of course. Have a seat."

I sat on his guest couch, and he sat in a wing chair next to me.

"You know the law firm Norcross and McKenna?" I said.

He raised his eyebrows. "Certainly." His voice sounded different now, low and disdainful. "I'd keep my distance, I were you."

"They're apparently the key to finding out who really

owns Slander Sheet. They're the firm that incorporated their holding company, the Slade—"

"That's all water under the bridge at this point, Nick. Slander Sheet is an object of ridicule. I don't really care who owns that piece of garbage."

"I do. Because last night, Kayla Pitts was found dead."

His large liquid eyes widened and his mouth came open. "*What?*" he rasped.

"She was in a hotel room adjoining mine." I explained about how she'd called and I'd gone to rescue her at the private airport. I left out where I'd gone last night afterward, breaking into Curtis Schmidt's house—that was irrelevant. And not the sort of detail he needed to know.

"Good Lord," Gideon said. "You don't think it could be a suicide?"

"Not given the circumstances, no."

"You think someone killed her."

I nodded.

"And staged it to look like a suicide."

"Right."

"So who would do such a thing?"

"Maybe someone who was afraid of what she'd expose. Which is why I want to know who the real owners of Slander Sheet are. And I think the answer's going to be found at Norcross and McKenna."

He nodded. "I know a lot of people, but I don't know anyone there. Which is no surprise—that's a highly secretive crew. I mean, they're doing all sorts of confidential work for tobacco companies, the nuclear power industry, gun manufacturers . . . but I'm not sure I understand what you're up to."

"If I find out who owns Slander Sheet, I'm one step closer to finding out who had Kayla murdered."

"Or Slander Sheet may have nothing whatsoever to do with Kayla's death."

"Maybe not. But I intend to find out."

"Well, you do what you gotta do. Though we can't keep paying you, you understand."

"Understood."

"Personally, I'm not sure what's to be gained by turning over rocks. Like they say, you lie down with dogs, you get up with fleas. Nick, the work you've done on behalf of Justice Claflin has been extraordinary. Let me tell you, Jerry Claflin will never forget what you did. *I'll* never forget it. What happened to that poor girl is terrible, but it's not your responsibility. You did nothing wrong."

"I don't agree, Gideon. That girl's death is on me."

"You're a compassionate man, Nick, I know that. But you shouldn't feel guilty. You didn't do a damned thing wrong."

I rose, put out my hand to shake his. "Thanks," I said.

"Hey," he said. He placed a hand on my shoulder. "You're a hero."

I smiled, and nodded, and didn't argue. But I knew who I had to see next, as painful as it might be.

My father.

49

For years, Victor Heller had been imprisoned in a Gothic redbrick medium-security prison called the Altamont Correctional Facility, formerly the Altamont Lunatic Asylum, in upstate New York. It wasn't convenient to get to—you had to fly to Albany and then rent a car and drive to the outskirts of a town called Guilderland. But that wasn't why I didn't visit him. Every time I saw him it felt like I gave up another piece of my soul. He was not a good man. I learned from him how to tell when someone was lying because he lied like he breathed.

I got a flight out of Reagan National Airport and got to Altamont around noon. He was waiting for me behind the long counter in the visitors' room.

He was wearing the prison uniform of dark green shirt and slacks. His hair had gone white, and he had a big, white Old Testament beard.

He didn't look well. His head lolled to one side. I was

surprised at how much his health had apparently deterio-
rated in the thirteen months since I'd last seen him.

When I'd called his lawyer to arrange the visit, he told
me that Victor was agitating for a compassionate release
on the grounds that he had senile dementia. That was
news to me. The few times I'd seen him he was as sharp
as ever. "Well, you'll see," the lawyer said. "He's not the
man he was."

I sat down at my side of the counter. My father was
mumbling something about ice cream and something
about shoes. I looked at him. His face above his beard
was raw-looking, with flakes of skin coming off. He had
a bad case of psoriasis, like a molting snake.

"Hello, Dad," I said.

He was looking off somewhere in the distance and
kept mumbling. More about ice cream and what sounded
like "laundry."

"Dad?" A little louder this time.

So much for asking for his help with the law firm Norcross and McKenna.

"Robert told me that you're applying for a compassionate release. Who has to approve it?"

He turned sharply and looked at me. "Bernie?"

Bernie was the name of his college roommate, with
whom he'd had a falling out before I was born. I'd heard
the name, and never in a positive way. Maybe I looked a
little like Bernie.

"You've got fourteen years left in here," I said. "That's
a long time. That's, what, fourteen times three hundred

and sixty-five days, which is . . . like four thousand—forty-five hundred days."

Victor, still looking off in the distance, rolled his eyes, and snapped, "Five thousand, one hundred, and ten."

Even at the dinner table of my childhood, Dad, with his slide-rule precision, could never stand to let arithmetic mistakes like this pass. I guffawed in victory.

He leaned forward, glanced uneasily at the guard who'd brought him out, standing about twenty feet away, and whispered, "What the hell do you want this time?"

"What can you tell me about Norcross and McKenna?"

"They won't represent you. You're not rich enough."

"What'd they do for you? Some securities-fraud allegation, right?"

"Is that what I told you?" He smiled wanly. "I needed to find a way to funnel money to a couple of politicians without having my name attached. They took care of it. Whatever black magic they used, I was able to make a couple of, uh, *gifts,* off the books."

"They're known mostly for handling dark money, right?"

"They do whatever their clients need. They assure you that your confidential files are protected. Most firms stow old files off-site at a storage facility, an Iron Mountain. But not these folks. Everything stays on-site, under their watchful eyes. They're very proud of their triple-locked strong room."

I knew then what my next step had to be.

"They don't still represent you, do they?"

"No. But if I called them up and said I needed help, they'd fall all over themselves to welcome me back."

"Huh." I thought a minute. Norcross and McKenna wouldn't believe me if I pretended to be there on behalf of my father. They'd see through it too quickly.

"Why are you so interested in Norcross and McKenna?"

"I'm working on a case involving Jeremiah Claflin and a gossip website called Slander Sheet."

He smiled his crocodile smile. "That's you?"

"You know what I'm talking about?"

"The sainted Supreme Court justice and the chippie?"

"You get the Internet in here, I guess."

He lowered his voice. "Amazing how far a pack of cigarettes goes."

"I want to know who owns Slander Sheet."

"Why?"

How much to tell him? That was always the dilemma. I didn't trust him, didn't trust his discretion, and I had no idea what his network was like anymore. How he got word to people on the outside. I never knew what his real, secret agenda was. The more I talked to him, the more corroded I felt.

"Someone had it in for the judge," I said.

He ran his hand over his eyes. "No doubt." He blinked rapidly, flecked away a few flakes of dead skin. "A man like Claflin is going to have some formidable enemies." He raised an index finger, and now he really did look like an Old Testament prophet gone mad. "But it's always your friends who do you in."

He should know. Several colleagues of his whom he called friends had cooperated with the prosecutors and provided the evidence that got him locked up for so many years.

As always, my father was talking about his favorite subject: himself.

50

Arthur Garvin, my retired police lieutenant friend, lived in an immaculate raised ranch in the distant Maryland suburbs with a lawn like a golf course. He was in overalls and a work shirt and was resealing his driveway. It looked like he was rolling black paint over the dusty asphalt. I parked on the street and strolled across the perfect lawn and waved hello. He waved back and made some sort of oblique hand signal that I assumed meant he needed to finish what he was doing. I sat on the front porch and watched. He'd been a workaholic, like a lot of homicide detectives, when he was on the job, and now he'd probably turned that prodigious energy to weekly changing the batteries in his smoke alarms and weeding. He was a widower, I remembered.

He disappeared into his garage, which looked pristine from here, and came around to the front door from inside the house. "Sorry to keep you waiting," he said. A strong chemical smell wafted from his clothes, from the driveway sealer. I sniffed. "That stuff can't be good for you."

"Good old coal tar."

"Isn't that stuff supposed to be toxic?"

He shrugged. He didn't care. He led the way to a dimly lit front sitting room and we sat down.

"You look good," I said. "Retirement is treating you well." He still had that wispy white goatee and the steel-rimmed glasses with lenses thick as an old Coke bottle. They magnified his eyes, insectlike.

"Retirement is hell," he said. "I'm going out of my goddamned mind."

"No consulting gigs on offer?"

"Unless I want to be an expert witness for the defense, and you know I couldn't stand that. Boston okay?"

"Sure."

"You miss DC."

"Like I miss a canker sore."

I told him about Kayla's death. He listened gravely, asked a few questions, shook his head. He looked amused when I told him about breaking into Curtis Schmidt's house.

"Let me see the picture," he said. He meant the photo of Schmidt and a buddy with a fish.

"It's on my phone."

I located it in the phone's camera roll and handed it to him.

He held it at arm's length from his face. "I see the bald guy, but I don't see his buddy. Let me get my reading glasses."

I took back the phone and swiped the photo and pinched and spread my fingers apart to magnify Schmidt's friend's face, then I handed it back.

"Oh, yes," he said at once. "Oh, yes." He gave a tart little smile. "Thomas Vogel."

"You recognize the guy."

"Vogel's famous."

"Oh yeah?"

"He was sort of the ringleader. Well, not sort of. He was the ringleader of the fake overtime pay scam. When he was on the force, he surrounded himself with a small group of alpha dogs, including your boy Curtis Schmidt."

"He get forced retirement, too?"

Garvin nodded. "He was a legend in the department, Vogel was. Thought he was smarter than everybody else, and he probably was. Did undercover work in narcotics and made some prominent busts. After he was forced out, he started this interesting kind of high-end VIP protection service, called Centurions. They're more like fixers than plain old security guards."

"'Fixer' can mean anything. What do they do?"

"They make scandals go away."

"For politicians?"

"Sure, and movie stars and rich people."

"You know this for sure?"

"All I know is gossip. A celebrity is found with a body in his bed, they make the body disappear. Some movie star has a problem with a stalker, they take care of the problem. No restraining order needed. A call girl threatens a congressman with blackmail, they handle it. They resolve the situation without involving the courts. They make problems vanish. They don't advertise, and they're not in the phone book. I doubt they have a website. I don't even think they have an office."

"How do they get clients?"

"Word of mouth. People just know about them."

"So," I said, "they're probably the ones who staged Kayla's suicide."

"Could be. Wouldn't surprise me. Question is, who hired them? That's what you really want to know."

I looked out the window at the perfect emerald lawn, the polished ebony of the driveway. I smelled the coal tar, astringent and medicinal. There were any number of directions I could have gone from there. But it was becoming clear, at least to me, that the answer might lie in the connection between the Centurions and Slander Sheet.

And that connection, if there was a connection, would require some serious digging. It wasn't going to be easy to find.

But I had an idea.

51

"Thank you for making time to see us, Mr. Troy."

I nodded, avoided eye contact, looked uncomfortable. Simon Troy was said to be uncomfortable around people.

The woman appeared to be in her midthirties and had glossy black hair. She was attractive, in a matronly way.

"Do you come to town often?"

"As little as possible." Simon Troy lived in Jenks, Oklahoma, outside of Tulsa, and rarely traveled. He was also a billionaire and one of the largest landowners in the United States and was known to be mostly a recluse. Very few photos of him could be found on the Internet. In truth, I didn't look very much like him, except for the gray hair and mustache I was wearing, and the black horn-rimmed glasses. But no one here at Norcross and McKenna was going to question whether I was Simon Troy or not. They wanted to believe.

We'd considered creating a false identity, but backstopping it—largely, seeding the Internet with enough plausible appearances—was time-consuming, and we didn't have the time. Whereas a billionaire like Simon Troy, seldom photographed and never interviewed, seemed relatively easy to impersonate. Mandy Seeger provided me with a download of what little information on him existed, and I studied it, hard. Dorothy then called the law firm from a spoofed Tulsa phone number to arrange this last-minute meeting.

"Well, Mr. Norcross was happy to clear some time in his schedule to meet with you."

We didn't talk again as she led me along a corridor to a corner office. A rotund man with a red face and silver hair bounded from behind his desk, his hand extended.

"A great pleasure to meet you, Mr. Troy. I'm Ash Norcross."

I gave him a limp, diffident shake, took note of the keycard clipped to his belt.

"Can we get you a cup of tea? I understand you don't drink coffee."

"Nothing for me, thanks."

"Thanks, Val," Ashton Norcross said, dismissing his admin. To me he said, "I understand you got my name—"

"I don't have a lot of time," I said languidly. "I have to get back to Capitol Hill. A few senators I need to see."

"Well, then, let's get right to it." He half-bowed and indicated a seating area with two brocade sofas. I sat, and then he sat across from me. I set down my briefcase to my left, close to him, a few feet away from his keycard. Close enough, I hoped.

"As you may or may not know, I tend to stay out of politics," I said. "In any public way, I mean. You won't find my name on any FEC databases, or at least not in a long while. But I've come to believe our republic is under assault."

"And so it is, Mr. Troy. And so it is. No argument here. In fact, we at Norcross—"

"But as you may know, I don't like to see my name in the paper."

"Absolutely."

"I stay as low profile as possible."

"Understood. You've come to the right place."

"Now, I've had a bad experience with one of our local law firms in Tulsa. Turned out that their security was lax. I want to know what precautions you take."

"Well, our security is state-of-the-art."

"If I were to become a client, where would you be storing the files you'd keep on me?"

"Oh, data security is paramount here, Mr. Troy. All digital client files are kept on a partitioned, air-gapped, encrypted server."

"What about paper files?"

"Kept in a separately locked, highly secured strong room."

"I'd like to see that."

"Certainly. In fact—"

Someone knocked on Norcross's open door. I turned. A trim guy around sixty with a thick thatch of gray hair stood there with a stupid grin on his face.

Ash Norcross waved him in. "Oh, Jeff, come on in, let

me introduce you to Simon Troy. Simon, this is Jeff Winik, one of our partners and a fellow Stanford grad."

Winik strode toward me, gave me a firm handshake, and said, "You were Stanford '79, right?"

I nodded.

"I was Stanford '80!"

"Oh yeah?" I said, smiling blandly as my stomach plummeted.

He went on: "Where'd you live freshman year?"

I regarded him for a few seconds. He wasn't challenging me, trying to determine whether I was really Simon Troy. He was genuinely attempting to bond.

It was not credible that "Simon Troy" would have forgotten where he lived freshman year in college. Several long seconds went by while I frantically grappled for an answer. A bead of sweat trickled down the back of my neck into my shirt collar.

Finally I said, "Larkin." The name suddenly popped into my head after the hours I'd spent cramming, poring over the Simon Troy dossier that Mandy had assembled for me.

"Oh yeah? I was in Branner!"

"Well, nice to meet you," I said, but Winik was not done with me.

"But then I got a bad lottery number," he went on, "and I ended up in the trailer park."

"Huh," I said. I had no idea what he was talking about. *Trailer park?*

"Ever used to hang out at the O?" he said.

The O? What was that, a bar? The freshman union? I

took a flyer and said, "I sort of kept to myself. I didn't really hang out." An all-purpose answer, but it seemed to satisfy him.

"Well, Mr. Troy doesn't have much time," Norcross said, blessedly cutting the conversation short. "He wants to see the strong room."

52

About an hour later I was back at the hotel. The dining table was covered with electronic equipment—cables and wires and little black boxes and white plastic cards and such. I set down the briefcase I'd brought into Norcross and McKenna.

"How'd it go?" Dorothy asked.

I shrugged. "Fine."

"No problem?"

"No problem."

"You get the briefcase close enough to a keycard?"

"I think so."

"Let's see what you got."

The day before, Mandy had made her own undercover visit to the same law firm.

She'd entered the building where the firm was located with the morning rush, tailgating on someone who was entering. She took the elevator to the fourth floor and briefly stood outside the firm's glass doors and took pictures with her smartphone, as subtly as she could, of the little black box mounted on the wall next to the glass doors.

Then she went right in to the firm's offices and told the receptionist that she lived just down the street and was looking for temp work, and asked what agency they used to hire their temps. She spun a story about having a young child at home and needing to find work in the neighborhood. The receptionist gave her the name of an employment agency but apologized that there was nothing available at the time, so far as she knew. Mandy thanked her, and that was that.

Now Dorothy examined the photos on Mandy's phone.

"Okay," she said, "this is good. They're using an HID system like just about everyone else uses. Almost certainly a low-frequency 125 kilohertz system. Like eighty percent of the keycard users in the world."

"Why is this good?" I asked. When it comes to technology, I long ago stopped worrying about sounding stupid. I ask, and Dorothy explains. This kind of technology is her forte. She enjoys being smarter than me, and I don't mind it a bit.

"Because a couple years ago there was an interesting talk at Black Hat USA about how to defeat it."

"How involved is this? You think we should bring in Merlin?"

Merlin's real name was Walter McGeorge, an old army

buddy who'd been a commo sergeant on my Special
Forces team and later became a TSCM specialist, an expert in technical surveillance. He lived in the area, in
Maryland. When I lived in DC I used to bring him in
frequently to help me on jobs.

"You don't need Merlin for this," she said. "I promise.
I can set it all up for you myself. Plug-and-play. Easy."
She tapped at her laptop. "Here we go." She turned her
laptop's display toward me. It was an eBay page with a
lot of listings, pictures of what looked like square boxes.

I recognized them. They were proximity readers, also
known as badge readers. They've become ubiquitous in
the corporate world. They're the little black boxes
mounted next to office doors at which you wave your
plastic keycard to gain entry. You also see bigger versions
of prox readers at the entrances and exits to parking garages. They allow drivers who have the right keycard to
pass right through.

"I know what a prox reader is," I said, "but I don't
see how that gets us in."

"Okay. I buy one of these long-range RFID readers
and do a trivial amount of futzing around to weaponize
it. Stick in a PCB, a circuit board, and twelve double-A
batteries. Like that. This thing can read a badge from
three feet away, normally. So pay a visit to Norcross and
McKenna, and you bring it in, in a backpack or briefcase,
and just make sure to be within three feet of someone
who's got a badge around her neck or on his belt."

"Then what?"

"You don't need to know how it works. It'll read any

Wiegand protocol card that gets close enough. It captures the data on the keycard. When you get back here, I download the data and write it to a blank keycard, and that's all she wrote. We've cloned the key to their front door."

"Hold on," I said. "Those things beep when they read a card. Am I going to be beeping audibly whenever I get near someone's keycard?"

She smiled. "You do think ahead. Good question, and thanks for mentioning it."

I shrugged. "Just another accidental flash of brilliance."

"I'll toggle a dipswitch in the thing to turn off the beep sound. Anything else?"

"Foolproof?"

"Well, idiot-proof. You should be okay."

She placed an order through eBay with a company in South Carolina and one in Eagle Mountain, Utah, and requested overnight shipping, and the next day several large boxes arrived at the hotel, and we were in business.

53

Now, Dorothy took the briefcase, unzipped it, and pulled out the badge reader. It was about a foot square by an inch thick. It was a long-range 125 kilohertz MaxiProx proximity card reader manufactured by the HID Corporation, the Texas-based company that makes most of the keycards and readers used in corporations around the world.

She turned the thumbscrew on top of the box and removed the front cover. She popped out the micro SD card and stuck it in her laptop.

She blinked a few times. Then she smiled. "You captured four separate cards."

"The receptionist, the partner—Ashton Norcross—and probably a couple of employees I was next to in the elevator on my way out," I said.

She nodded. "I don't know if there are levels of access, but Norcross is a partner, and he'll no doubt have the highest level. We'll clone his."

Dorothy and I went through everything I'd observed on my visit to the firm—the placement of the CCTV cameras, which areas appeared to be separately locked, and what kind of security protected the vault, which they called a strong room. "The vault is locked separately with a Kaba Simplex mechanical push-button lock," I said.

"Know anything about them?"

"Come on. This is why I want Merlin now. It's at least a two-man job."

She shrugged. "Okay. Now here's an extremely cool piece of hardware called a Rubber Ducky." She handed me something that looked like a thumb drive.

"A Rubber Ducky."

"Correct. I know it sounds silly, but it's dead serious. You plug this into the USB port of any of their computers and it goes to work."

"I'm going to need you to come along and help me deal with this thing."

"That's the beauty part, Nick. It's fire-and-forget."

"What happens when I plug it in and some antivirus program comes up? Which is likely."

"Someone's been paying attention in class. But that's not going to happen. This is configured to be an HID, a human interface device, like a mouse or a keyboard. The computer will detect that it's an HID and trust it."

"Okay. So I plug it in—then what?"

"It immediately injects code at a thousand characters a minute. It creates a shell on the network, and pretty soon it'll give us root-level access. It runs something called Metasploit that looks for weaknesses in the software. It creates a username and password. And then . . . I'll be able to get onto the Norcross and McKenna server from here."

I picked it up, toyed with it, and put it down. "If you're right, this really is cool. Just plug-and-play, huh?"

"Well, I've got to do a bunch of programming on it this afternoon to deploy the payload. But it will be."

Merlin—I never called him Walter—was short, maybe five feet seven, and lean. His physical type was surprisingly common in the Special Forces. He had a black buzz cut with some gray starting to move in, a pushed-back porcine nose, and a thin black mustache. The vertical lines carved into his forehead between his eyes made him look angry.

He had no family, as far as I knew, and one singular devotion: sport fishing. He lived in Dunkirk and kept a boat in the Harbour Cove Marina, in Deale, and was always out on the water. I reached him onshore, though, and told him about the job. It was a simple black-bag job of the sort he and I had worked several times before. I offered him a couple thousand bucks, double if we encountered any surprises, and he quickly agreed. His TSCM business was slow, and evenings he was never busy.

In the afternoon I did a bunch of errands, picking up everything we could possibly need. We rendezvoused at a dive bar in a strip mall in Leesburg around midnight.

He'd chosen it because it had a separately ventilated smoking section, which was permitted because of some loophole in Virginia law. Neither one of us had anything alcoholic to drink; wanting to keep sharp for the job, we both had Cokes. We sat at a booth. He smoked continuously.

I showed him the Halloween masks I'd picked up from a costume store, transparent masks, one of a young man, one of an old man. They both transformed our appearances, made us unrecognizable. Merlin insisted on wearing the young mask. In the bar's restroom we changed into the navy polo shirts with the Compuservice logo on the left. I had toolboxes for each of us to carry in.

This was the part of a black-bag job that always jazzed me: the preparations, thinking of every eventuality, everything that might go sideways. The high-wire tension. Assembling equipment, making lists, making sure that if we were caught, we'd have a way out.

But you can't ensure everything. Things go wrong.

Shit happens.

54

It was a few minutes after two o'clock in the morning. The parking lot was dark and almost empty. A cold wind whipped our faces. The only lights on in the building, as far as I could see, were in the lobby, where a lone security guard sat at a counter and probably was browsing aimlessly on the Internet.

The front door to the building was unlocked. We passed the guard, and I said, "Good evening, or is it good morning?"

The guard smiled and gave us a sort of salute. We were confident, we knew where we were going, and we looked like we belonged. He probably assumed we were computer nerds coming to solve some middle-of-the-night crisis. We headed for the elevators. That was the limit of building security. Easy.

We got off the elevator on the fourth floor. The hall was dimly lit. We quickly came upon the entrance to Norcross and McKenna. The glass doors were dark. Apparently no one was inside. That had been a worry of mine: Lawyers often work very long hours. At midnight I wouldn't have been surprised to find someone toiling there, a lone beleaguered partner, even several associates. At two in the morning, there was less chance of encountering someone.

I pulled our masks out of my toolkit and handed the young-man one to Merlin. I put on the old-man mask. I'd noticed earlier that there was a CCTV camera just inside the glass doors, pointed at the entrance. From now on we were being photographed. Our ball caps and masks made it impossible for the cameras to record our likenesses.

I waved my cloned keycard up to the card reader, a little black box mounted to the wall next to the glass doors. I bit my lip.

The little light switched from red to green and it beeped. I pushed the door and it came right open.

Until that moment, when something relaxed inside me, I hadn't been aware of how clenched with anxiety I'd been.

There was low-level emergency lighting here in the office, just like in the hallway, so although it was dim, there was just enough light to make our way. I knew where I was going.

I led Merlin through twisting corridors to the strong room. The door appeared to be wooden, mahogany, like all the other doors in the firm, but I knew that it was actually a sandwich of wood over several inches of high-grade steel. This was not a room you could slip into through the air-conditioning ducts and the ceiling tiles. There was no dropped ceiling. The wall, floor, and ceiling were reinforced concrete, Norcross had told me proudly, eight inches thick. Not only was the room fireproof, but it was protected against intrusion.

Merlin knocked on the door a few times and chuckled at its dead sound. He glanced at the steel lever attached to the Simplex lock, a vertical row of five steel buttons. He nodded and ran his fingers down the buttons. It was a familiar lock, the sort of thing you see inside all sorts of businesses, including jewelry stores and watch shops and casinos. FedEx uses them to secure their drop boxes.

"You start working on this," I told him. "I'll head over to Norcross's office."

"Don't go anywhere," Merlin said. "This shouldn't take more than a few seconds."

He unlatched his toolbox and pulled out a small cloth bag. From the bag he drew an oblong block of metal about two inches by three inches. "Watch," he said. He placed the shiny metal block on the side of the Simplex lock. Then he grabbed the lever and tried to turn it. Nothing happened.

"Shit," he said. "They fixed it."

"What are you doing?"

"This is a rare-earth magnet. Neodymium. A couple of years ago some security expert figured out that if you put one of these next to the Simplex lock, it messes with the combination chamber and unlocks it right away."

"Doesn't look like it's doing anything."

"Yeah. They must have upgraded to one that uses a non-ferrous metal inside. Oh, crap. That would have been too easy, wouldn't it?"

"Now what?"

"We do it the old-fashioned way." He pulled a folded piece of paper from a pocket. It had a long column of numbers on it. "This could take fifteen minutes or so."

"If you get lucky," I said.

Merlin grunted.

The Simplex had five buttons, which could be pressed in any order. But it had one rule, one weakness: Each number could be used only once per combination.

That meant that the Simplex lock had "only" 1,082 combinations. I don't know how this is calculated, but I know that math teachers sometimes give their students the "Simplex math problem" to solve: how to calculate the number of combinations for the five-button Simplex lock.

"I can shorten the time a little," I said. "I saw Norcross push four buttons, not five."

"Oh yeah?"

On the piece of paper he'd just taken out was a list of all possible combinations for the Simplex five-button mechanical lock. Now he was going to run down the list and enter each four-digit combination.

Seriously. I thought we'd be lucky if it only took him fifteen minutes.

I tested our walkie-talkies one last time and then left him there pushing buttons. I took out my penlight and wandered the corridors until I found Norcross's office.

The door was closed, as I expected. The plaque on the door said ASHTON NORCROSS in black letters on gold. I waved my keycard at it, and it beeped and the red light turned green.

There was no CCTV camera in here, as far as I could tell, but I didn't want to take a chance, so I kept my mask on. What if there was a well-concealed camera? Not likely, but possible, and I didn't want to risk being photographed.

It was starting to get hot and sweaty inside the mask. Perspiration was dripping down my face.

I remembered from my earlier visit that there was a credenza behind the desk that had books and keepsakes on display and a lower hutch section that looked like a file cabinet. I figured that might be where he kept active files on matters he was currently working on. It wasn't locked, but inside, disappointingly, were a few reams of printer paper and nothing much else. I turned around and surveyed the desk. There was not much on top of it except a pen set, a lamp, a few knickknacks, and a computer monitor.

I squatted down, searching with my penlight, and located a computer tower underneath the desk, pushed to one corner. It grunted quietly. I found a USB port and inserted the Rubber Ducky.

Dorothy had instructed me to keep it plugged in for at least ten minutes, though it would probably finish its work within five.

Then I stood back up and checked the drawers of

Norcross's desk, looking for a sticky note with numbers on it. You'd be surprised how often I find combinations to safes or passwords to computer accounts scrawled on Post-it notes or scraps of paper. We all have too many passwords and numbers to remember nowadays, and he couldn't be expected to have the combination to the strong room memorized. But there was nothing here. Good for him. He practiced good security hygiene.

Then again, I considered, there was his executive assistant's desk just outside, an even more likely place for one of those sticky notes. I left Norcross's office, headed to his assistant's desk, and searched her drawers, and the underside of the drawers, and her computer monitor and keyboard—all the usual places.

But nothing here either. Both Norcross and his assistant were good doobies.

So what about the other name partner, McKenna? Maybe he was sloppier.

I followed the corridor to the next corner office, and sure enough, the plaque on it read JAMES MCKENNA. I waved my keycard at the reader mounted to his doorjamb, but nothing happened. It was keyed separately, no surprise. I rifled through his assistant's desk. This one was sloppier, the desk drawers jammed with extra supplies like boxes of paper clips, printer cartridges, tape, staples. It took me longer to go through this cluttered desk, more false alarms, pieces of paper to examine, but I still ended up without the combination to the strong room.

I looked at McKenna's office door and stood there in silence, thinking for a moment about how I might try to get in.

Then my walkie-talkie came to life and I heard Merlin's voice. "I'm in," he said.

55

I took my toolbox and strode through the maze of hallways to the strong room. Merlin was holding the door open, and for an instant I was jolted by his strange appearance until I remembered we were both wearing masks. He said, "I knew it was just a matter of time. Can I take off this damn mask yet?"

"Not in here," I said.

"I know. You're right."

Merlin let the door close, with a pneumatic sucking sound, like opening a can of tennis balls, then a thunk like a car door closing. There was nothing else in this vault but a long row of black metal file cabinets. Then I noticed another keypad mounted to the wall next to the doorjamb. I noticed it because it had begun to beep, a slow, ominous, high-pitched electronic beep.

"What's that?" Merlin said.

"Oh, shit."

I had a good idea what this was, though I'd never

seen one before. Everyone entering the vault had to re-
confirm credentials by punching in a verification code.

Or else what?

I wasn't sure.

"It might be the same as the code that opened the
door," I said. "Do you remember what it was?"

Merlin unfolded his list of numbers. "Yes. Two nine
three five."

I spun around and pressed the four numbers. But the
beeping continued, a red diode flashing.

"That's not it," I said. "Shit."

"What's this, a secondary alarm?"

"Of some sort, yeah. Auto-activated at night, probably." I tried the standard defaults, 1111 and 9999 and
1234, but nothing halted the beeping.

Behind the mask, sweat trickled down my face. It was
hot, and damp, and uncomfortable.

"You want to try?" I said.

"Sure, but I'll just be guessing, too."

"Meanwhile I'll go through the files."

I stepped aside and made room for Merlin. He began
punching digits in no discernible order, faster and faster.

The beeping continued implacably.

I scrutinized the line of file cabinets. There were
twelve of them, four drawers in each, and they were arranged alphabetically. The first drawer was labeled "A—
Am." I wasn't sure where exactly I should be looking.
"S" for Slander Sheet? For the Slade Group? I moved
down the row of cabinets, found the drawer labeled "Sh-
Sy," pulled it open.

The files were marked with plastic tabs, names like Schuster Institute and Symons, Kendrick.

And there it was: Slade Group. I pulled out the brown folder, my chest tight. I opened it and found correspondence between Ashton Norcross and a woman named Ellen Wiley, of Upperville, Virginia. Ellen Wiley, whose name sounded vaguely familiar.

The beeping stopped abruptly.

"You get it?" I said, turning around.

Merlin shrugged, said, "No. It just suddenly—"

A metal *ka-chunk* sound.

"What the hell?" Merlin cried.

"Sounds like a relocking system. Spring-loaded locking bolts. Open the door—*now*."

He went right away to the door and turned the lever. But the door wouldn't open.

"What the hell?" Merlin said.

"I was afraid of that." The relocking system, I knew, was designed to block the door from opening. The sort of feature you might find in some safe rooms or survivalist shelters. In fact, I was pretty sure the strong room was actually a prefab, standalone safe room.

"We're locked in," he said.

I nodded.

"There's always an internal vault door release."

"Depends on how it's designed. Not necessarily."

He tried the door lever once again. "Shit. Well, screw this." He slammed a fist against the steel door, which did nothing but hurt his fist. He groaned and turned away. I moved in and examined the doorframe, noticed the silicon gasket. I took out a pocketknife, flicked the blade, and ran it along the gap between door and frame. It was tight. Every foot or so the blade hit something solid, which I assumed were the relocking bolts. I didn't see a way out.

Then I smelled smoke.

I sniffed, looked around, saw Merlin lighting a piece of paper, which he'd apparently grabbed from a file drawer. The paper went up in flames, sending up a plume of smoke.

"What the hell are you doing—?" I shouted as a loud klaxon began to sound.

"Check it out." He pointed with his free hand at the ceiling, at what looked like a smoke detector. Arrayed around the ceiling, every eight feet or so, were sprinkler heads, only they were hissing gas, not sprinkling water.

"What the hell are you doing?"

"That's going to automatically trigger the unlocking mechanism on the door," Merlin said with a crooked smile.

The sheet of paper floated away in a black wisp and danced through the air, the smoke now thick enough to sting my eyes.

"You goddamned idiot!" I said. "That's halon gas!" A label on the wall to the left of the door warned:

CAUTION

THIS AREA IS PROTECTED BY A HALON 1301 FIRE SUPPRESSION SYSTEM. WHEN ALARM SOUNDS OR UPON GAS DISCHARGE, EVACUATE HAZARD AREA IMMEDIATELY.

"They don't use halon anymore!"

"Yeah," I said. "Sometimes they do." Some years ago it was determined that halon damaged the ozone layer, and it was banned. But existing systems were allowed to remain in place. They were grandfathered in. It was still considered a superior alternative to water-sprinkler systems, especially in archives and places where water could damage paper records. Nothing as effective had taken its place.

Halon was not only bad for the environment, it was bad for humans. At high concentrations—in other words, in a few minutes, when enough halon had hissed out of the ceiling-mounted nozzles—it could cause permanent nerve damage and then death.

And we were trapped in here.

The fire suppression system didn't unlock the doors. The relocking mechanism on the doors had been triggered by our failure to disarm the secondary security system.

Merlin was coughing, and then I began to cough as well. I was furious at him for setting off the halon system, for doing something so impulsive without even checking with me. But even more, I was beginning to feel icy tendrils of panic seep into my bowels.

Because I did not see a way out.

56

Despite the deafening clang of the alarm, despite the hissing of the halon gas, despite my growing sense of claustrophobia, of being trapped in this steel-reinforced coffin, I forced myself to focus. To think.

It wasn't easy. I was steadily growing more and more woozy from breathing the halon, and I couldn't stop coughing. My body was desperately craving oxygen.

What Merlin had done wasn't, in fact, stupid. Setting off the fire alarm *should* have triggered the automatic un-locking of the vault doors. That's how it should have been, and probably what the fire code required.

But this setup privileged security over safety. Our fail-ure to enter the right code in the secondary panel meant we were locked in, whether that was against the fire code or not.

When I was a teenager living in the town of Malden, north of Boston, my friends and I used to hang out at the body shop of Norman Lang Motors, a used-car dealership owned by one of my buddies' fathers. There I learned, from a repo man, how to pick locks. I also learned the rudiments of electrical wiring, the stuff engineers learn in school. And I knew that the secondary alarm panel had to be connected to some kind of relay switch that triggered the relocking bolts. It didn't take me long to find what had to be the relay. It was a white-painted metal box about four inches square, mounted to the wall next to the door. Unobtrusive. Easy to miss. These relays always have an electromagnet inside, and the magnet either closes a switch or opens it. And that, right or wrong, was about the sum total of what I knew about relay switches.

Connected to the relay was white-painted electrical conduit about half an inch wide, which ran along the doorframe, then straight up to the ceiling. That had to be the power supply.

I handed Merlin the brown folder so I had both hands free. "Let me have your magnet," I said.

Merlin, no surprise, seemed to get why I wanted it. I'm sure he knew a hell of a lot more about mechanical engineering than I did. "You think—?"

He handed me the oblong chunk of rare-earth magnet. Neodymium, he'd said. It was extremely strong, but was it strong enough? I took it and knelt down. I pulled open the metal box and saw, as I suspected, a copper coil inside. The guts of the electromagnet. Then I placed the neodymium magnet on the exterior of the box and waited.

And nothing happened.

My chest had grown tight, and I was short of breath and light-headed, and my heartbeat had begun to speed up, not from adrenaline either.

"Nice try," Merlin said. "But the fire department should be here soon."

What I did next was out of desperation. I took out the Glock I'd stolen from Curtis Schmidt's house. I stood up, gripped the gun two-handed. My head was swimming.

"Heller, you're not serious."

"Stand back," I said.

I fired a round into the wiring conduit on the door-frame.

For a moment, nothing happened.

Then the bolts *ka-chunk*ed open. I grabbed the door lever and pulled it open. We both dove forward, out of the halon, and gulped air. I stumbled a bit, unsteady on my feet. I could hear sirens in the distance, which meant they must have been close to the building.

Merlin pointed toward a door marked STAIRS. We ripped off our masks so we could breathe better.

And we ran.

57

I screwed up, Nick," Merlin said.

"It was a good idea," I said. "It didn't work. That's not screwing up."

"No, I don't mean lighting the paper on fire. I thought that was pretty clever. I mean, I left the folder behind."

"Oh." I paused. "You did, huh? Yeah, that's a screw-up, all right." I felt a surge of hot anger but did my best to conceal it. Merlin looked so dispirited that I added right away, "But not a tragedy. We got the name and her location. We have Ellen Wiley and Upperville, Virginia. I remember that much."

"Okay," he said, sounding unconvinced.

We walked down a dark, wide street, moving from pool to pool of yellowish light cast by the sodium-vapor street lamps. Traffic was light, but not nonexistent. It was a little after four in the morning. Dawn was still a few hours off.

Merlin's mistake had put added pressure on us—"us" being me, Dorothy, and now Mandy Seeger, since I thought
of Mandy as being part of our team. Not only had we set
off the fire alarm and damaged the strong room door, but
at some point soon, someone in the firm would find the
misplaced Slade Group file folder, and that would start a
clock ticking. The fact that the file had been isolated and
removed from the secured file cabinets would tell them it
was probably important. That would point a blinking
neon arrow at Ellen Wiley's name. Maybe they'd alert her
that someone might be coming for her.

Because someone was.

I allowed myself five hours of sleep. That was about
the minimum I could operate on with my cognition
fairly intact. At ten in the morning, Dorothy, Mandy,
and I gathered in the living room of my hotel suite. I'd
given her the name of Slander Sheet's owner, Ellen Wiley, and she'd made a call to an old friend at *The Washington Post*.

"So it's Ellen Wiley, huh?" she said. "Amazing." She
was reclining in one of the big lounge chairs, one leg
tucked under the other. She was wearing black leggings
and a white button-down shirt. She wore her wavy hair
up. I couldn't decide if she was a redhead or a brunette
with coppery highlights.

"The shadowy owner herself," I said. "What do I
need to know about her?"

Mandy was looking over a sheaf of paper. "My friend at

the *Post* pulled a file on Wiley and e-mailed it to me. She's an interesting case, Ellen Wiley. Extremely rich—a tobacco heiress. She inherited a big chunk of the Philip Morris tobacco fortune. She's got homes in Upperville, Anguilla, Scottsdale, and a pied-à-terre in Georgetown. I'm pretty sure Upperville is her chief residence. A huge estate on two thousand acres in horse-and-hunt country. She's a big patron of the arts. Gives a lot to the Virginia Museum of Fine Arts in Richmond and the Oak Spring Garden Foundation in Upperville. Divorced three times, each time married to a younger man. She's not a recluse, exactly, but she's extremely publicity-averse. She stays away from the press."

"So why does she own Slander Sheet?" Dorothy asked.

Mandy riffled through the file. "That's a mystery."

"I need to see her up close. I want to ask her some questions. I'm fairly good at sussing out liars."

Mandy nodded. "Okay."

"So where is she now? How do we find out?"

Mandy smiled.

"At her estate in Upperville."

"You're sure?"

"She's hosting a fund-raiser tonight for wounded veterans at her house."

"So tonight's out. We go to see her tomorrow."

"I say we go tonight. You're a veteran, aren't you?"

"I wasn't wounded. Who's 'we'?"

Mandy smiled again. "You need a date."

"I wasn't invited."

"What's 'invited'?"

"I like your style," I said.

58

The drive to Upperville took a little more than an hour, straight down 66 west and then up north to Route 50.

I wore a suit—I had nothing fancier with me, of course, than the suit I'd worn on the way down from Boston—and Mandy wore a white zip-front peplum jacket over a matching skirt. She also looked like she'd spent some time putting on her makeup. She looked terrific, sophisticated and attractive.

I drove, and we fell into easy, companionable conversation. We talked for a while about her time working for *The Washington Post*, and about my time in Iraq and Bosnia. She seemed to enjoy bumping up against the barrier of what I couldn't talk about. I could see what a relentless reporter she must be. She told me about all the research she'd done on Justice Claflin when she was writing the piece about Kayla, and I asked if she wouldn't mind sharing her other files with me.

"Sure. There's all kinds of goodies in my files."

"Anything on me?"

"You flatter yourself. Slander Sheet was only interested in the powerful and the famous. The more lascivious, the better. Gideon's in there."

"Gideon?"

"Rumored to be something of a dog."

"He's seventy-five."

"Makes no difference. Did you know his sister was raped?"

I shook my head.

"Years ago. Helped shape the man he turned out to be."

"How so?"

"Apparently the rapist was a white guy. And they never caught him."

"Maybe there wasn't enough evidence. Or maybe they couldn't be bothered."

"Maybe. And the wife of the White House chief of staff has a shoplifting problem, apparently. And the number-two at the CIA may have plagiarized his Woodrow Wilson School master's thesis."

"Do you care about all this stuff? I mean, the gossip?"

"Not especially."

"Me neither. Did you ever care? Before you got fired?"

In a small voice she said, "It paid the mortgage."

I let the subject drop.

When we passed Manassas, she said, "So what's the game plan? Are you just going to ask her if she ordered the murder of Kayla Pitts?"

"You know the game: You go in at a slant. Get her to talk. Suss her out. Get a sense of how much she knows."

"And when she lies?"

"I get lied to all the time. It's my business."

"That must get depressing."

"Not really. You can learn a lot from a lie. Sometimes more than from the truth. If she lies to us, we'll learn something, too."

"But you don't think she ordered Kayla to be killed, do you?"

"I think she set this train in motion. I think her plan was to use this digital rag Slander Sheet to destroy Jeremiah Claflin, for some reason. She was doing a full-on Hearst—creating the news and then breaking it."

"You think?"

"Worked with the Spanish-American War, right?" She knew what I was talking about, how at the end of the nineteenth century a couple of newspaper moguls, William Randolph Hearst and Joseph Pulitzer, had their correspondents invent sensational, fictional stories about atrocities in Cuba, which eventually provoked the United States into going to war with Spain. Because Hearst and Pulitzer had their own war going on—over circulation. They did it to sell newspapers.

"Okay," she said, "but killing Kayla . . . ?"

"My gut says Ellen Wiley ordered up a scandal. Not a homicide. I think the thugs she hired just took things one lethal step further—killing the girl so she couldn't compromise them. At the end of the day, everyone saves his own ass first. Law of human nature."

"You think she knows her people did it?"

I nodded. "And maybe, just maybe, she'll feel a pang of guilt and come clean. Or at least open the door a crack. But I need to see her face-to-face so I know what she knows."

There was a long pause, and then she said, "Thanks for including me."

"In what?"

She waved a hand. "In all this. I need to put things right. As much as I can."

"I understand." I felt roughly the same way.

It wasn't until we'd been on Route 50 for a while and passed a sign for the Upperville Baptist Church that we realized we'd arrived.

"But where's the town?" Mandy said.

"Good question."

Upperville wasn't even a town; it was an unincorporated community, an assortment of old stone and brick buildings, most of them lined up along Route 50. There was a sandstone Episcopal church, a post office, a fire department. An inn once owned by George Washington, or so the Internet had told us. And horse farms. A lot of horse farms. A sign announced that this was the site of the annual Upperville Colt and Horse Show.

We stopped at a general store, and Mandy ran in to ask directions. Past the cemetery and then continue on for a couple of miles, she was told. On either side of the road were horse fences. There was a break in the fence and an unmarked road. We turned left there, as instructed. Soon we came to a stone fence. Inset in one of the pillars at the opening was a granite block inscribed ELM SPRING FARMS. Entering ahead of us were a Bentley and a Range Rover. We were obviously in the right place.

The road went on for a long while, jigging to the left and then to the right and then straight, lined with gracefully pruned elm trees and pin oaks. Just beyond the trees, on the right, was a clearing. In the gaps between the trees I could glimpse a long straight lane of asphalt paving, which I soon realized was an airstrip. It seemed to be about a mile long. The road continued another half mile or so. Finally it broadened out and the trees ended. Parked on either side of the wider road were a lot of cars.

Expensive cars, too. Mercedes-Benzes and BMWs and Range Rovers, Bentleys and Jaguars and Lamborghinis and Ferraris. And then there were the retro vehicles, the woody-sided station wagons, and the pickup trucks that probably belonged to the real hands-on horse-farm owners who had so much money they didn't need to impress you. A young guy in a valet uniform was guiding the cars into their slots.

We'd timed this well, in the middle of the arrival rush. We parked the Suburban and joined the parade of party guests walking down the driveway toward the extremely large redbrick Georgian house. I knew it was at least ten thousand square feet, on a two-thousand-acre plot of land that also included a private airstrip and stables and paddocks.

But when we got to the front door, there was a problem. A couple of pretty blond young women were sitting at a table just inside, handing out name badges and checking names off a list.

We were not on any list, of course.

"James and Lisa Grant," I said pleasantly.

Mandy glanced at me quickly. We hadn't discussed whether we'd pretend to be a married couple; I'd just improvised it, last minute, forgetting that neither of us wore wedding bands.

"Grant," one of the girls murmured, running her finger down a column. "Um, how do you spell that?"

"Like it sounds." Behind them was a painting of a white barn that I was pretty sure was by Georgia O'Keeffe.

"Um, I don't see a Grant here." She turned to the blonde sitting next to her. "Do you have James Grant?" They probably each had half the alphabet. The second blonde scanned her list, running an index finger down her list. She shook her head.

Then Mandy stepped forward. "I'll just write out our name badges if you give me a couple of blanks." As if the real problem was that we didn't have any badges. Not that we weren't on the list of invited guests.

The two blondes looked at each other, and the first one shrugged. You could see the conflicting instincts battling it out in their heads—*Only admit guests on the list!* versus *Never insult the guests!*

Never insult the guests won out, as I knew it would. How did they know the Grants' names hadn't been accidentally left off?

"Sure," the first blonde said uncertainly, pulling out blank name badges from a box and handing them to Mandy.

The entry hall, tiled in terra-cotta, gave way to a great hall with twenty-foot ceilings, very grand and formal. The floor was black-and-white harlequin tiles, the walls were painted oxblood, there were dramatic swags of drapery and gilt-framed equestrian paintings. The room was crowded. It looked like there were sixty or seventy people. We each took hors d'oeuvres from a waitress and flutes of champagne from a waiter and entered the fray.

It didn't take long at all to identify Ellen Wiley. She was a tall, attractive woman in her seventies who looked easily twenty years younger. She had the figure of a woman who did a lot of Pilates. She was wearing a long-sleeved gold evening dress with a diamond choker. Her hair, light brown with blond highlights, was styled in a short, flattering shag. She was talking to a silver-haired man who looked ex-military, and she was laughing, a deep swooping laugh.

"Now what?" Mandy said.

"We drink, we talk, we suffer through the inevitable pitch for money, and then we wait until we can get her alone."

Mandy and I talked for a long while, keeping to ourselves, like you weren't supposed to do at a party like this. Someone clinked a glass, then others clinked in response, and the room quieted. Ellen Wiley—we'd identified her correctly—made a speech about how for every US soldier killed in war, seven are wounded. She talked about the invisible wounds of war, like post-traumatic stress disorder, traumatic brain injury, and major depression. She introduced one grievously wounded soldier, recently back from Iraq, and he spoke a few words and reduced a few people to tears.

She finished speaking, and a few minutes later I saw her approach us. Her hand was extended. "You're the Grants, I'm told," she said, a smile lighting up her face. Her eyes were a bright blue.

"James Grant," I said and shook her hand. She'd been briefed. James Grant was a major donor to conservative causes.

"Lisa Grant," Mandy said and did the same.

Up close you could see the skillful plastic surgery she'd had, particularly in the tight lines around her eyes when she smiled. She turned toward me. "I understand you wanted to talk to me, Mister, uh *Grant*." She raised her eyebrows as she said *Grant*. "Happy to do so, when the guests have gone."

She smiled again and turned away.

A young guy in a blue blazer came up to us a few minutes later, introduced himself as Rico, and escorted us out of the great room and down a hallway to the library, which was only slightly smaller than the great room. It had large windows and whitewashed stone walls and built-in bookcases. The floors were painted wood. He gestured toward a round tea table with chairs around it in front of a large painting, a big red square that looked like a Rothko. "Mrs. Wiley will be with you soon," Rico said. When we took our seats, he turned without a word and left.

As we sat, uncomfortable on the hard wooden chairs, we said nothing to each other, because of the possibility of recording devices.

We waited uneasily.

Somehow she knew we wanted to see her. We hadn't said anything to anyone else at the party, or to the blond girls with the name tags.

I thought back to the folder that Merlin had left in the locked file room at the law firm and wondered whether someone at Norcross and McKenna had made the connection and warned Ellen Wiley. That seemed the likeliest explanation.

But if she knew we were there under false pretenses, why was she still willing to meet with us?

Mrs. Wiley appeared about an hour later. She began speaking as she entered the library, a good fifty feet from us.

"Finally!" she said. "*Now* the party gets interesting."

"Excuse me?" I said.

"Oh, I know every single name on my guest list. I didn't invite anyone I don't know. When I'm hitting people up for money, I prefer to know them personally." She tipped her head to one side, placed a hand on her hip, and smiled coquettishly. "The least you could have done was use your real names."

59

I stood up, and then Mandy did. "You're absolutely right," I said. "I'm Nick Heller and this is Mandy Seeger."

"So you're the one who torched my website," she said to me, wagging a finger, mock-stern. "I know who you are. You're a real troublemaker. And of course I know who your father is." She turned toward Mandy. "And you—aren't you the reporter?"

"Until yesterday," Mandy said, "I used to be an employee of yours. I wrote the piece on Jeremiah Claflin."

"I thought so. Ash Norcross warned me someone might be coming. But he didn't say they'd be crashing my party. Ballsy of you two to show up like this. I *love* it." She flashed a bright smile. "All right, somehow you two figured out who owns Slander Sheet. Now you know my deep, dark secret. So what the hell do you want?"

"I was going to ask you the same thing," I said. "What the hell do *you* want?"

"*Excuse* me?"

"Either you or your people are covering up the death of a twenty-two-year-old girl. Whether you ordered it or not, it's going to come back to bite you."

Mandy stared at me. I could almost see the cartoon thought bubble above her head: *So much for going in at a slant.*

"I don't know what on earth you're referring to." She seemed genuinely baffled.

"There was a call girl named Kayla Pitts, who was—"

"That poor girl killed herself!"

"I'm afraid not. Your people killed her because they were afraid she'd start telling the truth about the Claflin story."

"My . . . *people*? What in God's name—?"

"We know you hired the Centurions to eliminate a threat."

"Oh, do you? I know who the Centurions are, and no, I certainly didn't hire them."

"Then someone did."

She put out her hands, palms up, arms wide. "Well, then, you crashed the wrong party, because I don't know what the hell you're talking about."

"You wanted to bring down Jeremiah Claflin by any means necessary."

She pointed an index finger at me. "Oh, now, please. That's an exaggeration. Did I want to bring Claflin down? Hell, yes! Guilty as charged!" She gave a long sigh. "Do you mind if we sit down? I've been on my feet for three hours. No, not on *those* chairs. I don't have enough padding on my butt." She waved toward a grouping of overstuffed lounge chairs in front of a tall fireplace.

We walked over there, waited for her to sit, and then I sat closest to her, because my instinct told me she was one of those women who just prefers men. My instinct on this was rarely wrong.

She shifted in her chair until she was facing me, and only me.

Now she spoke more quietly. "That girl—the little trollop Heidi or whatever her name was—how do you know it wasn't a suicide?"

"I have sources inside the police." That was about as close to the truth as I wanted to give her.

"But why in the world—who?—I don't understand."

I answered her question with a question. "How did you first get the Claflin story?" I already knew the answer to that question, but I wanted to see if she knew, too.

"I own the website; I don't run it. *I* didn't get it. Julian Gunn told me about it. The prostitute contacted"— she turned to look at Mandy, seeming surprised she was still there—"*you*! Right?"

"That's right," Mandy said.

"We didn't search it out. It came to us. *You* didn't make it up, right?"

Mandy said, "Right."

"You didn't know it was fake when you wrote the story, right?"

"Right."

Satisfied, Ellen Wiley turned back to me. "You think I

wanted Slander Sheet to run a story that would only end up making us look ridiculous? I mostly keep my hands off. I'm not an editor. I let Julian do his thing. Oh, sure, Julian knows certain stories make my heart beat faster. He caters to my sweet tooth. He knows I like making mischief."

"Mischief," I repeated. "Is that what Slander Sheet is?"

"When I was a little girl and my mother put me in these perfect little dresses and pinafores, the first thing I'd do was run outside and roll in the dirt, or play in the barn. I always loved getting messy and dirty and it drove my mother right up the wall. That's why I had to buy Slander Sheet. Make a little mess. But you think if I knew the story was cooked up I'd *let* Julian run it?"

"If it forced Claflin off the court."

She laughed, a deep laugh that came from her chest. "Oh ho, is that what you think? Honey, let me tell you something. I won't deny I despise that man, Claflin. Ever since that ridiculous lawsuit in the nineties, with all those attorneys general going after the tobacco companies. When he was on the sixth circuit US Court of Appeals. Claflin's one of those prim-and-proper types who like to tell people what vices they're allowed to have. The nanny state and all."

"Then again, the lung cancer thing is kind of a bummer."

She laughed, and this time it was the coquettish laugh of a sixteen-year-old debutante. "The fact is, people do die from lung cancer, and you know what? It gets you pretty quick. Eight months or so. After you've lived a useful life, too—in your sixties or seventies. Smokers die ten years earlier than nonsmokers. That's ten years we all save on social security and Medicare and pensions. You want to know why our social security system is in such dire straits? It's that people are giving up smoking."

"Oh yeah?" I said.

"It's all this *fanaticism*. I say, make your choices, live your life. Now, I don't smoke. That's a decision I made. Maybe you do smoke. That's a decision you make."

"So that's why you own Slander Sheet—to advance the cause of smoking?"

"Oh, please. I was telling you why I hate Claflin and his ilk. You know, Nick, there was a time, not so long ago, when this country was in the hands of great men— men who believed in public service. They got us through the Depression and two world wars and the Cold War. Now look who's running the show. The likes of . . . Gideon Parnell! A man who used to be a protester! *Sit-ins* and such!"

Also a black man, I thought, but I just listened.

"So much for the WASP establishment, right?" she went on. "All gone. Our country is being run by people who don't really believe in America, do you know what I mean? Christ on a raft, they want to spell it with a *k*. They want to bring it *low* so we can all wallow in our sins. I'm about *saving* this republic of ours. Through tough love, if necessary. But when I see people who fundamentally *deplore* America's historical role in the world? When I see people who doubt the decency of the American soul? And now they're wandering around the corridors of power? Well, that's the *wrong* kind of mischief, I say. My attitude is, Get out of the goddamn cockpit, you people—you are *not* flying this plane."

I just smiled.

"Can we speak frankly, Nick?" She put a hand on my knee and lowered her voice to a confidential whisper. "People assume if you're rich you automatically have power." She gazed directly into my eyes and I could see what a minx she must have been in her prime. She was a very sexual woman. "Well, it sure doesn't feel that way. Getting your voice out there is harder and harder. I'm sure you remember this from what happened to your father, Nick. The way the press just *pilloried* Victor Heller."

"I didn't have a problem with the press coverage," I said. "The only one responsible for what happened to Victor is Victor."

She sighed. "You know, there used to be a saying, 'Never pick a fight with a man who buys ink by the barrel.' Now pixels are the thing, not ink. You want real power? You gotta control the flow of information. That's why I bought Slander Sheet. Stick it to all those hypocrites. And I won't deny I enjoy making a little mischief. But you ask me if I 'ordered' the death of this floozy, like I'm some . . . some mob boss? Why in heaven's name would I want to do that? To what end—to cast suspicion on myself?"

"Then who did?"

She was silent for a while. "Damned if I know. Someone who detests Jeremiah Claflin as much as I do—but didn't mind bringing down Slander Sheet in the process. Nick, how did you find out I'm the owner?"

"Norcross didn't tell you?"

She shook her head.

Norcross must not have wanted to admit that his law firm's vaunted security had been breached. He'd just warned her I was coming without telling her how I'd found out who she was.

I said, "I do my homework."

She laughed.

"Why do you keep it a secret?" I asked.

"Oh, it would be socially a bit *awkward* for me if people knew I owned Slander Sheet. Anyway, secret pleasures are always the best, don't you think? And I *don't* like having my name in the paper. I don't do interviews, and I don't want to have my name dredged up every time Slander Sheet runs a scoop. And now what are you telling me—that I'm under suspicion for this call girl's death? Nick, you strike me as a direct, honest, no-bullshit fellow. Plus, you're cute. I like the cut of your jib. If you're really trying to get to the bottom of all this, I'm willing to help you. Okay? In return, I ask that you keep the ownership of Slander Sheet a secret. Do we have a deal?"

I realized we really had the upper hand. She didn't want her friends to know she owned such a disreputable rag. I looked at Mandy, and she just looked back.

When we didn't reply, she went on, "I don't like being in the dark. I don't like not knowing. And I don't like having Slander Sheet turned into a joke." She turned to look at Mandy. "Now, I know Julian fired you because of this debacle. But I'm going to get Julian on the phone right now and tell him to hire you back."

"Don't bother," Mandy said. "Not interested."

"You don't want to clear your name?"

A look of irritation crossed Mandy's face. "Sure I do. But not for Slander Sheet."

"Then *I'll* pay you. Directly. You find out who did this to you, how this happened, I'll double your severance package."

Mandy barely hesitated. "Deal."

Turning back to me, she put her hand on my knee again. She smiled, a seductive smile. "You, too. What do you charge, anyway?"

60

S he likes the cut of your jib," Mandy said later.

I smiled and said nothing. I cut the wheel hard to the right and turned onto Route 15 South.

"I don't even know what a jib is, do you?"

"It's a sailing term."

"She was actually flirting with you! She thought you were cute!"

"Why is that so outlandish?"

"She's like a hundred and twenty years old!"

"I have to say, she looks awfully good for a woman of seventy-four."

"So now you're into her."

I said nothing.

"I could have been a potted plant in that room. A statue."

"You could have been the Venus de Milo, it wouldn't have mattered. She prefers men."

"Clearly. She's a cougar. She's also as crazy as a box of weasels."

"She's a complicated woman."

"I'll say. She's a racist. She doesn't like Gideon Parnell because he's black."

"Maybe. Or maybe because he marched. She doesn't like troublemakers unless it's her brand of troublemaker."

"I'll still take her money."

I smiled. "You did say yes awfully fast."

"Busted." She shrugged. "What can I say, I have a mortgage."

"Why did Slander Sheet never go after Gideon, anyway? Was it because they couldn't find any dirt on him?"

"Because there was nothing interesting to report . . . I was working on a story on him before the Claflin thing came in. There was nothing there."

"Did Julian tell you to do it?"

"He suggested it."

"Because his boss, the owner, wanted Gideon Parnell taken down."

She shrugged. "That was above my pay grade. But Claflin's a much bigger target."

My phone rang.

"Gideon," she predicted.

I took it out of my jacket and answered without looking at it first, because I was driving. "Nick Heller."

"Mr. Heller, this is Detective Balakian from MPD homicide."

"Yes, detective."

"I'd like to speak with you at your earliest convenience."

"What about?" Mandy was watching my face.

"Kayla Pitts."

"Is there a problem?"

"I just have some questions for you."

"I'm out of town and won't be back in Washington until late. How's tomorrow morning?"

A beat. "Nine o'clock at homicide branch, 101 M Street." It was an order, not a suggestion.

"I'll be there."

He disconnected the call.

"What does he want?" Mandy said.

"He wants this case to go away, but it's not happening anytime soon. He wants to talk to me."

"For what?"

"Just says he has questions."

"I wonder if he's getting pressure from above. All this conspiracy talk out there."

I thought for a minute. "Maybe. Maybe that's all it is."

61

We didn't get back to DC until late, almost eleven. I drove Mandy to her apartment, which was on Kalorama near Columbia, in Adams Morgan.

"As long as you're here, why don't you come up?" she said, touching my knee lightly. "You can pick up my Claflin files."

To my surprise, I felt my cheeks warm, and I was glad she couldn't see me in the dark. It was like that Shirley MacLaine line in *Terms of Endearment*, when she invites potential suitors to come up and look at her Renoir—a welcome invitation that confirmed the vibe that I'd wondered about between us. Apparently I hadn't just been imagining it.

"Sure," I said. "That'd be great."

"Thanks."

Her condo was on the third floor of a brownstone whose lobby smelled of curry from the Indian restaurant next door. She had three locks on the door.

"Apologies for the mess."

The place was small but smartly furnished, in IKEA simplicity. An open-plan kitchen with an island. It looked more spacious than it should have. Nothing was out of place. There was no mess. "Slovenly," I said.

She laughed. "Well, you know. Something to drink?"

"That would be nice."

"Coke or diet? Or seltzer? Or I can make coffee. Actually, mind getting yourself something from the fridge while I change out of these clothes?"

I located a couple of glasses and clanked in a few ice cubes from the freezer and poured us both some Diet Coke. I felt like having a real drink, but that wasn't going to happen. I didn't want to be the only one drinking anyway.

She emerged ten minutes later wearing skinny jeans and a black silk camisole with spaghetti straps. She was barefoot. She looked great. I had a fairly good idea she had the same thing in mind as I did. She retrieved her phone from the kitchen table and a minute later I could hear Art Pepper's silky smooth alto saxophone doing "My Funny Valentine."

"Nice," I said, handing her the glass of Diet Coke.

"You sound surprised."

"I love Art Pepper."

"You're not a big jazz snob, are you? You know, like, it's no good if it's not Django Reinhardt, or Thelonious Monk at the Blackhawk, nineteen sixty?"

"Not a jazz snob. That's not me. I mean, I don't know what mouthpiece Art is using, if that's what you mean."

I set down my glass on the kitchen island and excused myself to use her bathroom. When I came back, she was sitting in an armchair covered in a slouchy slipcover placed at a right angle to the couch. She'd moved my Diet Coke to the end table between the chair and the couch. I sat on the couch next to the end table, where she'd put a brown accordion file. She waved at it. "My Slander Sheet files."

"That's all?"

"That's the paper 'What If' file. The stuff I never got anywhere with. Rumors about everyone in Washington who counts." She'd put on perfume, something light and floral, maybe jasmine.

"Like who?"

"Your old boss, Jay Stoddard, for one."

"Whatever you have on him, no matter how kinky or disgusting, it's true."

"A lot of those leads never checked out. Never amounted to anything. Like ninety percent of them are just urban legends. But I never throw anything away. You never know when an old rumor turns out to be true."

"Thanks for trusting me with it."

"Before the Kayla debacle I was working on a story about a DC homicide that was allegedly covered up. A cold case involving some Washington bigwig."

"Who?"

"I never got that far. A retired police detective in Southeast, an old guy who's on his deathbed or close to it, supposedly covered it up and now he wants to talk."

"You have a working theory who the killer was?"

"Theory? Your friend Senator Brennan."

"Come on."

"A drunk-driving incident, maybe."

"You think?"

She shook her head. "I never got anywhere with it."

"Well, I'm not going to bring it up with him."

She stretched her legs. "You sure you don't miss living in DC? All the intrigue?"

"Not at all. You like living in Adams Morgan?"

"Where I am now, yeah. I used to live on Columbia and had to sleep with earplugs."

"The bar traffic."

"The drunken arguments, the smashed bottles, the sirens. The woo girls and the frat bros. But that was mostly Friday and Saturday nights."

"Any crime here?"

"I had a break-in a couple of weeks back, in fact."

"Were you home?"

"Nope."

"Get ripped off?"

"I don't know. The place was ransacked, but I haven't figured out what they took. They climbed in through the fire escape. I've changed the locks on the windows."

"When was this, exactly?"

She shook her head. "About a month ago."

"When you started working on the Kayla story?"

"Before that. Oh, hey." She got up suddenly and went over to the kitchen. I turned to watch. She wasn't skinny; she was curvy. Maybe voluptuous was the right word. Her legs were long and toned, like she cycled. She opened a cabinet and pulled out a bottle of Jameson. "I forgot, I keep some around for guests. If you want something harder than Coke."

"Not for me, thanks." As much as I wanted a drink, I also didn't want her to feel uncomfortable. "You can keep that stuff in the house?"

"It took a while. Now I'm okay with it. I really don't mind if you have some."

I hesitated, but not for long. "Then okay, I'll have a little. On the rocks."

She fixed the drink and brought it to me. I clinked with her Diet Coke and took a swig, felt the whiskey burn the back of my throat.

There was a moment of silence. She said, "So can I ask you something? When you were in Iraq . . ."

I waited for the inevitable question. *Did you ever kill anyone?* And *What was it like? What does it feel like to kill another human being?*

"Yeah?"

"Well, how did a rich kid like you end up in the army?"

"I wasn't a rich kid."

"You didn't grow up rich? Your father—"

"Yeah, till I was a teenager. Then my dad went on the lam."

"He got arrested?"

"Yes, but that was after a few years. He was a fugitive."

"I remember reading about him. What'd they end up getting him for?"

"Insider trading. Fraud. A bunch of things."

"Was he guilty?"

"Of that and more."

"Not a nice guy?"

I chuckled. "I wouldn't say so, no."

"But you still visit him in prison."

"He's extremely smart. He still knows people. Sometimes he helps, but it costs me."

"Costs you?"

"It's hard to explain. I don't visit him out of love or filial duty."

"How about your mom?"

"She lives outside of Boston. She's some kind of saint."

"Any brothers or sisters?"

I shook my head. Too complicated to explain about my brother Roger. "How about you?"

"Three older brothers."

"You were the baby."

She smiled. "I was."

"Little princess."

"Actually, I was a tomboy, until I discovered boys." She cleared her throat. "But you never answered my question. Why'd you enlist?"

"I didn't want to work for McKinsey."

"The consulting firm?"

"Yeah. I worked for them a couple of summers."

"Sort of an extreme way to avoid working for McKinsey, don't you think?"

"I *really* didn't want to work for McKinsey."

She laughed a little.

"I enlisted because I believed in it. Maybe I needed something like that, at that time in my life. I wanted to not be Victor Heller's son. I wanted to be my own man."

"I think I get it."

It was late and I was tired of talking. I stood up.

"Can I get you another Jameson?" she said, standing up as well.

"I'm good." I went to give her a hug, and her face turned toward mine, and somehow our lips met. Her hands came around to my back and pulled me in toward her. I could taste her lipstick and the Diet Coke. My tongue found hers. Our mouths melted into each other's. I slid my hands under her camisole and came around slowly to the front, felt the silky-smooth skin, her breasts.

She pulled back to take a breath and said, "God."

"Mm," I said.

"Heller, is this going to be a problem?"

"Hmm?" I'd gone from Nick to Heller. Interesting. Using just my last name connoted greater intimacy.

"You and me . . . ?"

"No problem," I said, and I kissed her again, my hands on her butt. Then I removed her cami and gazed at her full breasts, her nipples erect and pointed, and I sucked in a breath between my teeth.

Voluptuous. Yes.

I liked voluptuous.

62

I spent the night.

You never know the etiquette, after you sleep with a woman. If you leave right away, you're no better than a dog. But not all women want to wake up with a man in their bed.

We snuggled together, and I fell asleep, and I awoke sometime later to discover that it was early morning, though still dark. I got up quietly so as not to wake her and padded into her living room area where she kept the accordion file of her sources, her story leads.

The file was filled with tantalizing rumors. I pored through it. At one point I made coffee—she had a complicated Swedish coffee machine that took some figuring out—and when I was searching her cabinets for a cup, Mandy appeared. She was wearing the lacy panties she'd had on the night before, and a white tank top.

"Mmm. Could you pour me some, too?"

"Of course."

"The mugs are in the cabinet to the right of the stove."

"Good morning," I said, taking down two mugs. I took the one that had *The Washington Post* logo on it, in case it spurred bad memories, and gave her the one with the WAMU logo on it, the local NPR affiliate. The coffee was delicious. She got some milk from the refrigerator, offered it to me, and when I demurred she poured some into her mug. She took a sip.

"I enjoyed that," she said after a while. I knew she didn't mean the coffee.

"So did I."

"I hope you don't mind my asking: Are you involved with someone?"

I shook my head.

"Back home in Boston, I mean. Are you sure?"

"As far as I know."

"I was actually engaged."

"To who?"

"A lawyer at WilmerHale."

"It is Washington, after all. The odds are good you'd end up with a lawyer."

"We broke up around the time I got fired from the *Post*. That was another thing my drinking screwed up."

"Maybe it was just as well."

"He was a really nice guy."

"Then I'm sorry."

"He wasn't very interesting. But he put up with me, which is no minor consideration."

There was a long pause. Maybe she wanted to trade

ex-girlfriend/ex-boyfriend stories. But I didn't do that. I patted the accordion file. "Thanks for this."

"Find anything?"

"You're a really good reporter."

"Is there a 'but'?"

"You were working for a shitty website. But you're a reporter of an extremely high caliber."

"You already got into my pants, Heller. You don't have to be so nice."

I didn't laugh. Quietly, I said: "I think you were targeted."

"Targeted how?"

"I think you were given that Claflin story deliberately."

"I don't . . . follow."

"You were given a big story that was guaranteed to self-destruct. Just solid enough to withstand fact-checking by a smart journalist, like you. But with hidden fissures so that a high-powered investigator, with enough resources, would be able to take it down. Someone really determined."

"Like you."

"Like me."

"Meaning I got played."

"Maybe we both got played."

"What do you mean?"

"I've been doing a lot of thinking. I think you played your role and I played mine."

"Both of us? Why?"

"Because someone wanted you to stumble and fall."

"Who in the world cares enough about me to try to destroy me? That doesn't make sense, Heller. I'm just a journalist. Who'd been fired from *The Washington Post*. Working for a bottom-feeding website. Who would even *bother*?"

"You knew something. You had something. You had to be discredited. You and Slander Sheet both. The Claflin story was a booby-trap. A butterfly mine. You pick it up, and it blows up in your hands."

"Well, it worked, didn't it?"

"Perfectly. Whoever they were, they knew what they were doing."

"I'll play along. What were they so afraid of?"

"Well, let's think about what you were working on."

"Stories for Slander Sheet?"

I nodded.

"Half a dozen, maybe more. The chief of staff at the White House—"

"With the shoplifting wife?"

"Right."

"What else?"

"There's a B and D club in Washington, and it's rumored that a member of the Joint Chiefs of Staff belongs."

"B and D as in bondage and discipline?"

"Right."

"Did you have a name?"

"Members of the club wouldn't talk to me. So, no."

"You said something about a retired cop on his deathbed, something like that? A homicide by some Washington bigwig that was covered up?"

"Right. The Senator Brennan thing."

"How sure are you that it involved drunk driving?"

"Not sure at all. That was just my working theory."

"How sure are you that it involved Brennan?"

"That was just a theory, too."

I was silent. "Maybe it's that."

"Or the B and D club. Or any of a dozen stories I did."

"Possibly, yes."

"And maybe your speculation is wrong and I wasn't targeted."

"True."

"Maybe they were targeting Slander Sheet, and I was accidental collateral."

I remembered that Kayla said she was told to ask for Mandy specifically. "I'd say both you and Slander Sheet, at the same time."

"Still sounds like a stretch," Mandy said.

"Didn't it ever strike you that it was a little too easy?"

"What was?"

"What I was hired to do. Disprove the Claflin story you were doing for Slander Sheet. It should have been harder."

"How do you mean?"

"Look at it from their point of view."

"Who's 'they'?"

"Whoever was trying to bring Claflin down. They go to the trouble of booking hotel rooms at the Hotel

Monroe in Claflin's name. They actually have someone show up at the hotel and pretend to be him and check in. And then they don't bother actually going into the room. What's that all about?"

"They didn't know the hotel's keycard system kept track."

I shook my head. "I wonder. Then two of the nights Kayla was supposed to have met with Claflin she was actually in Mississippi."

"So?"

"We found out about the flights by getting into her laptop. But there are other ways we could have learned she flew to Mississippi to visit her sister. We could have gotten into her credit cards some other way. If I were trying to set Claflin up, I wouldn't have picked a couple of nights when she was *provably* out of town."

She looked at me for a few seconds. "You have a very conspiratorial turn of mind, anyone ever tell you that?"

"All the time," I said.

63

Dorothy was awake and working at the dining table in the suite's living room when I returned to the hotel with two coffees from Starbucks. I handed her one.

"Cream, two sugars, right?"

"Thank you," she said, taking it. She was wearing jeans and a T-shirt that said, JESUS IS MY ROCK AND THAT'S HOW I ROLL. "How was it?" She gave a cryptic little smile.

I had a feeling Dorothy was deliberately being ambiguous. Poking at me. She knew I'd spent the night with Mandy. She wasn't stupid. But I decided to ignore it. "It was interesting," I said. "I don't think Ellen Wiley was involved. Scratch that theory. But she wants to help us out."

"She does? Why?"

"She likes the cut of my jib."

Dorothy shook her head, as if to say *I don't know what you're talking about and I'm not going to ask.*

"I traced the tail number," she said.

"Tail number?" I'd forgotten what she was talking about.

"At the Middleton airport. The plane they were about to take Kayla away on."

"Right, sorry."

"It was a 900EX Falcon jet, made by Dassault, and it's owned by Centurion Associates Inc."

"Great. What about an address?"

"Just a PO box number in Langley, Virginia."

"Langley, huh?" That was where the CIA was located. "Was there an address on the Centurion Associates website?"

"There is no Centurion Associates website."

"What do you mean?"

"I mean, if you go to CenturionAssociates.com, you get a 404 error. 'The page you're requesting is not found.'"

"Maybe it's a different domain name."

"No, that's it. I ran a WhoIs search on it, and it's registered. It's a valid domain name."

"So who's it registered to?"

"All the registration information is hidden. It's registered to Domains by Proxy."

"So can you hack into it?"

She shook her head. "There's nothing to hack into."

"I'd call that low profile."

"As far as I can tell, they don't have an office either. Just a PO box."

"Interesting. Oh, I forgot to tell you. I left the Rubber Ducky behind on that job."

She exhaled. "Okay. If they find it, which might take a while, there's nothing on there tying it back to us."

"Sorry about that."

She shrugged. "It happens. They're cheap. No big deal."

"I should get dressed. Detective Balakian wants to see me."

"The homicide detective?"

I nodded.

"I thought he'd concluded it was a suicide."

"Maybe they're having second thoughts."

"New information?"

"That's what I want to know."

Detective Balakian was wearing the same outfit as last time, the white shirt with the skinny black tie, and I wondered if his wardrobe was limited. Or maybe he'd found his look and wanted to stick with it. He met me at the front desk of the police station, a converted old elementary school, and brought me to an interview room on the first floor.

There were four chairs at a rectangular table. He pointed to the one he wanted me to sit in.

"Is this being videotaped?" I asked.

"Do you have any objection?"

"No. I just like to know."

"Thanks. It's a lot less work than typing it up. Thanks for coming in." He sounded much more conciliatory than the night of Kayla's murder. Something had obviously changed.

"Sure," I said, instead of what I was thinking: *You didn't exactly give me a choice.*

"Coffee?"

"No thanks."

He sat in one of the other chairs and took out a small spiral-bound notebook. After a long pause, he said, "Why were you so convinced Kayla Pitts may have been a homicide victim?"

Now, finally, he was taking this case seriously. "Because I talked to her a few hours before her death. I told you that."

"Nothing else you might have heard?"

I shook my head. "I thought you decided it was a suicide."

"Toxicology came back."

"And?"

He hesitated. He took a drink of something brownish in a mug that was too light to be coffee. "There was a powerful sedative in her system."

"Ketamine," I said.

"Rohypnol, actually."

"Roofie. I thought tox results take weeks."

"We put a rush on it."

"Ah." Like he had the juice to do that. It must have been all the news stories that had put pressure on the MPD, convinced someone at the top to expedite it.

He knew I'd fixed a drink for Kayla, and giving someone a drink is the standard way to roofie somebody. So I wanted to make sure he could rule me out as a suspect.

"You've got the contents of the hotel wastebasket," I said. "Run a tox assay on the remnants."

"Already did," Balakian said. "Trust but verify, right?"

"Absolutely."

"You said she called you and asked for your help, the night of her death. Why'd she ask for you?"

We'd already been over this. Was he trying to catch me in an inconsistency? "We met after I tracked her down. She decided she trusted me. She knew I was an outsider, not with the people who were kidnaping her."

"That was the only time you two had met?"

"Right."

"You said she was being taken somewhere against her will. You don't know where?"

"Right."

"She didn't know?"

"She didn't."

"And you don't know who her would-be kidnappers were?"

"I have a pretty good idea. The tail number on their plane traces to a company called Centurion Associates of Langley, Virginia."

"The security firm."

"Is that what they are?"

He ignored my question. "Why didn't you tell me this when we spoke at the hotel?"

"I didn't know. We just found out."

He said nothing.

"Can I ask a question or two?"

"Go ahead," he said unenthusiastically.

"Have you looked at the hotel's surveillance tapes?"

"Closely. There's not a lot of them. Nothing in the elevators, nothing on the guest floors. This is a hotel that values its guests' privacy more than their safety. You can enter the hotel and head right for the elevator bank without being captured on video."

"What about the service entrance?"

"There's cameras there. But we don't find anyone entering there and taking the elevators up during that time period."

"What about the call she placed at eight forty-seven?"

"That went to a disposable cell phone. Which doesn't help us at all."

"Look, can we speak frankly?" I said.

"That's not what we've been doing?"

"You said it yourself, this looked like a 'textbook' suicide. The slit wrists and throat, the bathtub, the hesitation marks. Then there's the Rohypnol. Did she take it as a recreational drug? Most likely she was given a roofie to make her cooperate when they killed her, while she bled out."

He nodded.

"Whoever did this knows what a homicide investigator looks for."

He said nothing.

"This was a 'suicide' staged by a former cop, maybe even a former homicide detective."

"That's a wild allegation."

"No, it's a theory. One you should take seriously."

"Let's say I did. How does this help solve her murder?"

"It points to Centurion Associates. Apparently Centurion is staffed by ex-MPD cops."

"And you think one of them killed Kayla Pitts."

"Like I said, it's a theory."

"Huh," Balakian said. For the first time he didn't bat my suggestion away. "You may have something here."

64

Ellen Wiley's pied-à-terre in Washington was on N Street in Georgetown, a handsome Federal-style town house, redbrick with black shutters. The door was answered by a maid in a uniform of gray dress and white cuffs and bib apron. She took me to Ellen, who was sitting in a high-back tufted wing chair in her library, just off the front hallway. The room was lined with books, floor to ceiling. She was talking on a landline phone. She was wearing a black skirt with a white silk blouse cut low enough to show the cleft of her tanned bosom, and a string of pearls.

"But that's just it," she was saying, "he has no idea." She let out a whooping laugh. "Exactly." She saw me, smiled, and waved me into a nearby chair. "Sweetie, I have to go, I have a visitor." She paused. "Yes, a gentleman caller." She laughed again and hung up.

"There he is, Nick Heller!" she announced. "You're here a full hour early. He's not coming until eleven."

We had arranged for me to come by her house at ten, so I just nodded and said, "This shouldn't take more than ten minutes, then I'll be gone."

"Jorge," she called out, "can you bring this gentleman some coffee?" To me she said, "He makes the best sticky buns."

"Not for me, thanks."

"Are you sure? They're still warm. If I can't have them, at least my visitors can."

"Do you plan to meet him in here?"

"Sure, here or in the front sitting room."

"I'm going to need you to decide now where you'll meet him."

"Oh, heavens, then right here."

"Okay." I took out from my pocket an infinity transmitter, a small black GSM bug a couple of inches square. I'd already inserted a cell phone SIM card into it. "It would help if you decided now where you're going to sit."

"Ooh, spy stuff. I'll sit right here. He can sit where you're sitting."

"Okay, great." I looked around. The closest power outlet was some distance away. On the table between the two chairs was a brass lamp. I lifted it up. No room under the base. No drawer in the table. "I'm going to put it under the cushion in your chair. You'll sit there, right?"

"Honey, I don't even have to move. Do I have to do anything with it?"

"Ignore it. I'll call in to it just before he arrives, and it'll go right into transmission mode. I'll be listening in from my cell phone in my car."

"Anything you want me to ask him?"

"All I care about is that you seem genuinely interested in hiring Centurion Associates. That you have serious security concerns. The more complicated, the better. Maybe you have a stalker who won't go away. They pride themselves on being able to handle difficult cases. Just be a tough customer."

"Oh, that I can do," she said. There was a flash in her eyes, and she gave a fierce smile, and I realized that I wouldn't want to negotiate a contract with her.

I'd rented a silver Chrysler 200 because it was the most inconspicuous, anonymous-looking car I could find. I'd parked it across the street from Ellen Wiley's town house and about a hundred feet down the block.

I sat there and waited. The traffic on N Street was two-way, but it was light. At ten minutes before eleven, a white Cadillac Escalade pulled up to the curb in front of Wiley's house, slowed, and then moved ahead seventy-five feet or so and parallel parked. I took out my binoculars and focused on the vehicle. I saw two men in the Escalade, the driver and a passenger.

This had to be Thomas Vogel, accompanied by someone from Centurion Associates.

They were early. They knew who Ellen Wiley was and knew she represented an excellent business opportunity.

I continued to watch them through the binoculars. I could see the passenger talking to the driver. The body language indicated that Thomas Vogel was the passenger, talking to a subordinate.

At eleven o'clock exactly, Vogel got out of the Escalade, slammed the door behind him, and walked along the sidewalk to Ellen Wiley's town house. As he walked, facing me, I could finally see him clearly.

Vogel was tall, but not a giant, maybe around my height, six-four. He was wearing a good navy suit, white shirt, and red tie—very patriotic colors—and appeared to be powerfully built. He had salt-and-pepper black hair and a mustache. He walked with a confident stride. He was a man who was used to physically dominating those around him. I recognized his face from the fishing picture in Curtis Schmidt's house.

Vogel climbed the three slate steps in front of Wiley's front door and rang the bell.

The door opened after a moment, and the same uniformed housemaid let him in.

I hit a speed-dial button on my phone, which connected to the phone number on the SIM card in the infinity transmitter. It didn't ring. After a few seconds, I could hear faint voices. Then I heard the maid's voice.

"Wiley will be right down. May I bring you some coffee or tea?"

"Coffee would be great." A booming baritone.

"Please have a seat. Mrs. Wiley likes to sit in that chair, so maybe the one next to it?"

Then, much louder, Vogel's voice: "Thank you, ma'am."

Then silence.

At the same time, I kept watch on the white Escalade. The driver was talking on a cell phone. I hadn't expected a driver. This was too bad, because I'd brought a GPS tracker to affix to the car, and now I wouldn't have a chance.

Then I heard Ellen Wiley's voice, also loud and clear. "Mister Vogel, I'm Ellen Wiley."

"Nice to meet you. Tom Vogel."

"Stephen speaks very highly of Centurion."

"He's a valued client. My card."

"Oh, metal! How clever. You could cut yourself with this thing."

"It doubles as a self-defense tool," Vogel said, and the two of them laughed.

I couldn't see the license plate on the Escalade, so I studied the rear exterior for any markings that would help me later on. There didn't seem to be any. The vehicle looked new. There were no scuff marks or dents, as far as I could tell at this distance. No stickers or decals. Non-tinted windows.

Wiley and Vogel talked. He asked about her homes, and she told him about her art collection. He asked her about any thefts she might have sustained. "We're not like any other security firm you might have heard about," Vogel said. "There are plenty of good security and guarding firms—Triple Canopy, Aegis Defence Services, Pinkerton, Securitas—any of the top-tier ones. Well, we do VIP protection, but we're different. The thing you've got to understand is—we take care of problems. You want security guards? Hire security guards. You want a rent-a-cop? Rent a cop. We're not about patrolling a beat. You get me? We play offense, not defense. We don't stand at a wall and protect you from trouble. We make the trouble go away. It's a very . . . specialized skill set. If you've talked to your friend Brookhiser, then I assume you have some sense of what we deliver. Problem *solving*. Taking care of issues so they don't . . . exist anymore. And if I'm talking myself out of a job, so be it. It is what it is. What we do, it isn't for everyone. Not everybody has the need for it. Not everybody has the *stomach* for it, frankly. Mrs. Wiley, tell me this is making you the slightest bit uncomfortable, and I'll leave you in peace right now. This meet never happened."

After thirty-five minutes, Vogel emerged from Wiley's front door. I watched him descend the three steps and walk the seventy-five feet to the white Escalade and get in. Vogel and his driver chatted for about a minute. Then the Escalade pulled away from the curb and began making its way down N Street.

And I began to follow.

65

The trickiest part of a mobile surveillance is the very beginning. Start rolling too soon and the vehicle you're following will make you. You'll be burned even before you start. On the other hand, take too long to roll and you risk losing the target.

I'd waited until the Escalade was almost at the end of the block before moving. It turned right onto Thirtieth Street, and I followed. Thirtieth Street was two-way but narrow, with cars parked on either side. I tried to hang back, but even after slowing my speed, the Escalade was waiting at a long light at M Street. I pulled up immediately behind it.

I had no choice.

Now I'd have to disappear from view at some point soon.

I noticed the vehicle's Virginia license plate and snapped a quick picture of it on my phone. Then the light turned green and the Escalade turned left, without signaling.

M Street is fairly heavily trafficked, or was at that time of day. I turned left, too, and saw the Escalade up ahead. I slowed, pulled over as if double-parking, and waited for a few cars to pull ahead of me. When I could still see the Escalade, I swung back into traffic.

For several blocks, heading east, I kept a few cars between me and Vogel. We went over a bridge that spanned Rock Creek Parkway, taking us out of Georgetown and into the West End. The Escalade bore right onto Pennsylvania Avenue. I did, too, several cars behind, and soon we came to Washington Circle at Twenty-fourth Street, with George Washington University Hospital on the right. Traffic circles were a good place to lose a tail.

But the Escalade did not appear to be trying to lose me, which suggested that Vogel's driver didn't realize I was following. Which was good.

Washington Circle has traffic lights at every corner, which is annoying. Theoretically they're synced, but nobody knows what they're synced to.

In fact, Washington, DC, was deliberately designed to make it difficult for an invading army to move quickly from one side of the city to another, and to this day the traffic reflects that. Now a black Jeep was the only vehicle between us. That was fine with me. It provided cover.

At Nineteenth Street we bore left onto H Street, along with the rest of the traffic, because Pennsylvania Avenue is now closed to traffic in front of the White House. The White House was visible on my right, through Lafayette Park. On the left were St. John's Church and the Hay-Adams Hotel.

So far the surveillance was going smoothly.

Then, on H Street, an SUV barreled out of a parking garage immediately in front of me, without braking or signaling. I slammed on the brakes and cursed the guy. Living in Boston, I'm used to bad, or aggressive, drivers, but this was a close call. I veered around the SUV just in time to see the white Escalade turning left onto New York Avenue. I made it through the next set of traffic lights, but just barely. We passed the old Greyhound bus terminal, still recognizable even though it was undergoing construction to become an office building, like just about every other building in that part of town.

As we passed Twelfth Street, we entered Washington's small Chinatown. The FedEx Office sign was half in Chinese, though not many Chinese people lived here anymore. When the light turned green, the Escalade jogged left on Sixth Street, then right on K. I maintained a good distance from Vogel's vehicle, with two cars between us. I could afford to stay that far back as long as the Escalade was going straight.

I began to wonder where Vogel was going. We'd passed through the part of the city that most people consider downtown, which was the likeliest location for an office, I figured. Now we were entering a sketchier area. On the north side was Capitol Hill. I wondered if Vogel was heading to the Capitol, maybe to the Senate or House office buildings. But the white SUV kept going, into Northeast, still a few car lengths ahead of me. I still hadn't been made, as far as I could tell.

Then the Escalade came to a traffic light as it was turning yellow. It barreled right through the intersection, and the Audi right in front of me braked.

I was trapped on the wrong side of the light. The Escalade kept going straight.

On my right was a Citgo station, situated right at the southeast corner of the intersection. I swung into the gas station, cut through the lot, turned left and then right, and I was able to catch a glimpse of a white vehicle halfway up the block. I accelerated, wove through traffic, and confirmed that it was Vogel's Escalade.

We were driving through a landscape of liquor stores and car dealers and gas stations. The Escalade turned left on Franklin Street, and I followed, apprehensive. This was a lightly trafficked street in Brookland, the neighborhood around Catholic University. Even though I slowed to keep a good distance between us, I was still immediately behind them.

I didn't understand why Vogel's driver wasn't taking evasive measures. How could he not have detected me by now? I'd followed them for miles through the city.

Either he wasn't any good—not operationally skilled— or he wasn't looking for a tail. Which was sloppy. Maybe the Centurions' reputation for black-ops expertise was just overblown.

I passed by a block of connected brick row houses, each painted a different color. I followed the Escalade as it turned onto Rhode Island Avenue, which was heavily trafficked. I was relieved, because the traffic would provide cover. I let the Escalade get a few hundred feet ahead of me and watched it turn left onto Reed Street, which was small and not at all busy.

I hesitated. If I turned there, too, I'd be made right away. I'd already pushed my luck almost beyond the breaking point. Vogel's driver still apparently hadn't noticed me.

Unless he had.

And this was his attempt at a kind of countersurveillance called "dry-cleaning." And he was waiting for me to turn left onto Reed Street—at which point he'd have flushed me out.

Or maybe this was a trap.

So I had a decision to make. Abandon the tail outright, which seemed foolish after coming this far. Or keep at it, and risk a confrontation, possibly armed. Those were the only choices I could see.

I turned slowly into the narrow street. Just in time to see the Escalade turning left again, a few hundred feet away.

I accelerated up the street and then stopped at the point where the Escalade had turned. It wasn't a street so much as an alley, a cul-de-sac. On either side, a row of brick warehouses, hulking and dismal. Many of the windows looked broken. Some of the warehouse units appeared to be abandoned. But maybe not all of them. The Escalade had parked most of the way down the street, on the left. I saw Vogel and his driver get out of the vehicle and enter the last entrance to the warehouse row. Just before entering, Vogel glanced around.

The fact that the driver didn't remain in the car told me this was probably not a business meeting. Was this, then, Centurion headquarters, in this mostly abandoned warehouse building?

It seemed possible. If not headquarters, then at least some kind of rendezvous location, and it bore closer inspection.

I parked the car on Reed Street. There were no other cars in the alley; driving down the cul-de-sac and then parking there would be risky. Approaching by foot would be risky, too. But less so.

With the scope I examined the section of the building that Vogel and his driver had just entered. No movement that I could detect. Still, I waited about fifteen minutes. No other cars approached. No one else came in or out.

Curtis Schmidt's Glock was loaded—I'd bought a couple of boxes of ammo at a gun shop in McLean—but out of force of habit I checked again. Jacketed hollow-point ammo to increase the odds of stopping them. Then I pulled out my shirt and stuck the pistol under my belt, under my shirttails, and got out of the car.

I started out walking along the row of warehouses, keeping close to the brick wall, approaching slowly. When I reached the doorway to the last warehouse, I stopped, kept still, listened.

The distant low murmur of voices from within told me there were at least two men inside, Vogel and his driver. Maybe there were others, but at least the two.

Given the element of surprise, I could easily handle

two. More I could handle, just not as easily. After all, I wanted only to talk to Thomas Vogel.

I pulled out the pistol and, holding it in a two-handed grip, swiveled around to the entrance until I faced all the way in, the weapon at low-ready.

No one there.

Up six steps to a black-painted solid metal door. I stopped, listened. I heard the voices again, somewhat more distinctly. Shifting the gun to my right hand, I pulled the lever to the door. Very slowly. It moved; it was unlocked.

Now there was no turning back.

I made a split-second decision. The front doors of most homes swing inward, but the entry doors in most public buildings swing outward. For fast egress in case of fire. It's common fire-safety building code.

So with one violent movement I yanked the door open, the pistol trained on the area to my right.

I was looking at an office room of some kind, plain and functional. I processed the details at once: a metal receptionist's desk with a computer on it, a coat tree, a few chairs, gray wall-to-wall carpeting.

And on my left, a guy with a gun.

Pointed at me.

"Freeze," he said.

Now I understood.

66

I stood still, the Glock I'd confiscated pointed at the guy.

His weapon was a semiautomatic pistol as well. It was matte black and looked like a Glock, too. He was a young guy, in his twenties, with a military haircut, high and tight. He was holding his pistol two-handed, his grip and stance expert. But he looked tense. He was blinking rapidly.

I didn't like that. A tense guy with a gun could easily do stupid stuff.

"Put the gun down," he said. His voice was high and strained.

"You first," I said.

I was cursing myself for doing this without backup, a team, without at least one other guy. That had been both sloppy and arrogant. Or maybe I was simply being driven by my anger, which made me careless. Because I'd just walked right into a trap.

He blinked some more. "I mean it." There was a slight quaver in his voice. "Put the gun down."

"Or what?" I said.

I heard a door behind me open, and in my peripheral vision I could make out a human shape. I shifted my eyes to the right, keeping the pistol trained on the tense guy.

Without turning my head I couldn't see the new guy clearly, but I could make out enough to know he had a gun pointed at me, too.

"Drop the gun," the second guy said in a deep voice. He didn't sound nervous.

I calculated my odds. They weren't favorable. But it was the first guy, the anxious guy, that worried me. He was likely to have an itchy trigger finger. He looked like he wanted to shoot someone. That someone being me.

I didn't really have a choice, or at least not one that would end with me alive. I lowered Curtis Schmidt's Glock and then dropped it onto the floor, where it clattered loudly.

The two men moved in toward me, weapons still pointed, their movements coordinated. I turned to my right, finally able to look at the second guy. I recognized him as Vogel's driver. A man of multiple talents. He was pointing a semiautomatic at me, too, a Glock 26. I wondered where all the Glocks were coming from, whether there'd been a big sale, and then I remembered that Glocks were the Metropolitan Police Department's weapon of choice. Their service weapon was the Glock 17, probably the most popular law-enforcement pistol in the world. Off-duty, MPD cops were allowed to carry a Glock 26, the so-called baby Glock.

This guy looked around ten years older than the first guy, a little beefier, with black hair that was short but not military-short. He pointed a finger at the nervous guy and said, "Cover me." Then he slid his pistol into a holster on his right hip.

Coming closer to me he pulled out of his back pocket some long pieces of white plastic. Flex-cuffs. Disposable restraints. They were planning to cuff me, not kill me. Unless I struggled with the second guy. Then the itchy-trigger-finger guy would get to pull the trigger.

Therefore struggling was probably not a good idea.

"Front or back?" I said to the driver.

"Huh?"

"You want my hands in front or behind?"

"Behind. Let's make this easy."

"That's my plan," I said.

The driver came closer still and said, "Back up a couple of steps."

I did, and then he reached down and picked up the Glock. Then he set it down on a corner of the metal desk.

"Turn around."

I did.

I put my hands behind my back, wrists together.

"Palms outward."

I turned my hands. I felt him bind my wrists with a flex-cuff, then cinch it tight. I was a bit surprised they were using ordinary zip ties and not the law-enforcement-grade ones. YouTube was full of videos showing how to get out of zip-tie restraints.

Then he pointed to a metal chair nearby and said, "Sit, please."

It was the sort of chair that was made out of aluminum and manufactured by the hundreds of thousands during World War II for navy warships. Rustproof, non-magnetic, lightweight, and made to survive torpedo blasts. Now you see them in prisons and in chic restaurants.

I sat in the chair, my hands sticking out through the open back. He pulled out some more zip ties and looped each ankle to a chair leg. I think he even zip-tied my wrist restraints to eye-bolts under the seat. So much for YouTube videos. Getting out of this situation would take some time.

"All right," the guy said. "No trouble."

"I get it."

"Okay." He signaled to the first guy, who slowly lowered his weapon.

"Wait here."

He left the room. I looked at the first guy, who'd stayed behind. He was still holding his weapon, but down at his side. He glowered at me as if I were a stray dog that might be rabid, and he kept his distance. He didn't want to get close.

About a minute later a tall, bald guy with a shaved head and cauliflower ears limped into the room.

I smiled when I realized who it was.

Curtis Schmidt was wearing jeans and a black sweat-shirt. On his left knee was a complicated-looking ortho-pedic brace with buckles and hinges and Velcro straps. He had a gun holstered on his hip. His deep-set eyes glittered when he saw me.

I'm fairly sure he smiled, too.

He approached, limping, both fists balled.

"You're not seriously going to hit a guy who's tied up, are you?" I said.

He took a few steps closer.

"Isn't that cheating?" I said. "How about we make this even and you—"

Schmidt assumed a boxer's stance, his hobbled left leg forward, his right foot back, pivoting. His elbows in, his left hand up by his chin, he threw a right cross directly from his chin to my abdomen.

My adrenaline surged, and in that moment, every-thing slowed down.

I saw his fist coming at my stomach and I knew I had to relax my abdominal muscles, not tense them. I ex-haled sharply through my mouth at the same instant that his fist slammed into my stomach. Schmidt grunted loudly.

The pain was staggering.

Everything went white and sparkly. I gasped. For a long moment I couldn't breathe. My diaphragm spasmed, paralyzed.

I heard Schmidt chuckle.

When I finally was able to draw air into my lungs, I panted a few times. Then I said, "That all you got?"

But it came out in a high whisper, almost inaudible. Schmidt couldn't make out what I was trying to say.

He leaned in, close enough that I could smell his rank breath. "Huh?"

I whispered again, "That all you got?"

But it was still hard to understand, and he cocked his head, moving in close, listening, smiling. "Trying to say something, Heller?"

What I did next required every last bit of my remaining strength, and there wasn't much of it left.

I clenched my teeth, tucked in my chin, stiffened my neck muscles. Leaned back and abruptly snapped my head forward, crashing the crown of my head into his nose.

The crunch was audible.

All of a sudden there was blood everywhere. Blood streamed down his face as if someone had opened a faucet. It was a curtain of blood. He roared with pain and staggered backward, then crashed to the ground, his left leg straight out like a toppled bowling pin.

His hands flew to his face. He screamed, surprisingly high in pitch. Sprawled on the ground, he howled in pain, but I think it was something more than pain. It was humiliation.

Then he drew his Glock and, as he crabbed unsteadily to his feet, he pointed it at me.

The door opened and a second later I heard a voice barking: "Stand down, Schmitty!"

It was Thomas Vogel. He was still wearing his navy suit and red tie, and it looked like he'd freshened up. With his gray-flecked black hair, parted sharply on his left side, and his brushy mustache, he looked officious. He could have been a maître d' at an expensive restaurant or the manager of a Mercedes dealership. But there was something in his swagger, something about his barrel-chested physique that bespoke the confidence of some-one physically imposing, someone who was used to getting his way.

Schmidt lowered his gun at once. His left hand gripped his ruined nose. The blood kept flowing.

"Can I have the room, please?" Vogel said. His voice reverberated, adenoidal and powerful.

He looked at me, shaking his head slightly, while the two men exited, Schmidt trailing blood. Vogel looked amused and maybe a little embarrassed.

When the door closed, he said, "My apologies. I really should send Schmitty to anger-management school."

I had a headache, and I was still finding it hard to get air in my lungs.

"So you're Nick Heller," he said.

"I'd shake your hand but . . ." I managed to say.

"I know all about you. You're an interesting guy."

I took a few shallow breaths, the best I could do.

"A man of paradoxes, I'd say. I'm familiar with your army records. I know what you did at Kunduz. The blood on your hands." He shook his head again, and I couldn't tell whether it was with disapproval or admiration.

He was talking about an episode in my past that I never discussed and preferred to forget.

"You do what you have to do," he said. "You under-stand that, I can tell."

"What do you want?"

"Just a little talk. We're both busy men. We'll keep this brief."

"Okay. How about getting these cuffs off me?"

He nodded. "Sure. Soon." He scuffed the toe of his brown calfskin brogue at the edge of a little creek of blood that was already starting to dry. "You know, in our line of work, there's the sheep and there's the shepherds. Guys like us, we're the shepherds. We take care of the sheep. We protect them and make sure they live quiet, safe lives. Isn't that really what they pay us for?"

I looked at him and said nothing.

He went on, "You and me, we don't have an issue here. You may think we do, but we don't. We're like Germany and France—mortal enemies during the Second World War, and a few years later they're trading partners. History of the world."

"Do you have a point?"

He smiled. "We may do things differently, you and me, but ultimately we're on the same side. The problem comes when clients—civilians—distract us. Set us against each other. There's no reason for us to be at each other's throats."

"Is that right."

"Look, Heller, you have your soft targets. We both know that."

I just looked at him.

"There's that woman who works for you, Dorothy something. There's that nephew you're really close to.

The reporter from Slander Sheet. Hell, there's even your mother, back in Boston. Soft targets."

"Don't even think about it, Vogel."

"Man, I hate like hell to be talking like this. We should be working together, what I'm saying. Keeping the sheep safe."

"Uh-huh."

"You don't want to be on the wrong side of me, Heller. We work this out, same time next year I'll be sending you clients."

"Uh-huh."

"We don't? Get yourself a black suit. You'll be going to a lot of funerals."

His cell phone rang, and he took it out of his pocket. "Vogel," he said. "Yeah. Got it. I'm on my way." He turned around, called out, "Rafferty, let's go." Then to me he said, "I'm sorry, I've got a meeting."

He took out one of his metallic business cards and slid it into my shirt pocket. He waved vaguely at me, at the chair and the zip ties and everything. "We'll give you some time to think it over."

67

For a long time I sat there, zip-tied to the aluminum chair, thinking.

Vogel had left me alone in the empty warehouse, probably figuring that it would take me most of the day to get free. Maybe several days. I'd been bound with an excess of zip ties, one looped to another, which made it particularly challenging.

Not impossible, though.

Or so I told myself.

Unfortunately, I couldn't use Vogel's metallic business card, since I couldn't reach my shirt pocket. I looked around the room, poring over the metal desk and coat tree and floor, looking for scissors or knives or anything sharp. The desk had a drawer, and that demanded a closer look. So how to move around? My ankles were zip-tied to the front chair legs. I shifted my feet and discovered I had a little bit of play. Enough for me to lift my heels and push against the ground with my toes. That moved the chair only a few inches, though, and I had twelve or fifteen feet to travel to the desk drawer. But it was something. The journey of a thousand miles . . .

A kind of dazed calm settled over me, like a blanketing fog. A very useful sort of calm. Once I was helping my nephew, Gabe, assemble a fiendishly complicated play-set model of a hospital, and he cried out in frustration. That was when I taught him how to let the calm wash over you, and to focus on one piece at a time, breathing in and out, placid, *calm*. It probably took the two of us three hours to assemble this damned hospital, but high-strung, short-tempered Gabe stayed with it, and when the hospital was finished, he glowed with pride. So whenever he was faced with something perplexing and intricate, a physics problem set or a difficult math assignment, I would say to him, "Remember the hospital," and he'd instantly smile and nod, as if to say, *I got this*. When I'd see him about to blow his stack over an impossible jigsaw puzzle, I'd just say "hospital," and he'd smile and nod and try harder.

Now I said to myself *hospital,* and I smiled. I can do this. It'll be arduous and slow, but I can do this. I made myself enter the zone. *Calm*. I lifted my heels, pushed off with my toes, scraped the chair legs another two inches closer to the desk drawer. Two down, one hundred and seventy-eight to go.

My cell phone rang in my pocket.

As I slow-scuttled along the floor, the phone ringing, I worked on my hands. They were looped to each other at the wrists, and then each loop was connected to the chair's vertical struts. If you thrust in a downward direction with enough force, you can snap the cable tie's locking head and free yourself. But that wasn't an option.

Lift heel, press toes, and shove. Another two inches closer. Nothing was impossible. *Hospital.*

I had to get the hell out of here.

The phone continued to ring. I counted thirteen rings, and then it stopped for a moment, and then it started to ring again. Insistently, it seemed. Someone was trying to reach me with some urgency. Mandy? Dorothy?

Only then did it occur to me that my fingers were free to wiggle and move, and that was something.

Working by feel alone, I tugged at one of the cable ties with my fingers, a loop that connected the loop around my wrists to one of the struts. I was able to pull it around so that its locking head was nearest my fingers.

Now I inserted a fingernail into the tiny plastic box that forms the lock. Inside that little box is a pawl, a pivoting bar that engages with the notched end of the strap and locks it in place, keeps it from moving. With my fingernail I was able to pry the pawl upward to release the tension. Then, tugging with my fingers, I loosened the cuff, pulling and pulling until the end of the strap came loose.

Success! It felt like a major victory, like winning an Olympic gold medal. I didn't think about the fact that my wrists were still tightly bound together and my ankles were still looped onto the chair legs. That was negative thinking and wouldn't help me. Focus on one tiny victory at a time. *Hospital.*

The phone stopped ringing.

I crabbed the chair along the floor toward the desk drawer, another couple of inches.

Now I was able to grab the other loop with my scuttling fingers, pulling it around until I grasped the locking head, then I probed it with the fingernail of my middle finger until I felt the little locking bar. I pushed it up with my fingernail while, with the fingers of my other hand, I tugged at the strap and managed to pull it loose. My hands, though bound, were now free to range around behind my back. That was something.

Get the hell out of here.

I scraped a few inches more. I looked at the desk drawer and wondered what implement it might contain. Maybe scissors, maybe a sharp letter opener, maybe even fingernail clippers. Anything that could cut through the nylon straps and free me. Even a paper clip would be useful.

Eventually—it may have been another three quarters of an hour—I was close enough to the desk that, by thrusting my hands back and over, I was able to grab hold of the center drawer's handle and yank it open a foot or so. Slowly I turned around to look.

And the drawer was empty.

I cursed aloud.

I was frustrated and annoyed and out of ideas. The best I could hope for was that someone would come along, one of the Centurions, and I could attempt to strike a deal.

Then I noticed something interesting. The corner of

the metal drawer came to a sharp edge. It was a design flaw, and no doubt it had, over the years, inflicted countless injuries upon anyone bumping into the open drawer.

But sharp edges were good.

I shoved the chair back another couple of inches. Finally the backs of my wrists rested against the steel drawer and I slowly maneuvered my hands around until a length of nylon strap rested against the sharp burr. Then I moved my hands back and forth, back and forth, rubbing against the burr. I continued like this for maybe two minutes more, the steel edge abrading the nylon, until the strap had been worn through enough that I was able to jerk my wrists apart and snap the plastic strap open, and my hands were free.

I pulled them out from behind my back and massaged each hand with the other until the numbness began to recede. Then I reached down and pried open the locking bar on each loop around my ankle. Pulled each zip tie open.

Then I stood up. Free. And as I reached into my pocket to retrieve my phone it started ringing again.

Mandy.

I answered it.

"Oh, thank *God*," she said. "You're there. Where *are* you?"

I told her. "Where are you?" I asked.

Another call was coming through now. Washington MPD homicide. I let it go to voice mail.

"On my way to talk to that retired police detective. Remember—?"

"Wait. Meet me back at the hotel. We've got to talk."

"After I've talked with him."

"No. Before. Now."

"Why?"

"Because it's not safe," I said.

"Heller, I . . . Okay, thanks." And she ended the call.

68

I had three voice mails on my phone: from Mandy, from Dorothy, and from Balakian, the hipster cop I'd started to think of as Kombucha. I'd already talked to Mandy, and I knew that if there was anything urgent, Dorothy would have texted me. So as I pulled the silver Chrysler into traffic on Rhode Island Avenue, I called Kombucha back.

"There you are. Heller, we need to talk."

"I'm kind of busy. What's this about?"

A pause. "We may have a suspect."

"Who is it?"

"We need to talk," he repeated.

"Give me an hour."

"Sooner if you can, please."

"Okay. Homicide branch in Southwest?"

"Uh, no. Let's not meet at headquarters."

"Okay." Strange, I thought. "Who's the suspect?"

"We can talk about that when we get together," he said. "The sooner the better."

Kombucha was maddeningly cryptic. It occurred to me, fleetingly, that the suspect he had in mind was me. But he wouldn't handle it this way, with a polite request to come in. He'd have shown up at my hotel with a squad of officers.

Then what questions could he possibly have? And why did he not want to meet at police headquarters?

Back at the hotel suite, I arrived to find Dorothy beavering away on her laptop. She was wearing jeans and a blouse in a deep shade of oxblood. Her fingernails were the same color. Her bracelets rattled as her fingers flew across the keyboard.

"Where's Mandy?" I said.

"I think she's at her apartment," she said, not looking up. "She called me looking for you."

"Shit." I'd asked her to meet me at the hotel, where I could feel confident she was safe.

"Hey, what happened to you?" she said, staring at me. "My God."

"I had a disagreement with one of the Centurions. Name of Curtis Schmidt."

"Can I get you something?"

"I'll grab some Advil. I'm okay."

"You wanted me to find Thomas Vogel's home address."

"You got it?"

"It's a hell of a thing. No, I can't find it."

"That's impossible. He's got to live somewhere."

"There's one Thomas Vogel in Virginia, and he's not the one. Three in Maryland. None of them is an ex-MPD cop."

"He has to own a house or an apartment. A mortgage, a lease, utilities—you've checked all the usual places?"

"Nick, give me a little credit."

"Sorry."

"I assume his house is in the name of some corporation. The guy's a ghost."

"He's got to have a PO box somewhere."

"Probably, but I can't find it."

"I have his phone number. On his business card."

"Then you have more than me."

I handed her the metal card. She looked at it, then typed some more. After a few seconds, she said, "Nothing."

I looked for a phone number on my phone, then touched the number and the phone started dialing.

"Garvin."

"Art, Nick Heller again. I'm looking for Thomas Vogel's address."

"The man himself?"

"We're not turning up anything on the Internet."

"Doesn't surprise me. He keeps a very low profile."

"Why?"

"The story he puts out is that the narcos he busted have friends who want to track him down and give him his own personal retirement package. So he keeps himself unfindable."

"The department must have a good address for him somewhere."

"Don't count on it."

"Can you look?"

"I'll look. No promises."

"Thanks."

I ended the call, gave Dorothy a glance, shook my head. "That was my retired detective friend, Art Garvin. Doesn't look good."

"I'm not giving up."

I hit the speed-dial number on my phone for Mandy Seeger.

"Nick," she answered. "You back at the hotel?"

"But you're not here."

"I had work to do. Where my work stuff is. My little home office."

"I need you to transport your work stuff over here. Just until we're done."

"How do you define done?"

"Until we get an arrest in Kayla's murder." I thought, *If Kombucha was on the right track, that could be soon.* But I didn't want to tell her yet. Not until I talked to Kombucha.

"I think you and I are working on different things. I want to know who was behind this Claflin hoax that snared me. Who hired the Centurions."

"We may never know that."

"Speak for yourself."

I smiled with admiration. "Listen. I don't think it's safe for you to be out there investigating."

"Safe? Who's talking about safe? I didn't go into this line of work to be safe."

I heaved a long sigh. I thought: *soft target.* That was the phrase Vogel had used. *Guys like us, we take care of the sheep. We protect them and make sure they live quiet, safe lives.*

"I don't think you understand what I'm saying," I said. "Vogel's people have already killed one person, and I honestly don't think they'll hesitate to kill another one if they decide they need to."

She was silent for a few seconds. "And you think they're following me?"

"It wouldn't surprise me. I'll bet they've set up trip-wires out there. Certain people, if you go and visit them, talk to them, a wire gets tripped, a bell goes off some-where, and the Centurions go into action."

"It doesn't sound like you to admit defeat."

"I'm not. I'm not giving up." I hesitated, and then said it: "I'm talking about you. I can take care of myself."

"About me."

"Right."

"Is this—Heller, is this because of last night?"

"Of course not. It's because you've been at the center of this thing since the beginning, which makes it danger-ous for you if you stick your head up." But was it, at least in part, about last night? I couldn't ignore what I felt for her. That had to factor in. Would I be as protective of her if we hadn't been intimate? I didn't know. Maybe not.

But I knew what I knew, and I knew that Vogel's people were dangerous and probably knew no limits, and that she was a soft target.

"Nick, I've been threatened before. But in the end, you don't go after a journalist. You don't kill a reporter. That just doesn't happen."

I happened to know for a fact that she was wrong. I knew of several journalists who were killed investigating big financial scandals. I hesitated, considered whether to say anything, and finally said, "It does happen, Mandy. It has happened, and it could happen. Don't be foolish."

"Jesus, Heller. Now you're trying to scare me off?"

I was afraid she'd take it this way. Telling her about a genuine threat to her life was making her even more defiant.

"Let me pick you up. You can do whatever work you want to do here."

"No."

"All right, look. If you really insist on interviewing people, at least let me go with you."

"Are you serious? Like I need a bodyguard?"

"Would my presence be that odious to you?"

She laughed.

I said, "Think of it as teaming up."

"No, you know how I think of it? You want to chaperone me everywhere like I'm some Saudi woman, that's what it is. It's ridiculous. And I don't want any part of that."

"At the very least will you agree to work over here?"

"Yes. I'll do that for you."

"Great, let me pick you up."

"No need. I'll be over there soon. When I'm ready."

"Okay," I said, because I knew it wouldn't do any good to push it further. No sense in being overbearing. "I'll see you over here."

Looking back on that day, it pains me to admit that I should have been more insistent, more overbearing, refused to take no for an answer.

Unfortunately, I didn't.

69

A rt Garvin called me back about an hour later.

"All the MPD has on Tom Vogel is a PO box."

"Where?"

"Thurmont, Maryland."

"Shit. No street address?"

"No. Nothing. Buddy of mine who used to hang out some with Vogel says he built his house himself. He's some kind of gifted carpenter. It's big—he called it a compound. It's out in the woods, sort of a remote location."

I thanked him and hung up. Half an hour later, I met Balakian at a hipster coffee shop on H Street in a part of Northeast called the Atlas District. Indie rock on the speakers, exposed brick, and not a lot of seating. He was already at a table drinking something light brown in a bottle. I ordered black coffee, which seemed to disappoint the bearded barista, who probably wanted to draw a fern pattern in the foam of a cappuccino.

"Kombucha?" I said with a smile as I sat down with my coffee. I could smell the skunky odor of rotten oranges wafting from his cup, and I wrinkled my nose.

"Don't knock it till you've tried it," he said. He was wearing a tweedy checked jacket with a vest and a dark blue shirt and a scarf around his neck. "So, dude, I owe you an apology."

"Oh yeah?"

"We found a print."

"Where?"

"On a piece of broken glass."

"The wineglass?"

He nodded. "I went back to the MCL and asked them to look for prints, just in case. So they took the broken pieces of the wineglass from the bathroom and processed them in the superglue fuming chamber. Pulled up a couple of partials and ran 'em through NGI." NGI, for Next Generation Identification Program, was the turbocharged successor to the old national criminal fingerprint database, IAFIS.

"And you got a match."

"Right."

"Who?"

"One of ours. A retired MPD sergeant named Richard Rasmussen."

I shrugged. I'd never heard the name before. "Let me guess. He works for Centurion Associates."

He scratched his little beard and sipped his drink. He said nothing. My phone vibrated in my pocket.

"You have a print on what could be the murder weapon," I said. "Isn't that enough? Did you bring him in for questioning yet?"

"I think it's enough. I wrote out an affidavit. It's on my lieutenant's desk."

"When does it become an arrest warrant?"

"The lieutenant has to approve it, then it goes to the US attorney's office, then it goes before a judge."

"So you might not get an arrest warrant after all."

"Might not. Anyway, I'm still circling. Part of the reason why I wanted to talk to you."

"What do you want to know? I mean, I don't know the guy—never heard his name before."

"You're doing sort of a parallel investigation. What's your take on how it went down?"

"My take? The girl was paid to make a false accusation against Justice Jeremiah Claflin. To claim they had a sexual relationship."

"Paid by the Centurions?"

"That I don't know. I don't think so."

"Then paid by whom?"

"I'm working on that. She said it was an 'organization of businessmen' that paid her, that's all she knew."

"Go ahead."

"I think the Centurions were brought in at first to protect her, to keep her from talking to anyone. Then to deal with her. First they tried to get her out of Washington, but I got in the way. They were afraid she'd start talking to me, I assume. She'd become a problem that had to be eliminated."

"So why did she start talking in the first place?"

"I asked her questions. That was how it started. And she was scared. Maybe she felt bad about what she'd done. She had a conscience. Or maybe it wasn't conscience at all. Maybe she was just scared she'd been caught in a falsehood. Whatever the reason, she started talking, and she had to be silenced."

"And they staged it to look like a suicide."

"Not too badly either. It convinced you for a while, right?" My phone kept vibrating. "Any luck on the call she placed from the room phone?"

"Yeah. She called a friend. I guess she just wanted to talk. She was scared."

"And when she opened the door, at nine thirty-six?"

"Who knows. Rasmussen, probably. Maybe he said it was hotel security. Or the night manager. Or any of a number of things he could have said to get her to open the door. But open it she did. Then he left at ten twenty-five, when he was done."

He took another sip of the vile brew. I pulled out the phone and glanced at it. Mandy.

"If you have Rasmussen's print," I said, "why are you still circling? Why not at least bring the guy in for questioning?"

"Frankly, because I'm getting heat."

"From . . . ?"

"My bosses. My sergeant wants this case closed—he

doesn't want me to keep stirring it up. He doesn't want another murder on the books. I'm facing a lot of ridicule for persisting."

"So why are you?"

"It's . . . something just doesn't feel right about this case."

"Is that why you wanted to meet outside police headquarters?"

"I don't know. Maybe. I don't know how . . . extensive the Centurions' reach is."

"Within homicide branch."

He nodded, looked away for a beat. "There's a reason why I caught this case. And just me, solo."

"Why's that?"

"Because I'm a novice. They didn't expect me to push too hard. They knew I wouldn't make waves. And they could hang me out to dry if it came to that."

"And who's 'they'?"

He shook his head. "I know how it sounds. Paranoid or something. But . . . here's the thing. Somewhere between the lab and evidence control at the property division, the evidence got 'misplaced.'"

"The shards of glass?"

"Right." He opened both his hands, turned them up. "No one can locate it."

"How often does that happen—that crucial evidence gets 'lost'?"

"Once in a while."

"Not very often, I expect. Does that screw the case?"

"It's a problem, but not devastating. The shards were

photographed on the scene and the fingerprints were re-
covered and kept separately. If it goes to court, the defense will probably raise a stink, but it shouldn't make a
difference."

"So why are you still pushing? Didn't you get the
memo? The case is closed. It was a suicide."

He shrugged, shook his head. "It's not right."

"You know the name Thomas Vogel?"

"Of course. The Centurions."

My phone vibrated again. I took it out. It was Mandy.
"Do you mind?"

"Go ahead."

I answered it. "Hey, Mandy."

"Heller," she said. "I've got something."

I heard traffic noise in the background. "Where are
you?"

"Southeast. Anacostia. I just talked to that old cop."

"Mandy, I told you, I don't want you out there—"

But she spoke right over me. "Remember the retired
police detective in Southeast? This old guy who says he
covered up a homicide years ago?" I remembered: the
story she was investigating just before the Kayla story
broke, about some big-name Washington player. "Well,
you were right. And now I understand why I had to be
discredited. With that phony Claflin story."

"The homicide—who was it?"

She told me.

"Holy shit," I said.

"Hey," she said, her voice suddenly loud and sharp.
"Excuse me, what do you think you're—?"

"Mandy, you okay?"

"Hey!" she shouted. The phone made funny jumbled, crunchy sounds, as if it was hitting the ground.

"Mandy? Hello?"

But there was no reply.

70

I called Mandy back repeatedly, but each time it went right to voice mail, as if the phone had been shut off.

Something had happened to her.

Balakian was looking at me, alarmed. "Huh?" he said. "What's going on, Heller?"

I explained. "I'm going to need your help," I said. "I need you to ping her phone. I don't have the resources to do that."

"Man," he said. He shook his head, looked rattled. "I can do that, sure. But what if the phone's off? Or smashed?"

"That's possible. So at least we'll find out where it was last located. Which tells us where she was abducted."

"Right."

"If we can get a fix on where she was grabbed, traffic cams or other CCTVs might have captured a license plate or a face or something."

"That seems unlikely."

"This is the best lead we have at the moment. But you've got to do it now."

He nodded. He took out his phone and dialed a number and asked for a Detective Ryan. After identifying himself, he read off Mandy's cell phone number. A minute later they had the name of her carrier, AT&T.

In the meantime I called Dorothy and filled her in. By the time I ended the call, Balakian had something.

"AT&T says the phone's not active. They can't ping it."

"Like you said, it was probably shut off or smashed. Do you have a last known location, at least?"

"The last call—when she was talking to you—hit a tower near the Anacostia metro station. Martin Luther King Junior Avenue and Howard Road, Southeast."

I nodded. "Good. Now, I have another number for you to ping, if possible." I took out the metal business card.

"Whose?"

"Thomas Vogel's," I said. I looked at the card and dialed the phone number.

It rang four or five times. Then: "Vogel."

"It's Heller. Your guys have Mandy Seeger. If anything happens to her, you know what I'm capable of."

"I don't know what you're talking about, Heller."

There was a click and the line went dead.

I thought a moment. It was possible that his guys had grabbed Mandy and hadn't yet had the opportunity to inform the boss. But he'd hung up so quickly that I couldn't help but wonder. If he really didn't know what I was talking about, he would have pursued the matter.

Asked me some questions. So it didn't make sense. He had to know they'd taken Mandy.

The answer came about a minute later. Balakian was talking to his contact in the department about Vogel's phone when I got a text message. It was a link, a URL. The sender was a phone number, not a name, and I was sure the number was spoofed. I clicked on the link, and it took me to a website called Disappearing Ink. In the middle of a blank white page was a red button that said DOWN-LOAD DISAPPEARING INK. It was an app. I clicked the red button, which took me to an iTunes page and another button, and soon I'd installed it on my phone. It appeared to be an encrypted text messaging service of some kind. I signed in using my e-mail address, and the number *1* popped up on top of the DISAPPEARING INK button on my phone. I had a message. I clicked on it. It was from "ShepherdBoy." I thought again of Vogel's remark: *Guys like us, we're the shepherds. We take care of the sheep.*

The message said:

We had a covenant, and you know the terms. Ms. Seeger was in violation. You stand down, including your friends, and you'll see her again.

I stared at it. Vogel wasn't going to admit on a phone call to having kidnapped Mandy. That could be used against him, legally. So why was he sending an incriminating text?

After about five seconds, the message disappeared, and

I understood why he wanted to communicate this way. His messages were sent securely and disappeared as soon as they were read. I typed back:

```
Deal. Release her now or I'll come
after you.
```

Then I hit SEND. I looked at Balakian. He was still talking on the phone, shaking his head and saying, "Is there another way to try?"

Another text message appeared in the Disappearing Ink app:

```
MS will be released when you return
home, to Boston. Not before.
```

I tried to take a screenshot, but that message disappeared as well. No wonder Vogel was being this explicit. Screenshots didn't work. Even if I managed to take a picture of my iPhone's screen, there'd be no way to pin it on him.

I looked up at Balakian. "Did you ping him?"

He shook his head. "That's not his cell phone number."

"What do you mean?"

"It's a VOIP software-based number. Like Google Voice."

"Not entirely following you."

"It's . . . we can only ping real cell phone numbers. This is a software-generated number."

"But you can trace it, right?"

"Not this one. It tracks to a Tor-sponsored service."

"Tor, the anonymous network?"

He nodded.

My understanding of Tor was pretty limited. I knew it was a network that lets you be anonymous on the Internet. Much beyond that, and I'm useless.

"He's also using a VPN service with it, which further complicates our ability to track that number. So as far as we can tell, it's a black box. No luck."

"You know technology. That's unusual for a cop."

He shrugged modestly. "A decent basic working knowledge, that's all. I'm no hacker, trust me. What'd you find out?"

"They have Mandy Seeger, and they're not releasing her until I go back to Boston."

"*What*? Let me see."

"There's nothing to show you. The texts have disappeared."

"Disappeared."

"We're dealing with Tom Vogel. He's a clever guy." I checked the Disappearing Ink app again and found nothing. I typed out another message to Vogel:

Got an offer for you.

I waited. A minute, a minute and a half.

Finally a reply came back:

Fold up your tent and go home, and MS
gets to return to her life. Persevere,
and her death will be on you.

I showed the message to Balakian. He stared at it, said, "Jesus!" and handed it back. By the time I went to look at it again, it had disappeared.

"Please keep me updated, in real time, on what you find on the traffic cameras in Anacostia," I said. "It may be our best chance to find her."

"Heller, I don't know how easy you think this is, but the tower location we have is approximate. She could have been anywhere within a square mile, maybe more. That covers a lot of cameras. We don't have that kind of manpower."

"Or time. Look, just start with the traffic cams. I need to get going."

"I'll see what I can do."

"Thanks. I'll be in touch. I have an idea."

71

Walter McGeorge, a.k.a. Merlin, was doing a sweeping job at a law firm in Alexandria when I reached him. He called me back an hour later, when I'd returned to the hotel.

"I thought you were never going to talk to me again," he said.

For a moment I'd forgotten what he was so sheepish about. Then I remembered about the burning paper in the strong room at the law firm, and the file he left behind. It felt like months ago.

"Come on. Screwing up is part of the job. Keeps it interesting."

"I feel terrible about what happened. I'm really sorry."

"Well, now's your chance to make it up to me."

"Yeah?"

"I'm going to need a bunch of gear. A miniature tracker." I explained. "Any hunting stores near you? I need a tranquilizer rifle or pistol and maybe ten darts. A kit'll cost you a couple thousand bucks—do you have the cash?"

"I can charge it on my credit card as long as you pay me back soon."

"No problem. Now, this'll be the hard part. A couple sticks of dynamite."

"Dynamite?"

"Either that or ammonium nitrate."

"It's getting really hard to buy ammonium nitrate. I don't know, man. They're both hard. Dynamite or ammonium nitrate, this is going to take me a couple of days."

"We don't have that."

"When do you need it by?"

"Noon tomorrow at the latest."

"Impossible."

"Okay," I said, ignoring him. "And a couple of electric blasting caps."

"Blasting caps?"

"Electric. And zip ties. The heavy-duty kind."

"Okay."

"A couple of five-gallon cans of gasoline."

"This is a goddamn Nick Heller scavenger hunt."

"And a weapon. Semiautomatic pistol, if you've got one to spare." Like the others in my Special Forces team—operational detachment Alpha, as the lingo has it—Merlin was comfortable around weapons and kept some in his home, though in reality I'm sure he never had call to use one.

"You care what caliber?"

"No."

"How about a Ruger Mark II twenty-two LR?"

I smiled. That was what we used in the field. Same for Mossad. There's a general misconception about the twenty-two-caliber pistol, that it's not a serious weapon, that it's only good for plinking. Wrong. The truth is, both Special Forces operators and Navy SEALs use twenty-twos when they need to kill someone reliably and quietly. For subsistence hunting or sentry elimination. With a well-aimed head shot using twenty-two long rifle hollow-point rounds, the brain will explode.

"And LR hollow-points," I said.

"Okay."

"And some kind of piece for yourself."

"Why do I need one?"

"I'll explain when you meet me at my hotel. As soon as you can. Can you be here in two hours?"

"Not if I need to pick up all this crap, too."

"Okay. We've got tomorrow morning, too. Be here inside two hours. But one of the items I'm going to need for sure tonight."

"Which one?"

An hour and a half later, when I still hadn't heard from Kombucha, I called him.

"You know how many traffic cams the MPD has in DC?" he said. "I mean, total, everywhere?"

"No idea."

"Forty-eight. Total. In southeast, a grand total of seven."

"Shit."

"The closest one to the Anacostia metro stop is at Suitland Parkway and Firth Sterling, about half a block away. And I didn't find anything on that one. *Nada*."

"We need other cameras in the area. Banks and liquor stores and supermarkets and convenience stores and gas stations."

"Well, we've got an intel analyst unit now. Twenty-four-seven. I filled out a request. They'll search the area for known CCTVs and pull the footage and burn it onto a DVD for us if they find anything."

"How fast can they work?"

"I don't know, Nick. It's a laborious search. It'll take a while."

"I see."

"But there's good news. I have an arrest warrant for Richard Rasmussen. I haven't entered it into NCIC yet—I'm holding onto it, keeping it out of the computer for now."

"Oh, shit."

"What's wrong?"

"Don't arrest the guy yet."

"Huh?"

"Don't you want to get the ringleader? Give me a little time and you'll have Vogel, too."

Balakian expelled a mouthful of air. "Not the way I want to play it. Once I have Rasmussen, he'll give me Vogel. Or we'll serve a search warrant on him and maybe get the connection that way."

"Just . . . give me twenty-four hours."

"Give . . . *you*? Dude, you're not running this show."

I spoke quietly, but he could hear the banked fury in my voice. "You arrest Rasmussen now and Vogel has no more reason to make a deal. Which means he'll have his guys kill Mandy Seeger. She'll only be a witness against him. She'll have no more strategic use."

A long silence, then he said, "I'll think about it."

"Don't do it. You arrest Rasmussen, you're killing Mandy. I mean it."

By the time I hung up I felt fairly certain I'd gotten through to him. He agreed to hold off on arresting Rasmussen for the murder of Kayla Pitts.

That was a relief, but his news about the cameras was a big disappointment. That had been my Plan A. Now it seemed dubious. It was time for Plan B.

I turned to Dorothy, who'd been listening to my end of the conversation while munching on mixed nuts from the minibar. "Now it's crucial we find Vogel's home address."

"I'm on it, Nick, but it's not looking good."

"There's always a way. No one's entirely off the grid."

"This guy seems to be. Everything goes to his post office box in Thurmont, Maryland."

"The guy has electricity. And Internet. That's two utilities right there that require a service address. Time for a little social engineering."

She paused, shrugged. "Worth a try."

"Do me a favor and get me the customer service phone numbers for the biggest Internet providers in and around Thurmont, Maryland. Time Warner Cable, Comcast, DirecTV—let's start with the biggest ones.

Maybe we'll get lucky." I glanced at my watch. "Where the hell is Merlin? He should be here by now."

"Okay. What else you need?"

"Pull up all the pizza places in and around Thurmont. Can't be that many."

"*Pizza* places?"

"Yep."

"Pizza places, huh. Okay. What else you need?"

"Phone number for Southern Maryland Electric."

"That it?"

"Oh, and go down to the concierge desk and see if they have an express mail envelope."

"FedEx okay?"

"No, not FedEx. Got to be US Postal Service express mail. If not, see if they can find us one."

"How big?"

"Just a regular flat-rate envelope. But if Merlin's not here in the next half hour, we're going to miss the cutoff. But maybe I won't need it. Maybe we'll get a hit from the electric company."

"That it?"

"And order us some coffee from room service, okay?"

"Got it. You're moving into high gear."

"So are you."

"Nick," she said, and she seemed to hesitate.

"Yeah?"

"Can we talk?"

"Make it quick, sure."

Now she fixed me with a fierce look. "Do what he says."

"Who?"

"Vogel. He says he'll let Mandy go if you just go back to Boston? Go back to Boston."

"You don't think I've thought about it?" I said. "But I know people like Vogel. The things that trigger him, the small irritants you can't predict. Thing is, Mandy will never be safe. My nephew—a target, too, anytime the wind blows east and Vogel has a change of heart. I can't have these people walking around with a target on their backs. The sooner I move against him, the safer Mandy is."

She kept looking at me for a few seconds longer. Then, softly, relenting, she said, "Okay. I get it."

On my first phone call I got lucky, which only set me up for eventual disappointment. Thomas Vogel indeed had an account with Comcast for his Internet and his cable TV. I told them I was having trouble with my service. They asked for "my" date of birth, which I provided—I'd gotten it from Art Garvin—and then I asked, "What address do you have?"

This normally works. You give them enough information that identifies yourself and they tend to get loose with the information. People like to help. But she said, "What's your password, sir?"

"Password?"

"Your account has an extra security feature. We're not allowed to give out any personal information, including the address, unless we're given a password."

"Ohh—I've forgotten it, I'm sorry. But I gave you my name and my date of birth."

"I'm sorry, sir, I'm still going to need a password."

Vogel was smart. He'd taken precautions that ninety-nine percent of people wouldn't bother with. I hung up and called back, hoping to reach another customer service representative who wouldn't be as scrupulous.

But no matter how many times I called, I came to the same stopping point. They required a password before they'd give out the home address.

I was no more fortunate with the electric company. They, too, required a password before they'd divulge the home address.

Then came the pizza places. I called the first one, giving my name as Thomas Vogel, and said, "You have the address, I assume."

"No, sir. Can you give it to me, please?"

Normally this trick works. Pizza places, take-out places, restaurants that deliver—if you're a regular customer, and you order takeout from them a lot, they'll store your information in their databases. But I struck out with all five pizza places.

Either Vogel didn't have pizza delivered to his home—he picked it up or he just didn't eat pizza—or he didn't live in Thurmont. It was possible that he had his mail delivered to a post office that wasn't in his hometown but nearby. If so, he was even craftier than I'd figured.

Half an hour of this, and nothing. No luck finding his home address. Room service arrived with coffee, and then Dorothy came back with an express mail envelope from the concierge downstairs and the form that goes with it.

"For Thurmont, Maryland," she said, "they don't guarantee delivery until noon."

"So noon it'll have to be."

Then came a knock at the door. It was Merlin, holding a shopping bag.

"Hey, man."

"Thanks for coming. You got it?"

"I brought two, just in case you need a second one."

"I shouldn't, but I appreciate the thought. All right, hold on."

Merlin said hello to Dorothy while I called Ellen Wiley.

"I never heard back from you," she said. "I thought things might have gone sideways."

"Worked out okay. But I need one more favor from you."

"Whatever the hell you want, sweetie," she said.

When I'd finished talking to Ellen, I tried Mandy's cell phone one more time, but once again there was no answer.

Everything depended on one complicated plan with a lot of moving parts. With any number of ways it could go wrong.

72

This is the book you wanted, right?" Merlin said. "*The 48 Laws of Power*?" He pulled an orange hardcover from a plastic Barnes & Noble bag out of one of the duffel bags and set it on the dining table. Next to it he placed a small True Value hardware bag. "Razor blade and glue," he announced.

The book was a remainder, but it was a hardcover, which was the important thing. It had to be a hardcover book. "That's the one."

"What's so special about it?"

"Never read it," I said, absently. "It just seems plausible, and it's thick enough." I opened the book to the title page and scrawled, in loopy handwriting,

Contract on the way— meanwhile enjoy this.
XOXO
Ellen

It looked like a woman's handwriting, or close enough. Then I opened the razor blades' packaging and slid out one blade from the dispenser.

Dorothy looked at what I was doing and laughed. "Heller, you son of a bitch," she said.

We got to the big post office on Mass Avenue, next to Union Station, shortly before seven. Just in time to send off the package via overnight express mail.

In the car on the way back to the hotel, I sniffed the air and said, "You started smoking again."

"Couple days ago," Merlin said. "I feel lousy about it. Don't give me shit."

"Stressed?"

"I don't know. Nick, I gotta be on an FBI or DHS list somewhere, buying all this junk."

"You're nobody if you're not on a Do Not Fly list."

"Yeah. Uh, are you going to fill me in on what exactly you're planning?"

It was a reasonable question, but there was no quick explanation. I didn't finish outlining for him the operation I had in mind until we were back at the hotel suite.

"You don't even know for sure what to expect—what this guy Vogel's house is like, what kind of security precautions he takes. I mean, we're flying blind here."

"Not really. I know people like Vogel. So do you. I know what someone like Vogel would do. Which reminds me."

I took out my phone and texted Vogel, using that Disappearing Ink app:

> Wrapping up business. Flying back to Boston tomorrow morning. How is Mandy?

The answer came thirty seconds later:

> Alive.

I wrote back:

> Want proof of life.

The reply took almost five minutes. It was a picture of Mandy, seated. Her eyes open, obviously alive. Looking exhausted and terrified. There was a cut on her cheek. Her hands were at her side, probably bound. I couldn't tell where she was. Some kind of garage, maybe.

Then the picture disappeared.

73

Merlin drove home, and Dorothy and I talked for a while. We ordered some room service—a club sandwich for me, a Cobb salad for her. She picked at her salad; she didn't seem hungry. She had a glass of white wine, and I had a beer.

"Why are you so sure Vogel's going to keep Mandy alive?" she said.

"She's only leverage if she's alive."

"But for how long? Do we have till tomorrow?"

"He's planning on at least that long. Until I return to Boston, he said."

"Where do you think they're keeping her?"

"I don't know. It looked like she was sitting in a garage of some kind. There were garden tools hanging on the wall behind her."

"What you're planning for tomorrow—it's risky."

"No question."

"Are you sure it's . . . a good idea?"

"Vogel's the sort of guy who responds only to over-whelming force."

She looked into her wineglass for a few seconds, then set it down. "Can we speak frankly?"

I smiled. "Do you ever do anything else?"

"As long as I've known you, you've never been what I'd call cautious. You always seem to be willing to go to the very edge."

"Only when I have to. I don't play games, and I don't take chances when I don't need to."

She sipped from her wineglass, and I took a bite of my sandwich. "From where I sit, it doesn't look that way. You always seem to be pushing. Almost asking for trouble. I'm asking you to think twice, this time. Take some precautions."

"I always do."

She sighed. "You're not—afraid?"

"Of course I am. George Patton—I know, he was a jerk, but the guy was brilliant—said, 'I've never seen a brave man. All men are frightened—the smarter they are, the more frightened.'"

"These guys are ruthless, Nick. Just be careful tomorrow. You don't know what you're facing."

"You're right," I said. "I don't."

We both went to bed early. We had a long day ahead of us.

I was exhausted yet unable to fall asleep. I tossed and turned and thought about the next day's plans, rehearsing them, looking for holes. Then I tried to clear my mind. I breathed in and out. I stared at the clock on the bedside table.

My restless mind didn't give up the struggle until maybe two in the morning.

74

I got up early—I'd barely slept, actually—but Dorothy was already up, drinking room service coffee and staring at her computer screen.

"Where's the package?" I asked her. I knew she'd be tracking it.

She nodded. "Looks like it's in some sort of central sorting facility in DC. Any more messages from Vogel?"

"Not yet." My head was pounding, and my eyelids felt like they were made of sandpaper. I'd been too keyed up to sleep. I looked at the remains of our dinner, still on the dining table, with disgust. My stomach was tight.

"When's Merlin coming back?" she said.

"I'm meeting him at his place, in Dunkirk. He's got a garage where we can work."

I checked my e-mail and found a message from Merlin, listing which of the items from what he called the

"Nick Heller scavenger hunt" he'd found, and which he hadn't. He'd struck out on two of the most important things, the tranquilizer rifle and the electric blasting caps.

He'd e-mailed me before five o'clock, so I knew he was up. I called him.

"Morning," I said. "You feeling energized today?"

"Not yet. Mostly hungover. Too much Scotch last night."

"I need you battle-ready."

"I'll be okay after I've had some more coffee. I went through half a pack of cigarettes last night."

"You nervous about today?"

"I'm . . . out of practice. I do technical surveillance now, you know? It's tame stuff. Compared."

"You're not trying to worm out of this, are you?"

"I'll be there. For you. For a brother."

"I appreciate it. It'll be fine. Can't find a tranquilizer gun?"

"Incredibly hard to find, Nick. They sure don't sell them at Cabela's. I mean, they're sold to licensed veterinarians and wildlife rangers and zookeepers and whatever. Give me a couple of days and I can get one, but not this morning."

"Couple of Tasers, then. Police-grade if you can get it."

"No problem. I have a contact for blasting caps, now. A buddy just called me back. He can get us two."

"Two's enough."

*   *   *

I drove out to Maryland, leaving Dorothy behind in the hotel suite, stationed at her laptop. On the way I stopped at a Wells Fargo branch and withdrew a lot of cash.

Merlin lived in a small bungalow in a development in Dunkirk, Maryland, not far from the Patuxent River. He'd turned his garage into a workspace and parked his Honda in the driveway. The garage was immaculate, with a couple of workbenches and tools hanging neatly on pegboard mounted on the walls.

He'd already done some of the hard work. He'd popped open a couple of cheap cell phones and had fished out the wiring. Each phone was now connected by electrical wire to a blasting cap.

"Nice work," I said. On the workbench next to the blasting caps were two cylinders wrapped in brown paper on which was printed: HIGH EXPLOSIVE. DANGEROUS. 8 OZ. DYNAMITE. CORPS OF ENGINEERS, US ARMY. A couple of red gasoline jugs sat on the floor nearby.

"Where'd you get the dynamite?"

"I drove out to the Aberdeen Proving Ground. Pat Keegan still teaches there."

"Keegan. Of course. I should have thought of him. What about the stingray?"

"Hold on. It's in my car."

He returned with a piece of equipment—surprisingly old-fashioned-looking given how extremely sophisticated it was—the size of a small suitcase. It was white, with switches and LED lights and indicator dials on the front.

"Merlin," I said, "you got it! How?"

"Calvert County sheriff's office. They didn't need it today, so it's going 'missing' for a few hours."

"You're amazing."

"Nah. A guy there owes me a lot of favors, that's all."

The stingray was a powerful surveillance tool used by government agencies and law enforcement. But its existence is generally kept secret. Basically, it's a cell phone–tracking device that acts like a cell tower. It puts out a signal stronger than nearby cell towers, forcing mobile phones or devices to connect to it first, instead of to a real tower. So it allows you to capture cell numbers in the vicinity, and numbers dialed, and other data. The US Marshal's service uses stingrays in planes, flying over areas where they suspect a fugitive is hiding; they can nab their fugitive based on his cell phone number. It essentially lets law enforcement track your location without a warrant. It's real Big Brother stuff.

We fell silent for a moment, and then Merlin said, "Do we even know where his house is yet?"

My cell phone rang. "Maybe," I said.

It was Dorothy. "The package is in Thurmont."

"At the post office?"

"Right."

"That's early. Let me know when it moves again."

I ended the call and said, "Not yet. We will."

Working quietly, we assembled the components of two bombs, each in a cheap nylon duffel bag that Merlin had lying around.

Shortly after eleven thirty, my cell phone rang again.

"It's moving," Dorothy said.

"Out of the post office?"

"Yes."

"Okay," I said to Merlin. "It's time to get going."

"Can I smoke in your car?"

"Afraid not."

"Vape?"

"Rather not."

"Then hold on. I'm gonna need a cigarette first."

75

The night before, Tom Vogel had gotten a call from Ellen Wiley.

Her stalker problem was worse. Now her stalker had tried to break into her Georgetown house. She wanted to hire the Centurions to start immediately. Not in a week. Tomorrow.

He e-mailed her a contract, which she promised to sign and express mail back to him, along with a check. He'd given her a PO box. He was expecting the package.

He was not expecting what was inside.

Not a signed contract and a check, but a gift. A book Ellen thought he'd enjoy.

A hardcover whose spine was about an inch and a half thick. A book that might raise eyebrows but not provoke suspicion.

Because glued into its spine, and therefore hidden, was a small round flat disc no bigger than a silver dollar.

A battery-operated GPS tracking device. Whose movements Dorothy could follow on her iPad.

I'd considered staking out the post office instead, waiting for someone to unlock his PO box, and then follow him. Simpler, maybe. But these people were hypervigilant. Tailing people like this would be like putting a leash on a snake. It's just going to slip you.

No, this way was more sophisticated. I figured that Vogel wouldn't go to the post office himself. He'd send an underling. And the underling wouldn't open the package. He'd bring it right to Vogel.

But then Vogel, expecting a signed contract and a check, would pull out the book. A gift from Ellen Wiley. He'd consider it strange: idiosyncratic, but not alarming.

And if my intelligence was right, Vogel didn't keep a regular office. He lived in a compound. The express mail package would be brought right to his home. The tracker would tell us precisely where it was.

And then I was going to pay him a visit.

Dorothy called back about ten minutes later. "The package is leaving the town of Thurmont and heading to Gorham, the next town over." I hadn't even heard of these Maryland towns.

"Okay," I said. "Merlin and I have to go make a pickup. Keep updating me."

"On it."

She called back a few minutes later, when Merlin and I were driving in the Chrysler. "It's stopped moving."

"Where?"

"I have the location on Google Earth. It's pretty much what you expected—a large house surrounded by woods, fenced in."

"How many buildings?"

"Two. One small one that looks like a garage. Then the main compound."

"What about the entry?"

"As far as I can tell, just a gate."

"No booth?"

"Nothing that elaborate."

"Okay. Long driveway?"

"More than a driveway. A long road that winds through the woods and then broadens out to a clearing, where the house is."

"You have the street address. Can you get any info on the house from the county, or the town? Maybe even blueprints?"

"Give me five minutes. I'll call you back."

Merlin drummed his fingers on the dashboard as I drove. He was wracked with nervous energy. I could tell he wanted another smoke.

I said to him, "You know where we're going?"

"Yup. You got the cash, right?"

"Got it."

"You have the address now?"

"We do."

"So it worked, the tracker."

"Apparently."

"What if he discovers it?"

"I don't think that's going to happen. He'll see it's a book, open it, see the inscription, probably be a little baffled and a little annoyed."

"And suspicious?"

"Not likely."

"If he does? If he rips open the binding and finds where you glued the tracker?"

I shrugged, said nothing.

"Then he'll be waiting for you. For us."

"Let's just hope that doesn't happen."

A long silence followed. Then my phone rang: Dorothy.

"No blueprints online with the city or the county," she said. "But I found something interesting. A couple of building permits issued by the building inspector in Gorham. One was to build an outbuilding, a shed of some kind. The other was for the construction of a safe room."

"In Vogel's compound?"

"Right. On the ground floor. The walls are made of steel panels and ballistic-proof composite. It's got its own generator."

"Okay. Anything on the security system?"

"Nothing."

"Can you send me a screenshot of the house?"

"Sure thing."

I hung up. "All right," I said to Merlin. "Change of plans."

76

The UPS truck pulled into the private road and came to a stop at the gate.

It was a tall black wrought-iron gate, simple and spare, devoid of any scrollwork or curlicues. All along its top were sharp spear points.

The driver noticed the stone pillar on the left side of the gate, on which were mounted a camera and an intercom. He advanced his truck a few feet more, leaned out his window, and pressed a button.

After fifteen seconds or so, a voice came over the intercom: "Yes?"

"UPS. Package for Thomas, uh, Vogel. I need a signature."

Another pause. Less than ten seconds this time. "All right."

Slowly the gate slid to the right, and when it was fully open, the brown truck proceeded down the unpaved tree-lined road, which wound through the woods for quite a while. Finally the road opened up into a clearing, and there was a house, large and rambling, handsome, but not at all imposing.

It had a low-pitched roof, with generously overhanging eaves. Exposed, scalloped rafter tails. Dormers both gabled and hipped. The windows had single-paned bottom sashes with multi-paned top sashes.

The casing around the front door was wide, as was the casing around the windows, with their detailed mullion work. The house was built in the Craftsman style, and it was clearly done with great pride and attention to detail.

I was impressed. If Vogel had really built this house with his own hands, he did excellent work.

Merlin, who was driving, shut off the engine and handed me the electronic clipboard. While he went to the back of the truck to retrieve one of the duffel bags, I came around the hood to the front door. I rang the doorbell.

If Vogel came to the door, I was ready. But I didn't expect him to, and he didn't. Someone else opened the front door, a bulky guy with short black hair and a steroid-poisoned look. He was wearing jeans and a black T-shirt and had overdeveloped pecs.

"Thomas Vogel?" I said through the screen door.

"I can sign," the guy said. "Where's the package?"

"It's a big piece of exercise equipment. Before I take it down from the truck, can you eyeball it, make sure it looks right?"

The guy shrugged, looking a little uncertain, pushed open the screen door, and came out. I took a quick look at the small foyer inside, the living room next to it, and I froze the image in my mind.

I led the way to the back of the truck. There, I pulled open the roll-up door, and he saw the nearly empty cargo bay. All we had back there were the stingray and a pile of zip ties and one of the two duffel bags. Merlin had already placed the other duffel at the back of the house.

I saw Merlin approach but hang back, watching me.

The guy said, "What the hell—"

But my right arm was already swooping around his right shoulder and hooking his thick neck in the crook of my elbow. He flung his fists out and back at me, but it was useless. Grabbing my bicep with my left hand, I drew my shoulders back, and it tightened up like a scissor. I squeezed, compressing the carotid arteries on either side of his neck.

Within ten seconds, he slumped. He'd be unconscious for only a few seconds, really, but when he came to he'd be swimming out of a daze and sluggish. It took Merlin and me about a minute and a half to zip-tie his hands and legs, hog-tying him. I ripped off a length of duct tape and taped his mouth closed.

I left him on the ground. With the truck in the way he couldn't be seen from inside the house.

I picked up the electronic clipboard from the ground where I'd dropped it.

One down. The problem was that we didn't know how many guys lived or worked in the compound, how much protection Vogel maintained. But I was sure this guy wasn't the only one.

"Ready?" Merlin said.

"Just a second." I jumped into the cargo bay and found the Ruger .22. "Okay," I said.

Merlin punched a number into one of the cheap mobile phones.

He waited, looked at me. I could hear the distant ringing through his phone's earpiece.

Then came the explosion.

It was louder than I anticipated, an immense cracking, echoing boom that rumbled and roared and shook the ground. From where we were standing, we couldn't see it, but I knew the dynamite in the duffel bag had ignited the gasoline and created a vast fireball. The early-afternoon sky, already bright, blazed even brighter, tinged with red, and black smoke smudged the sky.

Whoever was inside the house would now turn their attention to the back of the house to see what the hell was going on. Probably most of the guards would race around to that side of the compound. It was a diversion bomb, which usually worked when I was in the country. A classic and effective technique. It would buy us a few crucial seconds.

I looked at Merlin and nodded. "I'm going in," I said. "If you don't hear from me in fifteen minutes, call the police."

While he stayed back and made sure that the guard remained bound, I hoisted the second cheap duffel bag and started toward the house.

77

Slowly, as if I belonged there, as if I owned the place, I walked around the back of the truck, to the front door, pulled open the screen door, and entered the house.

I was in the small foyer. There was a painting on the wall, something forgettable, an umbrella stand, a demi-lune table. All very ordinary and domestic. Nothing compoundlike about it at all.

Only then did I notice the closed-circuit TV camera mounted on the wall in the small foyer, pointed at the door.

If anyone was watching the monitors, I was in trouble. Especially if Vogel was watching. Because he knew my face. And although I was wearing a UPS uniform, I was not otherwise in disguise.

But maybe no one was watching the monitors. Maybe they were all investigating the bomb.

Or maybe not. In any case, I had to move quickly. I

had a choice between going left and going right, and I arbitrarily chose left. Into a small living room that stank of old cigar smoke. The walls were raised-panel wainscoting, stained dark walnut. Mounted to one wall was a huge flat-screen TV. There was no one here. I dropped the second duffel bag in front of a long, black leather couch.

Maybe the bomb had worked, and everyone inside the house was now focused on the fireball out back. Distracted, at least momentarily.

But not, as it turned out, everyone.

A tall and lanky guy appeared in the doorway. In a two-handed grip he was pointing a weapon at me, matte black, a semiautomatic. It looked like another Glock. Apparently Vogel had gotten a bulk price on Glocks.

"Freeze!" he shouted.

He was the smart one. He'd immediately connected the blast to the arrival of the UPS truck. He'd figured out where the danger was really coming from.

I froze.

"What the hell?" I said.

"Get *down!*"

I wasn't holding the Ruger. That was in a pancake holster concealed by my brown UPS shirt. I was holding the electronic clipboard instead.

For a split-second I considered pulling out the Ruger.

But the clipboard, used correctly, was the better weapon at that moment.

"I need a signature, right here," I said, thrusting the clipboard at him, as if trying to show him something.

All I needed was a moment of disruption. To disengage his brain from his trigger finger for a second or two. A break state, it was called. An interruption of thought, breaking the coordination between his mind and his weapon as he figured out whether I was for real. Because even though he'd deduced I wasn't a UPS driver, he wasn't entirely sure.

The lanky guy hesitated for a second. He glanced at my uniform, at my clipboard, in the space of maybe a second and a half.

I turned my left foot and flung the clipboard at his eyes. He jerked his head away. I thrust my left arm over his right, clamping down hard, while with my right hand I grabbed the barrel of his gun. I twisted it clockwise, up and away. He screamed as his trigger finger snapped.

Then I lunged at him, knocking him to the carpeted floor, my knee at his throat. I had his gun now and jabbed it into his forehead. He screamed again, said, "Jesus, no!"

"Where's Vogel?" I said.

"His . . . his wing."

"Where?"

He thrust his thumb to his right, my left. He indicated a set of double doors.

"Turn over. I said turn *over*."

I shoved him, and he complied. I yanked out a couple of the heavy-duty cable ties, but apparently he wasn't finished. He reared up, jerked his right hand back toward me, and I smashed the barrel of the Glock into his left temple.

He slumped immediately. He was dazed, semiconscious. I secured his wrists together, then his ankles. He didn't fight me anymore.

These particular zip ties he wasn't going to escape from.

Then I got up and went to find Vogel.

78

From the Google image I had a good sense of the house from above. I knew that the house rambled, and that there was a lot more to the house than the few rooms I'd passed through.

If this guy had told me the truth, these double doors led to Vogel's own wing. His residence, maybe.

Maybe.

Holding in my right hand the Glock I'd taken off the lanky guy, I opened the double doors with my left. Ahead I saw a long, broad hallway, with more wood paneling, chair-rail height. Here the wood was painted off-white, to match the walls.

On the right was what appeared to be a bedroom. The door was open, the light off. The bed was unmade.

On the left was another room, a study or office. More fancy woodwork here, and a long desk, cherrywood with scrollwork on the legs. On top of it, piles of papers. Cables and cords everywhere. In the corner of the room, a printer on a smaller table. The window had a view of the front yard. I could see the nose of the UPS truck. Here the lights were on. As if Vogel had been working there and left abruptly.

And then I saw Vogel.

And he saw me.

He was about thirty feet down the hallway from me, wearing a blue button-down shirt and a pair of dress slacks. He looked like he was about to put on a tie and go out for a meeting with a client.

I spun the Glock toward him. Vogel's right hand was moving behind him, to where he probably had a weapon holstered, and I said, "Don't."

Vogel smiled. His right hand stopped moving.

"What are you going to do, Nick?" he said. "Shoot me?" He smiled.

I came closer, the Glock pointed at his center mass.

He'd raised an interesting question. Was I really going to shoot Vogel? Or maybe shoot him in the leg, wound him?

"Release Mandy and you can walk away," I said.

He laughed. "Don't insult me."

"I'll throw you a phone. You call your guys, tell them to let her go. It's your only play, Vogel."

He smiled, shook his head, as if this was the stupidest idea he'd heard in ages.

"Put the gun down, Nick."

"First make the call. Then I'll put the gun down."

"I'm afraid that's not going to happen, brother."

I took a step closer. "Don't make me do it, Vogel."

He smiled again, the cocky son of a bitch. "You gonna shoot me, Nick?"

"Yeah, I am," I said, and I squeezed the trigger.

It was deafeningly loud in this enclosed space. Vogel bellowed. The bullet ripped through his shirt, tearing a small hole at the shoulder. A large bloom of blood stained the sleeve of his blue shirt. The round had creased his shoulder, inflicting a minor but intensely painful flesh wound.

"God *damn* you, you son of a bitch!" Vogel shouted. His right hand came up to grab his injured shoulder.

"What's next?" I said. "Your kneecap?"

I lowered the Glock and pointed it at his knee.

"Okay!" he said. "Okay! Jesus!" He glanced over my shoulder for just an instant, and then something came from behind my right side. A sudden movement, a shift in the quality of the light.

And in that same moment something long and cylindrical—I could just make out its shape—cracked into my right arm, causing me to drop the gun. My arm exploded with pain. I stumbled.

It was a baseball bat, wielded by someone who'd stolen up behind me.

The bat came up again, and I threw myself at my attacker, grabbed at the baseball bat. It cracked against my hands, a hot stinging, immensely painful, as I tried to wrench it from his grasp.

Out of the corner of my eye I could see Vogel moving away. But I was too preoccupied to stop him. The attacker roared, like a battle cry, as we struggled over the bat. Both of our hands were on it. He pushed it at me, and it cracked against my skull, causing a starburst of pain. With one great lunge, I shoved the side of the bat into his throat. I could hear the crunch of cartilage. He dropped to the floor, both of his hands grasping his throat, gagging, his eyes rolling up in his head.

I knew he was down, permanently.

I turned, saw the spatter of blood in the carpet where I'd shot Vogel. He'd left a trail of blood, which I followed down the hall and then to the right, along another hall, and then the spatters got denser and more profuse.

Right in front of a white-painted windowless steel door.

The safe room.

He was inside.

79

Vogel's voice rasped over a loudspeaker mounted high on the wall. "Backup's on the way, Heller. It's over. Go home."

"It's over when Mandy's released. Make the call, Vogel."

"Was I not clear about the terms of the deal? Go back to Boston, and Mandy walks free. Not till then. Enough of your games."

I saw a CCTV camera mounted next to the loudspeaker and realized that, though I couldn't see him, he could see me. I thumbed the magazine release on the lanky guy's Glock and saw that the magazine was empty. It was a Glock 17, the standard MPD service weapon, and its standard magazine had a capacity of seventeen rounds. With only one round in the magazine. And I had just fired it. At Vogel's shoulder.

Vogel must not have seen that the gun was empty, because he said, "Don't waste the ammo, brother. The walls are ballistic fiberglass and steel. You're going to need a howitzer."

He was telling the truth, of course. He was safe from bullets in there.

"Are you really going to hide in your steel box?" I said.

"You're locked out."

"Yeah? I think you've locked yourself in."

"You're wasting your time."

"Make the call," I said again. "Here's how it's going to work. Your guys bring Mandy to whatever intersection you want, in DC or wherever you say. I have a guy who'll pick her up and confirm she's okay." Balakian, a.k.a. Kombucha, was standing by, waiting for my call.

He gave a dry chuckle. "Or what?"

"Make the call."

"See, Heller, that's where your plan falls apart. You have no leverage and you never did. In about ten minutes, five of my most capable employees will be here. They're going to see an armed and dangerous intruder who's obviously just wounded several men and set off a firebomb on my property, and they're going to do what the law permits them to do: take you down. At that point, Mandy Seeger will be irrelevant."

I shoved the Glock into the waistband of my UPS uniform pants, as if it were loaded and could come in handy at any moment. Then I folded my arms. "Beautiful house," I said. "You build it yourself?"

"Most of it."

"The woodwork is extraordinary. It must have taken you years. It's a real shame."

He said nothing.

I took out my cell phone and held it up for the camera. "There's a phone number programmed into this phone," I said. "As soon as I hit the speed-dial, it will detonate the second gas bomb. Which is sitting in your living room. It's gonna turn your house into a fireball. The house that you built so lovingly. Within an hour all that beautiful woodwork is going to be charcoal."

Another long pause. I was about to resume speaking when he said, "I make one phone call and Mandy Seeger is dead."

"And here's the thing," I said, ignoring him. "Here's the best part. You're sitting in a ten-by-twelve-foot steel box. In the middle of a roaring house fire. Now, the average house fire burns at eleven, twelve hundred degrees Fahrenheit. And steel's a great conductor of heat. Your steel coffin will rapidly reach around two thousand degrees Fahrenheit. And you know what's going to happen to you?"

Silence.

"Well, first you'll start sweating. It'll be really uncomfortable. Then blisters will start breaking out all over your skin. By then you'll be in excruciating pain. If you're lucky you'll go into shock. It's probably the worst way to die."

Silence.

"Ever roast a pig in a box? That's what's going to happen to you. You're going to roast like a pig. Only you'll be roasting alive. Vogel—that's a German name, right?"

Silence.

"What does Vogel mean in German?"

Silence.

"It's been a while since high school German, but I'm pretty sure that Vogel means bird. So maybe it's more accurate to say you'll roast like a bird. Like a barbecued chicken. Human cremation takes place at between fourteen hundred and eighteen hundred degrees, so you're probably going to end up as just ashes. They probably won't be able to identify you by your dental records."

"You're full of shit, Heller. You're not going to do it."

"How's your shoulder?" I said, and I smiled. "You know about the blood on my hands. You know what I'm capable of."

"You're not going to do it, Heller. Because Mandy Seeger is being held in the basement. Right below me. And I don't think you're going to want to burn your friend alive, too."

I have a knack for recognizing lies. And I knew he was telling the truth.

80

I wanted nothing more than to run. To find the basement door and get down there immediately.

But I forced myself to backtrack down the hall to Vogel's office. There I looked around quickly and yanked the power cord from the desktop computer. The cord was six feet long and sturdy. Then I grabbed a couple of USB cables.

I returned to the safe room and looped the power cable around the door lever and looped that up to the mount for the CCTV camera. Pretty quickly I'd knotted the cables securely.

He wasn't going to get out of that safe room any time soon, and not without help.

I turned and raced back down the hall in the general direction of the front door. I flung open door after door, finding closets and bedrooms and bathrooms.

And finally the right one. The basement. I dropped the empty Glock and descended the stairs.

The air felt cooler. I smelled a dank odor as I descended the dimly lit wooden stairway. Lights were on downstairs. I heard low voices.

The basement appeared, on first glance, to have roughly the same footprint as the floor above. Bare concrete walls segmented it into a number of open rooms. It seemed to go on forever. It was, for a basement, relatively high-ceilinged: around nine feet. On the ceiling were soundproofing tiles.

The voices were a little louder, and I could tell they were coming from a TV in one of the open rooms. In the closest alcove were steel shelves that held white boxes marked with dates and letters. The Centurions' client files, probably. All along one wall were garden tools, neatly hanging from hooks on a long expanse of pegboard.

I sidled along the wall of tools toward the source of the TV noise, which seemed to be coming from the next alcove. There I saw what at first looked like chain-link fence. When I got closer—though still about twenty-five feet away—I realized I was looking at a holding cell. A twelve-by-twelve-foot standalone cell whose walls and ceiling were made of welded wire mesh. The sort of cage you might see in a small police detention unit. In one corner, a bare steel commode. In another, a sleeping bag on the floor and a steel bench.

And on that bench sat Mandy Seeger.

She was slumped, in a hooded sweatshirt, and looked weary and alone. She didn't see me.

About ten feet from the holding cell sat a very large

guy in a chair staring dully at a TV mounted on the ceiling. He wore a white short-sleeved polo shirt and a shoulder holster. He looked to be around three hundred pounds, much of it fat.

He didn't see me either. He was watching some reality show about deep-sea fishing.

The basement was soundproofed, and he was watching TV, but he still must have heard the bomb. And the shot I'd taken at Vogel. But he must have been ordered not to leave his post. He had a prisoner to watch.

"Yo!" I shouted, walking toward the fat guy. "Vogel sent me down here."

The fat guy turned to look at me, a guy in a brown UPS uniform. He whipped a Glock out of his shoulder holster and aimed it in my direction. "Who the hell are you?"

"Man, there's eighteen feds with windbreakers upstairs. You want to get out of this, follow me." I came closer. "Get her out of there and let's go."

"Huh? Feds? Where?"

Then a cell phone began ringing.

His.

With his free left hand he pulled out a phone. Then, with the thumb of his gun hand, he hit the ANSWER button, a neat little move. He must have done it before.

He answered it. "Yes, sir."

I knew who it was.

Slowly I drew the Ruger out from under my shirt and held it at my side.

As he listened, his eyes roamed the basement.

"Yes, sir. Yes, sir."

Mandy, in the cage, was watching me, frightened.

"Got it," he said.

Then he pocketed the phone.

"Stop right where you are," he said. His gun was trained on me. "Don't come any closer."

"Okay." I took another step.

"I said, freeze," the fat guy said.

In one fluid motion I pulled the Ruger up directly in front of my chest.

But the fat guy leveled his Glock and fired first.

Directly at me, from around twelve feet away.

Mandy screamed.

It felt like someone had slammed me in the gut with a baseball bat. I doubled over. The pain was immense. The wind was knocked out of me. I tumbled backward, against the wall of tools, grabbing my chest, gasping, as the Ruger flew out of my hands and went skittering across the floor toward the fat guy. All around me tools clattered to the floor. Something had gashed my neck.

The light body armor I was wearing was only 6.5 millimeters thick, weighing less than two kilograms, and it had saved my life. But it sure felt like I'd broken a few ribs.

I sprung to my feet, and I saw the fat man reaching down to grab the Ruger.

A stupid move. Maybe he thought I'd been seriously wounded or was even dead. But it gave me a couple of seconds that I needed.

I reached for the closest tool at hand, a long-handled

pair of garden shears with its jaws open. Grabbing it by one handle, I hurled it at the fat man like some ninja hurling a throwing star.

He yelped as one blade of the shears sank into the side of his neck. He fell to his knees, reaching for the shears, and I grabbed a large garden spade.

The fat guy fired at me again, but the round clanged against the steel blade. I pulled it back and swung it at the guy, hard. Though I was intending to land the blow on his chest, hoping to knock him to the floor, he had suddenly tipped forward and the shovel blade slammed into his ear.

There was a geyser of blood and I knew it had sunk in deep. The man collapsed onto the floor, the blood pulsing from an opening in his skull.

I grabbed the key from the retractable reel on the left side of his belt and yanked it off. I felt the spray of hot blood.

Mandy was screaming, and my ears were ringing, and I staggered toward the cage.

Even with the soundproofing, I could hear the faint distant warble of police sirens.

81

The beaten-earth yard around Vogel's compound was crowded with a fleet of police vehicles, mostly from the local Maryland force. Kombucha was standing next to his unmarked car in a black overcoat. He waved when he saw us emerge from the compound.

I was glad to see him. I never thought I would be.

"You look like you need medical assistance," he said, approaching.

I shook my head. "I'm good," I said. "Thanks."

I was in a lot of pain, but only when I breathed. I knew the wise course of action was to get to a hospital and get checked out and make sure I hadn't also injured my spleen or my lungs. I'd been shot while wearing a ballistic vest before. I knew what could happen.

The wise course of action wasn't what I chose, and Mandy couldn't persuade me otherwise.

She was okay, she insisted. She hadn't been injured or abused, beyond the discomfort of having to sleep on the floor in what was, after all, a cage, and the degradation of being forced to use a commode in front of a guard. I noticed Vogel's backup hadn't arrived after all. Maybe they were scared off by the police presence.

"Rasmussen?" I asked Kombucha.

He nodded. "Giving us the probable cause we need to search the compound."

"I think client files are in the basement," I said. "Will you excuse me a minute?"

Merlin was in the back of the UPS truck, and he looked antsy. "Nick," he said, "I need to return this thing."

"The truck?"

"The stingray. *And* the truck."

"Hold on. Help me up."

He extended a hand, and helped me up into the cargo bay of the truck. I was gritting my teeth and moaning as I climbed up.

"You get shot?" Merlin said, noticing the hole in the shirt of my uniform.

I nodded.

"Shit," he said. "I can't return it with a hole in it."

"How about, 'You okay, Nick?'"

"You okay, Nick?"

I nodded my head. I was still amped from all the adrenaline. But that was all right. It was probably keeping me from feeling much of the pain from the bruised ribs.

Merlin had been closely monitoring the stingray. I'd given him Vogel's mobile number, so he knew which of the many numbers the stingray had logged—including even distant neighbors—to lock onto. Once he did, he watched the list of numbers Vogel called grow.

"Seven numbers," he said. "Check it out."

I scanned the list of phone numbers.

One of them I recognized, as I was afraid I would, and I felt sick.

82

Mandy wanted to come with me, but I needed to do this alone.

Merlin gave me a ride back to his house, where I'd left the rented Chrysler. On the way we barely talked. I was tired. Vogel's men had worn me out.

I stopped at a Dunkin' Donuts and tanked up on caffeine, popped a couple of Advil, and drove to DC.

On the way I played a tape-recording of Mandy's interview in Anacostia. She'd recorded it on her iPhone and then sent me a link that, by means of some kind of iPhone wizardry, allowed me to play it.

I hit the ON button and put it on the seat next to me.

A very old man was speaking on the tape, an old man in a nursing home in Southeast Washington named Isaac Abelard. During the interview, she'd put the recorder on a bed tray next to the retired patrolman, she'd told me, with the result that her questions were hard to hear, but his answers were generally easier to make out.

Mandy: When did this happen?

Abelard: Oh, jeez, this must have been fifty, sixty years ago. Could it be sixty? I suppose that's right. Sixty. I was a young officer—in my midtwenties, must have been.

Mandy: (inaudible)

Abelard: Oh, I knew him from the neighborhood. He was a good kid. We all knew he was a good kid. I always thought he'd either end up doing great things or wind up getting killed. [Laughs]

Mandy: (inaudible)

Abelard: Oh, I had no idea.

Mandy: Why are you willing to talk about it now?

Abelard: Because I always knew I done a bad thing, covering it up. A wrong thing. I just thought I had a good reason to do it. (inaudible) Because his sister got raped. And when he found out about it, he went out and found the guy who did it and . . . he killed the man.

Mandy: How?

Abelard: A gun he must have bought on the street. It was easy to buy a gun on the street in those days, if you knew the right people.

Mandy: But how did you find out about it?

Abelard: His poor sister told her mother, and her mother told someone, and—I always had my ear to the ground. I had my sources, I had people in the community who'd talk to

*me, and . . . (inaudible) how I did my
job . . . I tracked him down and I said,
"Young man, is it true?" And he was crying and weeping and . . . he told me he
didn't think anyone would do anything
about it. He didn't think the rapist would
ever be arrested. I told him he was wrong, he
should have trusted the legal system, but . . .
but when I thought about it some more I
realized, he was probably right. The rapist
would probably have gotten away with it.*

Mandy: *(inaudible)*

Abelard: *Only his mother and his sister knew what
he'd done. And I felt for the kid. And for his
sister. The goddamned rapist had a rap
sheet longer than his cankered dick. Pardon
my French. Really bad news. So I made a
decision. It would go no further. If he didn't
tell anyone what he'd done, it would be like
it never happened. Well, his mother died,
and his sister died. I'm the only one left who
knows. And I don't have much time. And I
just—I just want to do the right thing.*

I didn't have an appointment, so I had to wait on one
of the sharp-edged, white leather sofas in the hard and
glassy waiting area for almost fifteen minutes.

He came out to meet me himself, not his receptionist,
which was unusual.

"Gideon," I said, "we have a lot to talk about."

83

"The whole point was to discredit Mandy Seeger, wasn't it?" I said.

I'd laid out everything I had on him, and now we were talking man-to-man. I wasn't wearing a wire; I'd given him my word on that. I made it clear that his best chance was to talk me through what had gone down.

Gideon looked visibly deflated, and ten years older.

He hesitated. "And Slander Sheet."

"You knew she was about to open that box. So you fed her a juicier story. Which was poisoned bait."

"Dear God, Nick, I didn't think—this is not the way it was supposed to play out. What they did to that girl—I had no idea. It sickens me."

"How did you know Mandy was about to talk to that old cop?"

"I still know people in Anacostia, Nick. I lived in fear of it coming out. I didn't even know Officer Abelard was still alive. He must be close to ninety."

"But there must have been rumors."

"There were always rumors. People knew my sister Olivia was raped when I was a teenager. I—I had such a temper back then. And you have to understand the times. When Olivia told me what had happened, I was sure he'd get away with it. He was a white man, after all. Is Mandy—Nick, is she going to use this story?"

"Of course she is. Ellen Wiley is paying her, and it's going to run in Slander Sheet. The whole story, beginning to end. Starting with the man you killed when you were sixteen. Are you going to deny it?"

"What if I did? You know how people are. They'll always believe the accusation against the so-called great man. That's what our society has come to. That's our culture. I never intended anything bad to happen to that poor girl. I never—*never*—thought anyone would be killed. My reputation—my honor—is vitally important to me."

"I understand. You know, Mandy didn't realize it was you."

"But it was only a matter of time before she found out."

I nodded. On the drive, I'd thought about what I was going to say. I'd put most of it together, but not all.

Two months ago, Mandy had heard a rumor about how some grand poobah, some Washington insider, had killed a man decades ago, but the murder was covered up. It sounded like a story for Slander Sheet, but it could also have been nothing, a waste of time. She made some calls. Located the source, a long-retired policeman now dying in a nursing home.

But she never got the chance to talk to the old cop, because a far more exciting story had presented itself. A story about a Supreme Court justice and a call girl. The story was false, of course, but it was made to withstand normal fact-checking by any good journalist.

It was also designed to fall apart when a dedicated, high-powered investigator dug into it. The story was made to collapse, to discredit both the journalist and the website. That had been my role. To undermine the story.

So that no one would ever believe anything this journalist ever wrote again. Or anything that appeared on this website.

It had almost worked.

"So what happened, Gideon? One night you and Jeremiah Claflin put away a bottle of Old Overholt between you, and it comes out. Anacostia. This incident from all those years ago . . . ?"

He stared impassively. A pause. "WhistlePig."

"Sorry?"

He spoke almost mechanically. "It wasn't Old Overholt. That's not my brand. The bottle in my office, that was a gift."

"And a few years later, Claflin's now the golden boy. He's the one being put up for the top job. You're not in the inner circle of consideration any longer. How'd that happen? Did Claflin whisper to one of the kingmakers that Gideon Parnell had a dark spot on his biographical X-ray?"

I waited. Gideon was silent for a long time. At last he said, his deep voice hushed, "I can't be sure. I've always wondered."

"And it ate at you, I'm sure. Which is why Claflin's name had to be dragged through the shit before he was vindicated. In your campaign to bring down Slander Sheet. And you know, the thing is, Gideon—you're probably too old to be named to the court. After all that."

Gideon just looked wounded. I thought of what my father had said. *It's always your friends who do you in.* Maybe that wasn't about himself after all.

"Vogel had probably done investigations for the firm, right?"

Gideon nodded. But his mind was somewhere far away. "The evil that men do lives after them," he said. "The good is oft interred with their bones."

I'd heard that before. "If you mean killing your sister's rapist, I think people will understand why you did what you did. You did a bad thing for a good reason."

"Do you know who Wilbur Mills was?"

"Yeah, vaguely. A congressman. A stripper named Fanne Foxe, the Tidal Basin, a sex scandal."

"And all anyone remembers about him is the sex scandal that ended his career. Then there's Clark Clifford."

Wearily, I said, "The BCCI scandal."

"John Edwards."

"The mistress, the kid. The wife with cancer."

"John Tower."

"Uh, Texas senator with a drinking problem."

"Yes. The list is long. All of them men who accomplished things. But how they're remembered? For some small-time scandal." He slid open a desk drawer and looked at whatever it contained. "A lifetime spent doing good works—to end up a figure of disgrace?" He drew out from the drawer a handgun, a nickel-plated revolver with a short barrel.

"You're not thinking straight," I said.

But he put the gun to his temple.

"Oh, for God's sake, Gideon!"

He closed his eyes. "How this story ends—how my story ends?" he said. "It's in your hands. And mine."

"Don't!" I jumped out of my seat and tried to grab his gun, but it was too late.

I saw everything as if in slow motion.

I saw the revolver, like a toy in his giant hand. Saw his manicured fingernails. Saw his index finger squeeze the trigger.

I saw the hammer pull back into the cocked position. Saw the fractional rotation of the cylinder as it lined up a new bullet.

Heard the metallic click. Saw the hammer slam forward, the firing pin striking the primer at the back of the bullet casing.

I saw the muzzle flash, the tongue of flame, and then the cloud of smoke as the gun recoiled.

Heard the explosion, so immensely loud yet not nearly loud enough for what it signified.

And I felt something moist and hot mist my face.

Epilogue

When I was finally released from the hospital, I couldn't wait to get back to Boston. But it wasn't to be. The US attorney's office needed me to attend Thomas Vogel's pretrial detention hearing. They weren't charging him with murder but with conspiracy to commit. Richard Rasmussen, the guy who actually killed Kayla and staged the suicide, had been charged with murder one.

They wanted to make sure Vogel remained in the DC jail through his trial. Which could be a year off or more.

So the government had to show that he might flee, or pose a danger to anyone in the community, or attempt to obstruct justice, or threaten a witness. The US attorney wanted me there, in case the defense put witnesses on. They'd parked me in a conference room next to the courtroom, where I paced like some caged tiger.

Vogel had hired the best criminal defense attorney in DC, a former federal prosecutor who was said to be a maestro of the courtroom. I was curious to hear some of the proceedings, but the courtroom was a media circus, packed with reporters and spectators, and I wanted to keep my head down and out of the way of the cameras. So I sat in the conference room next door and paced.

Suddenly it was over. I heard the explosion of babble and the clatter and the cacophony. I stood in the conference room doorway, trying to avoid the crush. Finally I caught a glimpse of the AUSA who was running the case. She didn't look happy.

Vogel was a free man. He was out on bail of half a million dollars, which was chump change for a man of Vogel's means and contacts.

On the way out of the DC Superior Court building, I saw Vogel, fifty feet away or so, as he was descending the front steps.

His eyes met mine. He gave me a firm, knowing nod—friendly, almost—and then, deliberately, purposefully, he leveled a pistol salute, making a finger gun with his thumb up, his forefinger pointing directly at me.

And he smiled.

I met Mandy for an early supper at Lobby, the dive bar with the license plates on the wall, the beer-sticky floor, the aroma of french fries. I had my go-bag with me, an aluminum Rimowa carry-on, which I stashed on the floor in our booth, at my feet. The speakers were blasting a David Bowie song. "Young Americans," I realized.

She looked pretty terrific when she showed up. She

had her hair up and was wearing pearl earrings, and her skin glowed. She had dark red lipstick on, which somehow complemented her coppery hair.

She ordered a Diet Coke and I had a Natty Boh, and for a while we watched the TV mounted to the wall, tuned to CNN. Jeremiah Claflin was being interviewed. I watched the fluid hand gestures, his sad eyes, the sententiously arched eyebrows, the drape of his hand-tailored suit. His perfectly knotted blue silk tie. The downward curve of his mouth as he spoke. His very white teeth. "He was the best of us," Claflin was saying.

He was canny, Claflin was. I admired his fluency, his almost-cloaked ambition, all those smooth traits that had pushed him to the high court. Because he knew the truth about Gideon Parnell, yet he was participating in the lie. Claflin, Senator Brennan had said, was known for clarifying the concept of *mens rea*. Which struck me as ironic, since in Washington, pretty much everyone had a guilty mind.

We'd met for a drink in his office the evening before. He wanted to thank me in person. I wanted to ask him about Gideon, about what kind of long-festering resentment might have led him to drag his protégé's name through the mud. But he feigned innocence. He didn't know what I was talking about. I wondered: How did he really feel about Gideon, after all that had happened? Curdled ambivalence, surely. But that didn't play well on TV. The lie was more convenient.

Now, on CNN, he was talking about Gideon and what a great man he was.

"He was, you know," Mandy said, turning to me with an even gaze.

"Was what?"

"A great man."

I nodded. The stories in *The Washington Post* and *The New York Times* and the Associated Press all mentioned the fact that he was known to be suffering from depression. Someone in his office had put that out, as if it lent his suicide a kind of logic. It wasn't true, as far as I knew.

The obituaries were all front-page, of course, and they all talked about how he'd marched with Martin Luther King and how he'd golfed with presidents. To me, the man was a heroic figure with a profound flaw, a streak of vanity that had propelled him to greatness and yet also propelled him to his destruction.

The waitress took our orders. We both asked for burgers. I got the fries, and she got the Greek side salad.

"Are you in pain, still?" she asked. She indicated the bandage on my neck where I'd gotten slashed struggling with the Centurion guy in the basement of Vogel's house.

"That's nothing," I said. "It's the bruised ribs."

"I always thought bulletproof vests protected you."

"It stopped the bullet. It can't stop the impact."

She put her hand on mine, warm and tender.

"Are you enjoying being on TV all the time?" I said, teasing a little.

"I guess so. I don't know. Part of me does. Part of me thinks I'm just a publicity whore."

"You can always say no."

She shrugged. "You say no too many times and they stop asking."

"That's the point." I smiled. "You're really good at it, Mandy. You're a natural."

"Thanks. You wouldn't believe the offers I've been getting. I've been talking to a couple of literary agents— one at William Morris Endeavor, and one at ICM. They both think they can get me a really nice book deal. I mean, a *lot* of money. Tomorrow I'm on *The View*. And I'm taping *60 Minutes*. Can I give them your name? *60 Minutes*, I mean."

"For what?"

"Don't be coy, Nick. You know damn well why. The mystery man behind a whole chain of events." She paused. "It would be great. For business, I mean. What do you think?"

I shook my head. "No, thanks."

"But this case was such a huge win for you."

I shrugged uneasily. With Gideon and Kayla Pitts dead and Vogel out on bail, it didn't feel like much of a win. "The only good part of this was you," I said.

She cocked her head, curious what I meant.

"You're safe, you're thriving, you're on fire. *60 Minutes, The View* . . ."

"Oh, and I'm in talks with TruTV—they want me to host a new true-crime investigative series they're calling *Spotlight*. How cool is that?"

"*Spotlight*, huh?" I laughed.

"Yeah, *Spotlight*. I know: just what you avoid. I mean, I realize it's not serious journalism or anything. It's journalism lite. But it could be a way for me to get back into the business."

"Sure."

She studied me for a long moment. "We really don't swim in the same waters, do we?"

I drained my beer. "How do you mean?"

"You're, like, one of those deepwater fish. Like a dragonfish or whatever they're called, that live a mile down, where it's almost totally dark and the pressure's intense and the water is freezing cold."

"Come on, Mandy, I'm just—"

"No, really," she said, interrupting me. "You prefer the dark. You're all about keeping secrets."

"Secrets are my business. I keep 'em or I find a new line of work."

"I thought lies were your business. Isn't that what you told me once?"

"Both, I guess."

In the last few days I'd been thinking about her a lot. If we lived in the same town, maybe we could keep on spending time with each other. But I was going back to Boston and she was staying in Washington. Our paths were diverging in other ways, too. Mandy Seeger, the kidnapped journalist, was becoming a TV personality, an instant Internet celebrity.

She was right, though. I preferred the shadows. That was where I belonged.

"How much longer are you in town?" she asked, playing with her straw.

"I'm flying home tonight."

"Tonight?"

I pointed to my carry-on, on the floor next to the booth. "I've got a lot of work to catch up on."

"And I've got to fly to New York early tomorrow morning. So . . . yeah. Wow."

I glanced down at the tabletop, at the gashes and wounds in the wood. I was feeling a little numb and more than a little sad. Maybe we both were.

"Next time I see you will probably be on TV."

"Don't let me read about you in Slander Sheet."

I chuckled. "Yeah, right. Come see me if you're in Boston."

"I will."

An empty promise, surely, but I let it lie.

Outside the bar we said good-bye beside my cab. We kissed, in a slow lingering way that I didn't expect. It didn't feel like a good-bye.

When we separated, she put a hand on my cheek. "Bye, Nick," she said, and she turned around and gave me a little wave.

Then I got in the cab. A motorcycle roared by at deafening volume. As we pulled away from the curb, I turned to watch her, through the rearview window, walking away. I was hoping to exchange one last glance, but she never turned around.

ACKNOWLEDGMENTS

Some very generous people helped me research and write this novel, and I want to thank them. They include, for much help on cell phones and computer forensics, Jeff Fischbach; on mobile phone forensics, Tom Slovenski; on computer hacking, Adam Hernandez, and especially Kevin Ripa. On perimeter security, locks, and lock picking: Marc Weber Tobias and, once again, Jeff Dingle and Kevin Murray. On hotel security: Jeffrey Saunders of the Saunders Hotel Group, Jon Estabrook of the Lenox Hotel, Jim McGlynn of Engineering PLUS, and Fred Juran of Kaba.

Jay Groob of American Investigative Services was again extremely helpful, as were Dick Rogers, Jack Hoban, Matthew Fleming; and Sean Murphy of *The Boston Globe*. In DC, my thanks to Kenneth Cummins of the Capitol Group, Robert "Buzz" Glover of the MPD, and especially James Trainum.

On gossip websites: Ben McGrath of *The New Yorker* and Gaby Darbyshire. For help with ecclesiastical Latin, thanks to Dr. William L. Daniel and Matt C. Abbott. I had legal assistance from Martin Garbus and, once again, Jay Shapiro of White and Williams; big thanks to the brilliant jurist Leo Katz of the University of Pennsylvania Law School for advice on *mens rea*. Clair Lamb was, as always, invaluable in all sorts of ways, including DC research; thanks as well to Karen Louie-Joyce; and to my good friend Rick Weissbourd, Stanford '79.

My thanks for the loving support of my wife, Michele Souda, and our daughter, Emma J. S. Finder. At Dutton, I'm grateful to Amanda Walker, Carrie Swetonic, Jess Renheim, and especially Ben Sevier. Finally, thanks so much to my terrific agent, Dan Conaway of Writers House, and my brother Henry Finder.

TURN THE PAGE FOR AN EXCERPT

When Michael Tanner accidentally picks up the wrong
MacBook in an airport security line, his curiosity gets
the better of him when he discovers that the owner is
a US senator and that the laptop contains top secret files.
Suddenly Tanner finds himself a hunted man, on the run,
terrified for the safety of his family, in desperate need of
a plan, and able to trust no one.

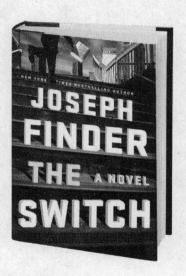

1

The security line snaked on forever, coiling around and through the rat maze of stanchions and retractable nylon strapping.

Michael Tanner was in a hurry, but LAX wasn't cooperating. Usually he went TSA Precheck, as well as Global Entry, and every other way you could speed up the security line hassles at the airport; but for some reason his boarding pass had printed out with the word *precheck* ominously missing.

Maybe it was random. Maybe it was just a personnel shortage. They never explained why. His flight was about to board, but he was near the end of a crawling line of harassed travelers trundling rollaboard cases and shouldering backpacks.

"Shoes off, belts off, jackets off, laptops out of your bags," one of the TSA agents, a large black woman, was chanting from the front. "No liquids. Shoes off, belts off . . ."

Tanner traveled constantly for business, and he was good at it. He glided through the lines, a travel ninja. But this time? Shoes off! Belt off! He realized he was out of practice. How long had it been since he'd gone through the whole indignity? He yanked off his belt, slid off his loafers, put them into the gray plastic bin, and shoved it along the roller conveyor, padding along in stockinged feet. He took his laptop out of his shoulder bag, put it into a gray bin of its own, watched it disappear into the maw of the x-ray machine. His jacket, too, he remembered. Pulled it off and shoved it into another gray bin. Tried not to slow down the line.

He glanced at his watch. His flight to Boston was boarding, had to be. If he re-shoed and re-belted and grabbed his stuff quickly and raced to the departure gate, he'd make it onto the plane before they closed the doors.

He patted down his pockets, found a few stray coins, took them out, and put them into a plastic bowl and onto the conveyor belt, to the apparent annoyance of the middle-aged, well-dressed woman just behind him.

Tanner passed through the metal detector without a hitch, and he was on his way.

Until one of the x-ray attendants on the other side of the conveyor belt picked up his shoulder bag and said, "Is this yours, sir?"

"Yeah," Tanner said. "That's mine. Is there a problem?"

"Can you pick up your things and meet me over there?"

Shit. Something in his shoulder bag must have looked funky in the x-ray machine. He couldn't afford this two or three minutes of scrutiny. But there was no questioning authority. He grabbed his stuff—belt, laptop, shoes, shoulder bag—and met the TSA guy at the metal table. The man pulled out a wand of some kind and ran it around the edges of Tanner's bag. The wand was connected to a machine that was labeled SMITHS DETECTION. It was obviously designed to check for traces of explosives. He waited patiently for another minute, suppressing the urge to make a crack, until the guy finally said, "You're all set," and handed the bag back.

Tanner unzipped the bag, slipped his MacBook Air into it, zipped it back up, slotted his belt into his pant loops while stepping into his shoes, resisting the urge to glance at his watch again.

He arrived at the gate to find no one waiting there, just a couple of airline personnel, a man and a woman, the man behind the counter and the woman next to it. "Flight three sixty-nine?" the woman said.

"That's right."

"All right, sir, you're the last to arrive." She said it disapprovingly, like she'd caught him smoking in the lavatory.

Finally he took his seat on the plane, sat back, exhaled.

He'd made it; he'd be fine; he'd get to Boston around nine thirty in the evening, and the next day he'd be back at work.

He wasn't sure whether the LA trip had been worth it. He'd had a pitch meeting with a famous celebrity chef, Alessandro Battaglia, star of the Food Network, Master Iron Chef, part owner of six restaurants. Chef Battaglia had said he cared about the quality of the coffee they served. Most restaurateurs didn't. When it came to coffee, they tended to care about cost and profit margins more than anything, even in the best places.

Those restaurants brewed generic swill from cheap blends, mostly Brazilian and Costa Rican, and their customers, sated from dinner, usually couldn't tell the difference. But Chef Battaglia knew what good coffee tasted like.

Tanner had brought a couple of different single-origins: a Kenyan, an Ethiopian, and a Guatemalan, each roasted differently three days ago. All ground fresh in a Baratza, in front of the chef, each poured over, each distinctly different, and each delicious. Tanner had come to LA himself—the founder and CEO of Tanner Roast—instead of sending Karen, his sales director. Battaglia was too big a deal.

Standing there in his green Crocs, Alessandro waited for the coffee to cool, knowing that the best way to sample it is at room temperature. He sampled them with a loud aerating slurp, like a pro. He liked the Kenyan best of all. Tanner agreed that was the brightest, best structured, most balanced.

Battaglia seemed particularly interested in Tanner Cold Brew, which was a coffee concentrate Tanner was proud to have invented. It could be used for iced coffee, for nitro, and for hot coffee, too, and without any of the usual bitterness. They sold it by the keg.

A lot of people made cold brew, but it was never quite right. It didn't work very well as hot coffee when diluted with hot water. But Tanner's did. He'd devised an original process. The result was a clear, bright flavor, fruity and floral and chocolaty. Not roasty and heavy like everyone else's cold brew. Way better than Stumptown's—no comparison, really.

Battaglia wanted that, too. All systems were go. A deal was at hand.

But Battaglia wanted to talk to his partners. Which really meant further haggling over price. He was no better than the manager of an Applebee's. Tanner Roast coffees cost more than institutional coffees, but all specialty coffee did. Chef Battaglia knew he was paying for individually sourced, impeccably produced, meticulously shipped green beans, roasted carefully in small batches . . . the whole deal. A cup of coffee from the Big Green chain usually tasted burnt. Compared to the Technicolor taste of a Tanner Roast, theirs was a black-and-white photograph. The expense was worth it.

Easy for him to say, of course.

Tanner was operating on a few hours of sleep. He was exhausted, so tired that he didn't need to take an Ambien.

He arrived at his South End house raw-eyed and headachy and punchy.

The house, five floors including the basement, seemed echoey with Sarah gone. He switched on some lights in the kitchen and, standing at the island, opened his laptop. He'd made some notes on it he wanted to e-mail to himself. The computer was off, which surprised him, because he rarely powered the thing down. Had he shut it off in the cab on the way to LAX? Maybe. Maybe he'd spaced out. It was no big deal. He pressed the power button, and a minute later an unfamiliar screen came up: a picture of a globe and the name "S. Robbins" and a blank for the password.

He stared at the screen for another minute or so until the realization sank in: this wasn't his laptop. In the rush to grab his possessions in the security line, he'd taken someone else's identical MacBook Air. Belonging to one S. Robbins.

While S. Robbins probably had his.

The perfect glitch to cap off a frustrating day.

There was a faint perfume smell to the laptop, a good and familiar white floral scent, a woman's perfume he'd smelled before. S. Robbins was probably female.

He closed the laptop, a little too violently, got up, and went over to the dry bar in the sitting room to pour himself a Scotch. Then he remembered, glancing at his watch. It was Thursday, which meant beer night at the Albion with a couple of friends. Which he'd been planning to skip, figuring he'd be too tired from the flight.

He was tired, yes, but even more, he needed a drink.

He took out his iPhone and punched the speed dial number for Lanny Roth.

Lanny answered, music blasting in the background. "Tanner! You still in LA?" For some reason, Tanner's closest friends, including his wife, Sarah, called him Tanner, and only strangers, or his employees, called him Michael or Mike.

"Just back," Tanner said. "Sounds like you're at the Albion."

"Coming over? I just got here. Brian already got dinged trying to pick up a BU girl, so the night is young."

"Save me a seat," Tanner said.

Something tickled at the back of his mind, and he picked up the MacBook Air. He'd remembered right: on the bottom of the laptop was a tiny pink square, a Post-it note.

He peeled it off the metal case and saw a jumble of letters and numbers.

342HART342.

He wondered . . .

He opened the laptop again and entered the characters in the password space, and sure enough, the screen opened up with the default Apple background photo of a mountain peak.

"Got it," he said aloud.

Then he closed the laptop and grabbed his car keys.

2

The baby had just fallen asleep on his mother's nipple.

Will Abbott lifted little Travis slowly from Jen's breast and carried him carefully, gingerly, across the darkened room toward the crib as if he were transporting a hand grenade with the pin out. It could go off at any second.

Because little Travis, six weeks old, hardly ever seemed to sleep. A few hours here and there, never more than that. And when he didn't sleep, his parents didn't sleep.

Travis had just had his last feeding for the day, or at least until he woke up at two in the morning, desperately hungry again. Right now he was the angel baby, flying through the clouds, making tiny fussing sounds in his sleep. At two in the morning, or maybe three, he would awake, ravenous and loud and beyond comforting.

Jen always got up and fed him, since the baby wanted

her, not him. And because Will had to go to work in the morning. Will could roll over and put a pillow over his head and fall back asleep while Jen nursed him. It was colossally unfair. Will, who worked on Capitol Hill as chief of staff to a senator, had by far the easiest job. But it was also the job that paid the rent on their Stanton Park apartment.

Will was always tired, always sleep deprived, since the baby was born. He'd taken a monthlong paternity leave—most chiefs didn't get that—during which he tried to take the baby as much as possible so Jen could catch up on sleep. But Travis always wanted his mother. Will tried putting the baby in his car seat and driving around, but that didn't quiet him down.

Jen's mom thought that Travis might have colic, but their pediatrician said colic was just an old-fashioned term for an inconsolable baby without any other obvious problem. It was probably abdominal pain, but he wasn't sure. He might just be a fussy baby. He was hungry a lot, but he wouldn't take a bottle, so they couldn't augment his feeding.

The room was filled with the whooshing of the white-noise generator in the corner near the baby's crib. The white-noise machine was Jen's idea. She thought it would mask traffic noise from the street.

Anything to keep the baby asleep a little longer.

Will walked back to the bed, avoiding the floorboard that always squeaked. When he reached the bed, his BlackBerry rang. His work phone. He kept it beside the bed, in its charger, because it rarely rang past nine at night. And if it did, it was the boss, which meant it was important.

As soon as the ringtone sounded—he'd forgotten to put it on vibrate mode—Travis awoke and started to squall. From the number readout Will saw it was the boss. It had to be something urgent. Otherwise, she'd just text.

"Hi, Susan," he said.

"Will, listen, I screwed up."

An ominous start. The boss was never self-critical, never self-blaming. She had a big ego and a maddeningly serene confidence.

"Okay," he said, switching into I-can-handle-anything, Mister-Fix-it mode.

"I grabbed the wrong laptop."

"I don't—"

"At the airport. I grabbed someone else's laptop. In the security line. And someone got mine."

"Okay. You flew American, right? I'll call their lost-and-found at National. Whoever took it probably brought it back—"

"This was in LA."

The baby was wailing now, so Will went out into the hall, one hand over his free ear.

"No problem, I'll call—"

"Did I wake you? You're not thinking clearly. The security line at LAX, Will. That means it could be anyone, on any flight, who took my laptop. Any of a thousand people. And"—she sighed heavily—"and you know damn well we can't call law enforcement."

For a moment he didn't know what she was talking about, and then it came to him. "Oh."

Icy tendrils gripped the pit of his stomach. "Oh, my God. It's—it's password-protected, right? I mean, no one can get onto your laptop without your password. Right?"

There was a long silence. Over the phone, Will could hear the distant clamor of airport announcements on speakers. He was about to repeat the question when she said dully, "Yes, it's password-protected."

"Great. We don't have to worry about it, then." The icy tendrils began to melt away. In the background he heard loud babble, people talking loudly, close to her.

"No," she said. "We have to assume the worst. We have to worry about everything as long as that computer is out there."

"Well, maybe whoever took it realized it wasn't theirs and brought it to the lost-and-found at LAX."

"Yeah," she said, sounding unconvinced. "How early can you get in tomorrow morning?"

"How early do you need me?"

Little Travis let loose with an ear-shattering, gut-churning yowl. Will glanced at his watch. Ten minutes after ten. Putting the baby down might take another half hour, and he knew it would be his job, not Jen's. If he was lucky, he'd get three and a half hours of sleep before the inevitable two A.M. awakening, and then another two or three fitful hours. Five or six broken hours of sleep, he calculated, before what was probably going to be a long and arduous day.

"Will, are you off the phone?" Jen called, voice taut with annoyance. That meant diaper duty.

"See you tomorrow," he said into the phone, then hit the red button to end the call. "Yep, I'm coming."

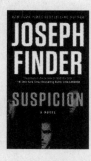
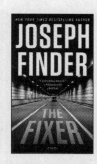
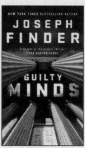
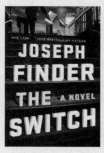